SCOURGE OF GOD

SCOURGE OF GOD

C. R. MAY

COPYRIGHT

Suddenly the barbarian world, rent by a mighty upheaval, poured the whole north into Gaul...

Sidonius Apollinaris

1

OTTAR'S CHARGE

Jutland
Harvest Month 450

A peek through lashes made gluey by sleep was enough
to reveal that the witching hours were behind him, and
Ottar listened hard as his mind sifted the sounds of the morn.
It would be a good while yet before his obligations would
drive him from his bed, but instincts honed over the course of
a lifetime spent in harm's way were difficult to ignore. As
host, the safety of them all was his responsibility, and Ottar
dragged himself fully awake as the others slumbered on. With
the candles guttering the firelight blushed the hall posts crimson, and reassured by the sight of the hounds stretched out in
the glow, the old campaigner's thoughts began to drift.

The night gone by had been a great success, he reflected
as he allowed his eyes to rest again, despite the nonappear-
ance of the reason for the gathering. Hygd had struggled to
hide her annoyance in front of their friends and kin, but Ottar
felt a smile play across his face as he recalled the sight of his
son after a summer away. He had been the first to spy the ship

coasting down the inlet, and the glimpse of a distinctive mop of hair had laid his concerns to rest before he had ridden back to spread the welcome news. He allowed himself a chuckle — it was always the same. Halga would be along later that morning, reeking of stale ale. But as the old chieftain settled, and his mind began to drift, the noise came again. Fully alert, he could place it now, and he felt the first sense of misgiving as he recognised the sound of running feet. Men were ringing the hall, and looking back towards the centre of the room he saw with mounting alarm that the dogs were at the door, the fur on their backs cock combs as the first growls cut the air.

Within moments, the sleepers were awake, blankets and coverlets cast aside as hands grasped spear shaft or sword hilt and groggy guests swapped anxious looks. Ottar was on his feet, and as the others reached for their shields, his sword slid free from its scabbard. He made his way forward, speaking in an undertone as Siward came to his side. 'Who is on guard?'

The big man glanced across: 'Hrafn.'

The pair, ealdorman and gedriht, shared a look. 'The new lad?'

Siward nodded, the growing realisation that they may have been betrayed reflected in his eyes.

Ottar spoke again. 'Fetch my helm and shield. If we are under attack, I would not ask any other to be first man to the door.'

Siward made to protest, but Ottar cut him dead. 'It's not Halga outside, finally pitching up after a night down in the burh to play tricks with his friends; the dogs have known their scents since puppyhood.' He clasped his hearth warrior's arm and fixed him with a stare. 'We may not have been the only ones keeping watch to see when the *Brimwulf* returned. If our enemies had lookouts posted, they will have seen the ship sailing down the broad yesterday, and know full-well that we would be holding a homecoming celebration last night.' Aware that others were listening in, Ottar softened his tone; panicky leaders were no leaders at all. 'If they are afraid to face us on equal terms, what better time to do so than at first light as we sleep off the effects of a night's heavy drinking? Retrieve my war gear,' he said, 'and let us see where we stand.'

Siward's frown had gradually recast into a look of resolve as he listened. 'If it is to be a fight in the dawn,' he growled in reply, 'let us make such as clamour as to wake the heroes in Valhall.'

The gedriht gave a curt nod as he turned to do his lord's bidding, and as he moved away, Ottar's gaze wandered across to the others. Despite the danger they found themselves in, he allowed himself a smile of satisfaction: they were a tough bunch, fighters any man would be happy to have at his side in a tight spot. He looked back as Siward strode through the hall, his earlier concerns replaced by a steely glare. As the gedriht reached the screen and took down his lord's shield and battle flag, the first fronds of smoke began to curl up from the eves of the roof thatch. Convinced now that they would soon be fighting, the rest of Ottar's hearth warriors were helping each other to arm, wriggling into shirts of mail and fastening helms. Ottar addressed the others as they did so. 'Friends and kinsmen,' he said. 'It would seem that I may have invited you not so much to a joyous occasion, but a hard fight. Let us discover the identity of those who wish us harm but are too shamefaced to announce themselves, before we look to our response.'

Siward arrived back as the ealdorman reached the door, his lord reaching out to grip the shield by the handle as a bodyguard levered up the locking bar and moved it aside. The pair exchanged a look, and Ottar motioned to the nearest warrior as he prepared to slip the latch. 'Grasp the dogs by the collar,' he said. 'They will have an important part to play before this is over.' The catch came up with a clack, the dogs now straining and beginning to slaver as a gust carried a whiff of strangers into the hall. As daylight striped the floor, Ottar moved into the opening, hunkering down until all that was visible to those who meant them harm were the slits of his eyes between shield rim and helm. A heartbeat later the ealdorman gave a stagger as unseen shafts thudded into the boards, and sure now that there were still men outside, his followers moved up to enclose him in a ring of steel. Ottar called out a challenge as they did so. 'Name yourselves — tell me who means to burn me in, or forever live in shame.'

The words of the response when it came dripped with hatred, and Ottar felt those around him stiffen as the leader of the burners revealed his identity. 'Garwulf, son of Guthlaf, is the name of your killer old man — point of spear and sword edge the cure for consorting with Angles and Danes.'

Ottar let out a weary sigh before calling out again. 'So, it has come to this Garwulf. Jute fights Jute, and the Saxons conquer us all?'

Garwulf spat a reply. 'The Saxons have no interest in our lands grey-hair. The Angles would have you fight their battles for them: it is they who are the enemies of our folk, as in the days of our fathers and their fathers before them — not those further south.'

'This is madness,' Ottar shot back. 'If we turn upon ourselves, only those who hate us can benefit, whoever they may be. Let there be a truce between us,' he pleaded. 'I will come across, and together we can plot a course for all our people.'

'It is far too late for that,' Garwulf snapped, 'you were

warned often enough. The time has come to pay the price for your disloyalty.'

Ottar sighed again, as he came to accept that only sword and axe play would decide the issue. 'And what of my women?'

'They remain in their bower,' came the reply. 'We came here to rid ourselves of traitorous men — we have no quarrel with your womenfolk.'

Ottar's eyes were darting about the courtyard as Garwulf spoke, and satisfied that he had gathered as much information as he was able, the ealdorman took a step back. The jeers and catcalls of his enemies followed him as he did so, and as the door slammed shut, Ottar stepped back into the shadows. As the foe's cries of jubilation carried to the hall, the old Jute turned his face to his companions. 'I wish that I could tell you we will be fighting our way out of this,' he said sadly, 'but you are not the type in need of coddling, and I would not want to give you false hope.' He switched his attention to a kinsman then, reaching out a hand as he did so. 'Osgar,' he said, 'lend me your spear.' The man handed it across, and Ottar took a pace back to open up a gap between them. 'I had a good look during my exchange,' he said as he began to sketch twin lines into the dusty floor, 'and our foes have taken up a strong position. Garwulf has two rows of sword and axe men on the far side of the yard,' he said, jabbing the ground with the heel of the shaft, 'here and here — with flanking bowmen to either side. Beyond them, a dozen horsemen are waiting near the hay field to ride down any who slip through.'

Ottar cast a look back into the depths of the hall. The fire had taken hold in the time he had spent at the threshold, with the higher reaches of the roof space now fogged by smoke. Here and there, the first tongues of flame were licking the thatch to send embers raining down onto tables and benches. They would have to make their move soon if they were to carry the fight to the enemy, or risk dying where they stood. He turned back to those who would share his fate. 'We may be heavily outnumbered,' he said with a look, 'but the gods have not deserted us completely. Garwulf's men have dismantled part of the paddock for use as firewood, and a pile of palings shows where they had hoped to find us in a drunken stupor. Fortunately, our alertness has denied them the chance to blockade the door, and I will not cower inside while my hall burns down about my ears. I am carrying the fight to them.'

His eyes flit from face to face, thrilling as he saw the same determination reflected there. 'Last night may have been a wild night,' he said, 'but I know of a place where the days and nights are wilder still. If I am fated to die this day, I mean to join my ancestors in Valhall.' He smiled a lupine smile. 'Who is coming with me?'

A roar of agreement confirmed what he already knew — no one there would die the death of a *nithing*. As his companions said their farewells and prepared to face their wyrd, Ottar's eyes swept the group until they alighted on the youngest. 'Oswy,' he said. 'Your duty today is to stay alive.' As the youth's features took on a look of horror, Ottar continued, forestalling any argument. 'I have no doubts that our enemies believe that Halga is among us. You know my son's habits better than most of us here, and whereabouts he is likely to be found. I made a point of checking while I was at the door. The bales and carts are still where they were left following the harvest, screening the drainage ditch we had the thralls deepen and clear out before the autumn rains.'

Creaks and groans above their heads told where the fire had begun to eat into joists and beams: a clump of thatch the size of a bushel fell flaming to the ground. Ottar glanced at the wolfhounds. Fiercer than the feral cousins they had been bred to hunt, the shaggy grey beasts had been a gift from a king in Hibernia. But ferocious or not, no animal would stand firm while flames raged around them, and it was all the men grasping the collars could do to keep them from bolting. 'Follow Grim and Gram,' Ottar said to the youth. 'The dogs will scatter the spearmen. Break out and make your escape using the gully. Get yourself down to Tiw's Stead and find Halga; tell him what has happened here and to look to his safety. With any luck, they will think he has perished either in the hall or the fight long enough for you both to get away.'

Leaving the youth to wallow in his disappointment, Ottar switched his gaze to those clustered about him. The men of his *comitatus*, his comrades — the fighting men oath sworn to him — had already formed an armoured wedge at the door as they waited for their lord to lead them through. His friends and kin with only their helms and shields for protection were clustering in their wake, ready to spill out and cut a swathe through the foemen as soon as Ottar's charge shattered the enemy ranks.

His face turned to Arékan then, a grim smile playing upon his lips despite the hopelessness of their cause as he recognised the war lust from old. The Hun was as handy with spear and sword as any man. But it was her skill with a bow that would be vital if they were to have any chance of breaking the enemy line that morning, and he tapped the stave with the flat of his blade as he gave his final order. 'I want you to use the cover of our shield wedge to take out as many of Garwulf's bowmen as you can when we cross the courtyard. Once we get in among them — fight as you see fit.' Arékan nodded as her hand went to the charm at her throat. 'I will go to Tángri Khan with a heavy heart at our parting lord,' she said. 'But I will tell the sky god and my ancestors of our deeds together, so they will come to know your greatness.'

Ottar dragged his eyes away from the woman as she hurried to retrieve her quiver, and seeing all was ready, the ealdorman turned back to fix Oswy with a look. 'All our hopes rest with you. If we are fated to die here, we go to Valhall, content that my son will wreak a terrible vengeance upon our killers.'

Men were beginning to choke as the smog grew denser: it was time to go. With a nod from their leader the door crashed inward, and as dawn's pale light flooded the room and the first arrows crisscrossed the air, the dogs bounded away. Ottar roared his defiance then, and as his closest companions gathered at his shoulder and brought their weapons to bear, he took a forward pace and broke into a run.

2

MANHUNT

Halga smacked his lips and belched. 'It's a funny thing,' he said as his tongue flicked out to brush the last drops from his moustache. 'If you carry on drinking steadily, you sup right through drunkenness and end up sober again.' Thera took a sip from the ale cup, her legs sliding forward beneath the surface of the tub as she threw him a beery leer. Surprised, Halga gave a start, the ale slopping over the rim to stain the bathwater as her toes moved in to stroke his cock. 'It doesn't seem to work that way with me,' she giggled. The pair leaned forward to share a fleeting kiss. Halga teased a wayward strand from her cheek as they drew apart. Freckles stippled a comely face, within a framework of hair the colour of fire. He shook his head as he drank in the sight of her. Aldred counted himself a canny trader, but the man was a fool. While he knew the value of every ell of homespun and amber trinket in his warehouse, he left his real wealth languishing at home.

His eyes went wide as her toes gave a squeeze. She pouted as she did so, but the gleam in her eye told a different tale. 'He's shrivelled a bit,' she cooed. Halga drained the cup and shrugged. 'What do you expect? He was up all night. Besides,' he said with a wink, 'the water is getting chilly; if he must get wet, he prefers it warmer.' They shared a smile as she began to walk her fingers along his thigh, but the humour evaporated instantly as the click of a latch resounded like a thunderclap from the room next door.

A fleeting look of horror and Halga was moving, the bath-water falling in curtains as he leapt from the tub and made a grab for the handle of his sword. Thera was recovering quickly, and as the blade slid from its scabbard, she pointed to the rear of the lean-to and hissed. 'Out the back — the locking bar is in place, nobody can get in. Gather your belongings and make for the strand. Hurdle two fences, and you are in the clear.'

Halga threw her a look, pausing midway to a chair festooned with his clothing. 'I am the son of the ealdorman. Tell me why I have to run from a trader?'

Thera stepped from the tub and padded across, laying a hand against the side of his face as she reached him. 'He is not just any old trader,' she pleaded, 'he is my husband, and he will not be alone. Yes,' she agreed, 'you are the son of the local lord, and as such you will end up married to a worthy woman and I shall be cast aside.' Halga made to protest, but Thera placed a finger against his lips. 'Let me enjoy our time while it lasts,' she said. 'The day will come soon enough when childbearing makes my belly suet, and saggy breasts will turn no man's head.' She gave his rump a playful slap, driving the melancholy away as she forced a smile. 'Now, go — I must open the door.'

The spell was broken as the latch fell back into place, to be replaced by the sound of hammering on the wooden boards. But the clamour that followed was not the roughly hewn cries of a trader and his oafish friends, and the pair shared a look as a crash from the side alley told where someone was already moving up to head off any escape. Before he could gain the rear door, the catch came up with a clack, and Halga took a firm grip on the handle of his sword as he prepared to fight. The door swung inward as he tensed, and as the early morning light flooded the room, Thera fled to the shadows. To Halga's surprise, the image that hardened from the glare was not the face of Aldred or one of his cronies, and he cried out as he dragged the sword thrust aside to bury the point in the planking an inch from the face. 'Oswy! You halfwit, I almost skewered you!'

Oswy's gaze swept the room, pausing only to blink in surprise at the sight of the redhead standing bare-arsed and wide-eyed against the end wall. 'We only have a few moments if we are to get away,' he babbled as he recovered his wits. 'Grab your things and follow me.' Before Halga could respond Oswy was gone, and as the door swung-to and the gloom returned, Thera was at his side. 'Something is wrong,' she snapped, scooping up his clothing to press it upon him. 'It is not Aldred and his gang who are banging on the door, whoever it is has come for you.' Thera gave him a lingering kiss as she stepped back into the tub. 'Follow your friend,' she said, as she lowered herself beneath the surface. 'I will wait until they break in, and then confront them. They will not expect to be challenged by an angry woman straight from her bath, and the surprise should delay them long enough to enable you to escape.'

With his arms full, it was all he could do to hook a fingertip between the jamb and the door to lever it open, and as he hastened into the yard the first sounds of splintering wood reached his ears. Up ahead, Oswy was across the first boundary and casting anxious looks his way, urging him on with a flick of his head. Halga was about to hurdle the line of fencing when the sight of it drew him up short. With armfuls of clothing and weaponry, he would have to throw a leg over before dragging himself across the roughly fashioned wattle. It was not the best way to start the day for a naked man straight from a warm tub. But the sound of raised voices and breaking pottery told where Thera was playing her part in the escape, and he knew that the pursuers were coming up fast. Halga took a rearward step as he eyed the hurdle before him, and as a shouted challenge came from the doorway to spur him on, he cleared the fence at a run.

The moment he landed, Halga was rolling to his feet, and as he clasped his belongings tightly to his chest, he lifted his eyes. A final fence stood between him and the wide open spaces of the quayside and strand beyond. Lower than the first, Halga prepared to put on a burst of speed to clear it, but as he did so, Oswy appeared and beckoned him aside. 'Not that way,' he barked. 'There are horsemen after us, they will ride us down in no time. Keep your weapons, but lose your clothes, they will only slow us down.'

Before Halga could question him, Oswy darted away, skirting the side of a building to emerge on the road that led to the dock. Halga cast about as his rescuer disappeared. If he tossed his clothing aside, it would mark his passage as clear as day. Directly ahead, the gable end of a smallholding blocked his view; but it was the doorway at its centre that grabbed his attention, and angling his run he made directly for it. The hinges were no match for the shoulder barge when it came, and as he crashed through in a cloud of dust and splintering wood, he saw to his joy that the front door was open to the street beyond. A momentary glimpse of a family sat breaking their fast, and he was through, tossing a plea to take care of the bundle he had thrown their way as he thundered past.

Back out in the open, Halga looked towards the centre of Tiw's Stead, and was gratified to see that Oswy was only a score or so yards ahead. The sounds coming from the direction of Thera's hall had changed from screams of womanly indignation to those of shattering wood, as the wattle fence that had caused him to pull up only moments before was beaten flat. With any lingering thoughts that this might all be a jape, a laugh at his expense by his friends and shield mates now driven from his mind, Halga ran on. A carter burst out laughing at the sight of the ealdorman's son pelting naked through the town, and he made a note of his face for a future visit. A portly woman nudged her friend, who turned his way to gawp. But folk were beginning to catch on that there was more to his nakedness than the results of a tryst gone sour, and laughter was turning to looks of concern as doors began to slam shut.

Oswy was a dozen yards ahead, and Halga put on a spurt. But the young Jute checked his stride again as his friend darted into an alleyway, and a heartbeat later, Halga saw why. Beyond a bend in the road, groups of spearmen were going from house to house. A haywain had been brought to a halt, the warriors working over the sheaves with the tips of their spears as they continued their search. Halga dodged between two huts, thankful that the wagon had shielded him from the searchers just long enough to enable him to remove himself from their line of sight. With the crashes and bangs made by Oswy at Thera's hall still fresh in his mind, Halga picked his way through the debris that always seemed to collect in such places as he sought another way through.

He had almost made it, when the sound of rough voices and the mention of his name from the courtyard at the rear brought him to a halt. It sounded like a pair, and with surprise on his side, Halga's hand went to the handle of his sword. But as he inched the blade from its scabbard and prepared to strike, he froze at the sound of others approaching. Once again he was heavily outnumbered, and with all thoughts of attack now driven from his mind, Halga searched about him for another way out. The walls to either side were unbroken timber, and the street beyond crammed with enemies. But just as he began to despair, his eyes picked out a lifeline. Nestling among the debris on the floor of the alleyway was a broken *kraki*, a type of pole ladder often used at sea, and Halga slid his sword blade home as he made his way across. Several rungs had broken off, and a jagged edge showed where it had lost its top. But the eaves of the hall came down to within a couple of feet of his head, and lifting the kraki clear of the floor he saw that it was enough. Within moments, he had propped the ladder against the wall and was climbing, throwing a leg onto the roof to heave himself up. Too caught up in their conversation to have heard the squeaks and groans made by the rickety old ladder, the pair were still chatting happily away, and Halga seized the chance to draw the kraki up onto the roof alongside him. He was just in time, and as the newcomers hailed the chatty pair, he worked his fingertips into the strands and held on.

'Had any luck?'

The first group chuckled as they replied. 'You could say that.'

With his hands occupied holding on to the roof thatch, the ladder, and his sword, there was little Halga could do. Trapped for now, he settled in to listen as he waited for them to move on.

'Where is he then?'

'No, that is not the kind of luck we meant — didn't you hear all the noise?'

'What, all the shouting and banging?'

The first pair laughed. 'Yeah, we scared some poor sod half to death, and chased him from his woman's tub. He must have thought we were the husband and his mates come to cut his cock off, so he scarpered out the back. We reached the yard just in time to see his hairy arse disappear over the fence.'

The newcomer spoke again. 'It could have been our man — didn't you go after him?'

'The Hunding brat? Halga? Not likely — he is already miles away,' the first man scoffed. 'Someone will stick a spear in the lad from the hall soon, and then we can all go home.'

Halga's stomach gave a lurch as the conversation confirmed his worst fears. Not only were dozens of warriors hunting him, but it sounded like they had already searched at his father's hall. He gripped the handle of his sword a little tighter, and continued to listen in.

'So, what was all the noise, then?'

'Lover boy left his gal behind when he ran for it. Fresh from the tub she was — ginger. Great tits, with a bush like an angry squirrel.'

The spearmen laughed again, and Halga found that he was smiling despite the danger he was in. They were his type of lads, and he was enjoying their banter. It was a shame they were here to kill him. The laughter trailed away as they began to move off, and the moment that Halga was sure he was in the clear, he raised his head to look. A dozen ridge lines stood between the place where he clung to the mossy thatch and the centre of town. Stretching his neck to peer into the street and backyards, he could see that there was little hope that he could evade the searchers if he left the rooftop. Equally, if he stayed where he was, he would be spotted long before they gave up and left. Oswy had been heading in that direction, and if he were to catch up with what was beginning to look like the only friendly face in town, Halga realised that he would have to use the heights to do so.

A brief look towards the roadway told him that the men there had just completed their search of the huts on the far side, and were coming across. To his right, a few spearmen were searching the bushes and undergrowth edging a drainage ditch that led down to the broad. They had their backs turned, and Halga knew that could change in a moment. But time was running out if he was to get away before he was discovered, and he knew that he would have to take a chance. The instant those on the road passed from sight, he was on his feet, sliding an arm through the carrying strap on his shield to hoist it onto a shoulder. With a final check, he leapt the gap, and following a moment of alarm as he began to slip back, he drew his dagger to drive the point deep into the thatch. Using the knife as an aid he crossed the first ridge, and as he moved from rooftop to rooftop he soon put the sounds of the search behind him.

As the silence returned, so did his confidence, and Halga dropped to the ground when only a handful of buildings stood between him and the main road down to the strand. Mindful now of the numbers facing him, he snatched a look around the corner of the building. Oswy was back in sight, his friend little more than a dozen paces further along the road, and he threw a look back the way he had come as he prepared to follow on. The cart remained where the warriors had ordered it to halt, and crouching low to peer beneath, Halga was sure that no one remained this side of the bend.

He was about to move away, when the sound of a shouted challenge stopped him dead. Near the dock road, a foeman had rounded the corner, his spear blade coming up as he caught sight of Oswy and realised who he was. But Halga's friend was the faster of the two, and the spearman's snarl became a bloody gash as a sword flashed in the soft morning light. As the enemy fell away, Halga caught a glimpse of a line of horses racked-up alongside a fence, and he put on a burst, leaping the body of the enemy to reach his friend at last. Oswy had already slipped the tethers from the closest pair when he arrived, and he threw an instruction over his shoulder as he bent forward, and the sword flashed again. 'Here,' he said, 'mount up!' Halga pulled himself into the saddle as Oswy moved along the rest of the line, chopping his sword in bloody arcs as he hacked at the hind legs of the helpless animals. The grim work took only a matter of moments. His sword work finished, Oswy mounted, the pair hauling the heads of the horses to the west as they threw back their heels to urge the animals on.

Shouts and cries of alarm came from the buildings and side roads as the horses gathered speed, mixing in with the agonised cries of maimed horses as the pair hunched forward over the necks of the beasts. Within moments the last of the huts were a blur, and as the dust and muck of Tiw's Stead receded to be replaced by ripening barley and the green fields beyond, the pair thundered on.

Within a mile, they were approaching the site of the *Thing*, the debating place for the freemen of the district, and with no sign of pursuit they felt safe enough to drop the pace to a trot. Reaching the Moot, they drew rein, hauling the heads of the horses around to stare back the way they had come. Even from a distance, Tiw's Stead appeared to be in uproar, as tiny figures scurried to-and-fro. But safe for the moment and with no one nearby, Halga finally grasped the first opportunity since the flick of a latch had interrupted his soak to blurt out a question. 'What is going on? I have only just got back, and everyone wants me dead.'

Oswy turned to face him, and Halga felt an ice-cold fist grip his guts as the morning sun revealed just how haggard and careworn he looked. 'We were burned in, Halga,' Oswy replied. 'It looks as if they are killing everyone who favours an alliance with the Angles.' He chewed at his lower lip, dropping his eyes to the ground momentarily before fixing Halga with a look. 'I am sorry,' he said, the anguish he felt clear by his expression. 'I think your father and the others are dead.'

3

GOD OF VENGEANCE

I t was a ride he had made a thousand times. Splashing through the ford, the track rose as it approached Hangman's Copse. It was a name so ancient now that nobody could recall just who the hanged man had been, though the aura of Woden — the god of the hanged — lay heavily upon the crossroads, and no traveller tarried there for long. Through the trees, the road took a dogleg to the right, before straightening to cross the hayfield and on to the hall. Dressed in borrowed clothing, it was not the homecoming he had envisaged when he had awoken in the byre that morning. But his weapons were at his side, and if the dun coloured workwear of a ceorl was coarse and ill-fitting, it was better than none.

Closer now, the distinctive smell of woodsmoke hung in the air; westwards, where the woodland edge came down almost to the paddock the trees wore a crown of rooks, the dark birds a cawing mass as they overlooked the devastation. Crossing the field, the horse slowed to a walk for the final few yards, and Halga's gaze took in the ravaging and the little group who awaited his arrival as he rode. Reaching the yard, the horse baulked as the ferrous tang of blood and death mixed with the reek from the remains of the hall, and slipping from the saddle he let the reins drop as he walked across.

'You are late, son,' she said. 'And thank the gods for it.'

Halga opened his mouth, but face to face now with the destruction of almost all he had held dear, the reply was stillborn. He tore himself away as the uncomfortable silence stretched, turning back to read the story of the fight from the telltale marks and bloodstains on the setts and grass. The men had erupted from the doorway, crimson speckles showing where arrows had flashed in to draw the first blood that morning: close to the barn, a strip of death still marked the battle line. Grim and Gram lay on the bank, what remained of them following the fight little more than ragged pelts and flyblown meat. He turned back. 'Where is my father?' She indicated the small building they had always called the women's bower with a movement of her head. The women normally shared the main hall with the men, only vacating it if a day on the ale would inevitably result in a night of male boorishness. Last night the coarse behaviour had saved them all. 'I had the thralls and field workers shelter our dead there,' she replied. 'I shall treat the bodies with the honour they deserve, until friends and kinfolk arrive to collect them.'

His eyes slid across to the paddock with its broken gate. 'You have sent out riders?'

'On the old nags they left us,' Hygd replied with a sour faced look. 'The best of the horses went south with the killers.' Her expression hardened as she continued. 'Our fighting men reaped a bloody harvest before they were over-whelmed by numbers. There will be twice as many widows lamenting Garwulf's cowardly raid, than among the followers of Ottar Hunding.'

Halga allowed the statement to hang on the breeze as they

walked across. Now that the moment had arrived he felt almost overwhelmed by a dreamlike daze, as if every step taken floated on air, and he was thankful that the door to the hall lay only a few paces away. Hygd stood aside as the latch went up, deferring to her son now that he was the head of the family, despite his youth. Two of his mother's menials stood watch over the bodies, and Halga saw the look of relief on their faces as they bobbed their heads and left a place of the dead.

Ottar lay at the centre of the room as was right, and as the pair moved deeper into the hall and the latch dropped back into place behind them, Hygd placed her palm on the head of her husband. Halga read the wounds on his cadaver. The broken shaft of an arrow protruding from Ottar's thigh told where his enemies had attempted to bring him down before he reached their shields, but raising his gaze, Halga was gratified to see that it had been in vain. At the shoulder the puckered kiss of a wound made by a spear point flanked the vivid gash of a longer blade, and steeling himself for the sight to come, Halga raised his eyes. Very little was recognisable of the face he had loved in life, the features of his father no longer distinct where weapons driven by hate fuelled spite had hacked them to gore and splintered bone. He raised his eyes again to peer into the face of his mother. 'Need I turn the body over?'

She fixed him with a steely look as she replied. 'Need you ask?'

Halga nodded, the pride they both felt shining in their eyes. Ottar had died the way he had lived his life — facing the foe, sword in hand. There would be no wounds to mark where he had turned his back on the fight. He looked for his father's broad blade as he prepared to take an oath of vengeance, blinking in horror as he came to realise the truth. '*Hildleoma*?'

'War-bright went south as booty,'

Recovering his composure, he reached out, covering his mother's hand with his own as he made ready to take the oath. As his right hand grasped the handle of a far plainer blade, he set his shoulders and made the pledge:

Vidar, son of Woden, Fenris bane: god of vengeance

Here, another man's son proclaims that he too is keen to avenge his father.

The vow taken, the pair took a rearward pace, and Halga paused to run his eyes around the room as his mother made her way back to the door. It was, as both *scops* and lesser poets would say, a company of heroes. To Ottar's right, Siward lay still in death, the rents that marked his torso no less savage than his lord's. Scattered about the rest of the hall lay the hearth warriors: kinsmen; friends of his father; men he had loved and looked up to for the entirety of his seventeen summers on Middle-earth. In their nakedness, it was obvious that someone was missing. 'Where is Arékan?'

Hygd had paused at the doorway, and the ghost of a smile played about her lips despite the grim surroundings as she replied. 'She was overwhelmed and carried south as a spoil of war.' The smile widened. 'We watched them ride away. Bound, gagged and thrown across the back of a horse, she still bucked and cursed like a wildcat.'

Halga nodded as his spirits rose a little for the first time since he had leapt from Thera's tub. But if there had been a survivor of the rout it was meagre fare, and Halga turned away, moving from body to body, marking the death wounds and swearing vengeance against the killers as he did so. The oaths taken, he retraced his steps to the door, pausing for a short time as his hand rested on the latch to fix the sight in his memory. It was an oft spoken saying of his father that even the longest roaming began with a single pace. Halga knew that he stood on the cusp of one such journey, and as the catch went up and light flooded back into the room, he gathered himself and took that step.

HYGD STRAIGHTENED UP, blowing out noisily as her hand went to the small of her back. 'Just there,' she said with a grimace, pointing with the toe of a boot as the thrall moved in to gently rake the embers aside. Halga looked on as his mother bent forward to probe the ash with an oaken wand, and moments later another blackened bone shard had made its way into the urn.

The wind had got up overnight, and the newly made widow appeared spectral in the sawing light as a pissy rain, maudlin and weepy, swept in to match the mood. Back in his own clothing Halga was once again beginning to feel like the son of an ealdorman, and surrounded now by his friends, he had the feeling that the world was beginning to right itself after the whirlwind of happenings since they had run the *Brimwulf* ashore, down on the strand.

The boys had come in dribs and drabs as word spread of the burning, and he was grateful for it. But the truth was that the attack had lopped the head from the leadership of the shire, and all their futures were as bleak as the scene playing out before them.

His mother sifted the hot ashes as she gave a final sweep, and satisfied that she had collected all that remained, she stepped back from the pyre and started across. 'You had best be on your way,' she said, with a glance to the East. 'Before the day breaks.'

Halga raised his eyes to peer across her shoulder as he

took the urn. Iron grey clouds were hurrying northwards, but the first pale smear on the horizon showed where dawn was not far off. 'What will you do while I am away?'

Hygd's eyes widened in surprise. 'Rebuild the hall, of course. My sons will need a place to call home when they return.'

Halga forced down the obvious retort. They had not heard a whisper of news regarding Oslaf or any of his crew for more than three years, despite questioning every trader who berthed at Tiw's Stead. It was clear to everyone except his mother that her eldest son had long since succumbed to foeman's blade or storm-driven wave. 'Of course,' he replied, 'and we shall all drink to father's memory together.' He lowered his voice to a murmur so that only she could hear. 'Are you sure you are not coming to the howe? You only get one chance at this, and you may regret it later.'

Hygd shook her head. 'I have duties here,' she said primly. 'Folk will be arriving to carry away the last of the dead. How would it look if they arrived to find their loved ones laid out in a side hall, and no one here to greet them and share their grief?' Halga nodded and turned to go, but she plucked at his sleeve and fixed him with a stare as she made a parting plea. 'I have played the part assigned me by the gods in this, yours is just beginning, son,' she said. 'But heed these words: beware of going where overwhelming force opposes you; there is more honour to be had gathering little by little, than by overreaching and falling down flat.' Halga confirmed that he understood with a curt nod. With Oslaf dead, he was the only hope they had of gaining vengeance on the burners. 'And don't forget Arékan,' she added with a look. 'She will need freeing.'

Halga nodded again, his irritation growing with every

instruction. His reply when it came was as sharp as good manners would allow. 'I know it.'

With a glance towards the east he turned to go, and as his friends came down to follow in his wake, he took the track that led downhill. Away from the circle of light his eyes struggled to pick out the path, but the sky was lightening quickly now as dawn approached, and soon the telltale line hardened from the gloom. Arcing away across a hillside made slick by the earlier rain, the trackway disappeared into the depths of a defile before reemerging a little way on to take a final zigzag up the steepening incline. Up on the headland the way ahead opened up, and as Halga emerged onto the summit the sun drew a line on the eastern horizon. The timing was perfect, and as he paused to allow those following on time to gain the ridge top, he drank in the view. With the sun now risen the waters of Tiw's Stead Broad took on the gloss of hammered iron, and as the workmen dipped their heads and cleared away, the first laments hung on the morning air. A woman came forward to chant a dirge. Keening of their loss, tearing at the sackcloth of her kirtle, she wailed and beat her fists; working grey ash into her hair, she mourned the death of a hero.

Oswy came across, and with the sun now rimming the horizon Halga unfastened the sword at his side, handing it over before making his way to the place where the ceorls had dug into the side of the barrow. With the sun directly behind him, the details of the chamber fell to darkness once again, and as he approached the entrance the slanting light cast a long shadow ahead. Flanked by walls of earth, he bent his head as he gained the burial chamber itself, cradling the urn to stoop as he reached the threshold. Even with the cell now open to the outside the atmosphere was oppressive, and as the fustiness of decades closed in, the young Jute moved along the side wall as he felt for a place to settle down. The instant his back touched the dank boards the sunlight returned, and as the details began to harden from the gloom, he ran his eyes around the room.

He was in a wood lined chamber roughly ten feet in length, a little less in width. Raising a hand, the pads of his fingertips came to rest against the roughly hewn boards above, and Halga felt the first feelings of disquiet at the closeness of the place. A dozen feet of rain sodden soil were at that moment bearing down upon the structure, and the thought threatened to overwhelm him. But he recalled just where he was and the company he kept, and he took a deep breath, filled his lungs with the fetid air and drove the fear away.

In the short time it had taken for him to enter the chamber and accustom his eyes to the shadowy interior, the sunlight on the far wall had moved an inch or two. Time was pressing if he were to accomplish his tasks before the darkness returned, and he shuffled forward towards the place where Ottar's ashes would join those of his ancestors.

The pelt of a bear dominated the centre of the floorspace, and at its head a curule chair took pride of place. Three earthenware urns of the type he now held in his hands already nestled upon it. Halga lingered a moment to cast his eyes over the runic inscriptions and triangular decoration that circled the rims of the containers, before reaching forward to place the newcomer among them. Four generations of Hundings now resided in the barrow, and he could not help but brush a hand lightly across the place where, if the gods willed it, a son not yet born to a woman unknown would place his own ashes on a far-off morning such as this.

With the first part of his burden completed, Halga rested on his haunches as he took a look around. A brace of shields stood propped against the rear wall, marks on the leather covering still displaying the evidence of their last fights. Resting on the boards before them several *angons*, the sturdy stabbing spears of the northern warrior lay in rows, while in the far corner were sheaves of the slender shafted *daroth* throwing spears. Boar crested helms rested on folded shirts of mail beneath a *cumbol*, the war banner of the Hundings, showing a leaping hound teased out in silken thread on a field of cherry red. Shielding his eyes against the sunlight streaming down the passageway, he shifted his gaze towards the eastern end of the room.

If the head of the chamber had been devoted to the trappings of war, the items collected here represented the joys of the hall. As his eyes slowly acclimated, shadowy shapes firmed into familiar objects. A lyre wrapped in the pelt of a wolf; a gaming board set on a trestle, the ivory pieces already in place and awaiting the game. At the centre of it all a krater and ladle, ready to dole out strong drink to gleeful men at the *Symbel*, the ritual drinking that would help to bind tough fighting men together in a brotherhood of warriors. Resting alongside the bowl were the golden rimmed horns of the aurochs, from which they would share it.

The sun had climbed a smidgeon while he looked, and Halga saw that the thing that he craved most of all was now bathed in its light. Immediately before the collected urns, with their precious contents, lay a long rectangular vessel fashioned from ash — the same wood from which the first man had been shaped by the god Woden and his brothers at the beginning of time. Nervous now, he wiped his hands on the legs of his breeks, and as he reached forward to draw the box towards him, he felt the weight of the moment keenly as he levered off the lid.

At first, the prize was hidden in shadow. But sliding his

hands beneath to raise it into the light, he let slip an exclamation of wonder at the work of craftsmen long since gone to graves of their own. The blade of the sword resided within a scabbard of blood-red leather, the golden point of the chape glinting in the sunlight for the first time in decades. Moving his eyes along the length of the piece, domes of gold and garnet secured silken peace bands close to the hilt. With a rising sense of awe, Halga teased them apart, as the thought came that he may well be loosening a knot tied by his grandfather, a man he had never known in life.

Halga paused to admire the handle, before drawing the sword from the scabbard. The grip itself was made of alternating bands of horn and bone above a guard of chased gold plates, but despite their splendour, it was the hilt that drew the eye. Halga drank in the beauty of the decoration, even as his hand closed around the grip. Kept greased and oiled by the fleecy lining, the sword hissed from its scabbard, and Halga thrilled to the sound as he imagined the ancient blade drawing the first breath at its rebirth after so many years beneath the soil. As the blade caught the light, and he gazed upon *Hildhete* — *War-hate* or *War-spite* — for the first time, Halga realised that he knew just what the sound had been. Rods of iron had been wound and worked in days gone over, and slowly the long lean body of a serpent had emerged from the hammering before a cutting edge of steel had been added to give the snake venom. It was cunning work, the work of a master sword smith, and Halga cradled the blade in his hands as he turned his face to his ancestors.

Now was the time he should be making a solemn vow, to replace the sword with *Hildleoma,* his father's blade, or never return at all. But the words would not come, however hard he tried, and Halga hoped that the look of determination he fixed upon his features would be enough. A change in the aura in the chamber seemed to confirm that it had, and lowering his gaze, he saw that the empty vessel had returned to shadow. The darkness of the ages was reclaiming the burial chamber as the sun rose higher, with little more than a rectangle of brilliance remaining at the entrance to light the way back to the world of men.

His gaze returned to the vessel that awaited its sibling blade. The lid was askew where he had woken *War-spite* from its long slumber, and he began to reach forward to slide it closed when he stopped. If words escaped him, he could still show his intent to the watching spirits of the mound by his actions, and he made a great show of removing the top completely and laying it carefully aside. It would be the first time that neither of the family swords had rested in the howe between their time above ground. If the weight of soil bearing down upon the chamber had made him feel uneasy, the expectation to retrieve the *lāf*, the heirloom left by his ancestor, was crushing. But a thought came then to drive the doubt away, and he sent an invocation to the gods or spirits from whence it came as he realised the importance. He was no longer adrift in life, just another footloose son seeking to make his mark upon the world. If the theft of his father's blade had brought shame upon his kin it had also given his life purpose, and he gripped the sword a little tighter, with a little more pride and confidence, as he made his way from the barrow.

4

DRIHTEN

Oswy wrinkled his nose as they approached the first huts, throwing Halga a look of distaste. 'Fish guts, muck and goat shit,' he spat. 'You can't beat that moment when you catch the first whiff of a town. How folk can bear to live in one is a source of never-ending wonder.' Halga's gaze drifted across the rest of the group, exchanging smiles as he recognised that they were all of one mind. Godwin, Beorn and Coella had been alongside Halga and Oswy at the barrow — just one more remained to be added to their number and the old gang would be together once again. 'We will not be here long,' he said. 'As soon as we collect Steapel and cobble together a crew, we can provision the ship and be on our way.'

It was the first time he had returned to Tiw's Stead since he had fled for his life from the tub. Halga ran a keen eye over the inhabitants' reactions as the roadway narrowed, the buildings crowded in, and the sea came back into view. It was testament to the popularity of his father and grandfather, that the majority looked pleased to see him fit and well after his brush with death that day. But there was an undeniable undercurrent to the mood in the town, and although he recognised the reasons for their anxiety, he found the openness of it more disappointing than he had expected. Many of the folk here he had known all his life. He had sailed with the men on the broad, laughed and drilled alongside them at the muster as they taught the youngsters how to stand shoulder to shoulder in the wall of shields. How to stab and parry with sword and spear. As another old friend saw their approach and darted into a side alley, Oswy spoke again. 'It's hard to blame them Halga, it is clear that Hunding rule is over for now. As soon as we leave, who will protect them?'

Halga nodded that he understood. But it was the group who had just rounded the bend that had his attention now, and any thoughts of conversing were forgotten as the riders followed his gaze. Oswy cleared his throat and spoke again. 'Come on lads,' he called across his shoulder, 'it looks as if we are not welcome in town any longer. Let's get ourselves up to Steapel's place, and then see to the ship. The quicker we put to sea, the quicker I will be able to sleep at night without worrying whether I have caught a whiff of smoke again.' Halga hung back as the riders urged the horses into a trot, guiding his mount across to the knot of women as they went. At his approach, the majority melted away until only a couple remained, and he gave a gentle tug at the reins to bring the horse to a halt before them. Thera turned her head aside to murmur to her friend, and as the woman walked on, she threw Halga a coy look as laughter danced in her eyes. With just Thera remaining within earshot, Halga opened his mouth to speak. But the words stuck in his craw as he saw the anger in her expression for the first time.

'What are you doing,' she hissed, 'trying to get me killed?'

Taken aback at her hostility, it was all Halga could do to

utter a reply. 'I wondered if you were all right?' The words
sounded feeble, even to him, but they were spoken now and
there was no point in wishing them away. He grimaced and
awaited her response.

'All right?' she spluttered. 'You wondered if I was all
right?' Thera glanced across to the rest of the group, pulling
a sickly smile and rolling her eyes as she did so. Halga
looked. The women were rapt as they shared whispered
comments. Most had a look of barely concealed glee on
their faces, but Halga noticed with a feeling of disquiet that
one or two looked more triumphant. He squirmed in the
saddle, as the realisation came that he may have delivered
her up to her enemies. Thera was rummaging about inside
the basket she carried when he turned back, and she added a
false jauntiness to her voice as she held up an item. 'Of
course, lord,' she said loud enough for anyone nearby to
hear. 'This will bring good fortune to you and your crew,
you have my word upon it — the finest amber all the way
from the land of the Balts, a gift from the gods, just for
you.'

Halga looked at her in confusion, but she held up the
pendant and made a show of placing it in his palm as she
lowered her voice again. 'Pay me then,' she spat through
gritted teeth. 'And then be on your way — there are more
eyes watching us here than you know.' Halga raised his eyes
to look, but a tug on his breeks brought them back down.
'Pay me and go,' she repeated, the fear she felt obvious in her
tone. 'You have enemies here, and you are making it unsafe
for us both. How do you think they knew where to come for
you that morning? If you ever harboured any feelings for me
at all, ride on and don't look back.'

An idea came as he rummaged in his purse for a fragment
of hack silver, and it formed itself into words and was spoken

aloud before he could think better of it. 'Come with me then,' he heard himself saying. 'You will be safe with us.'

Thera gasped, the pitch of her voice betraying her exasperation. 'Give up a husband? A home and a life of comfort and plenty to sleep on a beach? To help spotty kids bail bilge water from a leaky ship? Cheer you on, until some brutish Saxon makes you just another bloody corpse?' She made a show of biting down on the silver before popping it inside the pouch at her side. 'Ride away Halga — you were just a bit of fun, but the time for fun is over. It is time to grow up.'

Halga took a moment to collect himself as she walked away, patting her purse and throwing her friends a thumbs up as if she had made a killing on the trade. The lack of regard she had shown for his rank had revealed just how much damage the burning had caused. Tiw's Stead, the town he had known all his life, had suddenly become as unfamiliar to him as any he had visited on his travels. But the shock only lasted long enough for him to bring to mind the details of the night they had spent together, and as his eyes relished the sway of her hips, he gave a shrug.

Halga guided the head of the horse back towards the road, and despite the backdrop of feminine laughter, a smile was already playing upon his lips as he clicked the horse on. Before he had reached the outskirts the feeling had been replaced by one of liberation, and as the horse passed the last of the buildings and the waters of Tiw's Stead Broad opened up before him, he slowed his progress and savoured the view. The scene that presented itself was as familiar as the faces of his friends and kin. A steady breeze was driving the surface of the inlet northwestward towards the narrows, channelling the waters through to the place where it spilled out into the wider expanse of Lyme Bay itself. Across the water, the island of Moors dozed in the autumnal haze. A solitary *færing*, a four-ing, so-called due to the number of oars it shipped, bounded along in the swell, and Halga let out a chuckle of delight as he recognised the crew. He geed the horse on then, casting a final look as herring gulls shredded the air with raucous cries. Far from the stink of the town now, Halga filled his lungs as the salty zest of the sea returned, his nostrils flaring as a gusting breeze plucked at his cloak and trews.

Further along the path, the others had come to a halt, a canteen of ale doing the rounds as they waited for him to rejoin them. He allowed himself a chuckle as he imagined their faces had Thera taken him up on his daft offer, and climbed upon the horse's back. Soon he was among them, and he plucked the ale skin from the air with a shout of joy as Coella tossed it across. His old friend asked a question as Halga worked the stopper free and drank. 'How did it go?'

Halga pulled a face as he swilled the ale. 'She begged to come along, but I told her,' he said earnestly. 'There is no place in our troop for a woman.'

Their faces broke into grins as they shared enthusiastic nods. 'I imagine that went down well?'

Halga upended the skin, shaking it above his gaping mouth until he had drained every last drop. When he was sure the canteen was empty, he replied to the question with a shrug. 'There were a few sniffles, but you know — women…'

The group exchanged knowing looks, as secure in their understanding of female wants and expectation as any young men whose know-how invariably came in exchange for silver and ale. 'That's good then,' Coella said happily, 'we need to set sail. If the waters of the broad are choppy, we can expect to find white horses at sea.' The group looked as one. Coella was right: despite the warmth of the day the golds and russets

34

of autumn dappled the woodland canopy, and the first leaves were already littering the ground.

Halga urged his horse forward with a click of his tongue, and as the rest of the riders fell in behind, he raised his chin to peer ahead. The path rose slightly, before curving around to follow the beck the final few yards down to the place where Steapel's father had built his home and workplace long ago. Like all smithies, the squat building lay a good way from the hall and outbuildings — roof thatch and wattle fencing rarely mixing well with the white heat of a forge and clouds of windblown sparks. It was the reason ironworkers never set up shop within the boundary of any settlement containing more than a few rude huts, and following the awkwardness he had just left behind in Tiw's Stead, Halga was thankful. The sound of approaching horses had drawn the smith from his forge, and the young Jute found his good humour ratchet up a notch as he recognised the warmth in the welcoming smile. Moments later he was leading the horsemen into the yard, and slipping from the saddle he raised a hand in greeting as the big man came across. Stripped to the waist, with a muscly torso gleaming in the sunlight, Chad wiped the sweat and grime from his hands on an old rag as he came: 'Halga — lads.'

As they all acknowledged his welcome with a nod of their own, the smith spoke again. 'I was sorry to hear about your father, Halga,' he said. 'Ottar was a fine leader, and a finer man. I knew him for as long as I have lived in these parts, and I know that to be true.'

Halga dipped his head in thanks, but before he could reply, Chad spoke again. 'If you are here for Steapel, he is sailing the broad.'

Halga nodded. 'I saw him from the point. He was heading in, I expect he will be alongside soon.'

'When do you leave?'

'As soon as the provisions are aboard the *Brimwulf.* I have a man in Tiw's Stead seeing to it now.'

An outpouring of noise interrupted the pair, drawing their attention back to the hall. Steapel's younger siblings had erupted from the doorway to greet the family friends, and very soon they were engulfed in a screaming tide. The disturbance had served to chase away the stiffness that had come between them, and both men were smiling as Chad plucked at Halga's sleeve and led him aside. The pair shared a chuckle as the youngsters swamped the horses and riders, and as the women came from the hall carrying jugs of ale from the winter store, Chad lowered his eyes and spoke again. 'I see you wear your grandfather's sword at your belt,' he said. 'I was a young man myself the last time I laid eyes upon it, not much older than you are now. You will have to keep your wits sharp, and eyes open to danger at all times. A sword like that will draw covetous looks, and make you stand out from the crowd.' He hesitated as if reluctant to speak the following words, and Halga continued to watch the lads play rough and tumble with the young ones as he gave Chad time to order his thoughts. 'So,' the older man said finally, 'you will be going after your father's sword, I take it?'

Halga had the reply ready and waiting. Chad's concern that he would throw his lad's life away in an ill-judged quest for vengeance was obvious. 'When the opportunity presents itself, aye, I will. But *lāf* or not, you can rest assured I will not rush blindly in like a fool.' He fixed Chad with a look as he sought to lay the older man's fears. 'I will not waste my life, nor the life of my friends, to regain it — they are too precious to me.'

Chad's face creased into a smile. 'That is good,' he said, with an obvious sense of relief. 'Steapel may love you like a brother, but there is no greater love on Middle-earth than that of a parent for a child.' He snorted. 'Even when that child stands a head taller than his father!'

It was Halga's turn to snort. Steapel was the word for the central tower on the *hearg*, the temples dedicated to the gods among the Angles. He had picked it up on an earlier voyage to their southern neighbours due to his lanky frame, and the nickname had stuck to the extent that even the lad's family had taken to using it ever since.

Chad spoke again as the pair began to make their way back to the others. 'So, you will be sailing tonight?'

Halga shook his head. 'By the time we are fully provisioned, we will have missed the tide. We shall have to wait now until morning.'

Chad looked to the west. The day was drawing to a close, the lowering sun painting the base of the clouds with a fiery glow. 'Will you be spending your last night with your mother then? You are welcome to stay in my hall, of course. I would consider it an honour.'

Halga shook his head again. 'I have said my goodbyes at home, and I would not wish to place you in any danger by remaining here any longer than needs be.' The young ones had already sensed that the business between their father and their brother's friend had been concluded, and were beginning to swirl around them. Halga reached out to tousle an unruly thatch as the owner sped by. 'No harm will come to a smith,' Chad scoffed. 'Where would everyone be without a man to supply a barrel of nails or fix a broken ploughshare? I had hoped that Steapel would inherit my tools, but it is not the life for him. He has brine for blood that one, the boy is never happy unless he feels the lift and swell of the sea beneath his feet.'

Halga smiled. 'Then your loss is my gain, and it is a good

thing that the gods provided you with a healthy clutch of sons to make up for it.'

Chad laughed. 'Aye, it is that! Anyhow, rest easy; there is spell craft in smithing and no harm will come to me or mine. It takes a lifetime to learn Weland's work — we are not so easily replaced.'

Halga nodded. Everyone knew the tale of Weland, of how he had been hamstrung and forced to thraldom by King Niðhad. Weland's wizardry had cost the king not only the life of his sons, but the maidenhead of his daughter. Satisfied he had wreaked vengeance on the king for his wrongdoing, the smith had created a magical cloak from bird feathers and made his escape. Only a fool would invite such horror on their kith and kin.

Bawdy cries told where Steapel had finally made the yard, and Halga spoke again as Chad chuckled at his side. 'I am grateful for your offer, but there are still a few things that need to be attended to before we sail. If you can return the horses to their rightful owners, you will have done more than enough.' The sun had dipped below the horizon while they had chatted, and the shadows were gathering quickly — it was time to take their leave. 'We shall camp out by the barrow,' he said, jerking his head towards the nearby head-land, 'and be on our way at first light.'

'No wonder Halga left you at home last summer, just wait until we reach the open sea.' Beorn turned his head aside to throw his companions a wink. 'Mast high rollers shovelling under the stern: up and down you go: lurching and plunging — lurching and plunging…'

Oswy cast a bleary look towards the men he had mistak-enly believed to be his friends, and Halga struggled not to laugh as he saw the wretchedness there. 'And the wallowing,' Godwin pitched in, spreading his arms wide and swinging his hips from side to side, 'don't forget the wallowing.'

Wicked laughter hung in the air as Oswy's knuckles clutched the wale, and the laughter redoubled when he retched before turning his head to dry heave over the side. The gedriht had begun to feel queasy the moment he had stepped aboard, and by the time they had pulled into deep water, the contents of his stomach made a ribbon leading back to the shore. Halga laid a sympathetic hand on his shoulder as he walked aft. 'A couple of days and you will be in fine fettle,' he said with a gentle squeeze. 'As soon as you get your sea legs, you will wonder what all the fuss was about.' Skipping up onto the steering platform, he raised a hand to grip the backstay, swinging around as his eyes followed the ship's wake and its foul highlights back towards the town. The weather had turned overnight, and a sea fog had crept in to cloak Tiw's Stead Broad and the surrounding land in a mantle of grey. It would be thicker still in Lyme Bay where the waters were open to the sea, and Halga had sacrificed another suckling to Ran, goddess of the sea, seeking her aid.

But if the weather and poor Oswy were dour this morning his mood was anything but, and Halga reflected with pride upon the events of the previous night as he watched the oars rise and fall in time.

Returning to the foreland, they had drunk the ritual ale in the shadow of the howe, barrel following barrel, as they raised a horn to toast ancestors and gods. Even though he had no fine gifts, no blade, helm, or coat of mail with which to reward them they had come forward one after another: Oswy; Godwin; Beorn; Coella and Steapel swearing fealty to him and taking him as their *drihten*, their lord. It had been a humbling experience as they had placed a hand on War-spite's golden hilt, raising the fore and middle finger on the *swerian* hand to become his gedrihts, despite his poverty. It was a thing he knew he would never forget.

Despite a night of drinking, dawn's chill had found them already back on the strand at Tiw's Stead. Steapel had stowed the provisions as the crew came aboard, Halga allowing his eyes to wander over the town as he had wondered when he would get the chance to do so again.

At his shoulder, Steapel spoke, interrupting his thoughts, the tall steersman lowering his voice so that only they could hear. 'It's not much of a crew, lord,' he sniffed, 'but it was the best I could do in the time I had.' Halga nodded that he understood. With the fall of his clan and the lateness of the year, the man had done wonders to scrape together a crew at all. Even then, it had cost double the going rate. 'You did well,' he replied. 'As soon as I drop my guard, the burners will return, and silver is no use to a dead man.'

Halga lowered his gaze to take in the rowers as his gedrihts finally tired of watching Oswy's convulsions and began to drift aft. It was true, he mused as they pulled the little scegth through the swell, they were a scabby bunch — the scrapings of the shire. But if they got him clear of the kingdom it would be enough, for he had powerful friends abroad, and he was certain that with patience he would prevail.

5

SNAKE SHIP

The gedriht craned forward, knuckling his eyes as he peered into the sea fret. Halga ran a palm across his face, flicking the moisture away as his eyes became slits. He leaned in and spoke under his breath. 'You are sure it was a ship?' Beorn remained unmoving as he stared into the mist. Halga opened his mouth to repeat the question, but held his tongue as his friend turned back, and he saw the doubt there. 'I can't say for sure,' he murmured. 'I glimpsed something harden from the fret, but before I could make out what it was, it had gone.'

Halga patted him on the shoulder, leaning in to speak again. 'Keep a good look out,' he said. 'If it is a ship, it could be one of the last traders making for home before the weather turns.' They shared a look, and each man could see that the other doubted that was the case. Halga pulled a grim smile. 'But then again, it could be something far more dangerous.'

The others had gathered as they spoke, and turning away, Halga addressed them in an undertone. 'Beorn thinks he may have seen the outline of a ship in the fog bank, but he cannot be sure.' He ran his eyes around the group as he thought.

'Godwin, move forward and join Coella in the bow — if either of you see anything, raise an arm to point. Sound carries at sea, and we don't wish to draw attention to ourselves if we can avoid it. I will remain here with Beorn, that way we can cover the whole area around the ship and let Steapel know if he needs to alter course.' A snuffle drew their attention towards the place where Oswy lay dead to the world following his daylong exertions. They all shared a smile, as the sight of their exhausted friend lying on a makeshift bed of ropes broke the tension of the moment. 'What are we going to do about grunty?'

'I will cover him with a blanket to deaden the noise.' Halga's smile broadened into a grin. 'If he gets any louder, I will give him a kick.'

Halga followed on as Godwin made his way forward, squatting amidships as he explained their fears to the crew. 'Rest your oars, lads, but be prepared to pull for all your worth if you hear the order. There may be another ship nearby, and I am not in the mood to stop for a chat.' He left the rowers to their thoughts as he retraced his steps to the steering platform, exchanging a look with the helmsman as he reached the stern. 'I take it you got all that? What do you think?'

Steapel gazed to starboard before looking back. 'I think that you did the right thing last night, sacrificing to Ran to bring on this sea fret,' he replied. 'If that is an enemy ship and the mist had not rolled in this morning, the chances are we would be dead already.'

Halga moved closer so that only they could hear. 'What makes you so certain?'

'No one puts to sea in conditions such as these, lord, unless they have good reason. The fishermen back at Tiw's Stead told me a fret was coming before we shoved off, so no doubt the others scattered around Lyme Bay knew it too. An experienced trader would have known the signs, and beached the ship until the sun rose and burned off the mist.' He shrugged. 'Even if you know the waters well, why risk your ship and cargo to collision or sandbank, let alone your lives after a summer away, just to reach home a day earlier?'

Halga nodded. 'You are right, if there is a ship out there we have to assume that it is hunting us. You are the best seaman here, what do you suggest we do? Make a dash for the open sea, or ship the oars and let the ebb tide carry us clear?'

Steapel raised his eyes to the sky, teasing a few strands of horsehair from the backstay as he did so. Halga followed his gaze. A watery light in the sky to the south marked the position of the sun, and Halga looked on as his helmsman made a ball of the fibre and tossed it overboard. With the oars shipped and the breeze a cat's paw, the surface of the bay was as smooth as milk, and Halga watched in fascination as his gedriht calculated time and tide. After a few moments' deliberation, Steapel said. 'We should be within a couple of miles of Thorp Ness, and beyond that lies the open sea.' He was about to say more when he stopped and indicated ahead. Halga looked. In the bows Coella was pointing northwards, and following the line of his gedriht's arm he squinted in an attempt to pierce the gloom. Halga exchanged a look with his helmsman. 'I can't see anything, can you?'

Steapel shook his head. 'Banks of fog.'

Halga turned his face to the bows. Godwin had joined Coella now, and both men were staring northwards into the fret. He was about to leave the steering platform to ask what they could see, when Steapel grabbed his sleeve and hissed a warning. 'There she is!'

Halga turned back, the breath catching in his throat as a

snarling face slowly emerged from a belt of grey. Within moments the prow beast had been followed by the sleek lines of a warship, and as the cry of alarm carried across the water from the lookout in the bow, Halga turned his head aside and barked a command. 'Row!'

Banks of pale faces turned to the helmsman for confirmation, and Halga cursed himself for revealing his inexperience before them all. The sea was unforgiving, a place where Ran's daughters always lurked, ready to snare the unwary or just plain unlucky in their net. Every year the sea swallowed down men, dragging them beneath the waves to the undersea hall of the drowned. It was imperative that every ship had but one master as soon as it had left port, and it was clear that the rowers regarded Steapel as that man. Steapel had seen their reaction, and despite the danger from the other ship, he made a point of turning to Halga and awaiting his command. The instant his drihten gave a nod the helmsman's foot came down, and as the oarsmen stretched their backs to pull the first stroke Steapel's boot was coming up again.

Halga was about to recall the pair in the bow when Steapel spoke again. 'Leave them where they are, lord,' he said. 'We will need every oar manned if we are to have any chance of escape, and I will need a man to take soundings if I am to pull off what I have in mind.' Halga gave him a questioning look, and the big man explained. 'That is a *snaca* we are facing. Not only do we have no hope of outrunning her, but when they overhaul us the men it carries will outnumber us at least two to one.' He sent a gobbet of phlegm spinning over the side as his boot came down again to mark time for the rowers. 'Whoever is in command over there is a wily lad.'

'In what way?'

'By the looks of it, they intend to shadow us all the way to the Ness. They may be faster and carry more spears, but they also have a deeper draught. If they steer towards us, we will turn away and make for the shallows. Although we will be trapped, it will still be difficult to get at us. This way,' he said with a nod to the west, 'in time the trend of the Ness will force us to come to them.'

Halga looked outboard. The long sleek lines of a snake ship were emerging from the fret, the surface of the bay already beginning to foam as the rowers bent to their work. In the bows, the wan light of the sun was reflecting from helm and spearpoint, but he could see that the ship was holding its course and knew that Steapel was right. 'So, what do we do?'

'A mile shy of the Ness itself, there is a channel that traders use as a shortcut to save them from doubling the headland completely. If we can make it before they realise what we are up to, we have a chance. Once we reach the German Sea, we will only be a day sail from Angeln, and a day after that we will be in your foster-father's hall.'

Halga's eyes flashed. 'That sounds grand,' he replied, clapping his gedriht on the shoulder as he did so. 'Let us do all we can to make that happen.'

With the emergence of a plan, Halga's spirits rose, and as Steapel went back to marking time, he cast a look outboard. On the enemy ship, the spearmen had been joined by a man wearing the distinctive leather cap of a bowman, and he spoke a warning as he watched the cap come off. 'It looks like we are about to come under bowshot,' he said. 'I should just about have enough time to tell the lads for'ard what we are hoping to do, and get back to you here before the first arrow arrives.'

With the need for quiet now redundant, he snapped an order as he bounded from the steering platform. 'Beorn, we are about to come under attack by a bowman. Stand guard over Steapel until I return, then try to shield the rowers as best you can. If we lose our helmsman or start taking casualties among our rowers to well-aimed arrows, we lose everything.' Halga spoke words of encouragement as he made his way to the bow. 'Pull hard, lads,' he cried. 'There is a channel up ahead where the enemy cannot follow us; if we can reach it, we shall give them the slip.' Halga threw a look across his shoulder as he reached the mast. The snake ship was in clear air now, the water beginning to pile-up into a bow wave as she gathered speed.

Within a few more paces he was in the bow, and Coella spoke as he reached them. 'What's the plan?'

'Steapel wants one of you to take soundings as we go,' he replied. Halga switched his gaze to the man at his side. 'Godwin, you do that. Coella is the taller and has a longer reach, so he will protect you with his shield. We are only a short distance from a channel that Steapel thinks we can use to escape them.' The trio looked outboard. The snaca was still gaining on them bit by bit, but the water to either flank of the *Brimwulf* now seethed and fizzed as the rowers settled into their rhythm and the wide blades swept them on.

Near the prow, the enemy bowman was busily flexing the limbs of the bow as he attempted to nock the string. The bowstring was always in optimum condition, kept oiled and warm beneath the bowman's cap. But the chill of the morning had stiffened the yew of the bow stave, and Halga could see that he still had plenty of time to return to the steering platform before the first arrow arrived. Coella went to retrieve his shield from the wale, knocking free the wedges holding it secure in the rack, as Halga retraced his steps. Beorn had his shield ready by the time he made the steering platform, and the Jute grasped the handle as he flicked another look towards the snake ship. They were just in time, the enemy bowman now busily testing the pull of his bow before dropping his eyes to select a shaft from the quiver at his side.

Halga looked across to the sprawling figure of Oswy, still oblivious to the plight of his comrades, and thought to wake him. But a cry of warning at his side told him the opportunity had passed, and he raised his shield instinctively as his eyes moved up to pick out the incoming shaft. 'Where is it?'

Beorn snapped a reply, his shield held high as his eyes attempted to pierce the fret. 'Up high, lord. He is using the fog to make it difficult to track.' Halga shuffled rearwards until he felt the coils of rope on deck brush the heel of his boot. A few inches away, Oswy snored blissfully on as Halga stood guard. The shaft when it appeared had overshot, and he grasped the opportunity to unship his gedriht's shield from the rack before the bowman should let fly another. The arrow hit the surface of the water a dozen feet off the larboard beam, and a glance back from whence it came showed the bowman craning his neck as he looked to judge the fall of shot.

Halga was bent over, propping Oswy's shield against his body, when a cry from amidships had his head snapping back. An oarsman was on his feet, his features contorted in pain as he clutched at a thigh, and Halga shot a look at the closest gedriht as the man slumped from sight. Beorn threw him the ghost of a smile and a wink in return, and Halga stifled a laugh as he realised its importance. He turned his head to Steapel at the tiller, but the big man had already seen what had occurred and was subtly altering course with a flick of his wrist on the big paddle blade. With Oswy now protected from any arrows that got through, Halga crossed to the helmsman before the bowman could let fly another shaft. Despite the strain of the chase, Steapel chuckled as he came up. 'That was quick thinking,' he said with a nod towards the place where the oarsman was back at his station. 'I have altered course a touch, let us see if our friend falls for it.'

Both men turned their heads to the north in time to catch the enemy bowman nock and loose again, and as the arrow flew upwards to disappear, they held their breath and waited. Along the length of the *Brimwulf* gedriht and crewmen alike had their faces turned to the sky, and it was all they could do to smother a cheer when the shaft flashed down to strike the surface of the bay a good twenty feet beyond the wale.

Halga raised his chin to stare across at the enemy ship, as his friends began to congratulate the man whose trickery had played a major part in the miss. The snaca was shadowing the *Brimwulf*, the oarsmen keeping station with easy strokes as the little ship continued westwards, and a feeling of unease crept upon him as he looked. Halga asked a question without removing his eyes from the enemy ship. 'How far is it to the channel?'

Steapel glanced across as he brought the ship back onto its original course. 'Not far, lord — within half a mile, maybe less.'

The good humour had fled from Halga as quickly as it had arrived; something was wrong, and the drihten studied the snake ship as his mind ordered his thoughts. Clear of the fog bank now he could see that it was a fine ship — thirty oars a side with a crew to match, as likely as not a king's ship. It was inconceivable that such a fine vessel and the complement it carried would contain a single bowman within their ranks. 'This is too easy,' he said finally. 'If a man from far-off Tiw's Stead knows of this channel, you can be sure that those further south do so too.' Halga snapped a command as his mind reached the most likely conclusion. 'Dress for war,' he growled. 'We are being herded; there is another ship up ahead, and we will be fighting before we know it.' He threw a parting order across his shoulder as he began to make his way towards the bow. 'Beorn, take my place guarding Steapel — and wake Oswy. We will need every man who can use a weapon if we are to get through this.'

The rowers were craning their necks as he passed them again, following the fall of the next arrow as it cleared the ship. Halga spoke words of encouragement as he passed. 'Keep pulling, lads — we are nearly there.'

Coella and Godwin had seen him coming. 'Leave that,' he said as he came up. 'Arm yourselves while you still have the chance. I have a feeling we may be about to fight, and I want us to be prepared.' Coella opened his mouth to reply, but Halga spoke first. 'Go and do it while I take over here — and be quick about it. Steapel says that the channel is nearby, and they will have to spring any trap before we reach it.' The pair shared a look and Halga spoke again. 'The quicker you return, the quicker I can prepare myself.' He fixed them with a stare, barking a command as they continued to hesitate: 'Go!'

As the pair scrambled aft, Halga gripped the prow. To starboard the enemy bowman was busy selecting another arrow from his quiver, and satisfied that he was safe for now, he turned to peer ahead. A dark shape began to form from the mist, and the Jute's heart skipped a beat. But his fears proved ungrounded as the form revealed itself to be a toothy grin of age blackened beams, the wreck all that endured to tell the tale of a long forgotten tragedy. He turned back, cupping a hand to his mouth to shout a warning. A nod of recognition from Steapel cut him short, and he saw with satisfaction that the course adjustments were already in hand.

The look had confirmed that Coella and Godwin had gained the steering platform, and the hatch cover had already been laid aside as Beorn reached in to retrieve helms and war shirts of hardened leather. Oswy was awake now, sitting upright with his back against the hull as he gulped down water from a cup, and Halga realised for the first time what the earlier looks and hesitancy by Coella and Godwin had signified. It was the first time that he had faced danger as drihten, and he saw with satisfaction that the moment had marked the transition in their relationship to leader and led. They had been friends as long as he could recall: the old crowd. But they were no longer equals, and if he felt a momentary pang of loss that that life had passed, it was quickly subsumed by pride in what he had become.

As his concentration returned, Halga was pleased to see Coella and Godwin already cramming helms upon their heads as they hurried back, and as another shaft fizzed overhead to splash alongside he prepared to return aft and do the same. He was not a moment too soon. As the shipwreck marking the shoals came up on the larboard bow and Halga started back, shouts of success drifted across from the enemy ship.

6

FIRST BLOOD

As the rack of beams marking the shipwreck passed to larboard, Halga skipped up onto the steering platform. Turning back, he raised his eyes to look. A hundred yards ahead the mist was rolling away to reveal the withy that marked the channel south, and beyond that, the low sleek outline of a scegth much like their own squatted mid-channel. Halga's head snapped to starboard, and a quick check showed where the bows of the snake ship were already coming about as the enemy helmsman moved to slam the trap shut.

Already armed, Beorn stood before him, grim faced as he held out his lord's mail shirt. Halga dipped his head, throwing his arms forward before standing tall to allow the byrnie to unfurl down his body with a swish, and as he buckled his sword belt his gedriht stood ready with his helm. Halga cast a look outboard again as the helm went on, running his eyes over the snake ship as he secured the chin strap. The snaca was bow on now, the snarling beast head topping the prow standing out in stark outline against a seascape washed of colour in the fret. Halga's eyes moved across to Steapel at the helm as he rolled his shoulder muscles, anticipating the fight. 'Let me take the rudder,' he said, 'while you prepare for battle.'

To Halga's surprise, his helmsman shook his head. 'We don't have the time,' he replied. 'I am about to make a turn.' As the last of the wreck disappeared aft, he removed a hand from the big paddle blade to point towards the shallows off the larboard beam. 'I am thinking that our luck still holds,' he said. 'If the water is deep enough to swallow a neck that size, it should allow us to squeeze through.'

Halga looked. The clearing mist showed where the tide had stilled as it approached the turn, and a long bowshot to the south the ochre fringe of a stand of sea barley showed where they had almost reached the southern shore. Between the two, the low tide had revealed a warren of mudbanks and small islands, with a bevy of swans marking a deeper course as they dipped their long necks to feed. Steapel had the steering oar hard over when he looked back, and as the tall prow of the *Brimwulf* began to swing, Halga smiled for the first time since the snake ship had appeared from the fret.

Oswy appeared at his side, the gedriht bleary-eyed from his slumber as his mind attempted to understand what was going on. 'Arm yourself and prepare for a fight,' Halga said as the man's gaze went from ship to ship. 'Then join Coella and Godwin in the bows.'

With the *Brimwulf* now beam on to the blocking ship, it was clear they had done the right thing. Stout posts had been sunk into the mud on either side of the channel, and a chain ran from each to the stem and stern posts of the ship itself. Aboard the enemy scegth men could be seen moving fore and aft as they came to realise that their quarry had outwitted them, and as the glimmer of sunlight played upon the first of the muddy banks, Halga turned to address the crew. Without a breath of wind to propel them the sail remained stowed on the cross trees, and with the oarsmen sat facing aft they were reliant on others to tell them what was going on ahead. 'There is a ship blocking the main channel south,' he said, 'but Steapel has spotted another, and we are going to use it to give them the slip. Listen for his instructions; do what he says as soon as he says it, and I am confident that we will get through just fine.'

A quick glance outboard showed where the snaca was shearing off, reluctant to approach the muddy shoals now that the *Brimwulf* was moving deeper into the slew of small channels and mudflats. A look to the west confirmed his earlier fears, that the enemy scegth was letting slip the blocking chains and beginning to turn. Within a few paces, he was back at Steapel's side. 'How does it look?'

The helmsman raised his chin, his eyes following the stretch of water before moving back to the enemy scegth. 'The cut narrows up ahead,' he said, 'but if we can get through without too much trouble, we will reach the waterway before they can turn back and block us in.' Closer now, they could see that the mouth of the main channel wound about a mudbank, then snaked back upon itself. The other scegth would need to row away from them for a distance, before switching back and heading south. It was only a small detour, but it would involve course changes and sharp bends — it should be enough to give them the head start they needed.

An avian hiss followed by the beating of powerful wings showed where they had overtaken the swans. As the cob issued his challenge and the pen ushered the swanlings away, the ghost of a shudder beneath their feet showed just how little water remained beneath the keel. The pair exchanged a look — if they got caught here, they were dead men, switch-back or not. But the next instant the oarsmen had rowed the hull clear, and as the ship moved ahead and the pinch point came up Steapel called out an instruction. 'You will need to pole the ship through, lads. It is not far — a few shoves, and we should be in the main channel. Do it quickly now, before the way bleeds off the ship.'

Halga glanced across to the snaca as the crew of the *Brimwulf* hauled themselves to their feet. The outline of the big warship was growing indistinct as a bank of fog enveloped it once again, and another arrow appeared from the fret to hit the surface of the bay a good fifty yards to the north. Taken together they were indications that the larger ship and the warriors it carried could be safely discounted now that they were within the shoals, and with the main channel now tantalisingly close the rowers unshipped their oars. Moments later the first blades were disappearing beneath the ooze, and as the crewmen began to work hand over hand, the *Brimwulf* picked up speed again. Before the chasing scegth could gain the first bend they were through, the little ship shaking herself free from the cloying mud to slip into the deeper water that marked the main channel. Steapel called a command as the steering oar came into his chest to turn the bows to the south, and Halga matched the big man's smile as the tall prow came about. 'Back to your benches, boys,' the helmsman cried. 'Let us put as much distance between us as we can while they are navigating the bend.'

But if the feeling that they had escaped was welcome, one look at the rowers lowering themselves gingerly to their benches told both men that it was to be fleeting. 'They are all in,' Halga declared bitterly, 'some of them are blowing as hard as your father's bellows.' A quick look back showed where the enemy scegth had all but reached the channel, and turning his face to the sky, the drihten clicked his tongue as he thought. The fog was beginning to lift as the day grew warmer; finding a side channel to hide up in, and hoping that their pursuers would be too caught up in the chase to realise, was impossible. 'Our enemies are rested, and the boys have been bent over their oars all day, so we will be forced to fight,' he declared. 'But we need to choose a place that favours us — somewhere we can spring a surprise.'

He turned his face to Steapel as the boards beneath his feet gave a shudder, and the scegth began to move forward again. 'We have to assume that the rowers on the enemy ship have not only spent the morning waiting for us to appear, but were chosen because they can handle themselves in a fight. How well do you know the route ahead? Is there anywhere we can make a stand where we will not be quickly over-whelmed?'

Steapel whistled softly. 'I have never taken it before,' he finally admitted with a grimace. 'I have seen both ends — the bit in the middle?' He gave a shrug. 'Your guess is as good as mine, lord.'

Halga was already casting a look beyond the prow post as the helmsman made the confession. The detour through the muddy flats had not only avoided a hopeless battle on the bay, but had cut the corner nicely. A short dash away, the southern shoreline was clearly in view as the fret continued to lift. Steapel spoke again. 'Now is the time we could have done with a bowman of our own,' he said. 'If Arékan had been here, she would have picked them off one by one.'

Halga gave him a sharp look. 'If they had not carried Arékan away, she would have died alongside the others. Put her out of your mind,' he said, 'but I do promise you this. Her life is as precious to me as my father's sword, and if we survive this, you *will* see her again.' His hand moved to the amber charm at his throat as he made the pledge. Not only was the hammer the symbol of the northern thunder god Thunor, the Hun woman also wore a charm very much like it as the mark of her adherence to Tángri Khan, the sky god of her people. 'If one woman's help is beyond us for now,' he said, 'let us at least discover if Thera's parting gift brings us the promised luck or not.'

The *Brimwulf* had already made the marsh as they conversed. As the ship moved deeper into the interior and the ranks of sea barley gave way to the softer tones of hare's ear and marram grass beyond, Halga cast a final look to the north. The enemy scegth had doubled the last bend now and was coming on apace, and Halga gave the pendant another rub for luck as he saw that the fight was coming closer with every pull of the oars. Away from the sea the mist was lifting rapidly, and if the view ahead was of a landscape as flat as a witch's tit, it also revealed the thing that may give them a chance. Halga pointed as the *Brimwulf* cleared the first meander. 'There,' he said. 'Lay the ship alongside the jetty for as long as it takes for a few of us to scramble clear.'

Steapel looked aghast. 'You are leaving?'

Despite the dangerous straits they were travelling, Halga let out a snort of amusement at his old friend's expression. 'Not for long — follow the river, and we shall catch you up on the far side of the bend.' Halga grabbed the hatchet that all ships carried to hack away damaged rigging from the rack near the steering oar, and pushing the haft through his belt, he was moving forward before the helmsman could reply. 'Oswy — keep Steapel company: Beorn, grab your weapons and come with me.' The ship was already edging across to the end of the little jetty by the time the pair had gained the bow.

Halga addressed Coella and Godwin as he hooked an arm through the carrying strap on his shield and prepared to go. 'Come on, lads,' he said. 'Spears and shields — follow me, I have an idea.'

Halga leapt overboard as the stage came up, landing with a clatter on the rickety boards. Within moments, all four fighters were on dry land, and he shared a parting look and a nod with Steapel as the ship glided back into mid-channel. He judged the distance between them as it went. Built on the outer loop of a meander, the pier took up almost half of the usable watercourse. The flow became constricted on the far bank, where the current deposited its load of mud and silt, and Halga felt a tremor of excitement as he came to know that the plan just might work. But if he was not to win fame as the shortest lived drihten of all, he would have to move quickly. 'You two,' he said, turning to Coella and Godwin. 'Check the hut — Beorn, come with me.'

A mud brick shack stood within a circular area of beaten earth, and off to one side reeds lay stacked upon drying racks beneath a simple roof of weatherworn thatch. Coella was already reappearing in the doorway of the hut before Halga and Beorn had finished their sweep of the yard. He shook his head. 'It is empty.' Halga nodded as he lifted his chin to peer away to the north. Despite the harvest, the reeds had been allowed to grow tall here to act as a windbreak. But the low-lying salt marsh and lifting fog combined to allow the Jute to clearly see the mast of the enemy ship moving closer as it chased the *Brimwulf* down. 'They are coming on fast,' he said as the pair returned from checking the hall. 'Listen closely — this is what we are going to do.'

.   .   .

HALGA WATCHED the mast from the doorway, his eyes flicking left and right as he gauged the speed of approach. The fret had all but lifted now, and he turned his face skyward as a heron winged its way northwards with its distinctive bent necked flight. Some said the bird was a messenger from the underworld, sent forth from Hel's dank hall of the dead. But if it was a harbinger of death, the die was already cast, and he would have to hope that the errand was not for them. The instant the prow cleared the reed bed he drew *Hild-hete* with a swish, and as his gedrihts moved to his shoulders he spoke a single word: 'Ready?'

As expected, enemy warriors packed the bows of the enemy warship — spearmen, and axemen eager to be in at the kill. The midday sun glinted from mail and spearpoint, and he watched as they threw casual looks in his direction on the off chance that opposition was hiding there. Satisfied, they looked away, and Halga just had time to see them stretch their necks to peer across to the place where the mast of the *Brimwulf* was now within bowshot before they were swallowed again by the reeds. Halga tensed as the first crewmen hove into view, backs arching as they pulled the lithe craft through the water with steady strokes.

The instant the mast came abreast the landing stage, he took a breath and burst from the shadows. He was halfway down the little path before the first head turned, and as he reached the jetty and the crash of his footfall became a clatter on wooden boards, his eyes moved aft to search the steering platform. It was as he had hoped. With the nearness of battle only a single warrior remained to cover the helmsman with his shield, and Halga saw the moment when he realised the danger and the board began to come up.

As he reached the end of the landing stage, Halga dropped a shoulder and leapt, clearing the gap to smash into the enemy's shield as it came around. Knocked back on his heels, the warrior struggled to keep his balance as Halga made the deck, and before he could recover, *War-spite* was scything in to strike his shield arm above the elbow. Protected by his byrnie, the blade failed to penetrate. But the crack that echoed about the deck and the rictus of pain washing the man's features told of the shattered bone within, and Halga lowered his shoulder again to send him tumbling over the side. A last glimpse of the soles of the guard's boots disappearing beneath the surface, and Halga was turning, *War-spite* already moving as he switched his attack.

Caught in two minds between standing his ground or taking flight by the speed and ferocity of the surprise attack, the helmsman was staring open-mouthed as Halga came around. His sword swept down to carve open the man's shoulder — Halga worked the blade free, hacking down again and again as the steersman threw up his arms in a desperate attempt to ward off the blows. With every strike fingers and gobbets of flesh flew, and as blood spurted to redden the deck the helmsman quickly cast all thoughts of resistance aside to throw himself overboard.

With the steering platform secured, Halga risked a look for'ard. His gedrihts were strung out in a line the width of the ship, their shields interlocking as they moved forward step by step to spear one oarsman after another. Already the first to fall were littering the deck, and as those further on came within reach, Halga watched with satisfaction as they began to pile up amidships in their desperate attempts to escape. In the bows, the warriors were beginning to recover from their surprise. But with the deck between them and the attackers a scrummage of panicky men, Halga knew that he was safe for now.

He wiped the blood from the blade of his sword, replacing

it in its scabbard as he made a grab for the handle of the steering oar. He soon had it hard over, and as the bows moved around to point mid-channel and the stern ran aground, he whipped the hatchet from his belt and began to swing. It only took a handful of strikes to sever the leather band that secured the handle in place, and leaning over the wale, the braided withy that fastened the lower part to the frame of the ship itself quickly followed. As the big steering oar came free, Halga lifted it aboard before crossing the platform to heave it into the deep channel.

Carved from a solid piece of oak the rudder sank immediately, and satisfied at the stranding, Halga called out to the others. 'Coella, Godwin, Beorn — we are done here, let's go!'

The trio stepped up, and after a final flurry of hewing and stabbing, hurried aft. Halga indicated the bank with a flick of his head as they arrived, *War-spite* back in his hand as he covered their retreat. With the last of his gedrihts disappearing over the side, he took a final look at the chaos amidships before following on. The deck was slick with blood, the shock of the attack still reflected in the expressions of oarsmen and warriors alike, and Halga took a moment to wallow in self-regard before rejoining them on the bank. It was the first time he had led men into battle as drihten; the first time he had used his grandfather's sword in anger. His gedrihts had followed his plan, and they had inflicted a crushing defeat on an enemy more powerful than themselves — but more importantly, they had done so without shedding a drop of their blood. The foe had been over-proud and paid the price for the contempt they had shown, but the word would spread that they were not to be so lightly thought of, and they could take pride in that.

Halga jumped — Beorn throwing a meaty shoulder into

the stern post to send the scegth drifting back into the deepest part of the waterway, as he made the bank. Safely ashore, he shot them all a smile as Coella and Godwin clashed shields together to make a wall against arrows or spear shot. 'Let us repair to the ship,' he said as they began to edge away. 'Before the enemy can recover and follow on.'

7

HORSA

Oswy stepped back, tilting his head to admire his handiwork. Halga shared a look of amusement with the others, their smiles widening as their friend moved back to tuck a loose rope-end neatly away. Satisfied with his efforts to smarten up the ship, the gedriht turned his face to them. 'There,' he announced proudly, 'that looks better. Is there anything else you want me to do?'

Halga laughed. After a day and night at sea Oswy's seasickness had vanished as quickly as it had arrived, and keen now to make up for his earlier helplessness, the man was abuzz with energy and intent. Sadly, there were only so many things that needed to be tidied on a thirty-foot sailing ship. 'That will do just fine,' he replied. 'I doubt there are neater ropes anywhere at sea — coiled or cleated.' He turned his face to Steapel at the helm, and was about to ask if he could add anything to the conversation when the big man beat him to it. 'We have company,' he announced. The helmsman was leaning to starboard, peering past the sail and off to the south. Halga crossed the steering platform, craning his neck to look. A good head shorter than his gedriht the swell blotted out the view ahead, but as the *Brimwulf* crabbed up the side of the wave to perch on the crest, a handful of mast tops hove into view. Within moments the little scegth was careering down the back slope, and as the spars dipped from sight Halga and Steapel shared a look. The earlier humour had fled the faces of his gedrihts as they had noticed the pair training their eyes to the south, and looking amidships, Halga saw that the crewmen had put aside their dice to stare.

Halga looked eastwards as the ship began to climb the next wave. The coastline was an amber line on the horizon — if they held to this course much longer, they would lose sight of land completely. The crew were already skittish being out so late in the year, and although he knew there was little risk of them rising against his authority, he kept in mind that their willingness to put to sea had saved them all. He turned back to Steapel. 'Where are we?'

The helmsman replied instantly. 'That inlet you can see to the Southeast is Ho Bight, lord.'

'So, beyond that lies the Muddy Sea?'

Steapel nodded. 'It seems that we have made good time. This close to Strand, we can feel confident they are Anglian ships.'

The *Brimwulf* had clawed her way up the slope of the following wave as they had conversed, and the pair lifted their heads once again to stare. Southwards the sails of the vessels were clearly in view now, and Halga counted them off before the bow dipped again. 'Five snaca,' he said, flicking a look towards the man at his side. Steapel nodded again. 'That is what I saw too. If you ask me, they are Angles returning home from their lands in Britannia, lord,' he replied. 'This wind has pushed them a bit further north than they would have liked, but the next tack should see them safely home for winter.'

The steersman cast a look towards the place where the crew gathered amidships. They had been split into two watches, one group resting while the other worked the braces. It was heavy work, repeatedly angling the spar so that the big sail would catch the wind as it zigzagged south, but it also required a deftness to achieve that Steapel feared the crew lacked. He turned back, lowering his voice as he did so. 'If you were thinking of holding this course and passing astern of them,' he said, 'I doubt that these lads are up to working the ship to that degree. Beating to windward is a skill. In this sea, every time the sail luffs as we change tack there is a good chance they will make a mess of it, and then we will end up wallowing beam-on to the waves. If that did happen,' he said with a look, 'in this sea…'

Halga nodded that he understood. The only way a sailing ship could move quickly against the blow was to tack as close to the wind direction as possible. At the point during every turn where the ship was heading squarely into wind, the breeze would spill from the sail, causing it to luff or flap. Any hesitation in angling the spar to reacquire the wind would cause the ship to lose way and possibly founder, and although his gedrihts were experienced seamen, he was loath to use them to work the braces with unfamiliar warships close-by.

He looked outboard as he thought. The first spindrift was snaking back from the wave crests as the gusts began to build, and a glance upwind showed where the horizon to the Southwest was a rampart of grey. The weather was worsening. With a makeshift crew and not much more than a few feet of freeboard even in a dead calm, the little scegth would need all the luck it could get if it hoped to survive a full-blown storm. 'Head in,' he said finally. 'If we are already off the coast of Angeln, we can run her ashore if needs be and travel overland to my foster-father's hall from there.'

Halga explained to the others as the steering oar came about. 'There are a few ships ahead, but this close to Strand we have little doubt they are Anglian. Steapel is going to take us in closer to the coast. With the wind rising, we would rather be driven ashore than risk becoming swamped out at sea.'

As the watch worked the braces and the bows came about, Halga stretched to check on the position of the snake ships. It was as they had thought. Less than half a mile away, the last of the sleek vessels was coming about to match the course set by her companions, following on as they made the final course change to bring them back to port. Steapel let out a chuckle at his side. 'They are not too concerned by us shadowing them then, turning their backs to us like that.' They were close enough now to see the pale smudges of faces turned their way from the steering platform of the final ship in line, and Halga gave a snort as he replied. 'Maybe we could ram them if it came to a fight, but it's a long swim to shore. Just keep a steady distance between us, and we can explain who we are and why we are here when we come safe to land.'

Within the hour the treacherous shoals were behind them, and as the withy marking the safe channel came up on their larboard beam, Steapel brought the ship about to head on in. With the spar rattling down the mast and the oars sliding free of the hull the view ahead opened up, and as Steapel stamped a foot to mark time the rowers bent to their task. The turn had slowed the progress of the Anglian fleet, and Halga walked for'ard as the final ship in line came within hailing distance. Coella was lookout in the bow, and they exchanged a look as a curt challenge drifted across from the Anglian snake. 'Who are you?'

Halga cupped a hand to his mouth, filling his lungs to

reply. 'I am Halga Hunding — a Jute. I have come to call upon my foster-father, Hengest.'

'You are out of luck, Jute,' the answer came back. 'We parted company with Hengest a week ago — he is overwintering in Britannia. Follow us in,' the man continued, with a glance across his shoulder at his companions: 'you will be a lot easier to kill on dry land.' The sound of laughter carried to the men on the *Brimwulf* from the Anglian ship, and Coella spoke at his side. 'It doesn't look like we have much of a choice, lord,' he said, indicating to seaward with a flick of his head. 'I doubt we could make a run for it, even if we had the need.'

Halga turned back to look. The gull grey line of earlier had deepened in hue, and the first flickers of light pulsing along the storm front told of filthy weather to come. 'I have done enough running lately to last a lifetime,' he replied, 'and anyway we are among friends.' He clapped his gedriht on the shoulder as he turned to go. 'There is no chance that this crew would force a passage through weather as foul as that if we made a run for Britannia. Pay no heed to the Angle,' he said with a smile, 'they have a quirky sense of humour — it is how our lanky helmsman got his name.'

The clouds were directly overhead by the time Steapel worked the big steering oar to bring the ship prow on to the wharf. As the daylight fled and the nearby reed beds flattened in the blast, the first raindrops, the size, and weight of berries, swept in to spatter the town. Halga moved into the bow as the little scegth bumped alongside the nearest snaca, and as the crewmen began to stack the oars on the crosstrees amidships, another threw a bowline ashore. The rain had redoubled in intensity during the short while it had taken to guide the ship to shore, and Halga drew his cloak a little tighter as a voice hailed them from the quayside. 'Which one of you is Halga Hunding?'

Coella still had the watch, and Halga sensed his gedriht bristle at the lack of respect shown his lord. He laid a hand on the man's sleeve before he could bark a retort. 'Let it go,' he said. 'We need them far more than they need us, and I caught a glimpse of the man who sent him.' The clatter of wood told where the gangplank had bridged the gap to shore, and Halga was already treading the board before a crewman secured the hawser to the mooring post. The Angle was waiting impatiently on the dockside when he arrived, hunched against the downpour, and as another gust sent a sheeting rain to cleave the nearest roofline, he jerked his head and spat an instruction. 'Follow me.'

Halga stood his ground, and as his gedrihts hurried down the gangway to cluster at his side, he fixed the messenger with a stare. Flanked now by his hearth warriors, Halga recognised the moment the cockiness left the Angle's demeanour, and he lowered his voice to a growl as he made a reply. 'Tell your lord I don't take kindly to receiving orders from men who were raised in a swineherd's hovel. If he could send a man of the better sort with the manners to match, I would happily do what he asks.' After a short hesitation, the man turned to go, throwing a parting sneer as he did so. Within a few moments, the quayside was emptying quickly, as the last of the Angles came ashore and rushed to shelter from the storm.

Beorn cleared his throat as they did so, murmuring a question as the rain pelted down. 'You did think this through, lord? We are going to look pretty silly stood here in the rain if no one returns.'

Halga opened his mouth, ready to lay his concerns to rest. But a familiar figure ducked back through a doorway, and the retort never came. Flanked by two of the burliest warriors any of them had laid eyes upon, the Anglian lord splashed across, pausing only to throw a look of disgust skyward as he came. 'Halga!' he barked as he thumbed a drip from the tip of his nose. 'In case it has escaped you, it is slashing down, and all right-minded folk are undercover. We have just spent a week at sea, so do us both a kindness kinsman,' he said as his face broke into a grin, 'would you *please* come inside out of the rain?'

Halga returned the smile, indicating to his gedrihts that they follow on, as Horsa threw an arm around his shoulder and the guards began to relax. The Angle asked a question as they walked. 'So, these are your boys?'

Halga nodded. 'This is my comitatus — I am their drihten.'

Horsa shot them a smile. 'Welcome to Angeln, lads. Come inside and dry out, we will bank the fire and tap the barrels — just for you.'

The Angle cast a look across to the *Brimwulf* as they went. The crew had just finished constructing the tent amidships and were huddled together, knees drawn up out of the rain. 'Part timers?'

Halga nodded again. 'A scratch crew we assembled in a day or two,' he replied. 'Not many folk will risk setting sail so late in the season.'

Horsa patted him on the shoulder. 'With our ships arriving, I doubt there are many places for them to bed down on land tonight, so they will have to remain where they are. I will have Mildred send pottage and a barrel of ale out when I speak to her, and then you can tell me how your father died.'

Halga looked across in surprise — but the short walk had taken them as far as the hall door, and the Jute's reply remained unspoken as the big Angle stooped to disappear inside. Halga followed on, and the warmth of the hall found an echo within as he recalled the visits of his youth. Mildred's place was a heaving scrum, warriors scrambling for a place at the last free benches as serving girls flit between them like bees in a summer meadow. 'Here we are,' Horsa said as their eyes grew accustomed to the light, 'get yourselves in line. Everyone gets a kiss when they arrive safely home, even if they have only sailed down the coast.' With the snake ships long since emptied of men, the wait was thankfully short, and in no time Halga stood before her. Mildred clapped eyes upon him as she gave the last Angle a peck on the cheek, and Halga was grateful for the warmth he saw there after the trials of the past few days. 'If it isn't Halga,' she declared as the man moved away. 'And all grown up too! How long has it been *dēorling*?'

Halga smiled: 'four long years, Mildred.'

'That will be four kisses I owe you then,' she beamed. 'Bend your head.'

Horsa made a comment as Mildred puckered up. 'Less of the darling if you please — our Halga is a drihten now.'

She planted her kisses and took a step back. 'You will have to forgive me, lord,' she said with mock reverence. 'I am a wanton woman.'

Horsa gave her a squeeze and a kiss of his own. 'We are wanton food and ale, so we will leave his lads to introduce themselves while you smother them in spit. Come on,' he said, plucking at Halga's sleeve, 'let's join my boys.'

The Angle led the way, and Halga allowed himself a snigger as Steapel stepped forward and Mildred's head went back and back to take in his height. His eyes took in the room as they went. Bench after bench ringed the interior walls of the building, and the floorspace between was striped by more. A fire blazed within a nook at the gable end where a serving girl was busily arranging the sodden cloaks of the drinkers onto racks, the steaming mustiness adding another layer to the background fug made by hundreds of men just back from the sea. The Angles of Horsa's comitatus had bagged the prime spot in the room Halga recognised as they approached the bench, close enough to the fireplace to benefit from its warmth, but not so near that it would become stifling. It was a mark of his rank among the Anglian leaders in the hall, and he felt the effortless authority of the man coming off in waves as they crossed to their places.

A space had been left free at the centre for their warlord, but Horsa indicated they clear a gap at the end of the bench for the pair with a flick of his head when they arrived. As the men shuffled aside, pressing full cups upon them, Horsa settled in and spoke. 'So,' he said. 'Tell me how Ottar died.'

Halga took a sip, and was about to reply when he paused and sank a mouthful. He let out a sigh, cuffing the froth from his moustache as he celebrated the reality that he was safe at last and no longer a fugitive. 'That is my first sup since the night at the family barrow,' he said with relish, 'the night before we left. I never knew it could taste so fine.' The Angle listened patiently, only breaking eye contact to refill the young Jute's cup as Halga explained all that had happened since his return to Tiw's Stead. The burning: burial; oath taking and pursuits on land and sea. When he had finished, Horsa nodded. 'You were wondering how I knew your father was dead,' he said.

Halga replied that he was.

The Angle nodded towards *Hild-hete*. 'There are only two ways that a man gets to wear such a sword at his side; as *lāf,* or *eorle* slaying, and no word has yet reached my ears of Halga Hunding the hero killer.' Halga drank again as his kinsman continued. 'You know that my brother is in Britannia?' Halga confirmed that he did. 'What you don't know, however, is that Hengest has already sworn an oath and received a down payment from a warlord there for spear work this coming winter and spring.' Halga's shoulders sagged at the unwelcome news, and Horsa looked to reassure him. 'You have my word,' he said with a look. 'Your father will be avenged when the opportunity presents itself.'

'My father and friends lie in their barrows, and I am driven from my homeland,' Halga replied bitterly. 'Now I am being told that my foster-father cannot help me take vengeance for the slayings for another year. If that is good fortune,' he said with a frown, 'the gods have a wicked sense of humour.'

Horsa's gaze drifted across to the place where Halga's gedrihts were self-consciously sipping at ale cups, dwarfed by raucous Angles. His voice dropped to a burr. 'Listen to me, Halga. If you try to fight king Guthlaf, Garwulf and the plotters backed up by a gang of downy chinned youths in leather war shirts, the best chance you will have to kill them is if they die laughing.' The Angle leaned in, and Halga shifted awkwardly as he drove the point home. 'At the moment you are drihten and gedrihts in name only, and with that sword at your side,' he said, 'attracting every warrior, cutthroat, or drunkard for miles around you will be dead before Yule.'

Halga cleared his throat, his eyes dropping to the ale suds as his cheeks began to burn. It was clear now that the man had led him aside to spare him humiliation. But if all seemed lost at that moment, the Angle's follow-up rekindled the flame of hope. 'The warriors in a comitatus are a reflection of their lord's wealth and prowess. A drihten must be open-handed with his riches Halga,' the big Angle explained. 'What you need is a war, a place where you can gain experience and win renown. Do that and men will flock to your side; amass enough silver to equip your followers with the finest mail, helm, and weapons and many more will come. The gods are not mocking you, they are showing you the way,' Horsa said, leaning forward to prod him lightly on the chest, 'and you would be a fool to ignore them.'

Horsa drained the cup, smacking his lips with satisfaction before reaching for a refill. 'Actually,' he said as the ale frothed, 'you are doubly in luck; I am sailing to war in the spring.'

Halga cocked his head, his expression coming alive as he listened. Horsa was right, this was just what he needed. But there was a wrong that needed righting first, despite the Angle's well-meant advice. Halga listened intently as Horsa outlined his plan, and he awaited the opportunity to counter with one of his own.

'The king of the Franks, Chlodio, died earlier this year,' Horsa explained, 'and his sons have been fighting over the king helm all summer. Merovech is an adopted son of the Roman warlord Aetius, and with their help, he has driven the elder brother Gundebaud into exile. This Gundebaud has overthrown the aged ruler of their cousins, the River Franks, who dwell beyond the Rhine.' Horsa paused to sup, and his eyes took on a dreamy look as he anticipated the fighting to come. 'Roman help or not, Merovech expects to go up against the full might of his brother's new kingdom next year. He is looking to add numbers to his army, and willing to pay.' Horsa halted to glance aside, and Halga followed his gaze. A serving girl was hovering nearby, her reluctance to approach the famous warrior written on her features. Horsa beckoned her across, his mouth breaking into a smile as he reassured her with kindly words. He cut a hunk of beef as she retreated, wagging it to emphasise the importance of his offer. 'Spend a year with me, Halga,' he said. 'Lend me your oath, and by the time my brother is free to leave Britannia, I will have made you a warlord to fear.'

Halga took a sip from his cup as he ordered his thoughts. It was imperative he pitched his proposal well if he were to have any chance of success. 'You show me great honour kinsman,' he said finally, 'and I will gladly give you my oath. But there is a thing I must attempt before we go south in the spring if my word of honour is to count for anything at all, and I will need your help to achieve it.'

8

A YULETIDE VISIT

Halga buried his chin deeper within the folds of his sealskin cape, blinking away the raindrops as he peered into the gloom. Most of the men were sheltering from the downpour beneath the tent stretched out amidships. But as instigator of the midwinter trip he knew that it was his duty to be watchman, however hard the wind gusted, and the rain lashed his hide. Edwin, Horsa's gedriht, stood silently at his side, and Halga felt a pang of guilt that the big Angle was at sea while his hearth mates drank and feasted their way through the yule tidings at home. He thought to ask again if they could have drifted in the dark, but the question was made redundant as a light flickered on the distant shore, and he felt the warrior tense. A short while later the light flashed again, stronger this time as the flames took hold, and Edwin lay a hand on the Jute's shoulder as he began to make his way aft. 'I will rouse the lads,' he said as he went. 'They have rested long enough — it's time to get to work.'

It had been an indulgence to ask of his kinsman, to borrow not only a ship but the men to crew it at this festive time of the year. But with the discovery that his enemy was away, there was no questioning the fact that it was the ideal time to raid. Following his request for help at Mildred's place weeks before, Horsa had made a point of questioning all the travellers who called at his hall that autumn, and soon a picture had begun to emerge of the goings-on in Jutland to the north. Everywhere, they heard the same tale of woe. The length and breadth of Halga's homeland, the forces fighting against the conclusion of an Anglian alliance had brushed any opposition aside.

But if their success had been overwhelming it had also made them complacent, and confident that their enemies were either dead or driven abroad Horsa had learnt that Garwulf had let down his guard. To their joy, they had discovered that the fellow Jute and his greatest warriors had travelled south to spend Yule at king Finn's hall in Frisia. Distinctive due to her Hunnish features, Arékan was said by those who had travelled the Ox Way between the two kingdoms to have been left behind at Garwulf's hall. If that was the case, Halga had reasoned, a lightning raid at midwinter should not only free his dead father's gedriht, but inflict damage on his killer's property and reputation.

Halga thought back on the journey they had just made as the oars went to thole pins, and the scegth got under way. Travelling overland it had been only the matter of a few days before they had taken ship at the head of the great inland waterway of the Sley, and before nightfall they had made the sea. Two days later they were off the eastern coastline of their homeland, and after dropping Steapel and Oswy ashore, the crew had rowed for deeper water and begun to make their way northwards at a leisurely pace. If any watchers on land noticed the low outline of the little scegth they were far enough out at sea to be taken for *wicingas,* the raiders who infested the coasts and rivers of the North, and with the coming of darkness they had shipped oars and waited. Now, with the signal in sight, they were under way once again. All now depended on the success or otherwise of Steapel's visit to Garwulf's hall. Utilising his knowledge of metalworking, the gedriht had posed as an itinerant smith, pitching up just late enough in the day that the occupants would feel obliged to offer him shelter for the night. With an inside man to open the door, the plan was that they could quickly overpower any remaining warriors, free Arékan, and be away before any escapees could raise the surrounding countryside against them.

Halga glanced aside as Edwin returned. The signal light glowed steadily now, and he spared a thought for Oswy crouched on the rain-lashed shore, still unknowing whether help was on its way in the deep darkness of the midwinter night. 'Your man will be pleased to see us,' Edwin said, reading his thoughts. 'He did well to find his way on a night such as this.' Halga raised his eyes. A sickle moon shone dully, low in the eastern sky, its pale light barely enough to pick out the outlines of wind tattered clouds overhead.' If anyone can find their way through this unseen, Oswy can,' he replied with a smile. 'I am sure he was raised by a fox. I owe my life to his wiliness.'

Edwin nodded. 'I heard the tale of your escape, and I am sorry for your loss,' the Angle said. 'Let us repay them in part tonight so that they know this feud has only begun.'

Familiar with the waters of the Jutland coast, the helmsman was steering a steady course, and as a curtain of rain cleared away in the blow the river mouth came into sight. Muffled sounds from amidships told where the men were taking up arms as the scegth neared the shore, and the remaining members of his comitatus came up to join their drihten as a shadow flitted across the beacon ashore. Now was the moment of the greatest danger. Even if Oswy had been taken, Halga was sure that he would hold his tongue, however much he may have suffered. But with the roads and byways all but deserted as men celebrated the turn of the year at home, any travellers abroad would draw even more suspicion than usual. If that had occurred, there was always the slim possibility that he had been followed, and Halga's eyes probed the shadows as his hand moved to the handle of his sword. As they approached the shore the flames flickered out, and the moment the ship edged alongside, Oswy was at the bank. The bows had barely scraped alongside before the gedriht had leapt aboard, and as the steersman guided the ship back to mid-channel with a deft flick of his wrist and the oarsmen pulled again, Halga pumped him for information. 'How did it go?'

'Steapel is inside,' Oswy replied, throwing a nod of thanks to Coella as his comrade thrust a cup into his hand. He moved his head to indicate upriver as he swallowed a mouthful. 'Garwulf's hall is about a mile ahead, and from what we could see we were right; most of the inhabitants are away, celebrating Yule with the king of the Frisians.'

Edwin had returned, and the Angle asked a question of his own. 'How close did you get?'

'A hundred yards or so was the closest I could go,' Oswy replied. 'We couldn't watch from cover because the trees are too bare, but we made a tally of the horses in the paddock, and we are confident that only a hearth guard has been left at home.'

Edwin still needed convincing, and Halga allowed the Angle to ask another question as he listened in. As kin, Horsa had told his men that Halga was the leader of the raiding party and to defer to him, but the Angle was a warrior of renown and only a fool would discount his experience.

Besides, Angle or not, their lives were as much at risk as any Jute here. 'Could the horses have been sheltering in a barn or stable?' He cast a look of disgust at the sky. The incessant rain that had dogged their journey north was easing at last, replaced by the type of fine misting that would turn trews and cloaks into clingy rags in no time.

Oswy shook his head. 'The only outbuildings we saw were a byre — far too small to stable horses, and what could have been thrall quarters or maybe a storehouse. Those horses that remained were racked up beneath a lean-to along the northern edge of the paddock, sheltered from the rain but still fully visible from the road. This river,' he said with a sweep of his hand, 'separates the hayfield from the woodland edge, but it is only navigable for half a mile or so until it is cut by a road bridge. There is a small landing stage this side of the crossing, with a boathouse and a hut for the boat keeper. We will have to tie up there, and make our way to the hall on foot.'

Halga said. 'Was there any sign of life at this lodge?'

'No, lord: I watched from cover for a while before I followed the river course down to the shore. I saw no one come or go, and there was not a whiff of woodsmoke.' He shrugged. 'I wondered whether I should go across and make sure it was unoccupied, but in the end I decided it was too risky. That close to the road I may have been seen, and what was I to do if there was a family sat there? I would have had to bump them all off or bring them with me, and I didn't fancy doing either.'

Halga nodded. 'You did the right thing.' He, too, threw a look skyward; the rain really was letting up at last, the riverbanks either side glistening in the moonlight. 'Let us get this thing done and be away before the dawn. Even if for any reason we fail to free Arékan, we will do enough to let

Garwulf know that there will be an ongoing price to pay for his treachery.'

The conversation had eaten onto the time it took for the lithe warship to cover the distance to the bridge. As the river took a meander to the north and the bows came about, the outline of the crossing place and landing stage before it came into view. Halga opened his mouth to request his shield. Beorn had anticipated him, and his hand slipped into the grip as Halga stole a look astern. Horsa's men were ready: helmed, mailed and armed as the stern of the ship cleared the bend, and he looked on with admiration as they came up and made ready to storm ashore. A brief look to take in the preparedness of his own gedriht told him they were set, and as the helmsman worked the steering oar to bring the scegth bow on to the bank, he prepared to lead them forward.

The moment he felt the side strakes glance against the stage, he was moving, hauling himself up and onto boards made slick by the rain. The boat keeper's lodge was a score or so paces away, and Halga set off at a run as the sound of booted feet and the metallic chink of mail told where the ship was disgorging its deadly cargo. Within a few steps Halga was on solid ground, and as the surface beneath his feet turned from slippery wood to puddled earth he began to pick his way across to the doorway. Leaping from high point to high point he was soon there, and as he caught a glimpse of Edwin's Angle's pouring into the boat shed downstream he raised a foot to kick. The door crashed inwards, and a heart-beat later, Halga was stepping inside.

The interior of the hut was in total darkness, and although the lack of a hearth fire and the mustiness of the place confirmed Oswy's reasoning that the place was uninhabited, Halga dodged aside to deny anyone concealed inside a clear shot. His shield came up as he moved further into the room, and as he swept the interior with his spearpoint, his gedriht spilled through and did the same. A small wind-hole had been cut in the eastern gable of the hut to keep an eye on the boathouse, and although the moonlight barely lit the scraped hide covering, it was enough to confirm they were alone. Satisfied, he led them back outside, and as Edwin reemerged from the boathouse and led the Angles across, Halga summoned Oswy to their side. 'Give us a quick rundown — I want to attack straightaway.'

The roadway had been raised above the level of the flood-plain where it approached the bridge, hiding the fields beyond from view. Oswy ran the point of his spear along the line of the bank as Halga and Edwin listened in. 'Beyond that,' he said, 'the land rises gently up to the place where Garwulf has his hall. There is a spur leading off from the main road that cuts through the hayfield, and on into the courtyard. The hall itself is built on the highpoint, with the paddock and byre on its northern edge, sheltering the yard from the worst of the winter blow.'

'How far away are we?'

'Once we get up onto the road, it is only a dozen yards until the track branches off; then it is another hundred yards or so until we reach the hall.'

Halga chewed his lip, casting a look skyward as he thought. The rainclouds had all but cleared away now, and the moon was clear and bright. 'That's a long way to run without being seen, and we must assume that there will be a guard posted even though Garwulf is away.' He cursed. 'We could have done with the rain hanging around a little longer.'

At his side, Edwin cleared his throat, and Halga looked across. The Angle was staring upriver, and Halga followed his gaze. A pathway ran side by side with the river course, and raising his eyes he saw that it led to a series of well-worn steps cut into the side of the causeway. 'Where does that lead?'

'On the other side of the road there is a kind of towpath,' Oswy replied. 'They must use it to load and unload boats from the interior that can't get past the bridge.'

'Did it look waterlogged?'

Oswy shook his head. 'No, lord, it's raised above the level of the flood.'

Halga shot the Angle a look of thanks. 'That sounds just the thing. If I lead my men along there, we will take care of any guards and signal you to come forward when the way is clear.'

Edwin nodded that he understood.

'Right,' Halga said, fiddling with the chin strap. 'These can go.' He turned to the men of his comitatus as the helm came off. 'We are attacking along the line of the river, and with the return of the moonlight we can't afford any reflections to give us away.' He slipped the deerskin scabbard back onto the blade of his spear, as his gedrihts stacked their helms in a pile. 'Shroud your spear blades until we approach the hall, and leave the covers on your shields. If we are spotted before we are in position to launch the attack, we shall be fighting on a slippery slope until Edwin and his men can come to our aid. Keep low and make what use of shadow we can find.' He smiled. 'At least Steapel is already there — we shan't have to worry about the lanky streak of piss giving us away.' His gedriht returned the smile, but Halga recognised the worry that lay behind them, and knew that it must have been reflected in his own.

They had come a long way together during the past few months, he kenned. If they had been a solid band of friends before the attack that had killed his father and torched his home, the shared trials and dangers since that time had formed an unshakable bond. It was the longest period that any one of their brotherhood had spent apart since that time; if they had been only dimly aware of just how close they had grown together during that spell, Steapel's lone foray into danger no longer left them in any doubt. Halga threw a parting look at Edwin as sheaths slid onto spear blades. 'I will see you soon.'

As the Angle returned a curt nod and began to turn away, Halga set off down the track. A steady jog and the steps were rising before him, and gaining the roadway he paused to peer left and right. As expected, the only men mad enough to be abroad during the hours that were the domain of wolves and trolls were themselves bent on death and destruction, and he bent low in the moonlight as he doubled across. Within a few steps, he was safely descending the far bank, and as he moved back into shadow and the rest of his comitatus made their way across, the Jutish leader cocked his head and listened. Halga scanned his surroundings as he did so, rejoicing when he saw that Oswy had described it perfectly. The river with its towpath was a steely line in the light of the moon, and although the water meadow looked a boggy morass, Halga could see the pathway leading up from the watercourse was only a sprint away.

A quick check that all were there and Halga set off at a trot, back arched, spear held low as he made his way towards the footpath now tantalisingly close where it climbed the valley side. As he grew closer, the boggy ground fell away, and he gripped his spear shaft a little tighter as he cut the corner and leapt up onto the first step. Raising his eyes, Halga fixed his gaze upon the point where the steps reached the summit. He stared hard as he climbed. No face appeared there, and reassured that they had got this far unseen, he dropped his pace to a steady crawl as the gentle swish of their mail byrnies sounded unnaturally loud in his ears.

Halga was already slowing as the last of his men gained the foot of the stair, and the footfalls fell away as he came to a halt and risked a peek. With the moon now throwing the courtyard and buildings into stark outlines of light and shade, Halga quartered the scene as he searched for the guard he knew must be there. To his surprise, the yard before the hall appeared deserted. Switching his gaze across to the paddock, Halga's eyes stabbed the shadows as he attempted to pick out any sign of men among bulbous rumps of equine flesh. Halga hesitated, keenly aware that the success or otherwise of the entire raid rested upon the decision he made in the next few moments. When still no guard appeared, he glanced back as a hand moved up to slip the scabbard from his spear blade. Arrayed below him, the others were following his lead, their eyes fixed upon him as they tensed and prepared to dart forward on his command. Another look towards the hall — still nothing. He would have to take a chance.

9

A DISH BEST SERVED HOT

Every sense he possessed was keener than a blade as Halga rose from cover. But as he started to cross the moonlit square and hope began to build, the squelch of booted feet on muddy ground had his head snapping around. The sound was coming from the side of the hall, and Halga lengthened his stride as he sought to reach the point where the owner of the footfall would emerge into the clearing. He was almost there when the spearman appeared, his weapon wedged uselessly in the crook of an arm, mail coat hoist up and pinned beneath his chin as he fumbled with the ties on his breeks.

Sensing movement, the guard looked up, and Halga had the presence of mind to flash him a smile as the distance between them shrank. He had to assume the hall door locked and barred, but even a single cry of alarm from the man ahead would be enough to rouse the hearth guard against them. Halga saw the look of surprise in the young guard's expression replaced, first by bemusement as his mind attempted to fix the identity of the man before him, and then panic as he realised the truth.

But the moment of indecision caused by Halga's friendly smile had been enough to seal his fate, and the drihten levelled his spear as he spurred across the final few yards to slam the blade deep into his guts. Halga's hand was already moving from the shaft to draw his dagger as the man doubled over in agony and shock, and as the guard's head came down, the blade came up until steel and bone met with a sickening crunch. Halga reached behind the man's head as it was driven back up, dragging it into his shoulder to muffle his cries, pinning it there as the dagger came free. He managed a savage stab to the chest before the mail coat fell back into place, and as the sentinel's struggles began to lessen and his strength drained away, Halga twisted to bury the knife into his neck with a horrible squelch. Muffled by Halga's shoulder and cloak, the cries of the guard were becoming a pathetic mewl as death's doors opened wide, and as the sound became a rattle and his body went limp, Halga let him drop.

As soon as he was sure the man was dead, he tugged his spear free, his head turning this way and that as he searched for any sign that the man was not alone. Satisfied for now that the guard appeared to have been a singleton, Halga stepped back into the courtyard and raised his gaze. Twenty paces away, the top of Oswy's head was just visible above the lip of the rise, and Halga beckoned him across as his attention switched to the great double doors of the hall itself. If the sounds of the guard's death-struggle had alerted those inside, now would be the time when the doors crashed open to disgorge his hearth mates bent on revenge. Halga listened hard for any sign of a reaction within as the men of his comitatus began to cross the yard towards him, wiping the worst of the blood from the knife blade as they came up.

Oswy spoke in a whisper. 'Shall I make the signal?'

Halga nodded and turned away. 'You two,' he breathed, as

the gedriht loped off. 'Take a side each, and double check that our friend here was alone.' Coella and Godwin melted into the shadows as they went to circle the hall, and Halga crossed to the doorway as his hand went to the fire-steel on his belt. A quick glance towards the nearby roadway showed where Edwin was leading his Angles from cover, and as they gained the track that led to the hall, Halga turned his attention to the entrance. Both doors closed against a hefty beam that formed a sill at ground level, but there was enough of a gap further up between the door posts and the planking itself for what he had in mind. Sparks flew as steel came together, and Halga dashed the back of his knife blade along the fire-steel once more for luck before taking a rearward pace. As the tramp of booted feet told where Edwin and his men had reached the yard, the sound of wood scraping against wood came from the other side of the door as the locking bar slid from its bracket. Halga drew his sword as the door inched open, and an instant later a familiar face appeared in the gap. Seeing his drihten, Steapel hauled the door inward, and as Halga vaulted the threshold his eyes swept the room.

At first, the long hearth running down the centreline filled his vision. But as he moved further into the hall, the vista widened to reveal the ridge-like forms of sleeping men stretched out in the glow. The more alert were beginning to react, throwing coverlets aside to scramble bleary-eyed to their feet as the room began to fill with running men, and as the war cries of the Angles added to his own, Halga raised War-spite high. A face turned his way. Halga recognised the instant when fear and bemusement became the certainty of imminent death as the blade streaked down to make a horror of it. Halga reversed the blade, taking a backwards swipe to finish him off as he strode past and on to the next man. With all of his weight supported on one arm as he rose from the settle, it was clear where the next blow should fall. Halga brought his sword blade scything around to lop off the arm in a gush of blood. The point of War-spite had found the soft tissue beneath the man's chin before he hit the ground, slicing in open to pare flesh from bone.

Halga raised his eyes as the victim gargled blood at his feet. The room was filling with sword and spearmen, their reddened blades rising and falling in the firelight as they hacked at the struggling figures beneath them. The slaughter was almost over, and following a quick check that there were no enemies nearby, the Jutish drihten raised his gaze and looked about the room. Bloodied bundles showed where the hearth guard had been dispatched to Woden's hall of the dead. Scattered haphazardly between them, women lay frozen in terror, their arms held clearly in view as they placed their faith in the honour and restraint of blood-crazed men.

A high-pitched shout, and a woman's scream, as a lad of five or six emerged from a bower — sword held high for a killing stroke. But he had only gone half a dozen paces before an Angle ran him through, pitching his little body aside on the blade of his spear like hay at the making, as the war cry became a gush of bloody gore. The room from which the lad had emerged needed checking. Halga was about to move towards it, when he froze as he felt the cold steel of a razor sharp blade nick his throat. But if the fact that he had been snared at the moment of victory came as an unwelcome shock, the peck on the cheek and the words that followed replaced that feeling with one of elation. 'You took your time Halga,' she murmured into his ear as the blade came away. 'But I am glad to see you all the same.'

. . .

Steapel unhooked the iron ring from the nail, sorted through the keys and tossed one across. Halga went to catch, but another hand shot out to snatch it from the air, leaving him grasping at space. 'I will do this, if you don't mind,' Arékan said, working the key into place. 'Until you spend a couple of months chained up, you can't really grasp just how underrated the freedom to come and go as you please really is.'

The meaty thuds and anguished cries of men dying had faded now, replaced by the sobs of the survivors and a tortured rasp as wooden chests splintered. Halga spoke to Steapel as the lids came up, and the contents spilled out onto the floor. 'How did it go?'

'The plan worked well, lord,' the big man replied. 'I arrived far too late in the day to be sent packing, so they were obliged to offer me a roof for the night — what with the rain and all. The hardest part was bagging a sleeping spot where I could keep my eye on the door without arousing suspicion — that and lying awake all night, keeping a lookout for the signal.' He squeezed his eyes shut before making a great play of rapidly blinking them. 'I have that doorway imprinted on my mind now. I shall be seeing it every time I close my eyes for the next few weeks!'

Arékan was already rooting around the dead, rolling the corpses onto their backs and giving each face a cursory glance before moving on. Steapel spoke again. 'If she is searching for someone in particular, the gods would have done him a kindness if he is already dead.' The Angles guarding the prisoners had noticed too, and Halga hurried to lay their fears to rest as one of Edwin's lads levelled his spear at the strange woman. 'Stay your hand,' he said. 'She is with me.'

Oswy had joined them, and lifting his eyes Halga watched

as Coella and Godwin ducked in through the entrance following their circuit of the hall, the disappointment that they had already missed the killing etched on their faces. 'He is not too bright, that lad,' Oswy said, indicating the Anglian guard with a jerk of his chin. 'He knows why we are here — how many Hun women can you see?'

Halga snorted. Having shared his father's hall with the woman for the greater part of his life, he sometimes forgot how rarely the distinctive features of her people made an appearance so far north. Were it not for the Finns and Sami in the lands of ice and snow, they would be rarer still. As the spearman relaxed his guard and turned back, the woman hawked noisily and spat at a corpse.

Steapel said. 'It looks like she's found him.'

Arékan tugged down the dead man's trews as she drew his knife from its scabbard, and within moments something gory and pale was sizzling on the hearth fire. The Jutes shared a grimace, turning away as the Hun moved the blade up to pare away the dead man's nose. 'I have things to discuss with Edwin,' Halga said, as Arékan continued to cut and slice. 'You lads — make a search for my father's sword in the bower at the back.'

Horsa's gedriht was examining the plunder, as his men made a pile near the door. He smiled as Halga came up. 'That could not have gone better,' he said. 'A hall taken, a hearth guard slain — and none of my men took so much as a nick.' His eyes widened in question. 'Yours?'

Halga was about to confirm the same, when both men started as a high-pitched ululation cut the air. Both men looked. Arékan was standing astride what now looked like a butchered hog, her arm running with blood as she held a bloody ball aloft. Throughout the hall all eyes turned towards her, and Halga saw the colour drain from the faces of captives and hardened warriors alike as the Hun tore a strip from the dead man's heart with her teeth and began to chew. Edwin was the first to rediscover his voice in the shocked silence that replaced the woman's howl of vengeance. 'Fuck me, Halga,' he squeaked. 'Are you sure you are doing the right thing, freeing her?' Although the Angle's words had been spoken in little more than a whisper, the weight and implication behind them was clear. It was his raid, his insistence that they attempt to rescue his father's gedriht from captivity. The slaughterous retribution taken by Arékan on the body of Garwulf's man had driven the uneasy calm that had followed the killings away. The mood in the hall stood poised on a knife-edge, and it would only take a sudden movement or cry for the killing to recommence.

Despite his sense of shock at the blood-drenched rite that was taking place before them, Halga forced himself to act, and as he made his way across the floor of the hall he was painfully aware of a hundred pairs of eyes tracking his progress. Arékan still had her back towards him, the jerk of her head telling the tale where another gobbet of muscle had been stripped from what remained of the organ. His eyes moved to the bloodstained knife in her hand as he walked, and careful not to catch her unawares, he took a circular route before coming to a halt before her.

It was clear from the woman's eyes that her mind was elsewhere, and heedful of the bloody knife that was only feet away, he spoke slowly and clearly as he attempted to draw her back. 'Arékan,' he said, in a voice as calm as he could muster. 'It's over.'

Up close now, Halga noticed for the first time that the Hun was swaying gently as she chewed, and he held out a hand as those in the room looked on ashen-faced. 'Arékan, pass me the knife.' The second mention of her name began to clear away the mental fog, and Halga watched as her eyes slowly regained focus and fixed themselves upon him. He smiled, anxious that he be recognised as a friend. 'The knife, Arékan...' The woman raised her arm, and Halga kept the smile fixed upon his features as she did so. All at once, she came back, and Arékan returned the ghost of a smile as she handed the blade across before tossing the remains of the dead man's heart into the flames. The smile fell away as she spat a piece of meat aside, and Halga quickly moved the conversation on as Edwin's Angles went back to their looting. 'Garwulf not only carried you off, he took my father's sword. Do you know where it is kept?'

Arékan was fully aware now, and the Hun replied without hesitation. 'He keeps Hildleoma on him at all times, Halga,' she replied. 'It will be at his side.'

Halga nodded. Although it was as he had expected, there had been a small chance that he would find the ancestral blade in the hall, and the pang of regret was no less real. Arékan was bathed in blood, and he swept the room with a look as he explained the make-up of the raiding party. 'Most of these men are Angles, part of my kinsman Horsa's comitatus. We have a scegth nearby. Go and clean yourself up — we will be taking ship for Angeln very soon.'

Halga spoke a few words to the spearman guarding the women, children, and slaves as he crossed the hall towards the bower at the rear. 'Get these outside,' he barked. 'We are torching the hall.' Oswy was already exiting the room as he came up, and he threw his lord a savage grin as he pushed a man before him. 'Look who I found hiding out the back,' he said with a look of triumph. He grasped the man by the scruff of the neck, forcing him to his knees before his drihten. 'Do you want to kill him now, lord?'

Halga grasped the man by the hair, yanking his head back

to fix him with a glacial stare. The man went to open his mouth, but the look on Halga's face warned him off. Halga knew he was shaking, all the hatred he had for Garwulf and his burners now channelled into the fate of a single man. 'No,' he said finally. 'Hrafn deserves a far grimmer death, one befitting a man who betrays his lord and costs him his life. Bring him along until I decide what it shall be. Arékan says that Garwulf has my father's sword on him, so there is no more reason to stay. Get the lads outside, we are returning to the ship.'

Halga turned to Arékan nearby as she rinsed the blood from her arms in a pail. Hrafn's capture had gone a long way to making up for the missing sword, and his smile returned as his anger subsided. He took down a leather pouch from the wall. Halga had recognised it at once as her gorytos, the distinctive crescent bow case of the Steppe people in the East. 'I take it this is yours,' he said, propping it against a post. She returned the smile, and Halga gave a little shiver to see the white of her teeth flashing from a face made devilish by blood.

HALGA PAUSED at the bank and looked back. The blaze had taken hold now, and the causeway wore a corona of light. Arékan came across as the lads loaded the plunder aboard. 'Thank you,' she said, 'for coming for me.'

Halga shrugged. 'How could I not?'

They stood in silence awhile, watching the fire build. Soon great tongues of flame were licking the sky, painting the undersides of the clouds with their glow. There was something troubling her, and Halga watched the shadows dance as he waited for her mind to shape her thoughts into words. 'I was being made ready to accompany Nerthus in the spring,' she said finally, 'and the body I attacked belonged to the guda who was…' She hesitated as she searched in vain for the right word to describe all the things that had been done to her during her time in Garwulf's hall. Finally, she gave up, settling for the emphasis on an everyday word that would have to cover all the pain and indignities that had been forced upon her: ' — the guda who was *preparing* me to participate in the ceremony.'

The fertility goddess Nerthus lived in a sacred grove on an island off the coast. Each year she was drawn on a covered cart among representatives of the folk who worshipped her, before the slaves and captives who accompanied the procession were put to death by drowning. Halga gave a shudder: the secrets of gods and priests were best left that way. 'There is no need to explain,' he said. 'Too many men saw what happened to keep it quiet — but no stories will come from my men, and I will ask Horsa to speak to his.'

The matter out in the open, the Hun brightened. 'So,' she said. 'You are drihten?'

'I am,' he replied proudly. 'I have few warriors for now; but we are warring in the south next summer, and the loot and reputation I gain there will give me more.'

She smiled, running her eyes over him as a call from the riverside told them both that the ship was ready to sail. They turned to go, and Arékan spoke again as they walked. 'It suits you Halga,' she said, 'your father would be proud.'

'What about you? You are free to do as you please,' Halga replied. 'Where will you go?'

'My lord and hearth companions have been murdered, and the man who led the killers still lives,' she answered, the smile instantly replaced by a steely look. She slid the top of her bow from its gorytos, before slamming it home to reflect her resolve. 'My duty is as clear as your own.'

10

WITCHERY

'No, that's just an old oak,' Edwin said. 'That's the Woden Tree — there, where the roadway doubles the headland.' The young Jutes followed the line of his arm, gasping in wonder as they picked the old tree out, now gnarled and twisted by unimaginable age. Halga listened in to their excited chatter as the ship swept past, and the hint of a smile came to his lips as he recalled the first time he had seen the sacred bole, and heard the tale of how it was brought into being as a child. Hengest had brought him here, the first summer of his fostering, and in his mind he heard his foster-father speak again as the scegth cleared the promontory and the town of Sleyswic hove into view. The god Woden had visited the greenwood here in his journeying and hunted the great boar Spear-bristle. Brought to bay at this very spot, god, and beast, had fought a daylong duel before the deity had prevailed. Working a tusk free with his knife to carry off as a trophy, an acorn had fallen from the swine's mouth. As a tribute to a worthy foe, the All-father had buried both head and seed at the site of their struggle, and from that, the Woden

Tree had grown. It was a tale familiar to all who lived in the lands that hallowed the god, and Halga watched as the hands of Angle and Jute alike went to charms and amulets as the headland drifted astern.

With the narrows behind them, the Sley broadened again, and Halga took in the scene as the town came closer. With the midwinter festivities now behind them, the waterfront was abuzz, with the doors to the boat sheds flung wide as the vessels were run out to prepare for the trading and raiding season that would soon be upon them. Carpenters and ship-wrights, painters and sailmakers surrounded every hull, as the sound of hammering and sawing carried to the returning crew across the chilly waters of the firth.

Halga raised his eyes to the hillside beyond, as the helmsman worked the steering oar to bring her home. The huts, halls, and warehouses of Sleyswic ran upslope from the strand, the lime washed walls glistening in the weak winter sun beneath an ochre thatch of reed and hay. At the centre of the settlement, twin roads crossed. An east-west road that ran from coast to coast, and a smaller road, little more than a track, that led from the dockside and town up to the gilt columns and great hogged back of *Eorthdraca* — Earth-dragon — the hall of Offa, king of the Angles, perched upon the summit. As the shallows came up and the sound of gravel on keel told them all that the little ship had regained its port, he dropped his gaze again as crewmen tumbled over the bows to heave the hull ashore.

Halga shared a look with Edwin as dripping oars clattered onto the cross trees amidships, and the men began to collect weapons and belongings ready for the onward journey. 'Here they are,' he said. 'Come to welcome home the conquering heroes.'

Edwin tutted. 'Come to collect their share of the spoils, more like. They always did know the value of silver in Sleyswic.'

The crew had formed twin lines now, passing belongings and booty ashore, making a heap on the shingle where the newcomers had come to a halt. Halga spoke again. 'We had best get down there, before they take the lot!' The pair made their way forward as the helmsman shipped the steering oar, vaulting the wale to land in the shallows with a splash. Halga cast a look down the strand as he waded ashore. Already aware of the identity of the crew and the reason for their unseasonal voyage, the spearmen accompanying the king's reeve had brought a barrel down to celebrate the homecoming. With the barrel tapped and the first ale foaming, they listened in as their countrymen described the fighting in the hall.

Arékan had drifted aside as the others had celebrated the conclusion of a successful raid in typically boisterous fashion, tugging the captive Hrafn along on the end of a horsehair rope. Halga thought to follow on. But Oswy sought her out with a cupful, and he put her from his mind as he and Edwin made their way across the beach. The reeve threw the pair a welcoming smile as they came, sliding his eyes across to Edwin. Before he could utter a word, the Angle indicated the young Jute at his side. 'Halga Hunding is the leader of this war band; you should address any questions to him.'

The Anglian official tactfully covered up for the mistake with all the ease of a man long practised in diplomacy, and he instantly switched his attention. 'Welcome home, lord,' the reeve oozed. 'From the look of the items in the stack, you had an agreeably successful trip.' The smile faded to be replaced by a look of concern. 'Your casualties were light, I trust?'

Halga beamed, as he confirmed that they had rescued a captive, taken one of their own, and burnt his enemy's hall without suffering loss or injury. The reeve returned the smile as he offered his congratulations, before his sense of duty reasserted itself, and he held out a hand. 'You have the tally?'

Halga fished inside the pouch at his belt. The Angles had built something of a fort overlooking the place where the waters of the Sley emptied into the sea. All ships entering the firth put ashore there, where an inventory was taken of the items aboard. The reeve produced duplicate records — one for the shipmaster, the other to travel overland to the official's counterpart here in Sleyswic. If both records tallied, a tribute of one-third part of the imported goods or booty would be levied and sent up to king Offa's treasury in the hall overlooking the town. With the main north-south trading route of the Ox Way only a few miles further west, and a nearby portage linking the Sley to the inland river system and the German Sea beyond, Sleyswic was ideally placed to gather taxes. It was, Halga knew, a major part of what made the Angles such a wealthy and powerful people, despite the moderate size of the kingdom.

Satisfied that the two inventories matched and that no goods had been offloaded on the journey along the Sley, the reeve led the way across to the place where the goods looted from Garwulf's hall had been divided into thirds by king Offa's men. 'Assure yourself that all is in order here,' the man said, 'and you are free to leave.' With a third part owed by Halga to Horsa as his lord, and the final third due to be shared out among the men themselves, it took little more than a glance to confirm that the crew had watched the divvying up like hawks. Besides, he had rescued his father's gedriht from a grisly death in the coming spring, and although Hildleoma

— the sword War-bright — had gone south with its captor, they had struck a powerful blow against his enemy. The renown he would gain from the victory would far outweigh mere treasure. He turned back and gave the reeve a smile. 'That all looks fine,' he said. 'We will polish off the last of the ale, and be on our way.'

The reeve could not hide his surprise. 'You are not staying the night? We have a guest hall for travellers, and there is plenty more ale where that came from.' He pointed out a long, low building near the shoreline to the East. 'The Barley Mow brews the best ale in all Sleyswic.'

Halga's eyes glistered. 'Your brother's?'

The Angle laughed. 'No, my sister's place. But every word was true — she is as fine an ale-wife as you will find for a hundred miles around.'

Halga shook his head. 'Another time maybe — Edwin has already gone to retrieve our horses from the stable.' He raised his eyes. The sky was the washed-out blue of a fine winter's day, with only a streak of cirrus high up to the west to muddy its perfection. 'We are keen to return while the weather holds,' he added, 'our friends will be waiting, eager to hear our news.'

'Then I wish you well, Halga Hunding,' the reeve replied. 'May the gods continue to fight at your side.'

Halga watched as king Offa's official gathered his men and trudged from the strand, before crossing the shingle to rejoin his troop. Steapel held out a cup at his approach. 'That will make it easier to carry,' he said with a nod towards the much reduced treasure pile. 'It always irks you having risked your neck, only to give a third up on your return.'

Halga took the cup, savouring his first taste of ale for more than a week. He was about to respond when he realised the truth in the reeve's words: this was good stuff! He took a long pull and replied. 'No man enjoys paying his dues, but when foemen threaten and the king arrives at the head of an army, they see they have struck a good bargain. If only our king were so dependable — we should be safely at home, and my father still living.' Edwin reappeared with the mounts, chasing the awkwardness away, and Halga gave his gedriht a clap on the shoulder as they began to shoulder their belongings. 'Come on,' he said. 'Let's get moving.'

Within the hour they had loaded the panniers, and put the king's town behind them. Halga was leading the column with Steapel, Oswy and Arékan with the captive just behind, and the young Jute drank in the view as the land trended upwards, and they gained the hilly country to the west. It never ceased to amaze him just how quickly the countryside recovered from the dark days of midwinter. Only a few weeks into the new year the downhill slide into gloom and darkness had been replaced by visibly lighter days, and although the first green shoots of spring were still a way off yet, it seemed that every bird was busy pairing up and nest building. The track followed the line of the portage that ran between the River Trene and the Sley, the grassy line running arrow straight through the hills before descending to the carrying place at the Old Ford. Although they had the passage to themselves so early in the year, the hoof prints and runnels made by the oxen and their charges summer after summer was as clear as any road.

Beyond the Old Ford the track narrowed as it pushed out across the Polder, the lowlands where Horsa had his hall. Weighed down by the loot in the panniers, the horses were making heavy work of it, so it was a welcome moment when Edwin indicated the side track with a nod of his head. 'That's the place I was telling you about,' he said. He shot Halga a look. 'Are you are sure you want to go through with this?'

Both men cast a backward glance. Arékan rode grim faced a few yards to their rear, all the life seemingly washed out of her by the trauma of the past few months and the guda's spell work. The turncoat Hrafn looked even worse — riding with a noose around his neck. As Halga looked on, the Hun gave the short rope a wicked tug, jerking him sideways. Halga nodded when they turned back. 'If you had known the woman before all this, you wouldn't need to ask.' He gave the Angle a pensive look. 'We may have rescued her bodily from her torment, but I fear she will never fully recover unless we seek further help. I have spoken with her and, well...' He hesitated before carrying on. 'Let's say that she didn't say no. It needs to be done, and they should be satisfied with the exchange we are offering — a life for a rebirth.'

Edwin nodded. 'I will tell the lads. We will take your men and a handful of my own — we won't be in the type of danger we can easily fight off, so there is no point in taking any more, and it will give most of the men and horses a rest.'

The mood changed the moment the horsemen entered the woodland. Gone was the airiness of a winter day in the wide-open space of the portage, replaced by a feeling of dread as trees, gnarled and twisted by great age: oak; elm; beech, enveloped them. The nervous jokes and chatter quickly died away as they rode, and as the short day neared its end they were soon picking their way through a place of gloom and shadow. Halga shared their fear. The thought of spending a night inside the haunted woodland filled him with dread, so it was with a strange sense of relief when they came upon the skulls of animals and men fixed to the boles of trees. Halga glanced aside: 'Nice.'

The Angle pulled a sickly smile. 'None of your stick

shaking and crazy squeals here,' he replied. 'These witches are the real thing.'

The trees pulled back as they put the skull-field behind them to reveal a handful of huts, the thatched roofs indistinct where woodsmoke cloaked them from the hearth fires within. Beyond them, Halga could see the sacred lake, the waters taking on a steely sheen as a wintery sun sank in the west. The only sign of life came from a brace of crows, the dark birds cawing in the treetop as if to announce their arrival.

Edwin glanced upwards as the horses came to a halt. 'As I said, the girls here don't miss a trick.'

Halga said. 'Do you think they know we are here?'

Edwin snorted. 'Oh, they know all right.'

A more tangible answer to his question came within moments, as a group of women emerged from a doorway, crossing the open space before the huts to pitch up a half dozen yards before them. Edwin murmured an instruction as he began to dismount. 'Stay here, Halga,' he said, before adding more ominously. 'Let's hope we know what we are doing.'

The men watched as Edwin crossed the divide, holding his hands wide in supplication as he went. Halga risked a look at the women as he did so. To his surprise there were none of the crones and hags he had expected from listening to the old stories, and although their ages ranged widely from youth to middle age they were comely women. One in particular had caught his eye, and for an instant he thought it was Thera, his playmate from back in Tiw's Stead. But his stomach gave a lurch as she returned his gaze, and he quickly averted his eyes.

When he looked back, Edwin and the head witch were making their way across to the place where Arékan sat mid-column, and as the Hun dismounted to be led away the other women came across to mingle. Even sat at the front of the column, Halga could sense the unease among the men as they did so. Hard men, men with traces of other men's blood still staining their clothing, were clearly as afraid as they had ever been, and Halga too steeled himself as he sensed a witch stop at his side.

Despite his fears, his curiosity got the better of him, and he dropped his gaze to look. It was no surprise to find that he was looking directly into the eyes of Thera's lookalike when he did so, and Halga caught his breath as he was enveloped by a lustful wave. The memories returned with the familiarity of her features, the homely smell of woodsmoke in her hair: all combined to have the usual effect on his body. Still in the saddle, her face was at waist height to him, and he shifted with discomfort when he realised that she had noticed too. Barely a foot apart the witch was staring with an otherworldly detachment as she watched him swell, and when she was satisfied that it had reached its full extent she raised her eyes to his. 'Visit me,' she breathed, tracing a pattern with her fingernails along his inner thigh. 'Mayhap we can work a spell of our own.' Halga swallowed hard as she moved on, rejoining her sisters as they rifled through the panniers to carry away whatever caught their eye.

Edwin's shout broke her hex, and Halga's mind reaffixed upon the danger they were in as he listened to the Angle's instructions. 'Lead your horses over to the place they are marking out,' he bellowed. 'No man leaves the cordon until daybreak.' He looked across. Witches were moving near the tree line, corralling them into a place of safety using flaming brands. Further along, Arékan was halfway across the lake, looking back helplessly as the log boat moved towards a small island and the ramshackle hut perched upon it.

A voice came at his shoulder, dragging his mind back

from his thoughts. Coella had urged his horse alongside, and Halga nodded in agreement as his gedriht spoke again. 'Witches can sense a man's desires, Halga, and change their appearance to look like anyone. Every country boy knows it. If you go over there tonight, you will never be seen again.'

THE TWO LEADERS, Jute and Angle, exchanged a look as the town came into view. Edwin said. 'Well, it looks far busier than Sleyswic, we may have returned just in time.' Halga ran his eyes over the little port of Strand as the pair led the column along the waterfront road. Longships packed the wharves and jetties. The length of the hard, men worked to make vessels seaworthy after their winter slumber. Ahead of them, a line of workmen were carrying bundles of oars from storage; further out, sailmakers bent on sheets fresh from repair. The distinctive smell of tar hung on the salty air, and the sound of hammering and sawing told where shipwrights were busily closing seams and fixing leaky frames as they readied the vessels for departure.

Forewarned of their arrival by his guards, Horsa was emerging from a boathouse, wiping his hands clean on a rag, and as they reined in before him and slid from the saddles their lord flashed them a welcoming smile. The smile broadened into a grin as he raised his eyes to take in the column, and he exchanged a nod of recognition with Arékan before his gaze dropped to take in the bulging pannier on every mount. Riding in pairs, it was a simple matter for Horsa to tally the riders, and his eyes flashed as he turned back to Halga and Edwin. 'No losses?'

If it was the final act of his leadership of the raid, the confirmation that they had suffered no casualties was one of

Halga's proudest achievements. He stood a little taller as he replied: 'not a scratch.'

The Angle clapped each of his underlings by the shoulder. 'That's grand,' he said. 'With Arékan returned and a healthy profit, I doubt you could have done much better.'

Edwin spoke, the surprise obvious in his tone. 'The ships look seaworthy,' he said. 'Is it not a bit early in the year?'

Horsa indicated that they follow on, tossing the grubby rag aside as stable boys came forward to lead the horses away. 'We were only waiting for you lads to turn up.' He looked instinctively at the sky as he spoke. The pair followed suit. Gull grey clouds were ambling south through a wintery sky rinsed paler still. 'This weather set in a few days ago, and looks fixed to stay. It seems a shame to waste it. I don't need to tell you boys how fickle the weather can be in the German Sea. We can head down now and overstay with Hengest in Britannia, or trust our luck and risk a month tacking and wearing as we claw our way south in the spring. We heard you were back in the Sley a couple of days ago, so I ordered the ships run out and made shipshape for the journey.' He turned to face them with a glint in his eye. 'We expected you back yesterday,' he said. 'How was the Barley Mow?'

Halga and Edwin shared a look. Tales of shadow serpents and wolf eyes in the dark; of the deafening clatter of wings and animalistic scratching just beyond the flickering circle of light had seemed absurd in the dawn, even to them. But it was the sight that met their eyes when they had ridden from the clearing that really sent a chill through every man, as they exchanged fearful looks and recalled tortured shrieks in the night. Halga swallowed as the image flashed into his minds-eye again. If the bulging eyes still contained the ghost of all that Hrafn had suffered, the features twisted into a rictus of horror had them urging their mounts past the latest addition to the skull-field.

An agreement that it would be pointless to attempt to describe all the goings-on that night passed between them, and they drew a chuckle from their lord as Edwin replied for them both. 'It is fair to say that we had a night to remember, lord.'

11

MEROVECH

With the oars backed, the ship lost way, gliding to a halt within half a length as Horsa strolled to the bow. Halga followed on, shadowing his kinsman as the sentinel's admonishment carried to them. 'You are late; king Merovech is about to receive the oath.'

Horsa shrugged. 'In that case, how can I be late? All it needs is for you to lower the boom, and I shall be bang on time.'

Even from a distance of fifty paces, Halga saw the Frank roll his eyes at the retort, and glancing back he pulled a grin as he saw the smiles of the crew. The Frank called again. 'Don't tell me: Angles?'

Horsa cast a look back across his shoulder, taking in the mast top and the white dragon flag that flew there. Turning back, he spoke again. 'There are no flies on you, are there sunshine? I can see why they put you in charge of the final barrier and not the first. Are you going to lower the boom, or are we going to turn around and leave you to explain to the king why his Anglian allies sailed away?'

The crewmen on both ships turned their faces to the

guard, and Halga recognised the mirth there as they awaited the Frank's reply. They had already passed through a handful of barriers and checkpoints since they had entered the mouth of the River Scheldt earlier that day, and with the southern shoreline hidden behind a forest of masts, it was clear they had reached their destination. It was inconceivable that they could have rowed this far inside the kingdom if they had come with harmful intent, and they all watched as the Frankish leader turned his head aside to issue an order. A blue flag ran up the mast, and switching their gaze to the southern bank, Halga and Horsa watched as men sprang to. Within moments, the great chain spanning the watercourse had disappeared beneath the surface, as the locking bolt that held it secure was knocked away. As the order passed from man to man and Anglian oars dipped to stroke the ships forward once again, the bows came about and pointed to the bank. Horsa mumbled beneath his breath, shaking his head as he stomped aft: 'lackwit.'

Stretched out before them was a shelving riverside striped by hulls, and as a man on shore hailed the steersman and indicated the place to bring the great ship ashore, Halga reflected on the weeks and months just gone over. Despite the early departure from Jutland he had missed Hengest again, Halga's foster-father away in the northern reaches of Britannia dealing with a Pictish incursion. But the stop-off had carried them closer to the land of the Franks, and with their supplies topped up and another shipload of Angles added to the raiding army, the Jute had seen the sense. With Hengest gone, Halga and the men of his comitatus had enjoyed the spring months hunting in the great woodland the Angles called *Andreds Wold* after the Roman fort of Anderida that stood nearby, as Horsa worked to meld them with his own.

Despite the best efforts of the witches, Arékan was still

not yet back to her old self. But she was improving day by day, and Halga was glad she had elected to come along. Rewarded with silver for his oath, Halga had spent wisely, and he allowed his gaze to linger on his gedriht as they prepared to go ashore. Each man now wore matching cloaks of grey wool, the edges brightened by braiding in oxblood red. If their shirts were still a mishmash of colour and design, the matching brooches and the helms each man carried suspended from his belt told everyone they were hearth mates. His brief brush with wealth had not stretched to swords for the men, and they would have to make do with spears for now. But every man in Angeln had assured Halga that his kinsman had a nose for trouble, and the opportunity to acquire wealth and booty would arrive before the coming summer was out. Halga was certain that it was just what Arékan needed too.

A shudder of the boards beneath his feet told the young drihten that the ship had reached the bank. As his attention returned and mooring ropes flew, he waited as his band took up their belongings and began to make their way forward to join him. Horsa was first over the side, and Halga stationed himself in the bow as Anglian warriors vaulted the sides to splash into the shallows. Beorn was the first to speak when they arrived, his eyes flashing with the excitement they all felt to be part of such a thing. 'Best we catch up, lord,' he said gleefully. 'I want to avoid missing a single moment of a day such as this.'

Halga nodded as Oswy handed his lord's shield across. 'Got everything?' His gedrihts said that they had, raising their shields and angons as they did so. Halga raised his own in reply. Each shield face bore the white dragon of the Angles on a field of scarlet to mark them out as oath sworn members of Horsa's war band. But the rear of each shield bore the stal-

lion of Jutland to show where their ultimate allegiance lay,
and Halga threw them a smile as he bade them follow on.
'Good,' he said. 'Let's go and join the fun.'

Aware now of his rank and relationship to their lord, the
Anglian warriors paused their disembarkation to allow Halga
to lead his men over the side, and as the little group waded
ashore he raised his eyes to look. The field rose gently as it
drew away from the riverside, and outlined at the crest of the
rise, Horsa was deep in conversation with a Frankish official.
The man's clothing marked him out as a man of some importance, and as Halga waded ashore, he set off towards the pair.
The men of his comitatus trooped along in his wake, but if
Halga had thought to join the conversation, the scene that
revealed itself to him as he approached the ridge top drove
the idea away. Godwin let out a low whistle at his side, and
his follow-up remark echoed the thoughts of them all. 'I
never imagined such a thing.' The back slope of the hill was
thick with men, each company clustered about its sigil, the
Woden-hallowed war flag of the northern folk. The iron grey
setts of a Roman Road bisected the host, and following it
westward with their eyes they saw the walls and roofs of
Tornacum, the main town of the Franks, for the first time.

In the middle distance, an army was on the march, and the
Jutes looked on in wonder as it came on beneath a dragon tail of
flags. It had to be the king, and Horsa confirmed the fact as he
finished his conversation and came across flanked by his
heorðwerod, the hearth-troop of his personal guard. 'The
steward has gone down to make room for us among the host,' he
said happily. 'King Merovech will be here soon to address the
army and swear it in.' The Angle raised an arm to point. 'We are
the last to arrive, by the looks of it; the rest began to arrive more
than a week ago.' Halga looked. At the edge of the field, a
ramshackle collection of tents and soil pits showed where the

earlier arrivals had camped out waiting for the appointed day. Horsa spoke again. 'Let that be another lesson, Halga,' he said. 'Never arrive first at a meeting place. You may think that you will be pitching your tents in the choicest spot, but before you know it you will be ringed by shit-pits, middens and mud. A week of that and your men will start to sicken, just when you need them to be at their strongest. It is the reason I lingered at the temple.'

Halga nodded that he understood. The sanctuary his kinsman referred to belonged to the goddess Nehalennia, a protectress of seafarers and others who made their living from the sea. The temple itself stood on an island at the mouth of the Scheldt, the same river that had carried them inland to Tornacum. Angles making their way to and from the homeland and the new settlements in Britannia frequently called at the place to seek Nehalennia's providence, so it was entirely understandable that he should break his journey to honour her. Horsa's admission as to why they had loitered there for the best part of a week now made perfect sense. 'Come on,' Horsa said. 'Let us get down there, before the king arrives. I want you to remain close-by, Halga, so bring your lads down and form up at my shoulder. If I get the chance, I will introduce you to him.'

The Angle had turned away before Halga could reply, and as the big man led the way downslope, he hurried along. A glance to the rear showed where the Anglian host was following on, the hot southern sun reflecting gaudily from mail and spearpoint as each ship's company breasted the rise and marched down into the vale. Looking back, Halga saw that they were just in time. From his position mid-slope, he could see above the heads of the men already arrayed on the field below him. As the first horseman reached the plain and divided to left and right, his eyes sought the king. Time stretched, and the Frankish horsemen kept coming. But at the final instant before the slope bottomed out to blot out the view, a solid knot of riders appeared beneath a cloud of gaudy banners. As they did so, Halga lowered his gaze from the war flags, and was rewarded with his first glimpse of a southern king.

The steward from the hilltop had rushed down before them, and Halga saw the man and his helpers frantically signalling to Horsa where his host should form up. The Angles doubled across, and still in their ship's companies, it was a matter of moments before they filled the final yards between the left flank of the army and the rising ground near the river. Halga led his men to the front as ordered, and the breath caught in his throat as he saw the full extent of the Frankish deployment for the first time.

Fifty paces before them rank upon rank of heavily armed warriors stared back, and turning his head aside he looked in wonder as the formation crossed the ancient roadway and anchored itself against a copse. At the centre of the battle line, a deeper block of riders surrounded Merovech himself, and Halga thrilled to the sound as the king's warriors raised their spears and split the heavens with their roars of acclamation. A heartbeat later, the leading men in the allied contingent had walked clear of the line, raising their shields to beat out a staccato rhythm with their spear-hafts as they led their men in chanting the king's name. Halga felt the very ground beneath his boots shake as the shouts and war cries of the armies filled the air like rolling thunder. The hairs on his neck stood proud as the Frankish line split, and the royal party began to move forward beneath flags of red, blue, and gold. At the centre the war flag of Woden flew above them all, the black raven fluttering proudly as the cries rose in intensity, before dying away to leave the field captured in an expectant hush.

Halga cast a look across his shoulder as they came, and he let out a snort of amusement at the sight that met his eyes, despite the gravity of the moment. To a man, his gedriht looked stupefied by the events that were occurring all around them, and he spoke to break the spell lest others notice their moon-eyed bemusement and think them country rustics. 'Who would have thought we should be part of such a thing?' he murmured. 'But lift your chins and square your shoulders,' he gently chastised them, 'in case folk think we don't belong here.' Halga turned back before they could react, confident now that they would jump to do his bidding, only to see that the king's party had been swallowed by the crowd.

On the field before them, Frankish champions had dismounted, whirling swords and axes in a ritual display: stalking the ground between the armies, as they faced down armed men who had come into their land. Halga sensed spearmen bridle all around him at the challenge; but Anglian discipline held, and they soon quietened as the flock of war flags and banners approached.

Without further warning, Merovech was before them, and Halga looked on as the king's guards parted and men all around him drew a breath. In a day filled with wonders, the king stood out. Alone among the group, Merovech was without mail or war helm; but it was the finery of the king's attire that drew gasps, and Halga drank in the sight as Horsa lifted his chin and planted his feet foursquare. Dressed in gleaming white hose and a tunic trimmed by bands of crimson and blue, a brooch the size of a blacksmith's fist pinned a cloak of red and gold at the shoulder. At the king's side a fine sword, its golden hilt gleaming in the midday sun, hung suspended from a jewel encrusted baldric. But if the king's garb was an unmistakable statement of his rank, his features were more homely. Bull shouldered, strong jawed and with hair the colour of damp hay, if the gods had intended Merovech's appearance to be comely to womenfolk, the livid scar on his cheek told of a life spent in the hardy pursuits of war and hunting. Merovech spotted the Anglian leader as the guards moved aside, and his face broke into a smile of recognition as he did so. 'Horsa!' he exclaimed, his eyes already aglitter from the many excitements of the day. 'How many ships?'

The Angle bobbed his head before replying. 'Three keels lord.'

The king of the Franks came across, laying a palm upon his shoulder, and beamed. They were speaking Frankish, but it was close enough to Anglian for Halga to follow; he had spent a good part of his life in the southern kingdom at foster, after all. 'Three hundred Angles will reap a bloody harvest,' he heard the king say. 'Welcome back, old friend.'

Horsa indicated Halga with the sweep of an arm. 'And half a dozen Jutes, lord king. This man is Halga Hunding — my kinsman who leads them.'

Merovech switched his gaze, and Halga felt the aura of the man come off in waves as his eyes alighted upon him. 'Halga,' the king said, 'you are welcome here.' The Frank's eyes dropped to the hilt of War-spite as he spoke. 'That looks the finest of blades; will it fight for me?'

Halga raised his chin and squared his shoulders. There was something in the demeanour of the man that inspired fighting men to boast of the deeds they would accomplish in his name. 'Heartily, lord king!'

Merovech smiled again. 'Stout hearts should be rewarded.' The king held out a hand and within an eye-blink a retainer had placed a sheathed seax there, the short stabbing sword so lethal in the push of shields; the blade that had given the Saxons their name. Merovech handed it across. 'Here is part payment for your services, Halga,' he said, clapping the Jute on the arm as he went to move on. 'Use it well, and remember: strike true; strike hard; for Rhenish hides are as tough as old boot leather!'

Halga nodded that he would as Merovech turned back. 'Come Horsa,' the king said. 'Bring your banner man along, and we can quickly dispense with the oath taking. Once we do, we can begin to plan the war.'

The Anglian pair were soon surrounded by Frankish guards, and Halga watched as Horsa's stallion-headed Draco war banner joined those of the Franks and swept across the field. With Merovech retreating, Halga took the opportunity to examine the king's gift, cradling the seax in his palms as his eyes took in the embellishments on the scabbard for the first time. Stained a bloody red, the leather covering had been buffed to a waxy sheen, and Halga marvelled at the speed with which the king's retainers had produced the blade. It was obvious that the men carried a collection of scabbards with them, transferring the seax itself into the correctly coloured sheath as required; it was, he supposed, one of the details that set great kings apart from lesser men. The scabbard itself was decorated by a line of circular indentations running from tip to cross-guard. Lining the back edge a series of silver rivets embellished with a representation of the *francisca,* the throwing axe synonymous with the Frankish people themselves, allowed the sheath to be suspended from the owner's belt.

Drawing the blade for the first time, Halga marvelled at its finery. Pattern welded, a series of sinewy sweeps and whorls enhanced its thicker edge where the name MEROVECH had been inlaid in gold wire. The wording set off the gilt handle perfectly, and Halga welled with pride as he snapped the blade back. Within moments the gift had replaced his old seax upon his belt, and glancing behind he indicated that Oswy join him with a jerk of his head. He smiled as his gedriht came up. 'Here, 'he said, 'this is for you. Without your dawn run, I should not be here to witness such sights.'

Oswy inclined his head, his features breaking into a smile as he accepted the blade, and the smile widened into a grin when he realised that he had no place to hang it and stuffed it into his belt. Halga snorted. 'I shall pay for fixings when we get into the town. Stay with me, and we shall watch the swearing in together.'

The cloud of flags that marked the progress of the king had reached the midpoint of the Frankish line, and the pair looked on as the warriors took their places. The warlords stood proudly beneath their personal banners by the time Merovech had turned back to face them, and as guda summoned Woden and Tiw, the All-father and god of war to witness the pledge, a white stallion entered the field.

Garlanded by tiny shields and harnessed to a lead rope, the animal cantered between the armies as the men chanted and clashed their weapons. Halga made a study of the beast as it thundered past. With wildly staring eyes and flared nostrils, it was obvious that the horse had been well-prepared by the priests beforehand, and Halga stole a look at Arékan as memories of Garwulf's hall flooded back. She caught the look, shooting him a wink in return, and reassured by her good humour, Halga looked away with the trace of a smile. Back on the plain the priests were completing their invocations, and as the horse trotted across, an expectant hush descended upon the combined host. The white robed gudas move in at once, taking the lead rope to haul the horse's head forward and down. Steel flashed, and as a crimson jet pulsed from its neck to blacken the plain, the head priest moved around to open its belly in a gout of sheeting blood. Even as blue-grey ropes of gut slithered to the grass, the guda was reaching inside, thrusting an arm up to saw with practised movements at the heart. As the organ came free, and the blood-soaked man held it high for all to see, the godly group came together and went into a huddle around it.

But if the army of the Franks remained impassive as the priests made their deliberations, an expectant buzz built among the men of the war bands facing them, and as the sound grew louder Halga raised his eyes to look. Out beyond the place where Frankish war banners and spear points wooded the sky, another party of horsemen could be glimpsed riding hard along the road that led from Tornacum. The flags that flew above the newcomers were like nothing seen on the field — golden crosses, eagles, and dolphins — and as the head priest raised gore steeped arms to declare the omens propitious, the Franks shook their spears and cheered. But the answering cries from the allied host were thin and watery at best, and Halga felt the first signs of unease in those surrounding him as men closed ranks before the threat. Alert now to the change in mood, Merovech was casting rearward looks, and as the king's guards closed protectively around him, Halga looked to Horsa's men for an explanation. It was not long in coming, and the Jute witnessed the concern on his neighbour's features as he replied. 'The flags are Roman, Halga,' the Angle said, 'and men don't ride that hard unless there is trouble — and lots of it.'

12

INVASION

They all looked up as Beorn skittered downslope, curbing his headlong dash just in time to keep from crashing through them all. Halga pumped him for information. 'Any sign of Horsa's return?'

His gedriht shook his head. 'No lord, nothing.'

Halga raised his eyes skyward. It was growing late, the western horizon aglow. He switched his gaze to the ridge top, and the small lone figure outlined against a darkening sky. 'Well, let us hope that Arékan's turn to stand watch brings us better luck. If we are to fight against the *einherjar* themselves, I would rather know than sit here imaging worse.'

Oswy caused a rumble of laughter to roll around the group with his reply. 'Suit yourself, lord. But I can wait a little longer to find out what is going on, rather than fighting Woden's army of the dead.'

Halga snorted. 'Maybe I got a little carried away,' he admitted. 'But I am not the only one here eager for news.'

The men of his comitatus followed his gaze. Unlike the Jutes, the Angles sworn to Horsa had returned to their ships when their leader had accompanied king Merovech and his

Franks back to the city. All they knew was the message he had sent them by way of the returning banner man. A host had crossed the River Rhine and invaded Roman lands to the south, and as a sworn ally, they were calling upon Frankish help to eject them. With the completion of the swearing-in that afternoon that meant that Horsa and his oath sworn, which now included Halga and the men of his comitatus, would be as committed to serve Rome as any Frank should Merovech commit his army to the fight. But if the prospect thrilled and alarmed him in equal measure it was the reason he had followed his kinsman south, and Halga pushed the concerns away as a sudden peal of laughter reached them from an Anglian ship. Coella chuckled. 'It is that quirky sense of humour again,' he said. 'I will see if I can collect enough firewood to see us through the night; it looks as though we are in for a chill.'

Halga glanced upwards as the man rose to go. The sky to the east had taken on a magenta hue, with only a sickle moon low on the horizon to break the monotone. 'Make a wish before you leave,' he said. 'It is the beginning of a new month.'

They all turned to look, and Coella gave a wistful sigh. 'Aye, it is — Eostre Month. I would be in the midst of lambing now if I were at home.'

'They will be starting the dances now, lighting candles; leaving out blood cakes for the sprites,' Beorn added as they looked.

Oswy chipped in. 'And preparing to plough the first furrow at sunup on Eostre Day.'

Coella continued as if he had not heard a word, and they could all see that their friend was back in his father's fields in his mind. 'It was my job to skin the dead 'uns,' he said, leaning into his spear. 'My brother will have to do it now.' He gave a low chuckle. 'He won't like that, squeamish he is. He saw a scythe take a thrall's finger off once, and the silly bugger fainted!'

Halga listened in as his gedriht talked of home. As much as the times of shared danger and hardship, these were the moments when friendships strengthened, moments when men sat together and talked of nothing in particular.

Steapel added a question of his own. 'Why do you skin the stillborns, Col'?'

Halga took up a stick, snapping it in two as he listened in; tossing the pair into the fire, where they flamed and settled beneath a whorl of sparks.

'Occasionally we lose a ewe in childbirth,' Coella replied, 'but the lamb survives. So, where is it going to get its milk? As it is far more common that a lamb is stillborn or dies during the birth, we can skin it and tie the pelt to the one whose mother died. The ewe knows the scent of her own and lets the orphan suckle, so everybody is happy.'

'Apart from the dead sheep.'

Coella snorted. 'Well, yeah — but she does make a nice stew. Naught goes to waste on a farm.'

If thoughts of home and a mutton feast had caused the group to stare dreamily into the flames, the sound that carried to them a moment later from beyond the rise brought their minds sharply back. Halga spoke as the sound cut the air again. 'That is the leaders returning,' he said, as he pushed himself up. They all looked towards the crest; Arékan and her Anglian counterpart were dark shapes against the glow of the allied campfires, man and woman straining to peer eastwards towards the town. The sound of booted feet splashing into the shallows told them that the Angles had heard the horns too, and they all rose from the fireside as the riverbank began to fill. Halga spoke again. 'Come on,' he said. 'Let's see what we can see.'

Soon they were at the crest, and Halga saw that the field below was a heaving mass, as men left campfires and tents to await the return of their lords. He was about to ask Arékan what she could see when a knot of horsemen spilled out into the open from the road, and he looked on as the familiar figure of Horsa peeled away to canter across. The ridge top seemed crammed with Angles now, and as a final sunburst in the west heralded dusk, Horsa drew rein before them. Halga's hopes rose when he saw the excitement written on his kins-man's features, and his face broke into a smile as the big man called out to his troop. 'I have great news, lads,' he said. 'But, alas, I am too parched after my ride to tell you.'

A spearman doubled across as the host chuckled at their lord's good humour, unhooking a canteen from his belt as he did so. Horsa nodded his thanks, drawing the stopper with his teeth as an expectant hush fell upon them all. The Anglian leader took a sip, hesitated, and drank deeply as they waited, before replacing the bung and tossing the container back to its owner. He shot the warrior a smile as he plucked it from the air. 'Mead!' he declared. 'You are a canny one, Ochta!'

'I was saving it for a special day, lord,' Ochta replied. 'I was thinking this might be the one.'

Horsa was about to reply when a roar from the camp to the south caused him to turn. His face was aglow when he looked back, and he indicated the riverside with a nod. 'It seems that you may be right,' he said. 'Let us return to the ships, and I will tell you all I know.'

The patter of excited voices accompanied the men back to the bank, and Horsa dismounted as a clearly relieved group of guards came up to welcome him back. The bodyguards had looked on earlier as the lord they were oath sworn to protect had ridden away to a distant fortress without them, and even though their presence would have made little difference if treachery was intended, they had spent a guilt-ridden day awaiting his return nevertheless. At the riverside, brands flared into life, and as Horsa took his place among his men he was soon ringed by a circle of flame. Seeing all were present, he lost no time in beginning his address.

'I will cut straight to the nub,' he said. 'A week ago, Attila and his Huns crossed the River Rhine and invaded Gaul.' A babel of voices greeted the news, and Horsa waited for it to subside before he continued. 'In the first few days they stormed a settlement called Mettis, gathered booty and supplies and struck westward. The Romans seem to think that now he has stripped the Eastern Empire of every coin and silver plate the turn of the West has arrived, and he has brought his German subjects — Ostrogoths, Gepids, Alamanns and others, along for the ride. Aetius, the Roman commander, has negotiated an alliance with the Visigoth king, Theodoric, and is rushing north to confront the threat. But he will need to delay the Hunnish march if he is to arrive before they reach the coast. King Merovech is the adopted son of Aetius, and has been called upon to do what he can to delay the enemy. But there is a catch.'

Halga tore his gaze away from his kinsman as the Angle paused to take a swig of ale. The circle of faces looked hellish in the light of the flames, and he thought it unlikely that Attila possessed warriors to match them man for man. But the numbers they were likely to face seemed overwhelming, and he hoped for better news as Horsa continued.

'Gundebaud, Merovech's brother who lost the struggle to inherit the kingdom when their father died last year, has returned at the head of an army recruited from those Franks remaining on the far side of the Rhine. If he swings northward while Merovech and his army are in the south, the kingdom will fall. Merovech intends to lead an army consisting of picked men and his newly sworn allies — that's us and those lads over the hill — south, while his son the young prince Childeric commands the army here. That way he fulfils his treaty obligations, and hopefully has a kingdom to return to when this is all over.' Horsa ran his eyes around the group. 'That is as much as we know for now — does anyone have any questions?'

A voice came from the shadows, and all heads turned as an Anglian warrior spoke. 'Are we taking the ships inland, or do we have to walk?'

'The place where we are headed is located on the same river,' Horsa replied, 'but within a dozen miles of the source. Unfortunately, the Scheldt is too shallow and the surrounding valley too marshy for ships our size, so we will be forced to walk. Despite the additions, king Merovech is short of troops now that he is facing Attila and his host. He has been forced to split his army to protect the hinterland from raiders, and cannot afford to leave a ship guard. If the ships remain here, they will come under the protection of prince Childeric and his garrison, and free us all up to fight.'

Horsa raised his chin, sweeping the ranks with his gaze as he awaited further questions. Satisfied that there were none, he concluded his address. 'A pack train will arrive over the next few days to carry our arms and supplies, and following that we will move south to the city of Camaracum. From there we will send out mounted patrols, establish the whereabouts of the enemy, and hold out until Aetius and Theodoric arrive.'

. . .

HALGA WALKED in the front row, flanked by Steapel and Oswy. Twenty ranks ahead of them, Horsa's stallion-headed Draco hung limp in the still airs of a southern spring day; beyond that, the army of the Sea Franks and their allies stretched into the distance. Last to arrive for the swearing in, the Angles now found themselves bringing up the rear of the mighty column of troops, horse thegns, and carts as they neared the end of their two-day march — the city of Camaracum. Oswy cursed as he sidestepped another pat. 'So much for Horsa's idea that turning up last to the swearing in would keep us fresh and clean. He hawked and spat. 'If I collect any more dung on my boots, I may sow a crop!'

Halga cast a look behind. Out past the place where Arékan tramped along, happy in her own company, the majority of the Anglian host marched six abreast, spanning the roadway from verge to verge as they tramped south. Beyond them, the Frankish rearguard mounted on their big war horses blotted out the view. 'Well, thank the gods that king Merovech is an experienced campaigner, and had the vast majority of his cavalry bringing up the rear,' Halga replied. 'Otherwise we should be wading knee-deep in the stuff!'

Up front, the king and a hundred mounted men of his personal guard were riding at the head of the column, a full mile ahead of the place where Halga and the oath sworn of his comitatus trudged along in their wake. But with the ox drawn wagons and pack mules concentrated in the centre of the marching column, there was still more than enough shit to go around. His gaze slid across to the roadside as he turned back. 'Just be thankful that you are not one of them,' he said. Pinched, sullen faces stared back from among the folk gathered there as the locals fled the war. They all turned to look. Wattle sided wagons and hand drawn carts waddled by, piled high with the movables they had thought most worthy of saving: pots and kettles; workmen's tools; hens in wicker-work cages — snotty-nosed *kinder* and the odd prized porker. Even if Attila's vast army kept going southwest, they knew from experience their homes would have been picked clean by the time hunger or exposure forced their return. 'Aye,' Oswy replied with a sigh. 'It is a different type of warfare here in the south — much more than a coastal raid or the odd burned farmstead. It sometimes feels as though the whole world is on the move.'

It was late afternoon on the second day out from Tornacum, and the sky overhead was the vivid blue of a perfect summer day. The heavens echoed to the call of the wandering birds, now returned a full month earlier than they would at home, and the meadow to either side was a drugget of colour as the first blooms that year — corncockle, daisy, and harebell — drew butterflies and bees on delicate wings. 'It is a beautiful land,' Steapel put in, 'I will grant you that. But the richer it is, the more it will draw covetous eyes. There is a lot to be said for our homeland — it may be harder to scratch a living, but there is more chance of passing it on to your bairns.'

Trumpet calls from the head of the column interrupted their idle chatter, and Jute and Angle alike raised their chins to look. The line of alder and goat willow that marked the course of the River Scheldt meandered to cut across their path, and as they neared the crossing place the trees drew back to reveal their destination across the valley. Halga savoured the sight, as smiles illuminated faces all around: 'Camaracum.'

Set upon a ridge line half a mile back from the waterway, the limestone walls gleamed pink in a westering sun. Further in, red tiled roofs huddled beneath a mantle of woodsmoke as numberless hearths blazed to prepare a welcoming meal for the king and his host. Merovech and his heorðwerod were already in the town, the distinctive axe flag of Francia hoist above the highest point, indicating the presence of the king within the walls. Horsa led his shipmen between the twin columns marking the entrance to the bridge, sprits lifting as every thought turned to a hot meal inside them and a solid roof above, following weeks at sea and days spent on riverside and road.

Within twenty paces Halga was leading his Jutes across the span, and before long the roadway had crossed the marshy water meadow and was arcing around towards the town gate now clearly in view. Halga felt his calf muscles tighten as the road trended upwards, and he shifted the weight of the pack on his shoulder as he put the final few yards of the journey behind him.

Up close, the walls of Camaracum looked even more impressive than they had from the valley floor. Solid blocks of stone the size of a sea chest formed a firm foundation, with the smaller rectangular blocks he now knew were called bricks raising the walls to a height of twenty feet or more. Circular turrets guarded each corner, with another fighting platform topping the massive archway that guarded the gates themselves. Crenelations ran the length of the town walls, their presence all the proof that was needed that a walkway joined the towers for mutual aid and support should Camaracum come under attack. It was a formidable sight, and Halga sent a silent plea to the war god Tiw, that he would not be called upon to lead an assault against such a place before the summer's fighting was over. The road took a gentle dogleg to the right as it gained the crest, and within fifty paces they were swallowed by the shadow thrown by the wall. Up front, Horsa was through the gate, and as the men began to relax after the day march and final climb, Halga did the same.

Coming into the town, the Jute could see that the main roadway carried on as straight as an arrow towards the centre. Elevating his eyes to look, he recognised the roofs of the grand public buildings rising serenely above the mixed terracotta and thatch of the more mundane sort. But if his newfound experience of Roman building work had prepared him for the sights within the town, Halga was surprised by the equine smells that filled his senses. Oswy gave him a nudge and pointed out the cause. 'It looks as if we will be mounted,' he said joyfully. 'My feet will thank me, even if my arse pays the price.' Halga looked. A large area of holding pens and stables, no doubt intended for travellers and market days in more peaceful times, were crammed with horses nose to tail. Although a small area had been kept aside to accommodate those newly arrived with the king, Halga could see that there were still far too few to provide every man in the army with a mount. 'Don't get your hopes up yet,' he replied, 'those horses are intended for scouting.'

Oswy beamed. 'That's nice,' he said. 'I could do with a few days to rest up, while others spend theirs getting saddlesore.' The sound of doors clattering and banging carried to them from the roadway ahead. Turning his head, Halga saw that Horsa was leading a town official back down the column, parcelling the men of his comitatus into groups to be shown to their quarters by a Frank. Their turn came soon enough, and the Angle explained as he came up. 'One of these boys will find you a roof for the night, Halga,' he said. 'Make yourself at home, there is no telling how long we will be here.'

A man was waiting impatiently to lead them away, and Halga ensured that Arékan was in tow as they followed on.

After a short walk, the Frank ducked into a side alley, his eyes flitting from doorway to doorway as he judged the amount of room likely to be available inside. The passageway began to narrow, and Halga thought the man had missed his chance. But just as he began to doubt they would find a suitable place to take them all, the Frank pulled up and rapped on a door. Short of patience in what had already been a trying day, the Frank raised his baton to rap again. But he stopped just in time as the latch lifted, and the pale oval of a man's face appeared in the gap. The official lost no time in making his demand. 'How many can you take?'

Short, slight and pasty faced, it was clear to them all that the occupant's worst fears had been realised as he swallowed hard and squeaked a reply. 'Two, master — we can squeeze in two at a push.' He gave an apologetic shrug of his scrawny shoulders. 'I wish we could help more, but we are humble folk with little to give.'

The steward shoved the householder aside before he had time to add another word, and as the door opened wide, the official leaned forward to take a peek. He threw a look across his shoulder as he ducked back into the light, and Halga saw the man make a quick tally of their number as he did so. 'You're in luck,' he declared. 'There is just enough room for seven.'

13

CAMARACUM

'Well, this is comfy.'

Halga chuckled at Beorn's words as he glanced to either side. Racked up like sausages on a griddle, they awaited his command. 'Ready? Now!'

They leaned forward as one, reaching out to tear a hunk of bread from the loaf, before dunking it in the big communal bowl before them. Halga spoke again as the drips slowed and stopped. 'And — back!'

They all giggled with the absurdity of it, stuffing their faces as Halga raised his eyes and mumbled through a mouthful of mush. 'Your turn.'

With the only bench in the house taken up by Halga, Oswy, Beorn and Arékan, those opposite had different problems to contend with. Although there was more shoulder room, they had to make do with the floor, and Halga snorted again as he watched them shuffle forward to dunk. Coella and Godwin were on their knees, the taller Steapel resting on his haunches. Squeezed between them, two of the householder's older children bobbed into view as they made a grab for the loaf. Scattered around the sides of the room were several more, the younger ones making do with a bowlful each from which they slurped noisily from the rim, with their parents Glappa and Arlice completing the crowd surrounding the cooking pot.

Halga took in the room as he awaited his turn to come around again. A dozen feet in length and a little less in depth, with the addition of the Jutish lord and his fighters, the couple's home was packed tighter than a cowshed in a blizzard. Alongside the doorway through which they had entered, a small window near the top of the front wall was the only opening to the world outside. With similar dwellings to either side, there was no other source of light and air besides the single window and doorway; Halga could only imagine how drawn-out the long winter months must seem to the family cooped up in such a place.

Aside from a cup-board against the back wall, the only furniture consisted of a series of pallets for sitting and sleeping. Centrally, a smaller one catered for the needs of the parents, while a matching pair at opposite ends of the room allowed the boys and girls some degree of separation. With a central hearth taking up most of the room in between, it was clear that Glappa had been speaking truthfully when he had told the Frankish official that he only had room for a couple of additional bodies at most.

With the only free corner now piled high with spears, shields, helms, and other less warlike but necessary accompaniments for a war band on the road, Halga wondered how they would all find room to rest. Within moments, he had his answer. As the bottom of the cauldron appeared through the stew, Arlice made a suggestion as she began to clear away. 'Perhaps you could show our guests around the town, Glappa?' she said as the older children scrambled to help. 'That will give me the chance to tidy up after the meal, and free up as much floorspace as I can so that we all have room to rest our heads tonight.' She sniffed and glanced towards the place where their guests' boots stood in a row. 'Perhaps you will be able to find a water trough that is clean — I am sure our friends would appreciate the chance for a quick clean and brush up.'

Halga ran his eyes over the gedrihts sat opposite. Hungry and travel-weary, it was the first time he had thought to consider their appearance in days. Sunburnt and coated in a thick layer of road dust, not only was the distinctive smell of animal dung filling the tiny room from their boots, they probably added to it with their reek. Despite being the head of the house, Glappa deferred to Halga due to his rank, glancing across for confirmation. Halga nodded. He had never had occasion to wander a Roman built town, and in addition to opportunities for a wash and brush up, he was keen to discover what else they had to offer. He spoke as they rose from the hearthside. 'Leave your spears and armour here,' he said. 'Seax's for those that own one — otherwise, keep your daggers and eating knives to hand. There are thousands of armed men in town; let us put on a friendly face, but be ready for trouble if any occurs.' He looked across to Arékan, and was about to ask if she was coming along when the Hun supplied the answer. 'I will practice my bow,' she said. 'I saw a dozen butts outside the town walls, and I need the practice more than I need a wash.' The pair exchanged the hint of a smile as she spoke, man and woman fully expecting that a wash would be the last thing on their minds once they left the building.

With the promise of a night in town the others were already pulling on their boots, and as the door opened to flood the room with the soft light of early evening, Halga led them back out into the alleyway. He shuffled aside as the rest of his comitatus followed on, fixing his gaze on Glappa as their host ducked out to join them. 'Which way, friend? Back the way we came?'

The Frank shook his head. 'Head up that way, lord,' he said, indicating the opposite direction with a flick of his head. 'There is a short-cut I know that will bring us out near the centre of town.' Halga signified that the man lead on with a gesture of his hand. The meal had done far more than fill empty stomachs, he reflected as they walked. The act of sharing amid the close confines of the house had helped to chase away the natural feelings of fear and distrust the family must have felt towards the foreign fighters who had invaded their little world. Steapel had led the way. The eldest among a rampaging host of siblings back home at the forge, the Jute's eyes had lit up the moment he had entered the lodgings. In no time, his big-brother ways had encouraged the younger children to cast aside their fears. Soon the lanky steersman had come to resemble a maypole as the youngsters swarmed forward to festoon his limbs, and with the awkwardness of the moment chased away by childish squeals and laughter, adult reserve gave way to smiles and introductions. The family meal had done wonders for Arékan too. Although still not back to her old self she was well on the way, and although her ordeal had clearly left scars that would always remain, Halga was now certain that whatever had occurred on the island with the sorceresses had been worth the cost and effort. He was glad.

More mundane matters interrupted his thoughts, and Halga stepped aside as Glappa voiced a warning.

'Mind the gutters, lord.'

Halga looked. Surprisingly, for such a minor thorough-fare, the surface had been laid with stone paving. Shallow trenches had been sunk to either side, and from the look and smell it was here that the occupants emptied their pots and bedpans. 'The drains will not be flushed through until midmorning tomorrow, lord,' Glappa explained. 'Folk take it in turns to carry pails of water up from the river to wash them out.'

Beorn said what they were all thinking. 'So what happens to those who live further downhill?'

'They either do the same,' Glappa replied, 'or wallow in everyone else's shit — serves them right; their fathers should have fought harder.'

Halga was intrigued. 'How so?'

'Until twenty years ago, our people used to live further north, around the lower reaches of the Rhine and the River Maas,' the Frank explained. 'But king Chlodio, Merovech's father who died last year, conquered these lands from the Romans and rewarded the best of his fighters with homes in the towns or estates in the hinterland. I was only a lad at the time,' he added as he sidestepped a wayward turd, 'and to be truthful there was little fighting to be had. But my father must have caught someone's eye because he was gifted the house I now live in, when the time came to share out the spoils.' Glappa looked across. 'I know what you are thinking, lord,' he said. 'A single room without even a place to take a crap is not much of a reward, and if you don't mind me saying so, there is no reason why a man such as yourself should think anything else. But the point is it is my inheritance — it is mine. There is no rent to pay, and no boon work to do for my lord. Everything I earn is mine to do with as I please — it's much more than a room, it's my home.'

Halga's hand went instinctively to the handle of War-spite as he listened, and he nodded that he understood. The Frank's home may look lowly to a man of his background, but to Glappa it was *lāf*, as important an inheritance as the sword that hung at Halga's side, a thing of value to be handed down to those who came after.

The conversation had used up the time it had taken to wend their way through the warren of side roads and alleyways that housed the population of Camaracum. Glappa indicated that they follow on, as he came out onto the road Halga now recognised as the one they had used to enter the town earlier in the day. Unlike the smaller passageways, footpaths laid to stone flanked the main road into town, with the road itself maybe a foot or so lower. Every few yards, a series of stepping stones spanned the gap to enable folk on foot to tread clear of the rainwater and muck. At regular intervals, slab-like drinking troughs catered for the needs of draught animals and horses.

Glappa spoke again as Godwin began to roll up his sleeves. 'Not here, I will take you into the centre of town. There are several pools there, and it is only a little further.' They walked on, and Halga ran his eyes over the buildings fronting the road as they did so. The majority were shops and workshops of one kind or another, the families that worked them either living in a room to the rear of the working area or in a garret above.

The sun was sinking now, its light streaking the roadway where it found a gap between the buildings. Oswy came to Halga's side, and the big gedriht spoke a warning as the buildings began to draw back and the central area of Camaracum appeared in a sunburst of light. 'There are many warriors about, lord,' he said. 'It is best we stick together.'

Halga raised his eyes to look. They were approaching a vast open space, rectangular, with grand looking buildings built in the ubiquitous creamy coloured stone he had seen used on the older structures and town walls throughout Francia. The majority of the buildings were colonnaded, and although the traces of paint remaining on the sculpted figures and wording of the entablature above told of years of neglect, enough remained to give a hint of their splendour during the heyday of the empire, despite the heaps of guano. Roofs of terracotta gave an eye-pleasing contrast to the paleness of the stonework, and with the lowering sun bathing the whole, Halga could see by the looks on men's faces that the warmth of the day matched the mood. The walkways were filling up quickly as the men in king Merovech's army finished their evening meals and headed out seeking bawdier entertainment, and Halga gave a shrug as he sought to lay his gedriht's concerns. 'No one is carrying a spear, and only the leading men have swords as a mark of their rank. Relax,' he said with a smile. 'We are not the only ones to have spent the last few weeks aboard ship or in camp — there will be no trouble.'

Glappa had drawn ahead as they spoke, and their host came to a halt as they reached the edge of the square, turning back to throw an arm wide as he announced their arrival with a flourish. 'I hereby present the Forum Camaracum,' he said with an exaggerated sense of pomp. 'As you can see, we have it to ourselves.'

The group laughed — the large square that their host had called the forum was a heaving mass of bodies. Twin pools marked the limits of the space, each one already crammed to overflowing with naked men rinsing the road dust from hair and body. But if they had arrived a little late to be sure of a good clean up, Halga had already decided on a better use of their time. 'Those men,' he said, pointing out a large group stood sharing ale from a jug. 'Where did they get their drink?'

Glappa looked puzzled. 'From the tavern, of course, lord.'

Halga flicked a look at his companions: every man was

grinning. 'It must be their name for an ale house,' Coella said. 'Like Mildred's place, on the dockside back in Angeln.'

Halga grinned too. 'Point out this tavern to me. Better still,' he said as an afterthought, placing a palm on the Frank's shoulder. 'Show me.'

The Jutes followed on like lovestruck puppies as Glappa threaded his way through the crowd, and a short while later they were stood outside a doorway. Above the lintel, the image of a dolphin announced to the world the name of the establishment, and as the group stood aside to allow a busy serving girl to carry foaming jugs of ale to waiting customers, Halga slipped his arm through Glappa's. 'Come on,' he said, 'we owe you a drink.'

The Frank opened his mouth to protest — but Beorn had gripped his other arm before any words could come, and within moments they had frogmarched him through the doorway and into the gloomy interior. Safely within, Halga stood to one side as his eyes accustomed themselves to the light after the glare of the forum. While the front of the building had been stone-made to match the rest of those surrounding the great square outside, the interior of The Dolphin was more rustic. Oak posts supported a planked ceiling, no doubt the very same boards that formed the floor surface in the rooms above. Posts and panelling framed the walls above a stone laid floor, the flags polished to a waxy sheen by the footfall of centuries. Disappointingly, the tables seemed to be filled with drinkers; but Beorn spoke at his shoulder as he turned to go, and Halga snapped out as another group of men pushed through the doorway in a riot of sound: 'grab it!'

Halga moved his head to peer around a post as his gedriht took off. Nestling in the darkest corner of the room, what looked to be the last empty table in the entire place awaited its customers. A group of men — one of the Saxon tribes by the look of the side-knot in their hair — Chauken, Eowan or the like — were already making their way across. But Beorn was weaving through the tables like a sheepherder's dog at the round-up, and it was clear that he would win the race. The others had already set off, cutting the corner to back him up, and Halga relaxed a touch as he followed on at a pace more indicative of his rank.

The Saxons reached the table just as the last of his men slipped onto the bench, and Halga let out a snort of amusement despite the coming confrontation as he saw the look of terror on Glappa's face. Wedged between Beorn and Coella the scrawny Frank was obviously wishing himself far away as the Saxons towered over them all, and with the race won, Halga slowed his pace a touch to listen in as he came within earshot. As usual, the largest and fiercest looking warrior was to the fore, and Halga gave a snort of amusement as the first words passed between the groups. 'Shift yourselves,' the big Saxon ordered. 'We saw this first.'

Oswy threw the oafish leader a beatific smile. 'Seeing ain't having,' he said calmly. 'If it was, no doubt you would be accompanied by a bevy of beautiful women, instead of the gruesome gang.'

The room was quietening as word that a fight could be in the offing spread from table to table, and Halga weighed up his potential opponents as he drew nearer. The Saxon leader was tall and broad shouldered, layered by muscle. But there was an undeniable touch of the ploughman in his features and spade-like hands, and a quick look at his companions was enough to confirm Oswy's name-calling had been near the mark. These were tough lads though, if a little rustic, and although outnumbered two to one by Halga and his men they would do a lot of damage if it came to a fight. The rest of the drinkers had clearly decided the same, so it was with a feeling of alarm that Halga heard Oswy speak again. 'Now, if I had a face like a fishwife chewing a wasp I would drink outside in the sun, and leave my betters in peace.'

Halga picked up the pace again as smiles of anticipation spread around those listening in, along with a frisson of excitement at the nearness of violence. The Saxon's brows were furrowing as his mind sought to decide whether he was being insulted or it was just a vagary of this northerner's drawl. Thankfully, at the same moment his expression darkened, and a hand went to the handle of his knife, Halga arrived. 'I made it!' he exclaimed, throwing the men of his comitatus a smile. 'I thought the king would never stop! Now,' he said. 'Where is my ale?'

The mention of the word king and the obvious rank of the newcomer stilled the big Saxon's hand, and Halga threw them a questioning look as he slid onto the bench. 'Can I help you lads?' The commotion had drawn the proprietor across; it was obvious from the man's expression that he was about to order them all out, and Halga drew his seax from its sheath and laid it upon the tabletop. The sight of a weapon being drawn ratcheted up the tension in the room a further notch. The owner hesitated, and the Saxon's hand flew back to the handle of his own. Halga fixed them both with a stare. 'I was just saying to my lads,' he said, 'how much the king can jabber on when he is among friends — good friends.' He ran his fingertip down the length of the blade, making sure to underline the name Merovech inlaid there in bold letters. 'But he did gift me this seax,' he added with a disarming smile, 'and it's a wonderful thing — don't you think?'

As all eyes fixed upon the name of the king, Halga recognised the moment when the fight left their opponents. All that was needed now was a face-saving gesture on his part, and he turned his face to the proprietor and threw the man his warmest smile. 'Ale for us if you please,' he said, 'and a jug of your finest for our friends here, to show there are no hard feelings.' As the taverner summoned a serving girl across and the Saxons muttered their thanks, Halga addressed the table. The day had been hard enough, without the lads picking fights. 'Right,' he said, 'that's enough trouble — Glappa hasn't joined our little crew to crack heads, he has to be up for work in the morning.' The Frank pulled a sickly smile and began to protest. But the effort was half-hearted at most, and he slumped a little more as he resigned himself to his fate. 'We have come here to drink,' Halga went on, 'and I don't care what happens, or who says what. Should Attila himself and his army of Huns storm through that doorway, I don't want any more trouble tonight.'

14

OLD FRIENDS

Coella rubbed his belly and let out a belch, scanning the room with bleary eyes as the jug did another round. The tables in The Dolphin were largely empty now, as travel-weary men drifted away to spend the first night under a tiled or thatched roof in an age. Here and there, diehards drifted in and out, seeking to stretch their drinking for as long as they could. He snorted at the sight of their host. Even after witnessing the Saxon's face when the big oaf had finally realised what Oswy had meant with his wasp and fishwife remark, Glappa had been the best entertainment of all. Long before the first hour had passed, the Frank had been slurring his words, and from there on in his night had gone rapidly downhill. Trying to pick fights with amused Angles, warbling bawdy songs, spewing in the corner and serenading serving girls were only a few of the stories he would be hearing all about in the morning. Coella reached across to cover the man's shoulders with his cloak, like a mother tucking in her bairn. 'You sleep now, friend,' he muttered, turning the Frank's face aside to ensure there was no danger he would drown in ale spills. 'One way or another, you have a tough day ahead of you tomorrow.' He settled back again, content for the moment with his own company. To either side, his friends were as deep in conversation as only drunken men can be, putting the world to rights or anticipating the fighting to come. He left them to it, too ale-weary to join in.

A small group of Angles had settled themselves on the table opposite a short while before, and Coella allowed his eyes to wander across them as his thoughts began to turn to home. Lambing would be in full swing now, and he gave a sigh: raw winds and mutton stew. The sound of laughter came from the neighbouring table, and the vision vanished far quicker than it had come. He shot them a sour faced look: halfwits. The big one with his back towards them turned his face aside, throwing back his head as the asinine sound of laughter echoed around the emptying room once again. Coella concentrated harder — he knew the man. He was not one of Horsa's comitatus, of that he was certain, and he took another sip from his cup as he attempted to place him. Within a few moments, he had it, and he shot bolt upright to give Beorn a dig. 'Well, well — look who it isn't.'

Beorn screwed up his face. 'Look who what isn't?'

Coella pointed him out. 'The big man there — the one braying like a mule.'

Beorn sank a long draught from his cup as he looked across. Smacking his lips, he replied. 'Sure, I can play that game,' he said, clucking his tongue as he thought. 'It isn't… well…it isn't a nice plump ewe.' He tapped the side of his nose with a forefinger. 'Because if it was, you would be getting all hot and bothered.' Beorn attempted a wink, but his face seemed to have other ideas, and it came out more like a squint. 'We all know what shepherds get up to on a lonely moor, it's the reason sheep have horns.' He took another gulp. 'Your turn.'

Coella fixed him with a deadpan look. 'Ha, ha,' he said, 'very funny. Right then, now, tell me who he is.'

Beorn sighed and looked again, and Coella thrilled to the sight as he saw a look of recognition flash across his friend's features. Beorn placed his cup down on the table, and Coella saw the joviality had been chased away and replaced by the mien of a wolf. 'It's that bastard from last year,' Beorn growled. 'The one from the dockside in Angeln, the one who thought he could summon Halga like a dog.' The pair glanced across to the place where their lord had been having a drunken conversation with Steapel only moments before, only to find his place on the bench now empty. They exchanged a smile, and Coella spoke again. 'Halga said he wanted to avoid seeing any more trouble tonight, but he is not here, so he can't. That means we can have a bit of fun before he returns.' The crusty end of a loaf lay on a platter of half-eaten food, and Coella reached across to retrieve it as Beorn looked on. 'What are you going to do?'

Coella threw his friend a wink. 'Watch me.'

Tearing a coin sized piece from the soft inner, Coella rolled the bread into a ball before dunking it into an ale slop; squeezing the excess from the pellet, he took aim and threw. The ball flew true, arcing across the gap to land in the hair of the Anglian spearman, where it stuck. The Jutes sat there grinning, but as the time began to stretch it became obvious that the Angle had been out a good few hours too, and had not noticed a thing. Coella reached out and pinched another piece from the loaf, repeating the rolling and dunking before launching the soggy ball after the first. Larger than the previous one, this missile finally drew a response, the Angle raising his head to look about him. But even as the pair awaited the angry confrontation, the smiles slowly drained from their faces as the Angle shrugged and went back to his chatter. Beorn had waited long enough. 'Here,' he said, snatching up the loaf, 'this will get his attention.' Moments later, the bread was on its way, and the pair hooted with laughter as it caught its target a glancing blow before spinning away into the shadows. Beorn and Coella were on their feet and crossing the short divide by the time their target started to turn, and as the Angle's face came around and his companions stared open-mouthed at the surprise attack, Beorn clenched his fist and swung. The man's expression just had time to change from a belligerent snarl to slack-jawed shock before the punch landed with a tooth shattering crack. As the follow-up made a bloody pulp of his nose and the Angle staggered and fell, the men at both tables let out a roar and piled in.

HALGA RETRACED HIS STEPS, backing into the moonlight as he fumbled to retie his trews. He had pissed in some grim and dank places in his time, but none worse than the backyard of The Dolphin sprang to mind. Beer barrels had been sawn in half to act as what the taverner had called *latrina* — the piss they contained a nice little sideline that would bring in a handful of silver from the tanneries down by the riverside. But the sheer numbers of men who had cause to use them since the army had arrived that day, had long ago filled them to overflowing. With the courtyard awash with the overspill and the pungent stench assailing his nostrils, Halga picked his way through a ribbon of glistening puddles as he made his way towards the comforting light of the doorway.

The roar when it came stopped him dead, and a hand went instinctively to the hilt of his sword as he sidestepped a runnel and hurried across. The scene that greeted his eyes when he arrived at the doorway had him blinking in disbelief after the relaxed nature of the evening that had gone before. But he forced himself on as his mind scrambled to understand just what had occurred during the short while he had been away. An Angle lay sprawled beneath the table, the soles of his boots pointing towards the ceiling where his legs still rested upon the bench. Beorn was kissing his fist, the look of satisfaction on his face and the bloody smear on his knuckles all the confirmation Halga needed that it was he who had been responsible for laying out the stranger. Coella was at his side, guarding his comrade's flank, as Angle and Jute shrugged off the lethargy of a night's drinking to take up the fight. No one appeared to be in charge, so it seemed likely that the leader of the Anglian warriors was the one laid out beneath the table. Halga cursed as he came to realise that it would take far more than a jug of ale to smooth this situation over.

The space between the benches was a blur of pumping arms and balled fists. Certain now that it would take far more than a shout from him to end the fighting, Halga determined that he would ensure that his side won. As he searched about for a stool to wield as a weapon, Glappa unstuck his head from the tabletop. But the Frank had barely enough time to bring his eyes into focus before a savage blow sent him reeling from the bench. Steapel was rolling on the floor exchanging digs with an opponent and Halga made to help, but the flash of candlelight on steel caught his eye from the main fight to drive any other thoughts away. It could only have come from a blade, and Halga's eyes desperately took in the scrum of bodies as he searched for the source. This far from the fight, the drihten knew that he would have to react instantly if he picked out the knife again, but as his seax left its sheath the crowd pulled apart just long enough for him to spot the knifeman again. Halga prepared to throw as the

Angle lunged, and as his arm whipped forward to send his blade flying through the room, he held his breath and willed it to find its mark. The seax spun across the room, and time itself seemed to slow as he watched the two come together. Halga was no blade thrower, but to his astonishment and relief, his aim had been true. An instant before the Anglian knife blade plunged into Beorn's unsuspecting back, Long Knife flew in to pin the owner's arm to an upright by his wrist.

The scream of pain that followed was unlike the guttural cries and grunts of the fight, and as the combatants froze, Halga grabbed the opportunity, filling his lungs to bellow a command. 'Enough!'

The heft of his voice seemed far greater in the pregnant pause following the scream, and Halga made a show of drawing War-spite to emphasise his rank as he ordered the warring factions to part. He swept them all with an icy glare, making sure he spared neither group so that the Angles would know he would be even-handed in his judgement. He made a demand. 'What is the fight about?'

Both sets of men looked about them, and it quickly became clear that no one was really sure. Halga ran his eyes around the rest of the room looking for a witness, but the few remaining men appeared to be either asleep or drunk beyond the point of reliability. The serving girls had long since left them all to their drinking, and although the taverner was still lurking somewhere, Halga had no doubt that he had made himself scarce the moment the first punch had been thrown. Even as he watched, it was obvious that men who had only a short while before been intent on giving the other side a beating, were coming together in the face of authority; he would get no answers here. Angry now that he could not even take a piss without the world descending into chaos, Halga stomped across to the place where the knifeman still stood pinned to the post. Grabbing the handle, he brought his face in close as he fixed the man with a stare. 'I no longer care who or what started this,' he growled. 'But if you ever pull a blade on one of my men again, I promise you — I will slit your throat from ear to ear.'

The Angle winced, clutching the wound with his free hand as Halga tugged the seax from the post, and he turned his face to the men of his comitatus as he wiped the gore from the blade. Now that blood had been spilt, there would be little chance they could return to the idle drinking of before, and everyman there knew it; the night was over. 'That's enough fun for one day,' he said. He indicated the crumpled figure of Glappa, now sprawled in the corner where he had landed following the Angle's punch. 'Pick up our friend, and we will get him home.' The man under the table had recovered while they fought, and Halga gave him a second look as he began to clamber out; he had seen his face before, but couldn't place where. He gave a shrug: *who cares?*

Soon, they had negotiated the muddle of tables and upturned benches that was all that remained to tell the tale of the rowdy night before. Coming out through the double doors, Halga stopped and stared. Hilly outlines told where men had decided the journey back to their lodgings was too great to be worth the effort; hardcore drinkers snored in groups, reluctant to admit that the night was really over.

Steapel spoke, as Beorn carried the insensible form of their Frankish host through the doorway. 'It looks like it's going to be a fine day.'

Halga looked; to his surprise, the buildings at the eastern end of the forum wore a crown of light. Along with the sight of the returning sun, came the realisation that he was just about as tired as could be. They had marched for the entirety of the previous day, then drank through the night. His body and mind were crying out for sleep, and even if it promised to be a few square feet of Glappa's floorspace, he wanted away to his bedding. 'Yes,' he said as the first yawn came. 'That is enough fun for one night. Let's get back.'

THE KNOCK CAME AGAIN and Halga sighed. In truth, it was hard to feel any bitterness towards Arlice. It was her home after all, and she *had* taken her brood into town for the day, otherwise it was difficult to see how they would have got any sleep at all. Despite the hammering in his head, he allowed himself a snort. The woman's face had been a picture when they had arrived home in the dawn, Beorn pouring poor Glappa down upon the bed as sleepy children stared open-mouthed in amazement. It had quickly become obvious the previous evening that the Frank and strong ale were only occasional bedfellows. But if their presence had caused the problem, one look at Arlice's face had told them all that it was now saving the householder from a good tongue lashing at best. He smiled: it was not as if the man had not suffered enough already. With his shirt covered in puke and blood and black puffy eyes peeking out above a nose made jelly by a well-aimed punch, he doubted the Frank would be accompanying them when they went into town again that night.

The pounding came again, louder this time, more insistent, and Halga murmured to the man at his side without opening his eyes. 'Let them in, Godwin,' he said. 'You replaced the locking bar when they left.' Halga shifted as he sensed his gedriht haul himself up from the floor, pulling his cloak a little closer to his chin as he sought to wring every last moment of rest before the room became abuzz with youthful energy. But if the rattle of the window shutter and the shaft of light that followed caused them all to utter a curse, the words that followed tore the Jutes from their slumber. 'The alleyway's filled with spearmen,' Godwin blurted. 'Angles — and they don't very look cheery.'

Halga was on his feet instantly, and as his oath sworn rolled from their cloaks and leapt to their feet all around, he spat out a command. 'Arm yourselves — quickly! Mail, helms and shields, and be ready to defend the doorway.' Arékan was up, snatching her bow from its gorytos, fitting an arrow to the string as she covered the entrance until Beorn could drop the locking bar back into place. With a few more moments to collect his wits, Godwin was already sorting through the weapon pile, and before Halga could take the very few steps to close the gap between them, he had his drihten's byrnie held ready. Halga ducked his head, standing tall to allow the mail shirt to unravel down his body with a swish as he made a grab for his helm. Coella made a confession as Halga fastened the chin strap.

'I am sorry, lord,' he said. 'This is all my fault — I started it all.'

Beorn attempted to add his name to the list of the guilty, but Halga cut him dead with a look. 'It no longer matters who did or said what, does it?' he snapped. 'As soon as we spilt blood, it was never going to end there. They have rounded up their mates, discovered where we are staying, and come down to finish us off.' He indicated the sleeping form of Glappa, still dead to the world despite the mayhem all about him. 'Cover him with blankets,' he said. 'There is no reason why a family should have to eke out a living without a father due to your stupidity.'

Across the room, the hammering on the door was thunderous, the boards bowing inwards in a pall of dust under the pressure. Within moments the hinges would give way, and when they did their enemies will spill into the room, outflank them, and cut them down where they stood. They were out of time, and Halga barked a command as he moved back towards the door. 'Snatch up what you can and form the wall either side of me,' he said. Out of the corner of his eye, he noticed Arékan taking up a position on the flank, and he felt a wave of gratitude for her experience and good sense. The first through the door would pay with their lives as arrows sped from the gloom. With any luck, it would give him the time to seal off the entrance until help could arrive. But they would have to fight first, and he growled a command as the door flexed and splintered. 'Beorn, remove the bar — the rest of you, as soon as the door swings open, we advance to the doorway and fight them there.'

Oswy and Steapel hurried to his side, and the instant Coella and Godwin moved to flank them, Halga gave a nod. As the timber clattered to the ground, the door flew inward, and the Jutish line filled the room with a full-throated roar as they took a step forward to close the gap. Mindful of Arékan's bow creaking in the shadows, Halga stopped a pace from the threshold, weary eyes blinking in the bright sunshine as he hunkered behind the boards of his shield. But as the battle cry drifted away on the morning air, and he raised his sword for a killing strike, the expected rush of vengeful foemen became the tutting of a familiar voice. 'Yeah, yeah, yeah,' the voice said wearily, 'very frightening. I have just spent the best part of the morning paying wergeld, and persuading king Merovech to spare your sorry hide. Now, grab your gear and meet me at the stable.'

15

WAR AND CONQUEST

The noise of the city, combined with the brilliance of the southern sun, threatened to overwhelm senses dulled by too much ale and little sleep. Halga had led his band through the urban sprawl by the time Horsa and his men came back into view, and as the pace slackened and shaky hands raised flasks to parched and crusty lips, the main thoroughfare hove into sight. To his disappointment, the road was a heaving mass, warriors wandering in aimless groups or bartering for the goods that were pouring into the town to feed and entertain them. Annoyingly chipper following a full night's sleep Arékan had thankfully gone on ahead, and with news of Attila's incursion the talk of the town, Halga watched as folk drew back from the Hun as if she carried the plague. If it had been any other, he would have harboured concerns for her safety. But if her features made her lineage plain, her bearing, and the weapons she openly carried, told of her prowess as a warrior.

Oswy said. 'Did I hear Horsa mention weregild?'

Halga nodded. Weregild or man-price was the amount paid in compensation to a man's family or lord if they were unlawfully injured or killed. 'The Angle under the table was already beginning to get to his feet when we left,' he replied, 'so it can't have been Beorn's punch that caused the injury.' He took another pull on his flask, working the water around his mouth before drawing the obvious conclusion. 'The only man it could be, was the one I pinned to the post with my knife — it sounds like the fool may have died.' He shook his head and sighed. 'Now I have another reason to be indebted to Horsa — he must rue the day we sailed into Strand.'

The short conversation had eaten up the time it took to reach the town gate, and the Jutes pushed their way through the crowd towards the stable. Horsa's men stood around, talking in groups. Although Halga sensed the resentment in some that a few weeks of easy living had been curtailed by the events of the night before, the sight of a smile or two was enough reassurance that many were glad to be on their way. Like Halga's people, the greater number of Angles were rural folk, and although the temptations and entertainments of town life were fine for a day or two they quickly lost their allure. At the entrance to the corral, Arékan was also clearly buoyant that they would soon be putting the town behind them, and Horsa reappeared as stablehands began to emerge with saddles and tackle from the loft. He saw Halga and sauntered across. 'You are a lucky lad,' he said. 'Camaracum has been placed under what king Merovech called *Martialis,* while the town is full of troops. Any breach of the king's peace.' He shrugged. 'I don't know — knife fights that end in a death, for example — are punishable by hanging. Fortunately for you, the leader of the group you attacked spoke up and admitted that his man was the first to draw a weapon. It still cost me silver though,' he added with a look, 'and I offered to get you out of town so that there is no danger that minds sodden by ale will forget it has been paid over the coming days.'

Halga made to apologise, but the Angle waived it away. 'If a man pulls a blade in a fistfight, he deserves all he gets. Besides, it gave us the opportunity to leave this hole.' He cast a look back towards the centre of the settlement. Carts and wagons loaded with anything the army might feel worth their silver were still entering through the gateway, and a scuffle had broken out where the road into the centre of town narrowed as it reached the housing. 'Thousands living cheek by jowl,' Horsa spat. 'I don't know how they can stand it — the smell alone is enough to put me off.' The blankets and saddles were going on now, and the pair looked on as Arékan gave a low whistle. Within moments a horse was making its way towards her, nudging the others aside as it came, and Halga and Horsa shared a look as she leaned in to blow gently on its muzzle in greeting.

Horsa said. 'It looks as though someone spent time at the stables last night, making a new friend. It's almost as if she half expected trouble in town.' The pair shared a smile. Horsa spoke again. 'How is she getting on?'

'She seems happy enough, all things considered.'

'Do you think she will give you her oath?'

'At the moment we share the same aim,' Halga said with a shrug. 'But she is her own woman. What direction her life takes once Garwulf and the burners are dead, is for her and Tángri Khan to decide.'

The mounts were all but ready now, and Angle and Jute alike were busy slinging shields and weapons as bags of food appeared. 'Take as much as you can carry lads,' Horsa called out above the sound of horses, carts and the background hubbub of the city. 'Food will be hard to come by where we are going.'

Oswy had picked out a fine gelding from the herd, leading the horse across to his drihten for approval. Halga ran a practiced hand over the flanks and withers, nodding his acceptance as he bent to test the belly band. 'Wouldn't it be better to take pack horses along?' he said. 'We can carry far more that way.'

Arékan was the first to mount up, and she edged the horse across to reply. 'What if they are captured, Halga? Or we need to split our force? If we are going south, the land will be picked clean of anything edible by the invading army. This way we can divide our force instantly, and carry on independently without stopping to share our supplies.'

Horsa chuckled as he walked away. 'Listen and learn, Halga.'

Very soon the company mounted and prepared to leave. Arékan and Oswy urged their mounts alongside Halga, as they watched the Franks on guard at the gate clearing a passage through the crowd with their spear shafts. The trio ran their eyes over the streets and buildings of Camaracum as they waited for Horsa to lead them out. The sun was shining brightly in the sky to the south-east, the heat of the day already causing the big stone walls to shimmer in the haze. Enclosed by the defences, the air in the town was suffocating, the cooling breezes of the countryside beyond rarely felt in the man-made cauldron of stone. Oswy was the first to speak. 'It was fun while it lasted,' he said, echoing their thoughts. 'But one night was enough.'

A HORSE SNICKERED, the rider deliberately ignoring the dark looks shot his way as he leaned forward to run a calming hand over the beast's neck. Arékan slid from the saddle, jogging forward as lithe and noiseless as a cat as she went to lend a hand. At the junction, Horsa's scout went down on one knee, tracing the outline of a hoof print with his forefinger as he shared his thoughts with the Hun. Halga cast a look around as the Angle teased apart a ball of horse shit, offering it up to Arékan, who bent forward to sniff and nod. Every man in the column was as taut as a bowstring, their faces betraying the turmoil within, as eyes and ears strained for the slightest sound of the enemy. When he looked back, the conference was over, Angle and Hun seeking their leaders as they prepared to make a report. Within moments, Arékan was at his knee, her wide handsome face tilted up towards his as she held his gaze in her own. 'Two war parties,' she said. 'A party of Huns passed through some time ago, maybe as long as a month — heading west. Less than a day ago, around a hundred Germans came through heading eastwards, moving at a faster pace.'

Halga nodded. 'How do you know who the riders were from a hoof print?'

Arékan flashed a grin as she reached up to pat his belly. 'Germans are bigger and heavier,' she said, 'too fond of meat and ale.'

Halga returned the smile. 'Well, I did ask.'

A low whistle had him turning his head, and Arékan remounted as Halga urged his horse forward. Horsa was talking to Edwin, and the pair turned his way as he came up. 'What do you think?'

'Now they are engaged in a siege, they will have to range further and further to gather in supplies,' Halga offered. 'Maybe they are doubling back to see if they missed anything on the way through?'

Horsa nodded. They had come across another of king Merovech's war bands a few days earlier. Thankfully, the leaders had recognised the banners before the two columns had come to blows, and the Frank had been a welcome source of information. Attila and his allies had reached the walled city of Aureliani, which had closed its gates to them. Rather than bypassing it like most fortified towns on the westward march, the king of the Huns had chosen to invest the city. That the Hun advance had stalled before it reached the coast had been welcome news, but best of all, the Frank had been able to tell them that the Romans and Goths had finally joined forces and were rushing north to give battle. The giant clash of armies could only be a matter of time, and Angle and Jute alike had looked forward to finally fulfilling the reason they were here in the south: glory and loot.

Horsa said. 'Either they are foragers or Attila has got word that Aetius and king Theodoric are on their way to confront him, and he is pulling back. The land between here and Aureliani is hilly and wooded — unsuited for an army largely consisting of steppe horsemen. I fought here as a lad,' he added, 'a dozen years or so ago — when first Aetius and then Attila attacked the Burgundians and killed their king.' He rubbed his nose as he thought. 'A few days' march east of here, the woodlands give way to an open plain — if Attila decides to fight a big battle, that is where he will go.'

'So, we head back north and rejoin Merovech's army?' Edwin suggested. 'We have taken his silver, and if there is going to be a big battle he will need all the men he has got.'

Halga cut in before Horsa had the opportunity to reply. 'If Attila's horde is making its way towards this plain as you say, we have already missed our chance. We saw the way they moved forward on the way down here, splitting up into powerful columns and advancing on a wide front. It makes perfect sense,' he said. 'Use the roads for the slow-moving wagons and camp followers, and let the rest of the army feed off the land. It conserves the supplies they have brought along, cuts a swathe through enemy territory, and reduces the chance of a surprise attack on the core of the army to virtually nil.' Halga indicated the place where the paths intersected with a flick of his head. 'Arékan told me that a column crossed here moving eastwards less than a day ago. If that is the case, and it is part of the withdrawal, we are too late — they are either already past us, or we run the risk of running slap bang into more men than we can handle if we attempt to return north now.'

Edwin spoke. 'Maybe there are no more to come? When is the last time we found any bodies at a farm or settlement?'

Halga and Horsa exchanged a look, and the Jute watched as the Angle's expression slowly brightened. 'You are right,' he said, clapping his gedriht on the arm, 'several days ago.'

Halga began to smile as he too came to understand. It was a pattern they had come to know well over the past few weeks. The closer they rode to a walled town, the fewer bodies they encountered, as the folk in the hinterland fled to shelter within. A major settlement must be close by, and Horsa racked his memory as he attempted to work out how far they had ridden since they had left Camaracum a few weeks before. 'Well, we know we have crossed the River Aisne,' he said finally, 'because the Romans very helpfully leave a marker stone to tell us where we are when we use the bridge — but we have yet to reach the Marne. That means we should be within spitting distance of Remorum, a city that shelters behind some of the finest stone walls I have had the pleasure to see. If we rest up there and let the remainder of Attila's army pass by, we can link up with Merovech when he rides to join the Romans and Goths.' He threw them both a smile. 'We are already on the north-south road, and the mile markers will tell us how far we have to go. With any luck, we should be safely behind fortified gates before nightfall.'

. . .

THE LAND ROSE SLIGHTLY, the forest drew back, as the road-side stones counted down the miles to safety. There were still three to go when the summer breeze carried it to them, the sweet smell of death, a miasma that clawed at nostrils and throats in a sickening stench you could almost taste. Halga urged his horse to the front of the column, as the carefree chatter and lighthearted mood evaporated. He reached the head at the same time as the scout clattered to a halt before his lord, and the Angle blurted out his report straightaway. 'The city has been sacked,' he said. 'The walls look intact, but the southern gate has been forced. From what we can see without entering the town itself, there does not appear to be a building inside with its roof still in place.'

When no reply was forthcoming, Halga cast a look at his lord, staring in amazement as he saw Horsa blanch. For the first time he could recall since they had landed in Francia, Halga felt a knot of fear tighten in his guts. He watched as his kinsman forced his mind back to the matter at hand, which they all now knew was survival itself. 'Is there any sign of life?'

The scout shook his head. 'No, lord. As far as we could tell, there was nothing moving inside the city walls, and no sign of the enemy. It looks like Remorum was attacked some time ago.'

Horsa spoke again, and it was impossible to miss the sense of disbelief in his voice. 'Remorum is one of the largest cities in Gaul. You are sure it has fallen?'

The young scout stood his ground; Halga was impressed by the confident tone in his reply. 'Yes, lord,' he said firmly. 'There is no room for doubt. Remorum has been all but destroyed.'

Horsa nodded sadly. 'Where is your mate?'

'Still watching from cover,' the scout replied. 'If he spots any sign of movement in the ruins, he will gallop back and let us know.'

Horsa turned aside, and Halga felt his spirits lift as he saw that the spark of leadership had already reignited in his kinsman after the moment of shock and doubt. 'Ride back to your men,' he said. 'Pass the word that the city has suffered ransack. But that it was some time ago, and we are going in anyway.'

Halga gave a curt nod, hauling the head of his mount around as he did as he was bid. He cried out the news as he rode, the Jute allowing himself the luxury of revelling in the warlike demeanour of his Anglian allies as he went. If the careworn faces that stared back were grimy and sun blushed following a month or more living in a hostile land, their fighting spirit had been honed to a fine edge by the constant exposure to danger. Sure now that they could count on Halga and his Jutes they formed a formidable team, a fact that could only serve them well in the big fight to come. Arékan and Oswy were waiting, the other lads behind, and Halga called an order to those bringing up the rear as he slowed his horse to a walk. 'Coella, Godwin — did you get all that?' The pair confirmed that they had. 'Then ride and tell the rearguard about the situation up ahead. It is only a few miles to Remorum, we shall enter it together.'

The column was already moving forward again as the pair turned to go, and Halga slipped back into place at the head of his troop as they sped away. They rode in silence, each immersed in their thoughts as hands moved instinctively to check spears, swords, and shields. Arékan rode alongside, running a hand through her hair, before using oily fingers to lubricate her bowstring. He raised his eyes, taking in the canopy above, as he heard the bow slide back into its gorytos with a thump. Despite the sun being hidden by the dense foliage, shafts of light lancing in from the west showed the day to be well advanced. Overhead, a fragmented sky formed a brilliant, shifting, pattern of blue as he rode. Doves cooed in the branches above; somewhere in the middle distance, the staccato beat of a woodpecker carried on the muggy midsummer air.

In no time, they came to a stop again, and raising his eyes to look, Halga saw that Horsa had halted the march at the woodland edge. Every pair of eyes in the column fixed upon him now as they awaited a command, and following a brief conversation with what Halga assumed to be the remaining scout, Horsa raised an arm to order them forward. The procession split as it exited cover, dividing left and right before turning back to form an unbroken line overlooking the city.

From their vantage point at the crest of a gentle slope, Remorum lay spread out before them in its devastation. The road that had carried them there continued down a hillside made grey by a rain of ash, across a river and through the shattered doors at the centre of a magnificent triple arched gateway. Lifting his chin to look, Halga followed the line of the road on into the centre of the city, until it terminated at the usual forum and basilica. A flash of movement caught Halga's eye, breaking the spell, and he looked on as a strong party of Angles cantered downslope to sniff out any hint of trouble before they entered. Arékan guided her horse across as they waited. 'I was here,' she said, drawing a look of surprise from those within earshot. 'A few years back, with your father and my hearth mates.'

'Perhaps you should tell Horsa?' Halga replied. 'You may be of use to those lads.'

The Hun hawked and spat. 'Once you have seen one Roman town, you have seen them all: a gate at the middle of each wall; crisscrossed roads; forum, basilica, and temples in the centre.' She glanced across. 'Horsa's men are good.' She paused, before adding emphasis to her words. 'As good as any I have seen — and I have seen a lot. But Roman towns,' she shrugged, 'the least amount of time I spend in them, the happier I am. You must have noticed that I was a little underwhelmed by the prospect of a night out in Camaracum?'

Halga snorted, despite the grim scene spread out before him. 'Those Angles in the tavern don't know how lucky they were.'

She rolled her eyes. 'You forget, I have done all this before. I knew it would end in a pissed-up brawl.'

They sat in silence for a short while, until Halga spoke again. 'I was always told that your people were horsemen, ranging widely over limitless plains?' He indicated the place where a massive oak wood frame had been pushed aside, the heavy ram it carried still suspended within by ropes as thick as a man's thigh. 'The army contains many races,' she replied, 'even Greeks and Romans. Their engineers will have overseen its construction. Attila needed to make an example, to encourage others to open their doors to him. He is on the move and needs supplies, but also slaves and loot for his army; what better place to show his power, both his followers and those who may be preparing to offer resistance, than a city the size of Remorum?' Arékan raised her eyes, indicating the gateway with a jerk of her chin. 'That is Mars on top of the archway, riding his chariot pulled by fire breathing horses.' She threw him a look. 'The Romans always did love war and conquest — I wonder if the citizens appreciated the irony when the gates came down, and their buildings began to burn.'

16

FREYA'S VISIT

A sudden gust blew in from the west, uncloaking the hoof and footprints of an invading army as it ridged up the ash.

Oswy plucked at his sleeve. 'There is our man.'

Halga looked. Two riders had reappeared at the Mars Gate, quickly followed by others, as the scouts put back their heels to canter across the bridge and upslope in a cloud of cinders. 'Good,' he replied with a frown, 'let us get down there. The smell of rotting bodies will make a welcome change from shit and piss.' It had quickly become clear that the woodland edge had become the place to go when the men and women of the army of Attila had cause to ease their bowels. Although Horsa had moved the battle line downslope, the stench lay heavily on a land baking in the midsummer heat. The scouts were soon with their leader, and Halga looked on as they made their report.

Arékan said. 'It doesn't look good. We shall be looking for other lodgings tonight.'

Halga opened his mouth to query her, but the question was stillborn as the sound of his name carried across the slope. 'Come along,' he said. 'You know the town and may be of help.' The pair handed the reins to Oswy and began to trot across. They were using the horses as sparingly as possible now, dismounting at every stop, however brief. If the rivers were plentiful and the meadows lush with grass in this part of Gaul, the hard stone roads had worn horseshoes to slivers. Footsore and weary after a month of daylong use, the horses were in far worse shape than the men.

As ever, Edwin was at Horsa's side, and the Angles broke off their conversation as Halga and Arékan came up. Horsa came straight to the point. 'There are too many dead,' he said. 'If we spend even a solitary night here we will likely sicken, and I have not spent this long in a hostile land to lose a man unnecessarily.' He shot Arékan a weary smile: 'or woman.' The extended campaign had sapped them all.

Halga said. 'What do you intend?'

'It looks like another night spent sleeping at the roadside.' Horsa cast a look westwards, and the group followed his gaze. The sun lay on the horizon, the skyline aflame. 'We have — what, an hour of light? Enough time to retrace our steps and find another brook or river to water the horses.'

'There is an alternative,' Arékan put in. 'A hundred yards beyond the northern gate, there is an amphitheatre. It is disused now, but the circuit remains unbroken, and it is large enough to hold us all.' She indicated the river with a nod of her head. 'There is ample grass outside the walls and along the riverside, and if we take the horses upstream we can be sure that the water is untainted from the goings-on here.'

Horsa's eyes opened in question, and the Hun explained how she knew. 'I was here a while back,' she said, 'with Ottar Hunding and the rest of his comitatus.' The Angles shared a look. 'It will save the horses from another long ride, lord,' the gedriht said, 'and we will have a walled enclosure for protection.' He pulled a face. 'I might even get the chance to remove my boots. It will be the first time for days that we could relax a little.'

Horsa thought for a moment, and then nodded. 'I agree. It is late in the day. Even if Attila's army is retreating, they would have made camp by now. We will mount up, cross the bridge here and skirt the walls until we come to the amphitheatre. Once we are settled in, we can send men down to the riverside in groups to see to the horses.'

Horsa mounted with a grunt of effort, throwing them a self-deprecating smile as he settled into the saddle. 'You are right,' he chuckled. 'We could all use a rest.' Halga and Arékan retraced their steps as Horsa led his war band down into the vale. The men of his comitatus had already mounted when he arrived, and Halga hauled himself into the saddle as he prepared to follow on. Ahead, the Angles were funnelling back onto the roadway as they descended into the vale, and as Arékan explained their destination and the reason for it to his men, Halga led them across the bridge. A hundred yards ahead the great wooden doors of Remorum had been smashed to kindling by the power of the nearby siege engine, jagged shards clinging to wrought iron hinges all that remained of the barrier. With the great doors broken open, all eyes followed the roadway as men looked to catch a glimpse of the destruction beyond. Bloated bodies lay twisted in death beneath a hazing of flies; a pack of dogs, suspiciously well-fed amid the carnage all around, watched from the shadows. Above it all, Mars gazed down from the platform of his war chariot.

Turning the corner they left the ash field behind, and as the circuit of the amphitheatre hove into view, Horsa urged his horse into a gallup. A dirt track branched off from the main route northward, and as the entrance came up and men slid gratefully to the ground, a vanguard hurried forward to check the bowl for signs of opposition. They were back in no time, calling the war band forward with the sweep of an arm, and as they passed from light into shadow Halga allowed himself to relax for the first time in days.

Emerging into the centre of the arena, the Jute ran his eyes around the perimeter as he dismounted. Stone terracing enclosed the whole, rising in a series of steps for forty or fifty feet before ending in a crenelated battlement that he was sure had been intended more for decorative show than any serious defensive work. But it would serve them well if it came to a fight here, and with the entrance denied to any attackers by a hedge of shields and bowmen on the walls, it was as good a place as any to make a stand. He moved further in, picking out a position where the horses could rest up for the night. 'Here,' he said, 'grab that spot, before the Angles nab it.' Despite their tiredness, the comment caused a ripple of laughter among his men, and as he straightened from loosening the billet strap he grasped the saddle and lifted it away. With the saddle removed, Halga moved around the horse, running an experienced hand over knees, fetlocks and hocks, before raising each hoof in turn to check for pebbles or nicks. The stone setts of the Roman roads made for rapid movement in all weathers, but they were hard on horseshoes and wheel rims alike, and he teased the horse's ear as he made him a promise. 'You will be home soon, old fellow,' he cooed. 'Back in the stable for a well-earned rest.'

A shadow fell across him as he spoke, and he turned his head to find Arékan at his side. 'I need your help,' she said. Halga blinked in surprise, but before he could reply, the woman explained. 'I want to go a little way into the city and I need a companion, someone to watch over me while I am unable to defend myself.' She looked around as she saw his astonishment. The others were busily seeing to their horses. But the closest had heard her request and were glancing across, clearly as intrigued as their leader. Arékan was a woman who never asked for protection if she could help it, particularly from a man. 'There is something I want to do while we still have a little daylight,' she said. 'If you will help me, bring your weapons and I will explain as we walk.'

Halga nodded. 'Lead the way.' He caught Beorn's eye as he retrieved his spear. 'Take care of our horses, will you?' he asked. 'Take them down to the river to drink — I will give him a rub down when we return.' The last of the Angles were just clearing the passageway when they arrived, and within moments they were through and treading the path towards the city. There was a sharp edge now to the northeastern corner of Remorum's walls, the eastern defences dark and unwelcoming as they fell into deep shadow. But the setting sun painted the northern wall a fiery red, and Halga watched as Arékan made a shelf with her hand as she squinted to pick out the entrance. Satisfied that the doors were open, she turned to Halga and spoke. 'There is a lodge for travellers just inside the northern gate,' she explained, 'with a well, stable, and tavern. I need to go there and clean myself.'

'You heard me tell Beorn to water the horses,' he replied. 'Can't you go with him?'

She shook her head. 'Not for this. I have done so before, and it has caused problems. There are a few things I need to rinse out, too.'

Halga pulled a face, as he suddenly understood the reason behind the furtive trip. Arékan noticed, and a trace of impishness lit her features as she continued her explanation. 'It's not normally such a bother,' she said brightly. 'But what with all the riding and whatnot, the flow has been particularly heavy this month.'

Halga peered into the distance as she talked. 'Yeah, yeah — that's fine — yeah...'

Arékan laughed. 'Men,' she scoffed. 'Destroy a city and murder thousands. Spill a man's guts or pulp his head, and it's celebrated in song. Mention a few dabs of blood from something barely there, and they recoil in horror. Yes,' she confirmed. 'I have been visited by Freya these past few days. I have the flux, the flowers, or whatever it is you know it by. But trust me, you have nothing to fear. I promise not to let it blight the crops, cast a love spell over you, or dull the edge of your weapons.'

Halga looked sheepish, awkwardly aware that he had placed his body between the woman and his sword to protect the keenness of the blade as she had spoken. She gave a gentle laugh at his discomfort, surprising him as she went on tiptoe to plant a kiss on his cheek. 'Thank you for coming,' she said. 'Even near the gatehouse, the city will be a dangerous place. I would hate anyone or anything to creep up on me while I was squatting with my trews around my ankles, and my bare arse perched over a bucket. It would be an unfortunate way to die, after all I have been through this past year.' Closer now, they could tell that the background hum that filled the city was increasing as the night came on, as more and more mites and midges came out to feed. Halga shifted the weight of the sword in its scabbard as they reached the gate.

Passing through the archway, the road stretched out ahead, and the pair, Hun and Jute, paused to look. With the sun now low in the western sky, the main route to the forum was in shadow, but enough light remained to make plain the scale of the disaster that had overtaken the community. Not a roof remained intact the length of the route, each building wearing a skirt of debris beneath a skeletal frame of fire blackened beams. Littering the roadway itself, the bodies of those considered too old or young to fetch a decent price in the slave markets back east lay where they had fallen, scorched or overripe and bursting in the heat. Halga felt a tug at his sleeve. 'Come on,' she said. 'I can feel the eyes of the dead upon us — let's get this done and be away.'

The Inn stood just where she had said, on the far side of a courtyard backing onto the city walls themselves, and the pair picked their way across over a debris field of empty ale barrels and discarded cups. Arékan shot him a look. 'If you were hoping to find a spare barrel, it looks as if you are out of luck,' she whispered.

Halga snorted softly, replying in an undertone. 'It is as well that I don't. It has been so long now I doubt I could keep my wits, although arriving back having slunk away for a crafty ale with the only woman in the camp would be worth it to see the look on men's faces.' He swept the clearing with his gaze as they moved forward, his eyes flitting from window to doorway as he lowered the point of his spear. Arékan nocked an arrow, padding across the open space with the curious cat-like movement he had seen her use before. Closer to the Inn, dishes, cups, and barrels lay in drifts. The body of a man, stripped of anything of use or value, lay on its back, the eyes, face and softer parts of his torso long since pecked or chewed away. Ahead, Arékan had reached the well, and Halga watched as she slid a wooden cover aside and peered over the rim. The smile on her face served to confirm that the water below had remained untainted by the death and mayhem above ground, and he turned away as she laid her bow aside and a pail slid from sight.

Halga sauntered across to the lodge, poking his head inside the open doorway as the creaking of rope and the bump and clatter of a full water pail sounded unnaturally loud in the still evening air. The room inside looked remarkably ordered compared to the rest of the city. It took him a moment to realise that this would have been, not only, one of the last buildings reached by the invaders as they swept through the streets and alleyways of Remorum, but one of the last vacated as they moved on. As his eyes grew more accustomed to the gloomy interior, he could see where a pile of broken tables and chairs had been stacked against the far wall in a half-hearted attempt at firing the building as the army left. But the flames had soon puttered out, leaving little more than a few scorch marks and a sooty deposit on the wall behind to show that any attempt had been made at all. Straight ahead a staircase rose to the upper floor, flecks of dust dancing in the light showing where the shutters had been thrown wide by the rampaging Huns. He cocked an ear, listening intently for the slightest sound; none came, and satisfied that the building was unoccupied, he resisted the temptation to search for a wayward barrel and stepped back into the light.

Arékan was splashing away, and he only resisted the urge to steal a look with difficulty, as the thought of her nakedness a few feet off triggered the idea that it was not only ale he had gone without for a good while. The stables and tack room were on the far side of the yard, and he fixed his eyes upon them as he passed her by. Within a few yards, she was left behind, and it was as he moved his eyes from stall to stall that he saw it for the first time. Their eyes locked, and Halga knew instantly that they were in danger. He glanced aside as his hand moved across, untying the silk peace bands holding his sword secure in its scabbard. 'Are you done?'

Arékan looked up, squeezing reddish water from a strip of linen, as she recognised the concern in his tone. 'Almost,' she replied. 'What is wrong?'

'You need to dress yourself,' he replied. 'We may be in trouble.'

When he looked back, the dog had gone, and he trotted across to the end of the courtyard as she tugged up her clothing. A brief look up and down the roadway showed him that they were once again alone. But there had been something in the dog's demeanour that had caused him alarm, a cockiness in its eyes that told the Jute that the animal had lost its fear of man. Arékan came up, plucking at her trews as she attempted to unstick the material from her damp skin. She nocked an arrow and squirmed again. 'What is it?' Before he could reply, she had her answer, a handful of dogs scampering from cover to come to a halt between them and the city gate.

Halga said. 'How many shafts did you bring?'

She glanced down. The Hunnish gorytos had a smaller pocket on the front for storing arrows ready for use. More would be carried in a quiver to replenish it in a fight, but they both knew that had been left with her spear, back at the amphitheatre. 'Six,' she replied.

A drawn out howl had him switching his head back to the road. The first dog was back, and Halga made a plea as the dogs nearer the gateway took up the cry. 'Shut that bastard up,' he growled. 'If anyone is going to die here, he can be the first.' The dog's head snapped back, sensing danger as the bowstring twanged. He barely had time to move a muscle before the arrow buried itself deep inside his chest, and Arékan nocked and loosed gain to send the largest dog in the archway group flying backward with a yelp. But if the pair thought they had dealt with the threat, they were to be quickly disappointed. As howls and barks filled the air above Remorum, more dogs began to arrive in pairs and small groups, with the space between Halga, Arékan and the outside world shrinking with every moment.

'We have to get out,' she said, 'before they can surround and overwhelm us. I will cut a path to the wall, and we can move towards the gate from there.' A brutish beast, thick set and droopy jowled, the type the Roman's called a *molossian,* was barring their way. Arékan loosed, the arrow flying true to punch a hole squarely between its hate-filled eyes. 'Run!'

They reached the city walls before the dogs had time to react, and Arékan strung another shaft and took aim as the remaining dogs regrouped and surged again. Within moments the two fiercest dogs had joined their predecessors bleeding out in the dust, and as the attack faltered and the remaining animals gathered in wary groups she spoke again. 'That was the last,' Arékan said, as she raised the bow and drew the string. 'Let us hope that they are not sharp enough to notice that the bowstring is empty.'

As Halga led the way, edging along the inside wall towards the hoped-for safety of the meadow outside, the boldest dogs began to make darting runs, each time finishing a little closer to what they obviously considered fresh meat. When no arrow came they grew braver still, and despite Halga lunging forward to skewer another with his spear, it was becoming a matter of time before they broke through the defence. Halga handed the bloodstained weapon to Arékan as the dog dragged itself away, drawing War-spite as the hunters began to close in, sensing a kill. Another molossian dodged Arékan's spearpoint, all muscular torso and slavering jaws: Halga brought his sword crashing down to split its skull like an egg, stepping in to finish the beast off with a downward stab to the throat. At his side, Arékan's spear shot out, sliding along the flank of another to pare flesh from bone before piercing its belly to leave it yowling as it dragged itself clear. Halga raised his eyes as the attackers regrouped. It was still a fair way to the nearest arch, and switching back, he was dismayed to see yet more dogs galloping into view.

Beside him, Arékan began to laugh.

Halga stole a look, suspecting she had given up or lost her mind.

She laughed again when she saw the concern written on his features. 'Can't you hear it, Halga?'

Halga cocked an ear, turning back as he made ready to fight off another onslaught. To his astonishment the dogs had drawn up, milling around in uncertainty; now they were slinking away, melting back into the shadowy recesses of the shattered city from which they had appeared only a short while before. He listened again, thoroughly bemused by all that was happening around him. This time he heard it. A horse army was approaching, the drumming of hooves on the sun-baked ground building like distant thunder. Hun and Jute shared a look, and Arékan shook her head in weary resignation as the sound of a war horn confirmed that the manner of her death had merely changed. She circled the yard, plucking arrows from the dead: wiping canine gore on still warm pelts as she went. 'That's no raiding party,' she threw over her shoulder, teasing the fletching on the arrows to ensure they would fly true. 'If it's not Attila and his horde, it will be one of the subject kings and his army.'

Halga crossed to the archway, peering outside as she planted the sole of a boot against her final victim and jerked the arrow free. Now that the great mass of masonry no longer muffled the sound, he could pinpoint the direction from which it came, and he turned back and flashed a grin. 'That's neither Attila, nor one of his German underlings,' he said. 'The army we can hear, is approaching from the North.'

17

THE WOLF-TAILED STAR

He had heard the scops and poets use the description and always thought it flowery and absurd, but if anything, to describe the silence that lay upon the meadow as deafening felt inadequate. The war host of the king of Francia appeared dumbfounded to a man as they stared away to the east. It was only when a guda, Woden's rune-man, shattered the peace, leaping and cavorting as the singsong note of his voice filled the air that the spell was broken. Halga had been as rattled as any when men had pointed out the wolf-tailed star. But he dragged his gaze away as a voice came at his shoulder, and he turned to come face to face with a grizzled Frankish veteran. Here stood the type that had seen everything worth seeing long ago, his deadpan expression confirming that he was completely unfazed by the fact that the sky was afire. 'Halga Hunding?'

A curt nod was enough to confirm that the messenger had got his man.

'King Merovech has summoned you, lord. If you accompany me, I will lead you to him.'

With all eyes turned to the heavens it was a difficult task

to push through the crowd, but they were soon approaching the amphitheatre within whose defences the king had set up his tent. Halga glanced across to the roadway as they walked. The last of the stragglers were emerging from the woodland edge, footsore and weary following the long march down from Camaracum, and Halga watched as they too paused to gape and point at the eastern sky.

They had been arriving for the best part of an hour now, and the meadow had quickly become a heaving mass. The mounted men followed by the wagoners, with those on foot bringing up the rear, as each component of Merovech's mighty army came on at their best speed. But if the mood had been breezy, the appearance of what men were calling the wolf-tailed star had dampened their zeal, and Halga wondered what the reaction to the new addition to the night sky would be within the king's inner circle. As the entrance to the amphitheatre loomed over him once again, he knew that he was about to find out. Well-known to the guards, the pair were immediately waved through, and Halga ran his eyes around the bowl of the building as they emerged into the central ring. Horsa and his men had already been ejected from their bolthole by the time Halga and Arékan had returned from the city, the leading element of the Frankish force as quick to grasp the defensive potential of the place as the Angle had been earlier. Although they now faced yet another night sleeping in the open, they all agreed that to do so in the midst of so many friendly spears was as good a trade as they were likely to get following weeks spent in enemy controlled land.

With the stored up heat of the midsummer sun radiating from the stonework all around, and not a breath of wind pene-trating the building, the king's tent flaps had been tied back. Halga was pleased to see the figure of his kinsman among the fighting men as he was led within. King Merovech was off to one side, deep in conversation with a man whose russet coloured clothing and travel-worn appearance marked him out as a scout. Halga glanced down, wincing at the awkward realisation that he must look much the same to the fighting lords of Francia, dressed in their war glory. The guard who had fetched him halted a respectful distance from his lord, and Halga felt a chill despite the warmth of the night as the king lifted his eyes, and his face became a frown.

'Halga Long Knife!' the king exclaimed. 'You are becoming a problem.'

Halga swallowed hard, his mind scrabbling to think of anything he could have done. The men in the tent stood stony-faced as the king went on. 'I gift you a fine seax, and you use it to kill my allies; now my men tell me that you were seen sneaking back into camp with a Hun in tow.' The king held out a hand, indicating that Halga give up the seax. Halga attempted an explanation as he handed the blade across. 'Arékan is attached to my war band, lord,' he said. 'She was a member of my father's comitatus.' He glanced across to Horsa, expecting his kinsman to back up his story, but to his dismay, the big Angle just gave a shrug and averted his eyes. Taken aback by the refusal of his lord to corroborate his story, Halga saw no alternative but to reveal the reason they had gone into Remorum, but even as his mind began to shape the words he knew how ridiculous they would sound. Dazed and caught off guard, he flushed as he realised that his tongue had gone ahead without him, and he was gabbling like a fool: 'we were just — she wanted — needed to — and then some dogs...'

Halga's gibberish was finally too much for the king, and he led a chorus of laughter as he spun the blade, plucked it from the air, and handed it back by the hilt.

'Horsa has been singing your praises,' Merovech admitted, 'and thrilling us with tales of your efforts on my behalf here in the South.' He swept the room with a look of amusement, clapping the Jute on the arm. 'If you can fight as lustily as we have heard, and still retain enough for a tumble at the end of the day, you are just the type of man we want on our side. Come,' he said, leading Halga across to the rear of the tent, 'join our war council. There is always a place for a man of vigour alongside us as we make our plans.'

Halga shot Horsa a look of incomprehension as the king led them across, but the twinkle in the Angle's eye gave him away. Halga stared wide-eyed as he began to suspect the truth: *he knew all along why we had gone into the city.* As he watched in disbelief, the mischievous look became a smirk, and Halga shook his head as he realised that he was smiling too: *you bastard...*

The king had reached a wooden trestle table by the time the pair had composed themselves, and the high-born Franks crowded around as Merovech deliberated. He glanced up as Horsa, Halga and the other hireling leaders managed to bag a spot at the end. 'This is a map of the area surrounding us,' the king explained, shooting them a look. 'Study it well: we may become split up when the fighting starts, and it will help you fix where you are.' He switched his gaze and spoke again. 'Dagmer — perhaps you would be kind enough to describe what we see here so that there is no room for misunderstanding?'

The Frank came forward, clearing his throat as he did so. Halga joined the others, listening intently as he ran through the highlights of the map before them. 'This is where we are — Remorum,' the steward said, pointing to a mark on the chart, 'and this is the road that we took to travel down from Camaracum, the Via Agrippa that snakes across central Gaul from northeast to southwest.' Halga looked at the map in wonder. The city outside had been drawn in detail, with the Mars Gate, and even the amphitheatre in which they stood, clearly recognisable. Although he would never have admitted it to those crowding around, it was the first time he had seen a map. Even as he felt a twinge of shame at his lack of knowledge, he recognised a keen desire kindle within him that he should learn more of the marvels of the southern lands before he left for home. 'A few miles to the south we have the cities of Senones and Tricassium,' Dagmer continued. 'Connected by a good Roman road that takes advantage of the valley of the River Vanne to cut through the hilly, wooded terrain, before reaching Duro Catalaunum and the great plain that takes its name from the settlement — the Catalaunian Fields.'

Merovech placed a hand on Dagmer's shoulder as a signal that he had said enough for the time being, and the king raised his eyes to the rear of the tent, clicking his fingers to summon another as the man stepped back. The scout hurried across, cuffing a well-earned drop of ale from his moustache as he did so. Merovech spoke. 'Use the map to tell my lords what we discussed earlier.'

Surrounded by his king and the most powerful men in Francia, the young man gulped as he turned to face them. His voice was calm and measured when it came, and Halga could see that all those present looked impressed. But if their expressions were of satisfaction at the calibre of their fighting men, they quickly changed to looks of incredulity as the scout shared the electrifying news. 'King Attila and the bulk of his army are already past us and have reached the edge of the plain.' The revelation caused a stir among the fighting lords of the Franks, and a whistle came from the crowd, followed by an observation they all clearly shared. 'Attila is really driving them hard!'

Merovech held up a hand for quiet. 'It's clear that he intends to fight Aetius on the Catalaunian Fields, where his horsemen can manoeuvre in the open.' He turned back to the scout. 'Where is he now?'

'At Duro Catalaunum, lord.'

'And Aetius and his army?'

'Still a day's march east.'

Merovech clicked his tongue as he thought, before raising his eyes to sweep the room again. 'Attila has to fight,' he said. 'He has drawn upon practically his entire strength for this invasion — men will be expecting to return east weighed down with treasure, slaves, and tales of glorious conquest. He was unable to fight in the wooded country to the west and still be sure of a victory, so he is leading them back to a place that will suit their fighting style.'

Merovech called Dagmer forward again. 'It looks as if we have our battlefield, perhaps you could run through the main points for us?'

'It seems clear that the enemy is looking to make a stand with his back to the River Seine. The east-west road they used for the retreat spans the river there at Tricassium. But there is a smaller crossing place a few miles north that would permit Attila to make a fort of his wagons,' Dagmer went on, 'whilst at the same time providing easier access to water and forage. It is here I think he will make his camp.'

Merovech asked. 'How far is it from the woodland edge to the river?'

'A little over five miles, King Merovech.'

'And how far are we from Attila now?'

'If the Huns are at Duro Catalaunum? Twenty-five miles lord.'

The reply drew a gasp from the Frankish lords, and Halga listened in as a spokesman formed all their fears into words.

'We are standing here chatting within twenty-five miles of Attila's yurt?' The man exchanged a look with his fellows. 'If they discover we are here, the Via Agrippa could bring them crashing down upon us within the hour.'

To their astonishment, Merovech met their fears with a smile. 'Well, unless they have set off already, they may yet be disappointed when they arrive.' He indicated the tent flap with a nod. 'Follow me outside — you too,' he added, glancing towards the scout, 'and I will explain.' The king led the way, and as they all filed out, Halga and Horsa shared a look. From the sound of it, they would be fighting a battle of gargantuan size within the next few days, and the Jute noted that the reality had driven any jokiness from his kinsman's expression. To everyone's surprise, the king turned aside the moment he was through the tent flaps, and as he climbed the theatre steps they scrambled along in his wake. Reaching the parapet, they formed a line, gazing out across the Frankish camp as they waited for the king to speak. The last of the daylight had been driven away while they had been deliberating inside, and the moon and its newfound companion were brilliant beacons to the East and the West. Covering the meadow below them, the encampment basked in their steely glow, with only an occasional watchfire marking the perimeter providing a warmer light. After a while, the king spoke again. 'What are the men saying about our new friend in the heavens?'

Their eyes turned skyward once again as the Frankish lords offered their replies. Halga looked. He could barely make out the stars, such was the dazzling radiance emanating from the twin sources of light, and he listened in as the Franks spoke. 'The men are calling it the wolf star or the wolf-tailed star lord,' one was saying, before adding to his reply with obvious reluctance. 'Many are saying it heralds the death of a king.' Another added: 'I heard it said that it is Woden himself, riding at the head of his spectral army, and that the upcoming battle is the final clash at the ending of the world.'

Merovech nodded as he listened. When his underlings had exhausted their supply of tall-tales and hearsay, he spoke again. 'If the hunters are saying these things about the appearance of this wolf-tailed star, how must the hunted feel? Put yourselves in their place. So much for the easy pickings they were promised; it must appear to them as if they are fleeing for their lives, despite the reassurances of their leaders and the promises of a great victory to come on the banks of the Seine.' He lifted his chin towards the east as he continued, seemingly as much to himself as those around him. 'Romans, Goths, and Franks snapping at their heels, and now Woden rides from Valhall to lend a hand.' The king stared out over the army, before turning back to summon the young scout with a click of his fingers. 'Finish your report,' he said. 'Tell my warlords what you told me in the tent.'

'The enemy left a rearguard ten miles west of Duro Catalaunum, blocking the road that Aetius and Rome's allies are using to chase him down. That road,' he said, 'pointing across the river to the south, joins up with it a couple of miles from their position.'

Halga glanced aside at the news, and was encouraged to see that Horsa had formed the same idea. The Angle gave a subtle nod that the Jute speak on their behalf. 'We know that road lord,' Halga said. 'It's the direction from which we arrived at Remorum only a few hours ago.'

Merovech smiled. 'I appreciate the offer, Long Knife, but I think we can follow a road without a guide.' Gentle laughter accompanied the king's remark, and Halga pushed down his anger at the thought he was being mocked or taken lightly. He spoke again, more forcefully this time as he sought to make himself clear. 'No, you don't understand. We know this region well; we have crisscrossed it this past month and there is another route south, a woodland track that leads away from the main roadway towards the west. If the rearguard is ten miles from Duro Catalaunum, as your scout says, this path will join the road a few miles to the rear of their position.'

Fury blazed in the visage of the Frankish lords as they rounded upon him, but as hands flew to sword hilts at the disrespect shown their lord by the foreigner, the king spoke soothing words. 'Let him be,' he said. 'If he forgets himself, he only does so out of a desire to further our cause.' Merovech turned back to the scout. 'Do we know who forms the rearguard?'

'They flew the Raven flag of Woden, alongside another showing a Bison on a golden background lord,' he replied. 'The bull heads and background colour repeated on their shield facings.'

Merovech switched his attention back to Dagmer. 'What can you tell me about them?'

'They are Gepids, lord,' the steward replied. 'The Gepid contingent of Attila's army has been estimated at seven to eight thousand spears, led by their king, Ardaric — one of Attila's closest allies.'

Merovech pumped the scout for more information. 'How many did you see?'

'We counted three thousand mounted men, King Merovech.'

Dagmer asked a question of his own. 'Did you see a Bison standard? It would look like a shaggy bull head, mounted upon a flagstaff.'

The scout shook his head. 'No, lord.'

Dagmer pressed him. 'You are certain?'

It was the young Frank's turn to make a forceful reply. 'If it was there, we would have seen it.'

King and steward laughed at the young man's testy response, and Merovech glanced Halga's way. 'It would appear that impertinence is catching; never mind, you have done well,' he said, clapping the scout on the arm. 'Return to your drinking while you can, we may have further use for you tonight.'

The men glanced up as a brace of wood pigeons clattered into the air from a nearby tower, beating their way skyward before gliding across to the woodland edge. Merovech turned back, and every man there saw that the joviality of a moment ago had been replaced by a look of determination. 'It is so light, even the birds think it is daytime,' he said. 'We must take advantage of it, or forever rue the missed opportunity. If the scout is correct, the Gepid rearguard contains less than half of their army, and the absence of the bull standard indicates that it is commanded by someone besides the king. Without his presence, they will be much more likely to break and run if we can get in position, and hit them hard before they know we are there.'

He cast another look to the west. The wolf-tail star appeared larger still, the stars paling to insignificance in its glow. Merovech shook his head in wonder. 'Whether we are about to be joined by Woden and his einherjar or not, it is certain that the gods fight at our side — the conditions are perfect for a night attack. What is more, the enemy will never suspect that such a thing would be attempted during the depths of the witching hours. I will outline my plan, then you will each return to your troop and tell them to be prepared to ride within the hour. If we can gain a victory before the Romans and Goths arrive, we can put heart into our army, bring glory and renown upon ourselves, and put the wind up the enemy at the same time.' King Merovech's gaze shifted from face to face, pausing a heartbeat when it reached Halga before moving on. The king's stare had taken on a steely look, and the Jute revelled in the force of the man as he addressed them once more. 'We are attacking,' he snarled, his decision made. 'Tonight!'

18

GEPIDS

All heads turned again, tracking the owl's flight as it ghosted by on silent wings. Halga spoke in an undertone. 'Keep your eyes and ears open; there will be time enough for bird watching once the fight is over.' The road shone like a silvery wand, the woodlands to either side walls of stygian blackness where the light from above failed to penetrate the summer canopy. A little way off Arékan was poised, her bow held low, the bowstring slightly flexed as they waited. Halga squinted, the light reflecting from the stone setts just enough for him to pick out the shadowy figures in the tree line opposite. Horsa raised a hand: Halga smiled; they were set. The screech owl returned, heading back to the east as it continued its nocturnal beat, its head bent low as it scanned the roadside verges for any signs of movement. Halga's mind wandered as they waited, his thoughts drifting to the nighttime ride that had carried them here, despite his remark to the others.

They had left the campsite outside Remorum as soon as the Frankish leaders had gathered their troops. Crossing the river at the Mars Gate, they had struck out south, heading back down the very same road that had led Horsa and his oath sworn to the city only a few short hours before. Within half a dozen miles they were back at the crossroads where Arékan and the young Anglian scout had held their conference, and Halga stood momentarily stupefied that the meeting had taken place less than a day before. His mind ran through all that had occurred since that moment as they waited: the ride north; their horror at discovering the great city sacked and ruined. The fight with the dogs, followed by the arrival of king Merovech and his army of the Franks; the appearance of the wolf-tailed star and the certainty that the greatest battle was only a day or two away.

A hand plucked at his sleeve, dragging him back to the present, and Halga turned to find the honest round face of Coella close to his. 'The owl, lord,' he breathed. 'It's not returned.' Halga had grown to trust his gedriht's countryman ways implicitly, and he nodded that he understood. He turned to Arékan, but the Hun had either overheard or recognised the importance too. 'Make sure you don't let fly directly across the clearing,' he warned. 'Remember, Horsa and his men are there.' Her eyes rolled, and he recognised the pitying look which followed. 'I will try,' she said, the sarcasm dripping from every word. 'But I can't promise my aim will not suffer if they forget to do the same.' The wolf-tail light glinted on the woman's thumb ring as the stave came up, and every man strained to hear as the bowstring creaked. All of a sudden, it came, the staccato drumming of hoofs on stone growing louder by the moment in the muggy air, and Halga tightened his grip on the shaft of his spear as he prepared to dash forward.

A flash of movement off to the west and Arékan stepped from cover, and as the bowstring twanged and the first arrow sped away, she was already nocking another. The second shaft was on its way before the first had struck its target, the horseman one of a pair, and as an arrow flashed in from the opposite side of the roadway Arékan's first found its mark. Punched back by the force of the strike, the rider's hands were scrabbling to cling to the reins as the second pierced his eye, the arrowhead reemerging in a spatter of blood as he was thrown from the saddle. At the same instant that a cry of pain told them all that the Angle's arrow had struck home, Arékan released again. A fourth shaft nocked the bowstring, and as the Hun tracked the speeding horse through the clearing, she waited until the second rider's back came into view before releasing again. Halga watched spellbound as the missile sped through the night, silver dart and galloping horseman coming together to meet at a fixed point ahead. It was the first time he had been in a position to fully appreciate Arékan's skill with a bow, but the thrill it gave him was tempered by the reality that it appeared likely they would soon be facing thousands of Huns just as deadly. The Gepid rider twisted as the shaft buried itself in the small of his back, and a heartbeat later another loosed by Horsa's man on the far side of the road threw him to the ground.

With both men unhorsed, Halga sprang from cover, racing across to the roadside where the first Gepid to fall lay sprawled upon the grass. The man lay on his back, pink froth bubbling at his lips showing where an arrow had pierced a lung, and Halga stabbed down with his gar to put an end to his writhing as his gedriht rushed up to cluster around. Halga threw a look to the right. Angles were standing over a shadowy hump on the floor, their spear shafts rising and falling as the Gepid leader went to join the first in Heaven or Valhall. Coella had the first rider's horse by the bridle, calming the animal with a stroke of its muzzle and a string of soothing words. Satisfied that the enemy encampment would not be alerted by the arrival of a rider-less horse at night, he picked out Horsa from the crowd. Halga walked over, stepping around Arékan and the Anglian bowman as they trotted across to retrieve their arrows and swapped congratulatory banter. 'That's the first part done,' the Angle said as Halga approached. 'Now we move up and wait.'

Halga nodded. 'Do you still wish me to lead?'

Horsa confirmed that he did. 'If you ride at the front of the column with Arékan alongside you, it will add a touch of familiarity to any Gepid looking on. They are used to seeing Huns and Germans riding together, and men in the thick of it have a habit of seeing what they expect to see. We only need them to believe that we are a relief force for a few moments, and we will be close enough to join the attack.' The Angle glanced aside as a few of his men passed with one of the Gepid dead slung between them. 'Merovech was right,' Horsa said, his gaze switching back and forth. 'We do look alike — it can only help.'

Halga looked, and saw what he meant. Whereas the Franks were fresh from a month spent lazing in Camaracum while they awaited the arrival of the Romans and Goths, the Angles and Jutes had lived a life not far removed from that of the invaders. Days spent in the saddle, eating whatever you could scavenge, gave a man a lean and grimy look that was as hard to feign as it was easy to recognise among men who had just endured the same. Halga said. 'How long shall we wait?'

'It is a quick ride from here to the main enemy camp,' Horsa replied, 'so the rearguard would be expecting any help to arrive soon after our two friends here raised the alarm. If they have sent for aid, we can be sure that Merovech and his boys have already arrived.' He worried his beard as he thought. 'We will ride a little closer to the place where the rearguard has deployed. As soon as we hear the Franks attack, we will carry out our part of the plan.'

Halga nodded that he understood, turning aside to whistle up his men. 'Mount up,' he said, as faces turned his way. 'We need to get going.'

Arékan was deep in conversation with her Anglian counterpart, holding up her bow to show him a fistful of arrows, and Halga pushed the thought of the big battle to come away again as he walked. Oswy had Halga's horse by the reins by the time he arrived near the trackway, and as he hauled himself into the saddle and turned its head to the west, the Hun come jogging across. He threw her a smile. 'Teaching our friend new tricks?'

'He is a fine bowman,' she said as she mounted alongside him. 'They were difficult targets. But if he is about to go up against Attila's army, he will need to up his shot count.' Halga nodded as the Angles began to spill from the woodland edge. The Huns and other Steppe bowmen held up to half a dozen arrows in the same hand that they used to grip their bow. The moment one shaft loosed, another slid quickly into place, more than doubling the rate of shot compared to bowmen who kept all their arrows in a quiver slung at their side.

The force was splitting as it left the cover of the woodland track, dividing into equal parts to hasten the ride forward. Halga took up position at the head of the nearest troop, his chest swelling with pride as he prepared to lead battle hardened men to war. A glance to the left and Horsa gave a nod, and both sets of horsemen urged their mounts into a trot as they headed back to the west.

With the iron-grey spear that was the Roman road to guide them the distance rapidly shrank, and when the first shouts and hollers reached their ears both men drew rein.

Within moments, the crash of wood on wood replaced the sound, as shields clashed and the Frankish attack went in.

All eyes were on Horsa now, the Angle glimmering in mail and helm under the light of the wolf-tailed star, and the instant that he judged that the Gepid defenders must be fully engaged he rose his sword arm high. Horsa's blade flashed, dazzling as he swept it in a wide arc, and as the sword chopped down to signal the advance, Halga put back his heels. With the need for stealth gone, both leaders led their columns from the verge and back onto the road, and as the muffled hoof fall of nigh-on a hundred horses became a resounding clatter, Halga raised his eyes. The road took a gentle curve to the north where it squeezed between the river and a wooded knoll, and as they swept around the bend his heart leapt as the fight came into view half a mile away.

Seeing the Gepid rearguard and the fighting up ahead, Horsa slowed his mount, and as Arékan urged her horse to his side Halga searched for the enemy leader. A heartbeat later he had him, fighting beneath the banners at the centre of the line where any good leader should be, and he began to slow the horse to a trot as he approached their backs. Beyond them, the Franks were surging forward again, Merovech clearly visible beneath the raven flag of Woden. But if the original plan had been for the Jutes and Angles to attack the Gepid leader and his hearth guards and link up with the king, Halga could see at a glance that they would be unlikely to succeed.

Blocking the valley at another pinch point where a spur of higher ground almost reached the water's edge, the enemy had chosen the ideal defensive position to throw up their wall of shields. Three thousand strong, the Gepids were arrayed across the width of the pass at least a dozen men deep, and with the centre packed by higher numbers still, Merovech had stumbled upon a foe far tougher and better organised than he had allowed for. Halga's mind raced. The success of the entire attack could very well depend upon the action he took in the next few moments, and he scrabbled about for an answer as he threw out an arm in the hope that Horsa would stop his charge.

A party of Gepids jogged across, the leader's gaze flying from Halga to Arékan and back as he led what the Jute knew must be the enemy reserve. But even as the man opened his mouth to sound him out, he realised what he must do. 'King Ardaric sent us,' he bellowed above the din, 'he is gathering his hearth warriors and following on.' Halga drew his sword as the man hesitated. 'Come on, man,' he barked. 'Or shall I tell the king who was responsible for the position being overrun when he arrives? Where do you need us?'

Shields crashed with a noise like thunder, and as the Gepid shield wall bowed alarmingly and men threw their shoulders into the rear of their boards to heave again, the man pointed his spear southwards. 'The wall is thinnest at the river's edge,' he cried, his caution thrown to the winds not just by the strength of the enemy attack, but the thought that he would be the one to shoulder the blame should the Franks break through. 'Head down there and lend them a hand. I will remain here, in case I am needed to shore up the line at this end.'

Halga nodded, hauling the head of his mount around as he pointed with his sword. 'This way!' he cried. 'Follow me!' It was the matter of a few moments before the river hove into sight, the waters glimmering like silk under the twin lights above, and Halga unhooked his shield from its carrying place as Horsa reined in at his side. 'This is the weakest part of their defence,' he explained as the Angle came up. 'If we can break them here, we can turn inwards and roll up the line.' Horsa nodded, throwing a question over his shoulder as horsemen strained to hear all around. 'Edwin, do you still have the flag?'

The gedriht nodded. 'Yes, lord.'

'Raise it then,' Horsa said, 'and my Draco too!'

Horsa turned back as the Angles retrieved the war banners, and shook them free of their bindings. 'Halga,' he said. 'You have carried us this far, kinsman — lead the attack.'

A glimpse of the standards as they rose into the midsummer air, and he was turning, firming his grip on the reins and sword handle as he urged the horse forward. Below him grins and smiles were turning to open-mouthed horror as the nearest Gepid spearmen recognised the war flags for what they were, and before they could shout a warning Halga was among them. With no time to turn and face the threat, the first men were bowled aside as Halga urged the horse deeper into their ranks, War-spite hacking down to the left and right as it reaped a bloody harvest. With all semblance of order disintegrating around them and little chance of swinging around to face the new threat in the crush, the Gepid shield wall was already beginning to collapse as men fell beneath his blade or were sent spinning away by the muscular chest of his horse.

Movement to his left — Oswy was at his side, and as Arékan's ululating war cry chilled men's blood, a roar came from the Frankish attackers and they burst forward again. Steapel and Beorn found a gap and pushed their way past, their sturdy angons stabbing down at any Gepid who came within reach, and left without an opponent as the defence began to collapse Halga raised his eyes to look. His Jutes were in the forefront of the fight, hacking and slashing at Gepid shoulders and heads as they beat a bloody path north. Edwin was riding at the head of Horsa's named men, the best of the best, riding down the first to flee beneath twin standards sapped of colour by the ethereal light. Further off, Halga's kinsman was riding at the head of the remainder of his comitatus, striking out to either side as they worked towards the heart of the defence.

Gaps were beginning to appear all along the line now, the rising and falling of blades showing clearly where Frankish heroes were forcing their way through, and as the Gepid defenders wilted beneath the onslaught the dam suddenly broke. Like a dyke overwhelmed by a surge tide, a flood quickly followed the first breaches as the trickles widened, coming together to form an unstoppable torrent as the Gepid rear ranks broke and ran.

A fleeing spearman, his face a mask of terror, crashed into the shoulder of Halga's horse; the Jute's sword chopped down again and again, hewing his features into a bloody hash as cries of victory filled the air. Horsa swept by at the head of his host as the first Franks appeared among them, wild-eyed and frantic as bloodlust drove any thoughts of caution away. The foemen in the front line, the better fighters, were cut off now that the rear-rankers had fled the battle, and Halga looked on as they backed together to form shield forts and prepared to fight on. Halga knew their reasoning; if they could just hold out until the first fugitives arrived at Attila's camp, they may still survive to see the sunrise. They had to be crushed before victory was certain. Every man had seen his attack, and word would spread that he had led the break-through. But Halga knew that he needed more. This was his chance, the moment of which every young warrior dreamed; the eyes of important men were upon him: a king; eorles; men of renown. He had to make the most of the opportunity that may never come his way again.

Halga dropped to the ground, sheathing War-spite as he retrieved his shield from its carrying place. An instant later he was moving, drawing his seax, Merovech's Long Knife, as he ran. An enemy shield fort was forming half a dozen yards ahead, their spears coming up as they moved shoulder to shoulder. Halga knew that he had to reach them before they were set, and he increased the pace as the first faces turned his way. A heartbeat later he was there, his shield sweeping across to open a gap between the spear points, and as his seax came up he lowered his head and leapt. The sound of breaking bone filled his ears as his helmeted head struck the Gepid full in the face. The man staggered, his gasp becoming by a cry of horror and pain as he felt Halga's powerful thrust burst through the links in his mail, and the seax slide into his guts. The short sword came up as his first opponent slumped, curving upward to open the next man's throat. Blood pulsed as he pushed forwards, a hot gush drenching his face and shoulder as he threw his weight into the back of his shield and pushed again. Halga's boot scrabbled at the turf, the sole wedging against a tuft to drive him forward, and with a final heave, he burst through the defence to find himself facing a line of mail clad backs.

Halga knew that if he faltered, even for a moment to catch his breath, the Gepids would turn and overwhelm him. Hunkering into his shield, he raced forward again, the steel dome of his shield boss cracking a rib as he buried his seax in the next man's neck. Barged forward by the force of his attack, a Gepid warrior threw a look across his shoulder, blinking in astonishment as he saw an enemy face inches from his own. Halga's head slammed forward again and again, shattering teeth and bone as his seax found the man's belly, and the sour stench of loosened bowels filled his nostrils.

And then, with a suddenness that was as disorientating as it was unexpected, he found himself alone, gulping down great lungfuls of air as he stood panting and heaving like a war horse run hard. Men were milling around, hanging back until the madness that had gripped him ebbed away. Merovech was there surrounded by his guards, the hoary veterans bristling with menace as they drove men back with a scowl. The enemies had gone, and the faces that ringed him belonged to his friends: Horsa; Edwin; the men of his comitatus; Arékan holding a bloody sword. The king spoke. 'Long Knife,' he said, a look of incredulity painted on his face. 'You fight like a demon.'

19

THE FLAMES OF MIDSUMMER

Horsa cleared his throat and sniffed. 'This is where we will fight.'

Halga nodded, his heart in his mouth as he gazed upon the army of Attila for the first time. From the crest of the rise, what he now knew to be the Campus Mauriacus stretched away before him, the line of trees that marked the course of the River Seine five miles distant a verdant blur in the summer heat. Covering the grasslands, mounted divisions of enemy riders swept to and fro, Huns and Germans alike delighting in giving the mounts their head after the constrictions of the retreat.

Coella broke the heavy silence to murmur. 'Like starlings...'

Halga replied without taking his eyes from the breath-taking sight before him. 'Like starlings?'

'In autumn,' his gedriht explained. 'When they wash the evening sky in waves.'

Halga replied in an absent-minded whisper: 'oh...'

Away to the south, the road that had carried both armies the hundred and something miles from Aureliani raced away towards the city of Tricassium, before becoming temporarily hidden from sight behind a long grassy ridge. Reappearing beyond it, the last of Attila's wagon train were clearly in view as it took advantage of the paved way, almost reaching the city walls before turning north to follow the river to the camp.

Horsa was the first to shake himself from their collective reverie. 'That's enough daydreaming,' he said. 'We are here to do a job.' He turned to Halga, indicating their surroundings with a flick of his head. 'Many a night we two have sat around the campfire and talked of other battles; now's the time to put that knowledge to the test. Look at the landscape,' he instructed with a sweep of his arm. 'You are Flavius Aetius, *Magister Militum*, General and overall commander of the army of Rome and her allies. What are you going to do?'

Halga had been studying the ground since they had come to a halt, and he replied straightaway. 'This is our front line,' he said, 'right here — lining this shallow ridge of land. It is the perfect defensive position, running from north to south, from woodland edge to woodland edge. Anchor the flanks with your best troops. One wing with the *comitatenses* of the Roman field army of Gaul and their federates and allies: Burgundians; Franks; Saxons; Angles and Jutes.' He flicked a look at his kinsman as he did so, sharing a chuckle at the mention of his nation's contribution to the great war, a mighty army totalling six youths and a Hunnish woman. 'The opposite flank I would entrust to Theodoric's Visigoths, who will almost certainly dismount and fight in a shield wall.'

Horsa nodded. 'Who would you task with holding the vital centre of your position?'

The track that crossed the grassland to the place where Attila was marshalling his forces took advantage of a natural cleft in the ridge line on its passage down the plain, neatly dividing the higher ground in two. It was likely that the main blow would fall here if the battle did indeed take place at this location, and Halga had already decided who would offer the best defence if it did so. 'Sangiban and his Alans,' he replied confidently. 'They would be almost impossible to shift — even the horses sport armour, and their long lances will hold the lighter Hun horse at arm's length. With the army secure behind their defences, I would support the shield walls with the bowmen, slingers, and crossbowmen. Upslope, they can aim over the heads of the front line — while keeping the Roman and Gothic cavalry back as a reserve, ready to shore up a leaky defence or exploit a breakthrough.'

Horsa nodded, indicating away to the south with a jerk of his head. 'What about our friends over there?'

Halga raised his eyes to stare. Overlooking the likely battlefield on that side was a far higher ridge, the crest rising gently to end in a summit on the southeastern skyline. He waited, his patience finally rewarded as the flash of sunlight on steel showed that armed men were there. 'I would then detach a mounted force, to drive the enemy off the high ground,' he admitted with a rueful look.

Horsa nodded as his gaze flitted about the field. 'Well, it's a good plan,' he said finally, before indicating that Halga follow him with a flick of his head. 'Come, let us take a look from the enemy perspective — just we two. Then we had better get back to camp; even though only half of the army had arrived when we left, I have a feeling that we will be back here tomorrow in far greater numbers.'

The pair urged their horses downslope, and Horsa threw a parting command across his shoulder as they descended to lower ground. 'Keep a sharp lookout, lads,' he said. 'I don't want any nasty surprises — there may be stragglers or enemy foragers in the area.' As soon as they were out of earshot, the Angle spoke again. 'I brought you down here so that the others will not hear what I am about to say. Leaders should have a degree of infallibility about them, an aura that the men will trust implicitly. Then, when you are in a tight spot and tell them to do something that might appear reckless, they snap to it without stopping to ask why. Your disposition was sound, Halga,' he continued as they reached the bottom of the slope, 'and any fighting man would be thrilled to have such a strong position to defend. But I want you to think like a commander, and I will tell you why I think Aetius will move down from the high ground to the edge of the plain below.' The pair walked their horses in a circle, taking in their surroundings before drawing rein and looking back upslope. They sat in silence awhile, both men studying the ground until Horsa spoke again. 'What can you see now, Attila — king of the Huns?'

Halga looked, and saw immediately that his kinsman was likely to be right. 'An unassailable position,' he sighed. 'The flanking woodlands force a frontal assault, upslope into the teeth of the defences. Not only will the mounted Hun bowmen have to urge their mounts up and down hill all day long, tiring them out, but the narrowness of the position will take away their room for manoeuvre.'

'Which was the whole point of their retreat from outside Aureliani, a hundred and thirty miles through hills and woodlands to this open plain,' Horsa agreed. 'You said that you would place the bowmen, slingers, and crossbowmen further upslope, where they can see over the heads of their shield wall. What would happen to the attackers' arrows?'

Halga nodded; it was obvious from the foot of the slope. 'Any that missed the front rank, would sail off skywards and do no harm at all.'

Horsa said. 'At the moment Aetius leads a hastily thrown together alliance of bitter enemies — Romans, Burgundians,

Franks, Alans, and Goths. If he can keep them on the move while offering them the chance of a glorious victory, the allied kings may well swallow their usual enmity for the common good. But the moment men have time to stop and think, he is in trouble. Attila knows this, he is no man's fool and has never suffered a defeat in battle. Safe down there,' he said, turning to peer at the riverside camp, 'he can afford to wait. He will have resupplied from Tricassium, and there is ample water and grazing for his horses and draught animals.' Horsa turned back, raising his chin to look upslope. Leaderless, their men were getting fidgety, turning this way and that as if they expected Attila himself to come crashing from the tree line at the head of his horde at any moment. 'Having brought them to bay, Aetius *has* to force an engagement. If they remain in camp, men will start to fight, someone will die, and all his hard work will begin to unravel before his eyes.' Horsa threw Halga a look. 'I don't need to tell you that. How long were we in Camaracum?'

Halga snorted. 'Just long enough to kill a man in a drunken brawl, and wreck another man's marriage.'

They both chuckled before Horsa went on. 'If Aetius advances and his position is so strong it appears impregnable, Attila can just leave him sitting on a hilltop in the midsummer sun until thirst drives him off. Our army camped at the last watering place between here and the Seine; that's why the Huns occupied it before we chased them away with our little victory last night. The Roman needs to leave the heights and take up a position that is still strong, but not so strong that he will dissuade the Huns from attacking.' Horsa tugged at the reins, guiding his mount around to face back eastwards. 'There,' he said, pointing with an arm. 'That's where we will fight, at the edge of the plain. Anchor the left wing against the woodland spur, and the right against the hillside. It's strong,' he said. 'But not so strong that Attila will think he has no chance to win.'

SANGIBAN and his army of Alans had appeared a fearsome sight when they arrived the previous afternoon; dressed now in their battle garb, they looked demonic under the harsh light of the wolf-tailed star. If any had considered the tales that the horsemen used the skins of their enemies to make harnesses and saddlery far-fetched, the sight of the flayed and preserved necks and faces of the unfortunates proudly displayed from the horses's *antilena* had laid any such doubts to bed. Halga gave a shudder as he recalled the sight, and they began to exit the camp. Dressed in the scale armour he now knew the Romans called *squamae* beneath a conical helm and aventail, the swarthy warriors looked as heavily armed as they were armoured. A long sword hung at each man's side, while a composite bow and arrow quiver hung from the saddle. But it was the lance that drew the northerner's attention, and he marvelled at their length as Sangiban drank a final toast to victory and was swallowed by the gloom. Fully fifteen feet in length, the heavyweight weapon looked as deadly as it was impressive, and he idly wondered if he would face another like it in battle later that day.

The riders looked magnificent, but they were arguably outshone by their mounts. An iron scale trapper covered the horse from nose to tail, a type of armoured blanket that hung as low as the hocks. Laced together front and rear, the trapper fully enclosed the torso in an armoured skirt. Above this, a shorter type did the same for the neck, while faceplates of mail or highly decorated steel protected the head. These were the super-heavy horse warriors known as *clibanarii,* the type that would be defending the centre of the allied line if the army set up as he expected, and Halga wished them good fortune as he turned to go.

Oswy and Beorn had tagged along, the pair as thrilled to be part of great events as he was himself, and the bear-man spoke as the first suggestion of daylight edged the horizon to the east. 'This time last year we were raiding up in the Vik,' he said, 'chasing fishermen and ransacking farmers' holdings.' He shook his head as he looked about. They had put the Alan and Roman horse warriors behind them now, and were trudging past rank upon rank of *pedes* in their distinctive circular felt caps, the tough foot soldiers of the Roman field army. These were the fighting force that Horsa had called the comitatenses when they had ridden out to view the battlefield the previous afternoon. Beorn shook his head as he continued. 'Look at us now — not only about to fight in an army containing more men than I thought existed on Middle-earth, but against a foe that will likely outnumber us.' He cast a look skyward, squinting at the sight that greeted his eyes. The wolf-tailed star had grown brighter still that night, bathing the army in its spectral light. 'Maybe it's true,' he said, 'that *is* Woden riding at the head of his army of slain heroes, and it does herald the start of the wolf-age? Perhaps we *are* about to fight at the end of the world?' He set his face, recounting a verse from a gods' tale known to all as *The Prophecy.*

> Brothers will do battle unto the death,
> sons of sisters fight their kin,
> the world has turned harsh,
> an axe-age, a sword-age;
> shields are cleft,
> a storm-age, a wolf-age,
> before the world tumbles.

'They could be telling it like it is,' Oswy chipped in, as he prepared to recount a verse of his own. 'The country folk we have come across down here; maybe Attila and his host are serpents and devils. They invaded Gaul from the right direction, after all.'

> Hrym drives from the east,
> his shield before him;
> the mighty serpent writhes in fury,
> the snake thrashes the waves,
> and the eagle grows joyful;
> pale-beak plucks at corpses.

Halga rolled his eyes. 'Such a joyful lot — I am glad I brought you along.' The strident blare of war horns told them all that Flavius Aetius was approaching under a cloud of banners and Dracos, Rome's ablest general riding to war in the midst of his oath sworn, the *bucellarii*. The Jutes moved aside, clearing a path as the army commander swept by accompanied by hundreds of Huns and Germans, their bearing and quality of arms telling any man who cared to look of the high regard in which they were held by their lord. He turned to Oswy and said. 'If you think easterners are serpents and devils, maybe you should ask Arékan, I am sure she will put you right. Or better still, flag down one of those lads — Huns who will be fighting alongside you later today?'

The Jutes stood and watched as they passed. The Huns had very possibly lived within the empire their entire lives, and if their physical features told of their heritage: short, stocky and with the raven coloured hair typical of their folk, their arms, and armour were Roman. Beorn spoke again. 'The world is a mad place here in the south. The general leading the fight against invading Huns is protected by a hearth guard consisting mostly of the same folk. Attila's most trusted men are Germans: Sea Franks fight against River Franks; eastern Goths go up against western Goths, and all for control of an empire that has its heart beyond the Alps.'

Halga shrugged. 'There is wealth and reputation to be made here,' he said, 'that's all I care about.' He stood to one side, taking in their war gear as he did so. 'You were not complaining last night when we shared the spoils — come on, let us get back to the others. The Goths, Alans and now Romans have left the camp and are already on their way to the battlefield, it must be the turn of the Franks to follow on.' The Jute thought back to the end of the previous night's fighting as they walked. As a reward for Halga's lone charge into the heart of the Gepid shield-fort, king Merovech had forgone his share of the spoils, insisting that Halga had earned them by right of conquest. It had enabled him to finally fulfil the promise he had made to them, that night back in Jutland where they had pledged him their oath and become his gedriht in the shadow of his forebears' death-mound. Now, every man in his comitatus sported the accoutrements of war: a fine helm; mail shirt and a patterned sword, and his stock among the Franks and Angles was sky-high. Halga spotted the others up ahead, raising a hand in recognition as the Roman column tramped eastwards. 'Do you have them?'

Steapel held up Halga's shield, turning it so that the inside boards were facing him. 'All fixed and ready, lord,' he said happily. 'I have just spent the best night since we rowed south, helping the smiths hammer out the heads for them down at the forge.'

Halga took the board as he came up, running the pads of his fingertips over the wooden fixings as he did so. 'Did we all get the same?'

Steapel nodded. 'Half a dozen each, Halga, and we will be resupplied the same as any Roman if we run short.'

Halga slipped one of the darts from its bracket, weighing it carefully in his palm and finding its point of balance. 'It seems simple enough,' he said. 'At least we will have the opportunity to hit back at the attackers after throwing our javelins. They will be much easier to throw in a scrum of bodies, too.' Steapel was passing the darts around, and Halga took the opportunity for a closer look at what his helmsman had told him were known as *plumbatae*. A tad shorter than his forearm in length, the darts consisted of an iron head fixed to a wooden shaft — much like a short arrow. Like an arrow, fletchings at the rear helped to guide the missile in flight, while a lead weight had been attached to the shaft to act as a counterweight, giving each plumbata the balance required to be used as a hand-launched weapon.

The tramp of booted feet came again, and Halga raised his eyes to find that his earlier prediction had been correct. The Frankish host was exiting the camp, Merovech a point of light amid the muted colours of the predawn at their head, and the drihten's heart swelled with pride as the king singled him out among the crowd of fighting men lining the route for special praise. 'Long Knife!' Merovech exclaimed with a smile. 'You had best hurry. I doubt that Aetius would wish to start the battle without you!'

Halga dipped his head, acknowledging the honour as the king strode by, and as the meadow all around became a muddle of scampering men, he led his gedriht to the rear. Horsa was there, slipping free the leather mantle that protected his shield on the march: flipping up the cover on the sheath that contained his daroth; tallying up the northern throwing spears the Romans called *veruta*. The big Angle's face creased into a smile at his late appearance, and as his head shook in mock admonishment, the smile became a laugh. 'I thought our little talk yesterday had scared you off,' he quipped. 'Shame — it would have allowed others a sniff at gaining glory too!'

Halga left the Angles as they sorted themselves into ranks, walking across to the place where his horses were casually pulling at tufts. 'Goodbye, old lad,' he said, laying a hand on the velvety softness of the animal's muzzle. 'Wait for me — I will see you tonight.' The Roman commander had decreed that only army leaders and cavalry could ride to the battlefield, citing the plausible reason that it was better that they remain close to a source of water than ride out onto the barren plain. But if there was a good reason for the decision, it fooled no one. If the battle went badly, and they were driven from the field, barely any of the men on foot would escape the swarms of mounted Huns. It was a powerful incentive to stand firm and fight, however hard the day went.

All was ready, and he took a moment to stare away to the east as the others stamped down the pegs pinning the reins to the turf. The band of light had widened there; higher up, the moon was paling as daybreak approached.

Coella spoke at his shoulder, making him start, and they exchanged an awkward chuckle as they returned their gaze to the sunrise. 'Arékan's not returned yet,' he said.

Halga replied. 'She will be back — it's not like her to miss a fight. Besides,' he continued with a glance towards the horse line, 'her horse is still here. She will catch us up on the march.'

Coella lingered, and it slowly became obvious that their Hun friend had not been the reason he had approached his drihten after all. Halga returned his attention to the east, taking the time today to marvel at a scene he had witnessed hundreds of times before and thought little of it, as the first sliver, ox-blood red against the lightening sky, showed where innumerable men's last day on Middle-earth had finally broken.

'The campfires last night — they made me yearn for home,' Coella finally admitted, dropping his voice to an undertone.

Halga tore his gaze away from the dawn to throw him a look of surprise. 'There were thousands!'

'But today is midsummer eve,' the gedriht explained. 'Tonight, fires will be lit everywhere, scattered among the fields and hilltops throughout Jutland and beyond to usher in High Summer.'

Hearing it, Halga also felt a pang of homesickness. But he pushed the thoughts away as the men, *his* men, began to dress themselves for battle in a rattle of leather and mail.

Coella spoke again, even softer this time so that none of his mates could hear. 'I am scared, Halga. I thought sixteen was old enough for all this,' he said, sweeping the campsite with an arm. 'But I was wrong.'

Halga felt a lump in his throat. The fight against the Gepid rearguard had changed them all. It was the first time they had fought in anything greater than a skirmish, and despite the victory, it had felt nothing like the poems had led them to expect. Now, they were marching out to fight at the ending of the world. Halga placed a hand on his lifelong friend's shoulder, lowering his voice as he replied. 'Don't worry,' he said, 'you are not alone. Although we try not to show it, deep down we are all shaking like a tree in a gale.

20

A TROOP OF GLORIOUS MEN

Halga's stomach gave a lurch, an involuntary gasp carrying on the breeze as men all about him sucked in air at the sight. Lining the edge of the Campus Mauriacus, almost filling the space between the woodland and the foot of the hogback ridge, the army of the West was arraying itself for battle. Oswy spoke at his side, and for an instant, he was back in his father's hall in far-off Tiw's Stead. The long hearth was burning, flames flickering, turning the scop a hellish red as he recounted a battle tale to the wonderstruck warriors lining the benches:

> Fyrd sceal ætsomne,
> tīrfæsta getrum...

> The army shall come together,
> a troop of glorious men...

Further on, Horsa turned his head, throwing the Jute a grin and a wink as the battle line revealed itself. Halga laughed aloud at the sight, acknowledging that his kinsman had the right of it when he had pointed out the spot the day before. Taking the easy route after the five-mile trudge from camp, the column followed the line of the track down the cleft and onto the plain. Halga ran his eyes over the allied disposition as the trees pulled back, and the view ahead opened up.

At the centre of the line, Sangiban and the clibanarii sparkled and glimmered like sunlight on ice, their banners and Dracos a brawl of colour under the hot southern sun. To the right of the Alans, guarding the entire southern wing of the army, Theodoric: his Visigoths set in their shield walls, rank upon rank of spear and swordsmen facing east. Further back, closer to the main road to nearby Tricassium, Gothic horse warriors stood beside their mounts. Ready to counter any enemy successes, see off a sneak attack using the ridge for cover, or pour forward to exploit an allied breakthrough.

Aetius had mirrored the deployment on the northern flank. The Roman field army anchoring itself against the woodland spur Halga had seen the previous day, backed up by the mounted elements of the comitatenses, the heavily armoured cataphracts and light cavalry known as equites. With the Roman standards placed at the centre of the line, that left twin gaps to plug between the comitatenses, the Alans in the south, and the other Roman elements in the north. A brief check towards the head of the column confirmed to Halga that they were headed in that direction. Other allies were almost there, and Halga told off the flags one by one as he made a note of the folk who would fight alongside his men.

At his side, Oswy was following suit, and Halga glanced across as his gedriht exclaimed in surprise. 'More Saxons, Halga! Where did they come from?'

Halga said. 'Don't worry, they are not from the Saxon

homelands, so hopefully they are more accepting of Angles and Jutes. Horsa told me they travelled from a province neighbouring the Goths — it would seem that the Romans have trawled the whole of Gaul to build this army.' As they looked, Roman riders cantered across to the front of the column, and Halga spoke again as the Saxons angled their march northeastward. 'It appears that the Romans are aware of our rivalries in the North after all — look.' It seemed that the Saxons had been instructed to fill the gap in the line between the Roman flank and centre, and Halga's suspicions were confirmed when other equites rode across to lead the Angles towards the southern end of the wing.

It was midmorning. They were already sweltering under a fiendish sun by the time Horsa led his Angles into the gap in the position, and as the column divided to fill the front line with northern spears, Halga gathered his comitatus around him. 'Oswy,' he said, as they awaited his instructions. 'If we find ourselves in the shield wall, I want you as my righthand man.' The big gedriht nodded, the pride he felt shining in his eyes. A fighting man held his shield with his left hand, leaving the warrior's right flank unprotected as they fought. It was the duty of the man on the right to cover him with his shield, as it was the warrior to his right to protect him, and so on until the end of the line was reached. Halga continued to arrange his dwarfish contribution to the Roman cause, as the sound of his kinsman's rousing speech carried from the front line. 'Steapel,' he said. 'You take my left flank, and I want Coella directly to my rear as *cumbolwiga,* with Beorn and Godwin to either side. They all shared a smile, the northern term for standard-bearer a balm for their ears after a day spent hearing only of *signifers* and *draconarii.*

Halga puffed out his chest, running his eyes around the little group, as a great roar and the clatter made by hundreds of spear shafts on shields told them that Horsa had finished his address. 'Well,' he said, 'here we are, on the cusp of battle. I have neither the skills in warfare nor honeyed words to exhort you to do this and that — and you know it. This time last year, we were a group of backwoods friends; but you know why Horsa placed us in the second rank — to watch and learn. If they break through, or we are called forward to shore up the defence, rally to the *cumbol*, and we will fight for all we are worth.'

Halga's gaze drifted across to the neighbouring soldiers of the comitatenses and back, as the long wait to see whether the enemy would respond to their challenge began. His kinsman had described the typical formation of the Roman army in defence the previous evening as they had ridden the very same fields, and he looked on with interest as the Angles mimicked the formation and dovetailed with the Roman battle line on either side. The first half a dozen ranks comprised the toughest fighters, the veterans of both armies. Heavily armed and armoured, they would fight with spear and shield, interlocking the boards to present an impenetrable rampart to any attackers. A few feet behind them, Halga and his comitatus stood amid the younger Angles in the first line of the second rankers, men desperate to prove themselves and earn renown and reward in the post-battle storytelling and gift giving that followed every fight. Further back in the phalanx, blocks of men stood ready beside stacks of veruta throwing spears, ready to hurl their weapons over the heads of their comrades when the attackers came into range. As the ranks closed in behind him, Halga stood on tiptoe to study the rear. With no specialist bowmen of their own, the Romans were thinning the ranks to support their barbarian allies, the *sagittarii* lolloping across laden down by bows, crossbows, and armfuls of arrows and bolts. More ominously, Roman troops, both mounted and foot soldiers, were beginning to form up to the rear of them all. These were the file-closers, men whose job it was to keep the formation tight, and stop any faint-hearts from escaping before panic spread and became a rout. Further off, ox drawn wagons were trundling across the field, carrying water and rations to the army now that they were set in their ranks.

With the host now in place, word passed from rank to rank that the men take their ease, and as the plain filled with the sound of thousands of men lowering themselves to the grass, Halga turned at the sound of a familiar voice. Arékan had resurfaced, just in time by the looks she was getting from the file-closers, and he chuckled along with his friends as they watched her argue that they let her through. With the oxen and their charges drawn closer now, the words became lost in the din. But the body language was familiar to those who knew her, and the chuckles turned to laughs as they watched her shove a guard aside and stomp across. Following a brief stop at one of the supply wagons, Halga looked on as the Hun picked her way through the ranks. Very few were on their feet now, the five-mile march that morning under the midsummer sun enough to send even the hardiest of men to ground the moment the opportunity arose. Halga amused himself by picking out the old hands from the inexperienced as she came. To a man, those used to campaigning were already stretched out and snoring, or sitting with their backs facing south as they rested beneath a sunshade made from cloak or cape.

He smiled as she came up. 'Where did you get to?'

'I was with the Goths,' she replied, unslinging a leather canteen from her shoulder and passing it across. Halga prised away the stopper, wincing slightly despite his thirst as the contents washed down his throat. 'Warm water?'

She gave a shrug. 'No doubt it was cool when it started its journey.'

'I thought the Romans drank watered wine?'

'I doubt that would be a good idea today, do you? Imagine an army of tired men, laying all day in the hot sun drinking wine.' She screwed up her face. 'Wouldn't be much of a battle, would it? When Attila turned up to find them dozing and fighting among themselves. Here, I got you one of these,' she added with a look, 'as you are so grateful.' Arékan handed over a cake of *bucellatum*, the standard fare of a Roman army on the march. 'Wheat biscuit and hot bacon fat,' she explained. 'Get it down you, you may need it when I tell you who I saw there.' Arékan glanced down as she did so, leaving Halga wondering what she could mean; to his knowledge, he had never so much as spoken to a Goth. The others were sitting like expectant puppies, their faces just beginning to display the devastation that only a growing lad could feel when they realised there was no food for them. 'Sorry boys,' she said, somehow making it very obvious that she was not feeling truly sorry at all. 'I have only got two hands. You will have to wait until they fetch yours across.'

Halga was already eating when she looked back, blowing gently on the salty fat before nibbling a rim from the hardtack. 'I have been with your brother,' she said casually, before gnawing at her biscuit. 'He is one of king Theodoric's oath sworn.'

Halga blinked in surprise. No one had heard anything regarding Oslaf's whereabouts, nor of any adventures of his, for nigh on four years now. Very few doubted that he was a permanent guest of the gods — either in Valhall with the All-father, or Wade's undersea hall of the drowned. If any time was suitable to joke about dead kinsmen, the hours preceding a great battle was arguably the least of all. Halga said as much, stifling a gasp as the woman answered his protest with a shrug.

Arékan broke another piece from her hardtack. 'Well, he looked in rude health,' she spat through a mouthful of crumbs. 'I would say that death suits him. I told him you are fighting alongside Horsa and the Angles — he is going to seek you out when this is all over.'

HALGA SQUIRMED, arching his back to dig yet another stone from the sunbaked soil.

Arékan gave him a poke and a withering stare. 'What's up?'

'Funnily enough, I can't sleep,' he snapped. 'Can you think of any reason why that might be?'

The Hun rolled her eyes and turned her back to him, shuffling to get herself comfortable again as his mind went back to sifting his thoughts. Oslaf's reappearance changed everything. Not only was he no longer the rightful heir to the ealdormanship back home, as head of the clan even the sword at Halga's side belonged to his brother by right. Did that mean that he was now absolved of the responsibility of retrieving his father's sword? What about replacing it in the barrow, as he had promised the spirits of his ancestors before he had left them? He shifted again, drawing an exasperated grunt and an ill-tempered wriggle as he accidentally kneed her in the arse. Arékan had told Oslaf about the death of their father, and the identity of the burners...

So many thoughts were swirling in his head, that the fact that men were climbing to their feet all about passed him by. It was not until the light of the sun was extinguished, that he realised the background hum made by dozing men had been replaced by a buzz of excited chatter. He opened an eye to peep. Oswy was looking down at him, the thrill in his features obvious to even a mind fogged by uncertainties and a lack of sleep. 'Come and see, lord,' he said. 'The Gothic horsemen are attacking!'

The electrifying news had him on his feet instantly, and as his gaze followed the pointing arms to the south, he searched for signs of fighting. Steapel stood a head taller, and he leaned across to point them out. 'Not on the plain, lord,' he said. 'They are climbing the ridge.' Halga switched his gaze, shielding his eyes with the ledge of a hand. The clibanarii were standing in a solid block of armour and horse flesh a short bow shot in that direction, the sun shining upon their armoured heads and flanks making it difficult to see through the glare. He squinted and waited. An instant later, he had them. Halga turned to Arékan as she scrambled up to his side. 'You know the Gothic banners,' he said. 'Who is leading the charge? Is Oslaf there?'

She tutted. 'You will have to wait awhile, or describe what you see, Halga,' she replied. 'If Steapel had to point them out to you, and you are a foot taller than me, what chance do I have?'

Halga returned his gaze to the hillside. The leading riders were clearly in view now, urging their mounts along the ridgeback beneath a cloud of flags and banners, and the Jute waited until the steepening gradient had teased the Goths apart before picking out the man at their head. A draconarius rode at the man's shoulder, and Halga described the flowing banner to the unsighted woman as the hum of excitement all around them turned to animated cries. 'The leader is riding beneath a Draco with a head of gold, and a tail of red and green.' He glanced down, eager to discover if his brother was likely to be among the attackers. 'Is it Theodoric?'

Arékan shook her head. 'No — if the king rides into

battle, he fights beneath a dragon that is gold from snout to tail. If the sock is green and red, that will be the king's son, Thorismund.'

Halga realised then that it was to be a day of mixed emotions. Before he had discovered that his brother was on the field, every warrior dear to him: Horsa; Arékan; the men of his comitatus, were within spitting distance. Not only was it likely he would share their fate, but he had the opportunity to come to their aid if need be. For his brother to return from the dead, only to die for certain before he even had the chance to exchange a word, would too much to bear.

On the ridge Thorismund had led his Goths up on to the heights by the time he looked again, and Halga thrilled to the sight as flashes of light showed where swords and spears had been drawn. The fighting erupted an instant later, as a cloud of Hunnic horse warriors appeared from the back slope and crashed into the Gothic flank. The sudden appearance of their foe on the nearby hilltop — the first sight of the enemy that day — caused the men in the allied army to catch their breath. But the shock lasted barely a heartbeat, and the plain soon shook as the shouts of encouragement became a roar. The Hun counterattack had been well judged, and the army looked on moribund as Thorismund and his draconarius were enveloped. But they found their voices again as the Gothic prince fought his way clear, Thorismund reappearing in a blaze of colour against the skyline, as he turned his horse back to the fight.

Free from the constrictions of the narrow path, the Gothic horse swept onto the summit, rushing forward to drive the Huns back towards the drop from which they had appeared only a short while before. As more and more Goths gained the heights, the crest shimmered in the midday sun as long blades hacked and slashed. Halga tore his eyes away from the spectacle unfolding before them, looking to judge the reaction of those around him. As he had expected, the lads looked as thrilled as could be at the drama unfolding on the hilltop, and Arékan's eyes seemed to shine no less brightly than the flashing blades themselves. But it was Coella's reaction he had really sought following his friend's self-confessed doubts in the dawn, and he was pleased to see that his new standard-bearer looked as intoxicated by the sight as any. The gedriht sensed him looking, and as his eyes flicked down to lock with his own, Halga gave the ghost of a smile and shared a nod.

Reassured that his banner man had rediscovered his courage, Halga returned his gaze to the mount. The Huns had been driven back by the ferocity of the Visigoth assault, and the last men to stand and fight were about to pay the price for their bravery as allied riders curved around to cut off their retreat. Further downslope, their countrymen were fleeing as best they could, twisting in the saddle as they rode to send flights of arrows back at any pursuers.

A drawn-out wail drifted across to them then, the distant note of the recall the first sound to carry to those on the plain since the beginning of the fight. As the report faded and Thorismund's men mopped up the last of the resistance, war horns blared out a salute all along the allied line. Oswy gave him a nudge, indicating the Roman divisions to their left with a flick of his head. 'Here he comes,' the gedriht said. 'Ready to bask in the glory.'

Halga looked across. Flanked by king Merovech and the Saxon leader, Flavius Aetius was guiding his horse through the ranks, out onto the grassland to the acclamation of the army.

Halga switched his gaze to the east as the general began his address.

A dark line on the horizon was growing by the moment.

As yet it was an indistinct shimmer in the heat of midsummer eve, and although a man rode before the Roman to speak his words in the language of the North, they were lost on him as he prepared for battle. The rhythmic thrum of weapons beating on shields drew his eyes to the south. King Theodoric was riding there, rallying his Goths for the fight. Halga's eyes flit from face to face, eager to catch a glimpse of his brother. Before he could fully focus, Sangiban's Alans mounted as they too readied themselves for war — masking his view.

When he looked back, the Roman front lines were dividing once again to allow the leaders to pass through, and Halga exchanged words with Oswy as a deathly hush descended upon them. 'What did he have to say?'

'The Huns were hoping to resupply at Tricassium and wait for us there, but Aetius sent word ahead that he was hard on their heels and to close the gates. When Attila pitched up expecting a comfortable night, someone called bishop Lupus shouted from the walls that he was the scourge of God, and told him to get lost.'

Halga snorted. 'Well, I know at least one Christian who is on his knees at the moment, praying hard for our victory.'

21

SHIELDS AND SPEARS

Horsa was making his way through the ranks, his easy movements and the pitch of his voice contemptuous of the fast approaching threat. 'Remember what we said, lads. It is a day for shields and spears.' He shot them a grin and a quip as the ground beneath their feet began to tremble, drawing nervous laughter from the younger members of the comitatus as he walked. Halga watched intently, contrasting their reaction with that of the veterans. Grim-faced and alert, as the outline of the Hun riders and their mounts began to harden from the haze.

Arékan said. 'I will leave now, Halga. You boys will have enough to do soon, without having to worry about protecting me.' They exchanged a meaningful nod. Forced to shoulder her shield to use her bow, she was far too vulnerable to stand in the phalanx. Halga watched her go, threading her way through the ranks of stony-faced men as she sought the sagittarii at the rear.

Movement caught his eye as he looked, and Halga watched as the Alan clibanarii lowered their long contus as one. A flash of gold further south showed where the Visigoth king stood beneath his banners, surrounded by the men of his hearth guard. His mouth was drier than old bones, and he felt the urge to piss. It was too late now, and he shook all other thoughts from his mind as he gripped the handle of his shield and his left foot slid forward to brace. 'Ready boys? It's going to be a long day. Keep your wits about you, and you will have a tale to bore your grandchildren rigid when you are old and grey.'

A deep-throated howl drew his attention back to the front. The Huns were closer now, their faces dark smudges haloed by leather and steel as they urged their horses forward with the mesmeric bobbing motion of their breed. Enemy war horns keened again, adding to the wall of sound washing over the allied ranks. Roman discipline held, and they stood stock-still, without a whisper, as they prepared to face down the threat. Halga felt the need to answer the challenge in kind, to clatter his spear shaft against the rim of his shield as he too bawled and yelled. But they had all agreed to put up a united front, to follow the Roman custom of meeting an attack in silence the previous night around the camp fires, and he could see the sense in it now. Tens of thousands of men, standing in ranks as quiet as the grave, could be as unnerving as any amount of war cries.

Halga cast a look skyward. The heavens were a vault of the purest blue on this midsummer eve, with only a swelling cloud of vultures to break its completeness; riding the updraft on ragged wings, the dark forms a sinister reminder of why they were there.

A shouted command from the Roman centenarii carried across the allied ranks as the Hun bows came up:

Parati…

As the order to make ready hung on the sweltering air, shields were hefted, and spears slid proud to make a war hedge all along the line. A quick glance towards the position of the sun told Halga that it was early afternoon, and as the muffled clatter of hide-bound shields told him that the defenders were preparing to face the onslaught, he raised his arm and followed suit. The Huns were coming within bowshot, and as Oswy and Steapel overlapped the rims of their shield with his own, he spoke a final instruction. 'Unless you are tracking a particular arrow,' he said, 'follow my actions. If we can present a solid front, we shall win-out, however many shafts they loose against us.'

The background rumble of a horse army on the move had become a tremulous roar now, and Halga took a peek over the rim of his shield as he waited for the first arrows to arrive. All along the battlefront, Roman commanders roared again:

Adiuta...

Already practiced in the response, the allied formations added their voices to the reply, and the answering cry from the army of the West rend the sky as they roared as one:

DEUS!

Again and again the call and response thundered across the plain:

Adiuta...

DEUS!

Adiuta...

DEUS!

Save us...

OH, GOD!

Save us...

OH, GOD!

All around him, Jutish and Anglian hands were going to good luck charms and pendants as they sought to invoke the protection of the gods of the North. Halga found a fleeting moment to call upon Woden, the All-father, as Attila's battalions filled his vision.

Spear-shaker: Victory-giver; Battle-wolf...

As the Western army's invocations to the Christian God rolled away, the leading enemy riders let fly the opening salvo that day as javelins darkened the sky in reply. Halga watched their flight carefully as they came, shaft following shaft to bury themselves in the shields in the front line as Horsa and his Angles hunkered into the wide boards. Another volley came, then another, and at almost the last moment, just as he feared that the horses would continue their mad dash to oblivion, the enemy column began to divide — paring away like a newly ploughed furrow as those following on sighted and loosed. The Huns were almost within touching distance of the Anglian shield wall by the time they straightened up, and as the familiar muskiness given off by a horse run hard drifted across on the breeze, Halga watched and waited.

Frustrated by the effectiveness of the Anglian wall, a Hun raised his face to look. Halga recognised the instant when his eyes fixed upon the leaping hound banner and Coella beneath. His arm drew back and released. Halga went to move as the arrow sped towards them, but an utterance at his side, perfect in its brevity, stayed his hand. 'Mine.' An instant later, the missile had buried itself in the lime wood of Oswy's shield, the head punching through to come to rest a hand's width from his gedriht's shoulder. Oswy drew a smile despite the mayhem all around, as he gave it a contemptuous look and spoke again. 'That's handy — somewhere to hang my hat.' The first Hun attackers were curving away now, hauling at the reins to double-back towards the main body of their formation, as they twisted in the saddle to let go a Parthian shot over the rump of their horse. As they did so, those following on sighted and loosed in their turn, as the air between the armies became a latticework of flying missiles. A Hun concentrated on his target a little too intently and paid the price, as a javelin flashed in to pluck him from the saddle. A crossbow bolt hit another, the powerful strike making a horror of a Hunnish face as it buried itself to the fletchings.

The view ahead was filled with Huns now, with what appeared to be the entirety of the Campus Mauriacus a mass of cantering horses sweeping to and fro. Forewarned by Arékan of her compatriots' tactics, Halga forced himself to concentrate on those who posed an immediate threat, as the bulk of the attackers became little more than ghosts — shadowy shapes, half-glimpsed within the pall of dust kicked up by the hooves of their mounts.

The next Hun entered the fray, loosing an arrow before guiding his horse to run side-by-side with the Anglian shields with a squeeze of his knees. Halga fixed him in his gaze, following his movements as the next arrow slid across from the hand gripping his bow to be nocked and drawn. The horseman sighted, his head moving freely as he sought an opening in the linden wall flashing by at his side. His arm went back, ready to release. With all his attention fixed upon the target, he never saw the arrow which took the nose clean off his face. Stunned and blinded by the strike, the Hun dropped his guard. The rider's shock and confusion lasted little more than a heartbeat, but it was enough, and before the Hun could recover or retire from the battlefront another shaft had buried itself in his thigh. Sensing an easy kill, every man within throwing distance singled him out, weapons raining down on the hapless rider as he struggled to get away.

Halga grasped the opportunity to hit back, plucking one of the plumbatae from the rack on the rear of his shield as the Hun ducked and weaved. The Jute tracked the rider as he weighed the dart in his hand, making small adjustments until he knew he had found the point of perfect balance before opening his body to throw. Oswy had seen his lord's action, and the gedriht took a pace forward, angling the face of his shield as his eyes quartered the air, sniffing out any hint of danger. The instant the plumbata was balanced his arm went back, and as it flew forward to release the dart his shield was already coming back up. Oswy was back at his shoulder as the dart flew true, but as it looked as if they had finally taken the chance to strike back at their tormentors, the Jutes gave an involuntary gasp.

The Hun was out of the saddle, launching himself through the air to land with a crash on the Anglian frontline. With the integrity of the wall cast to the four winds by the rider's suicidal leap, other horsemen appeared from the whirling mass to rain arrows into the breach. Witnessing the attack, the allied rear redoubled their efforts, filling the air with javelins, arrows, slingshot and plumbatae as the veteran fighters at the front struggled to close ranks. Ahead of Halga, men were stepping up, raising their shields to protect their head and upper torsos as they stabbed down at the figure struggling in their midst.

With the sealing of the breach in the defences the rain of missiles from the rear drove the horsemen back, and as they began to circulate once again the Angles closed up. As the fight settled back into its familiar rhythm, the first of the wounded passed through to the rear. Here the Roman specialist, the medicus, and his helpers would do their best to tend to wounds and return as many men as possible to the fray. Warriors in the second rank were scuttling forward in ones and twos to take their place, and Halga felt the eyes of his gedriht on him as they went. He shook his head and held his ground. 'Our place is here unless there is an enemy breakthrough,' he said. 'This is only the first attack, there will plenty more to come.'

A GENTLE BREEZE had got up, just enough to draw the veil of dust aside. Halga snatched a look to the south before the next arrow arrived. As far as he could tell, resistance to the Hun attack remained robust all along the battlefront. King Theodoric and his Visigoths were immobile as they anchored the line to the hillside and the brook that ran at its foot. Between the Roman comitatenses and the Goths, the iron fort that was the Alan clibanarii for the most part projected like a rocky headland on a wave lashed shore — massive and unyielding. But here and there knots of riders had allowed themselves to become teased out from the fabric of the defence, and Halga felt a pang of disquiet as his head snapped back to the front. Like all elite mounted forces, clibanarii attracted a certain type to their ranks, men of wealth and a keen sense of bloodline and honour; they existed to attack the enemy wherever they could be found. But the same blend of aggression and resilience that made them the spearpoint of many eastern armies also made them loathe to remain inactive as the enemy rode within feet of their ranks. The formation was becoming increasingly ragged as Sangiban's blue-bloods led their oath sworn out to attack, and even to Halga's inexperienced eye it was becoming clear that the Huns knew it too.

A shoulder barge from Steapel brought his attention back, and he shook all concerns for other parts of the line from his mind as the big man plucked an arrow from the air on the face of his shield. To the fore, the Huns were still whirling about in what appeared to be a disorganised mass, but was, in fact, a carefully thought-out battle tactic. Tipped off by his

Hunnish friend, Halga knew the manoeuvring was designed to cause confusion within the enemy ranks, while at the same time enabling the highest number of bows to bear on their formation at any given moment.

Despite his earlier lapse in concentration, Halga and the men of his comitatus were moving smoothly now, snatching or deflecting the incoming Hun arrows with ease. With the Angles of his kinsman's oath sworn protecting their flanks in similar manner, the predictability of the attack had made the fight almost routine.

Halga snatched a look to the south once again as the latest Hun passed them by, blinking in surprise when he saw the position of the sun. Although he was not fool enough to risk raising a hand to gauge its passage since the start of the fight, he was shocked to realise that a couple of hours had already passed. But if the look had provided a jolt in one respect, it only confirmed his fear from earlier. Hunting packs of clibanarii were moving forward from the Alan position, the great lengths of their lances driving the light horse warriors facing them further and further away. Halga fixed his shield at head height as he looked, confident that the men to either side would protect his body while his attention lay elsewhere. In the short time it had taken to do so, the situation to the south had developed as he had feared. Drawn further and further out onto the Campus Mauriacus by the retreating Huns, blinded by the dust made by a million hoof falls over the course of the fighting and the incoming arrow storm, the Alan horse were in danger of becoming cut off from the rest of their host.

Looking at the faces of men around him, it was clear that they realised it too, and the army of the West looked on in impotent frustration as the Hun trap began to close. The bravest among the Huns began to drive their attacks between the rear of the outlying formations and the greater mass of Sangiban's host, ignoring the undefended backs of the clibanarii to pour a withering fire into the main formation. The trickle of horsemen grew by the moment, to become a torrent, and then a flood. By the time the Alan attackers saw the danger that had developed to their rear, it was clear to any observers that the realisation would come far too late to save them.

A familiar voice sounded in Halga's ear as Coella leaned forward to speak. 'They are making me all wistful again, lord,' he said. 'The Huns are like a shepherd and his dogs, cutting out a sheep from the rest of the herd for slaughter.'

As news of the success in the centre spread through the Hun ranks, the attackers immediately to the front of the Roman and allied shield walls began to draw away. Moving back beyond missile range, they turned their heads to the south, ready to reinforce the assault if the cutting out developed into a breakthrough.

Safe from attack, Halga made a rough headcount of the stranded clibanarii, sucking at his teeth in wonder as he reached a total. They had been fighting in near silence now for hours, and knowing that the others were likely to be doing the same, he asked a question of them — as much to hear his voice than to confirm the tally. 'How many do you make it?'

'About a hundred,' Godwin replied. 'Give or take.'

Grunts of agreement told Halga that they agreed with his estimation, and Beorn added a reminiscence of his own as men took advantage of the let-up to move through the ranks with pails of water. 'It reminds me of a time I was crabbing as a lad,' he said, 'off the beach near Tiw's Stead knob. I was doing so well I wanted to fill the bag, and although I had a vague awareness that the tide had turned, I just got carried away. When I turned back, the channel had filled behind me, and a tidal race was running full pelt — there was no way that I would have made it back. Luckily for me, old Deorstan appeared around the point in his boat, or the crabs would have been eating me later that day.'

Halga raised his chin to peer away to the south. The Alan horsemen had become stranded in deep water themselves now, outliers of the dead for all their glittering steel. A fresh-faced lad appeared before him, nervous glances thrown to the rear telling the tale that he was eager to be off. Twin pails hung from a wooden yoke across his shoulder, and Halga waited patiently as his lads cupped their hands to drink. Soon it was his turn to dip, and even warm and mixed with other men's spittle, his senses came alive as the water refreshed his parched throat as only water can on a sweltering day such as this.

Beorn spoke again as the lad scurried off. 'This should be interesting.'

Looking back, Halga saw that a lone clibanarius had fought his way clear of the encircling Huns. Although the breakthrough had cost him his contus, his spatha was holding any pursuers at bay for the moment as the long sword swept to the left and right. Denied a route back to his countrymen by a wall of Hunnic horse, the Alan was cantering along the allied line as he sought an escape from the baying mob. Although the rider's desperation and terror was hidden from them by the impassive steel face-mask he wore, Halga could guess his mien within.

Roman, Angle, and Jute alike thrilled to the sight as the horseman rode by, a glittering point of light at the head of a darker tail as the Huns gave chase. A break appeared in the chasing pack, the lie of the land forcing the Huns to divide. The Alan snatched at the chance, hacking a path through. The way was open now to the allied line, but as he approached,

Halga watched the Franks deliberately close ranks, raising their shields and spears to make the front line an impenetrable barrier. The Alan had seen it too, and the rider pulled up short of the bristling wall, hauling at the reins to turn his mount in a circle as his mind scrambled for a way out. His pursuers had already recovered from their misstep, unhooking lassos from their carrying places as they crept within range of Frankish weaponry — taking a chance, following the Franks' open hostility towards a supposed ally.

An eerie hush had descended on the immediate area as thousands of men watched the armoured giant at bay, a throwback to the Roman arenas of old.

The distinctive sound of rawhide ropes filled the air then as the Huns whirred the lassos above their heads, and as the first arced across, the world seemed to catch its breath. The Alan saw it coming, sweeping his spatha across to swat the rope away. But others were following close behind, and soon the clibanarius resembled a glimmering spider at the centre of a dun coloured web.

With the rider their captive the Huns put back their heels, the Alan shooting over the rump of his horse as the lines grew taut and the victors cantered away. An animated chatter got up among the men in the Western ranks as the Huns whooped and hollered, their conquest bouncing and slithering in their wake as they returned south with their prize.

Oswy spoke as they watched them go. 'It's fair to say that the Franks and Sangiban's men don't get along, then?'

Halga shrugged; he had enjoyed the sight as much as any man there. 'Neighbours seldom do.'

22

EORLES

'Here,' Halga said. 'Dip your head.' A rumble of laughter followed from the lads and the surrounding Angles, smiles illuminating weary faces as he reached up to tap the egg against Oswy's helm. The Jute picked at the broken shell with a thumbnail, tutting at the final pieces that flat-out refused to budge. In the end, he decided he couldn't be arsed. He took a bite, his eyes going wide as his mouth filled with warm yolk. 'Still runny,' he said in surprise. 'Get stuck in, boys!'

Arékan was back bearing welcome gifts from the wagon line: boiled eggs; hard cheese and harder bread. The Angles beamed with pleasure as she shared the remainder among them. The water boy from earlier was back too, parched men clapping him on the shoulder — tousling his blonde mop in gratitude as they waited to quench their thirst.

Halga turned back to Arékan, bumbling through a question as he picked a shard of eggshell from his tongue. 'You staying?'

Arékan nodded. 'They will not be back,' she said, indicating the mass of Hun horsemen assailing the centre of the allied line. 'They have tasted blood, and they want more.'

Halga followed her gaze. Reacting to the earlier success, Attila had shifted the focus of the assault to the centre, sensing weakness there. Despite their training, the Alan horses were getting jittery, and the immobile fortress of steel and horseflesh was a thing of the past. The edges of the formation were becoming increasingly ragged, as Hun attackers took advantage of any opening to land a hit with arrow or lash. Several of Sangiban's clibanarii had already paid the price for a nervy horse or a moment's indiscipline, as they were lassoed and hauled out to be instantly swamped by their sprightly enemy. He nodded down at her bow, and the arrows clutched in her hand. 'Are you planning on using that here? We can't spare a man to cover you with his shield, especially when that lot gets here.'

The comment drew both their faces to the east. The River Franks had just about formed their battle line now, king Merovech's brother, the pretender Gundebaud, clearly visible beneath his war banner at the centre of the formation. 'You will see,' she replied. 'I will pick off a few as they approach, and then take up my shield and spear before the franciscas arrive.'

Away to his left the Sea Franks were already calling out taunts and insults to their riverine cousins, and despite the relentless pounding given them by the Hun riders, Halga could see that the worst of the fighting was yet to come. Folk wars were often the bloodiest, when kin fought kin as a requirement of their oath. Halga knew that to be true as much as any man, it was the reason he was here on this southern plain, and not back home in the northern lands after all.

Horsa was walking through the ranks, Halga's kinsman all smiles and words of encouragement as he went. He threw them all a grin as he came up. 'Still with us?' he quipped, drawing a chuckle from the Angles surrounding them. He stretched his shield arm and winced. 'I thought they would never go away; holding my shield up for hours on end — I half expected to look down, and find that my arm had dropped off!' The Angle opened his mouth to speak again, but the sound of war horns in the east stopped him dead. Halga raised his eyes, sweeping the enemy formation with a look. Eorles, the champions of the northern armies, were strutting clear of the River Frank line, raising shields, spears, swords, and axes high as they called out insults and issued their challenges. From further north the thunderous sound of shield walls clashing told where Ardaric's Gepids, the folk whom Halga had battled the night before, and Attila's other German allies: Thuringians; Alamanns; Heruls, were already fighting. Assaulting the western position, they were fighting to drive a wedge between them or turn the northern flank. Either outcome would be a disaster for the Roman cause, and hearing it, Horsa lowered his voice and spoke again. 'It's time I got back, kinsman. Fight well — defeat this lot, and then we can sail north and retrieve your father's sword.'

The mention of *Hildleoma* brought Halga up with a jolt, and he thought to call after the Angle as he made his way back towards the banners. Horsa was almost there now, and to cry out would have been as pointless as it was impractical. He turned to Arékan, blurting a question as a buzz of excitement ran through the army. 'How could I forget to tell him that my brother is alive, and fighting with the Visigoths?'

Halga was taken aback as she answered with a shrug and a question of her own. 'Maybe you are just not very bright?'

It took him a moment or two to recover, and he flashed a look at the men of his comitatus standing nearby in case they had overheard to judge their reaction. To a man, they had their faces turned to the east, and the moment passed quickly as he responded with a snort of amusement. It was still an unspoken thing between Jute and Hun, whether she was tagging along for convenience until she had avenged the death of her lord, or if she was considering offering him her oath. But even as he considered the insult a jest, he realised that it was a mark of just how far he had come since he had been turfed out of Thera's bathtub less than a year before. Months had passed since he had been shown anything but deference and respect, and he realised with satisfaction that even the Angles of Horsa's oath sworn, tough men whose esteem was always hard-won, unquestionably regarded him as drihten now.

Halga turned to follow their gaze. In the dead space between the armies, the champions of the River Franks were singing their war songs, each rendition accompanied by the clash of steel on shield or the distinctive burr of a bearded axe as it cut the sultry air. But it was the emergence of the men who were responding to the challenges that had caused the buzz of excited chatter to run through the ranks of the Sea Franks and their allies. Halga raised his eyes to follow their progress, as they made their way into the open. With the men on both sides chanting the names of the eorles, Halga thought that he saw a look of dismay appear on the face of the nearest enemy — an instant of hesitation that caused a jerkiness to appear in his movements. The man recovered even as he watched, repainting his face with a snarl.

A heavy silence fell upon both armies then, all talk forgotten as the eorles came face to face, with only the recounting of their lineage and deeds adding to the sound of fighting drifting from north and south to break the spell. Halga listened in, straining to hear as the breeze picked up the champions' words had carried them away, but with his head still encased in the steel shell of his battle helm it was a hope-less cause. He thought to ask those around him if they had had better luck. But the hush was broken by a cheer, and he turned back to see that the fighters had already dropped into a fighting stance.

Halga turned his gaze on the closer pair as the first sounds of combat resounded across the grassland. It was to be a trial of differing styles. The brutish strength of the axe man against the skilful use of sword and shield, and the Jute looked on as enthralled as any man as the battle axe began to swing in wide circles. The Sea Frank withdrew before the whirring axe, his slow retreat matching the Riverine step by step. Oswy spoke out of the side of his mouth as he came. 'Who is your silver on, lord?'

Halga studied the pair, clicking his tongue as he thought. 'If they retain their current positions,' he said finally. 'I think the swordsman has the edge.'

'It doesn't look that way at the moment,' Oswy scoffed. 'He will run out of space before he gets a strike in.'

The Franks were fighting still, the axe man scything the air with his deadly blade, as a roar from further up the line told where an early slip or mistake had already sent the first man to Valhall. Halga explained his reasoning as the Riverine finally landed a blow, his Frankish cousin turning the blade aside with a deft flick of his wrist. 'Our man has the slant of the land in his favour,' he said. 'It's not much of a slope, but it's enough to add a little to the force of the strike and help tire his opponent out. Both men know it, so the axe man is hoping for a quick victory. If he can get past and switch posi-tions, he will become the favourite, but the swordsman looks a canny lad — I doubt it will happen.'

As Halga finished speaking, the Sea Frank made his first attack, stepping inside as the axe blade continued its circuit.

For an instant, it looked as if the counterattack had been perfectly judged; but the Riverine was no fool, and he threw his head back as the sword blade flashed by within a whisker of his chin. The easterner danced aside as he recovered, darting to the right as he saw the chance to outflank his opponent and gain the higher ground. But the sword stroke had been a ruse after all, a feint to open up his defence, and the armies looked on as the sweep reversed to draw a line across his calf. The effect was immediate, the axe man staggering to one side like a wagon shedding a wheel as the strength ebbed away from the ravaged muscle, and the men in the western army roared their support as their champion danced out of range.

Before the wounded man could turn to claim the high ground the Sea Frank was back, swinging around to face downslope as his shield came up to parry. Even at a hundred paces, Halga could see the desperation on his opponent's face, the blood draining from the big man's features as fast as it was from his leg. The bottom of his trews were stained black with it, and the warrior's *winingas*, the silk bindings that crisscrossed the trouser leg below the knee, were cut through and trailing behind in bloody ribbons. With the axe man's strength ebbing as every heartbeat sent a cupful of blood pumping into the dusty soil of the Campus Mauriacus the River Frank attacked again, swinging the great blade down in a diagonal cut towards his opponent's shoulder.

The westerner dodged aside with ease — but it was the River Frank's turn for trickery, and the butt of the haft stabbed out to send the man staggering backwards as the breath exploded from his lungs. Now was the time to strike, to follow up the attack with the bone crushing force of the long hafted battle axe. But the sword cut had already done its work, robbing the Frank of the agility needed to land the killing blow, and Merovech's eorle squirmed aside to catch his breath in safety.

Oswy spoke again as the Frankish pair eyed each other from a distance. 'It looks like you had the right of it, lord,' he said. 'That was his chance, and he messed it up.'

Halga nodded. 'The moment that gash appeared in the axe man's calf, it was always likely the fight would only go one way.'

The men standing in rank on both sides of the clearing were far quieter than Halga had expected, given the bloodletting that was being played out before them. As his mind began to pick at it, a sudden move from the coastal fighter drove the thought from his mind. The sword flashed out again, driving his opponent back down a slope made greasy by his blood. Without a shield for protection and growing weaker through blood loss, the axe man swatted the first lunges away like a troublesome wasp. Despite the skill and ferocity of the sword work, it was his leg ties that finally undid the big man's defence, as the bloodied strips became entangled in his feet. By some miracle, the Frank managed to maintain his balance, but as he came back to an even keel, his opponent's spatha was already driving in. Caught unbalanced, it was all the Riverine could do to watch in horror as the wide blade entered his chest, bursting through the links in his mail coat and on through mantle, muscle, and rib to reappear from his back in a gush of blood.

Another duel was over, and Halga noted the muted nature of the Sea Frank celebrations again as the axe man grimaced. To his astonishment the victor dropped his guard then, walking forward to embrace the vanquished, and as the sword man helped to lay his opponent to the grass a pregnant hush descended over both armies. The shock of his death wound had caused the axe man to drop his weapon, and Halga watched as his killer gathered it up and pressed it to his hand. There was a concern and tenderness in his actions that was baffling, and Halga turned to Arékan at his side as he sought an explanation. Fresh from her position among the sagittarii at the rear, the woman was wearing the leather cap typical of bowmen, her ears still free from the sound muffling constrictions of the steel war helm. Maybe something had been said in the opening exchange between the eorles that would explain the odd behaviour? His question when it came was as brief as the reply. 'What is going on?'

Arékan tore her eyes away from the death scene, and Halga felt shock again when he saw tears welling in the toughest woman he had ever known. 'They were father and son, Halga,' she said flatly. 'Oath sworn to different kings.'

Halga felt a knot of emotion building in his chest, as the strange goings-on out on the Campus Mauriacus were explained. He returned his gaze to the front, as a sudden roar reminded them all the fighting to the north and south was ongoing, savage, and unrelenting. It would have been natural for a trusted retainer of the elder prince of the Franks to wheedle a place for his son in the hearth troop of his lord's younger brother. No one could have foreseen that the king's sons would fight to become his successor on his death, and a sworn oath to a leader always eclipsed kinship, however close the ties.

If the tragedy played out on the grass between the armies had been keenly felt among the fighting men of both Frankish kingdoms, it was now clear that it had not gone unnoticed among their leaders. Warlords were striding clear of the battle lines, urging spearmen to recall their oaths; pointing out heroes from the crowd to honour as they regaled all within earshot with tales of past deeds and the warlike fury of their clan.

A noise went up then, and a thrill coursed through Halga and turned his blood to fire as he recognised the beginnings of the barritus. Birthing as a low hum, little more than the background drone of a meadow in high summer, the famous war cry of the North slowly rose in strength and intensity as men amplified it on the boards of their shields. Within moments the buzz had become a roar, thundering like a stampeding herd as men threw back their heads to whoop and bawl.

If the noise was said to bolster the host fated to conquer that day and drive the courage from their foe, Halga had to admit there seemed nothing to choose between the two as the enemy took the first steps towards them. With the gradient in their favour, Halga and the men of the West watched them come, peering over the heads of the leading ranks and between the gaudy war flags as they sought to estimate their strength. 'Steapel,' he said, throwing his gedriht a look. 'You can see better than us. How many are there?'

'I gave up counting when I reached the twentieth rank, lord,' the big steersman shot back. 'It felt like the right thing to do.'

Arékan was cramming her helm onto her head, fixing the chin strap and stringing an arrow to her bow. Further along the line, Halga was aware of faces turned his way, and he realised for the first time that the Angles surrounding him were looking to him for leadership. He gave a nod and a smile he hoped was reassuring, even though his mouth was as parched as a wind dried codfish, and his tongue felt about the same size. Looking back, Gundebaud's Franks were halfway across the field. Picking up the pace, they prepared to charge, the king himself shining like the morning star beneath a cloud of banners as the men surrounding Horsa closed up and braced.

A strung-out heap of horses and men formed an irregular barrier between the armies, the pitiful remains of the Hun attacks earlier that day, and Arékan stretched and released as the first to reach them leapt the obstruction. With his head down and his shield arm thrown wide for balance, the Frank never saw the arrow in flight. But he felt the hellish pain in the guts well enough as the arrow hit, and he was down and sprawling in the dust before the following shaft took out another. Satisfied with her tally, Arékan slid the bow back inside its gorytos, and with an invocation to Tángri Khan she hefted her spear and stared ahead.

As the Frankish charge became a sprint, the Angles set up a chant of their own, the age-old war cry that had resounded over battlefields throughout the North as they beat their shields in time:

Ut! Ut! Ut!

Out! Out! Out!

The battle cry petered out as the attackers hurled their distinctive throwing axes, the franciscas suggestive of their name. Halga instinctively withdrew his head into his shoulders, making himself as small as possible as a rolling wall of steel thudded into the Anglian line. When he raised his eyes again the enemy had become a sea of snarling faces, spittle flecked and crazed as they threw themselves forward in a frenzy. An instant later they hit, the front ranks clashing in a sky ripping welter of sound as Horsa's men threw their shoulders into the rear of their shields, dug in their heels and heaved.

The Anglian position began to bow inward as more and more Franks slammed into the backs of the vanguard, and Halga knew that the time to move up in support had arrived. Lifting his spear, he raised it high, savouring the moment as he felt the eyes of hundreds of fighting men fixed upon it. For a heartbeat, Halga felt giddy with the power of it. But the counterattack could not be long delayed if they were to save the day, and the instant his arm came chopping down they gave a cheer, bellowed their war cries, and hurled themselves into the fray.

23

SCOURGE OF GOD

Half a dozen paces, and he ploughed into the back of the Angles. Halga just had time to move his shield across as the Franks drove them back on their heels, aiming the boss so that it would wedge itself between the bodies of the two men immediately before him. The big steel cone was a weapon in itself. Ending in a disc-tipped prong designed primarily to deflect or trap sword and spear blades, the boss had been known to become the only part of a warrior's shield remaining to him in a hard fight. An armoured fist covering the hand grip itself, it remained a formidable weapon, able to smash teeth or hook out an eye even as the wooden boards surrounding it were hacked away bit by bit.

Another shove, powerful and irresistible, came from the front, and Halga felt the soles of his boots scrabbling for grip on the flattened grass beneath them. But the slide was beginning to slow as more and more men crossed the shrinking gap behind, throwing their shoulders into their boards to lend their weight to the push. At last, as the breath wheezed from his lungs in the crush, the Jute felt the Frankish tide still and begin to ebb as the Anglian battle line recovered.

With his face pressed close to the back of the man in front, Halga could barely see. But Oswy and Steapel were either side, Arékan beyond, and he dug in his heels to heave again and drive the Franks back. A shadow told Halga that his standard-bearer had remained with him, Coella rediscovering his courage after revealing his fears back at the camp, and the fight settled down into a shoving match as he forced his head up to look.

A dozen paces away the frontline was a snaking mass, as first one army and then the other gained a foot of ground. Locked together, shield on shield, the heads of the foemen in contact could be seen ducking and weaving, their shoulders working as they attempted to find a gap through which to stab their knifes and seaxes. Above them, the air was latticed by spear and sword blades as the men in the following ranks thrust their weapons over the heads of their countrymen, probing and jabbing as they sought to pierce the faces of the enemy. Higher up, a nightmarish rain of javelins and darts crisscrossed the air to fall upon the heads and shoulders of men too caught up in fighting to look.

With the battlefront stabilised, the pressure fore and aft eased off as both sides settled down to fight. Halga took half a pace to the rear as his hand moved up to release a plumbata from the bracket secured to his shield. Immediately behind him Coella had seen the action, and the banner man twisted his upper body, angling his shoulder to give him room. As soon as he found the point of balance Halga's arm went back, and his eyes searched the enemy lines for a target as he prepared to throw. A Frankish standard in gold and red hung limp in the still airs of the day, the design itself unknowable within the folds. But even as Halga's gaze dropped to the group fighting beneath it, he knew that he would have to look elsewhere. With the frontlines now intermingled as the fighting sawed back and forth the chances that the shot would fall short were very real, and he raised his eyes with reluctance from the juicy target as he searched out another. Straight ahead, a cluster of banners showed where the enemy were gathering opposite the place where Horsa stood resolute beneath his stallion-headed Draco, and Halga let fly as he picked them out before reaching for another. The dart flew true, arcing down to disappear in their midst, and as the front ranks continued to push and shove he grasped the opportunity to throw again.

With a shout the Franks pushed forward once more, and all thoughts of hitting back fled Halga's mind as he threw a shoulder into his board. After the first desperate defence the men were finding their rhythm, and as Halga called time Angle and Jute dug in their heels, held them, and slowly drove them back again. It was clear now that the momentum had drained from the Frankish assault, each push of shields now noticeably weaker than the last, and it came as little surprise when war horns blared and the pressure in front suddenly eased. Halga raised his shield as the air once more filled with deadly missiles, his eyes scanning the sky for danger as the enemy rear covered the retreat. Dropping his gaze, he could see the Frankish frontline glaring back from behind a wall of gaily coloured shields, their shoulders heaving as they gulped down air and recovered from the fight. Ahead, Horsa was addressing his men — calling out words of encouragement, and singling out individuals for praise.

Everyman there knew the respite would be brief, and as men sipped from canteens or restored the edge to gory blades, more wounded began to make their way to the rear. The ranks parted as the medicus's helpers hurried forward to guide them away before the fighting recommenced, and Halga studied their wounds as men clapped them on the arm and uttered words of encouragement. The vast majority were to shoulders and heads, mail shirts rend where spears had punched through steel links and into the muscle beneath, or a livid gash to cheek or neck from a glancing blow. Following the injured, the bodies of those less fortunate were dragged or carried through the ranks, freeing up space for their replacements and ensuring that there would be no cause to trample the dead underfoot when the next attack came.

A roar, and the clatter of spear shaft and sword pommel on wooden boards told them all that their brief rest was about to end. Halga worked his neck and shoulder muscles as he prepared for the hard work to come. His shield arm felt like lead, and he tried to think when he had last put the heavy boards down before realising he hadn't a clue. But war was the great leveller. It paid no heed to privilege or rank, and as the sound of Frankish war horns added their voice to the din, Halga swapped smiles and nods with those surrounding him as he hefted the thing once more. 'Ready lads,' he cried. 'Here they come again!'

HALGA STEPPED UP, exchanging a look with Horsa as one of his men helped a wounded friend to the rear. 'It has been a long day, lord,' the Angle remarked to his leader as he passed.

'The longest,' Horsa replied grimly, patting the man on the shoulder as he went.

'It almost is the longest day!' Halga exclaimed, as his weary mind recalled its importance. Battles came and went; men would still celebrate the solstice in king's halls and hovels, when everyone here was dust. 'I completely forgot until Coella reminded me this morning. Tomorrow is the longest day of the year.'

Both men turned their faces to the sun. The orb lay on the western skyline, the trees that crowded the higher ground throwing long shadows out onto the plain. 'Well, there is not much of midsummer eve remaining,' Horsa replied. 'If either side is going to win the day, whether it is almost the longest or not, they had best get a move on.'

Frankish horns sounded once more. Halga grimaced with the effort as the shield came up yet again, casting a weary look as he asked his kinsman a question. They had lost so many men in the fighting that day that Halga and the men of the reserve were now only a half dozen ranks from the battle-front. And still, the Franks came on. 'Will they break through?'

Horsa shrugged. 'I can't promise they won't,' he replied, as he too hefted his shield and sniffed. 'But I *can* promise, they will not break through here.'

Horsa's oath men Edwin and Osgar had been listening in, and Halga committed their response to memory as their lord's words caused them to cast off their weariness, lift their chin, and stand a little taller.

The Frankish charge was a shadow of its former self, the field of dead and dying forcing them to pick their way through before closing with the Anglian shield wall, robbing the attack of its cohesion and momentum. They, too, had suffered grievous losses in the daylong battle, and although they came on no less boldly than before, it seemed clear to Halga that his kinsman's confidence was well-placed. The River Franks had already lost the best of their fighting men — there would be no breakthrough here.

A plumbata thunked into Oswy's shield, drawing Halga's attention back to the front, and he nodded in agreement as the gedriht watched it fall to the ground. 'One of our old darts, lord,' he said. 'The point was bent out of shape before they threw it.' Every man listening in knew the importance of the discovery, and took heart from it; the Franks were as low on throwing weapons as themselves. If they were forced to fight back with what came to hand, they could finally concentrate on the threat before them, a threat that was closing in once again with every passing moment.

The front ranks crashed together for the umpteenth time that day, and Halga hunkered into the back of his shield, looking on as the familiar see-sawing of blades resumed over their heads. Directly to the fore, he picked out a giant of a man staring his way, the Frank's eyes twin pools of malice above a beard as dark as jet. Halga got an uncomfortable feeling that this attack was about to pan out differently. An instant later the Franks made their move, the front ranks drawing aside as the big man darted forward. The rays of the sun flashed red on the blade of a poleaxe, the weapon sweeping down to burst the head of an Angle in the front rank like an overripe pear. Halga braced as the Franks let go a roar, barging the stricken warrior aside to pour into the breach.

With surprise and momentum on their side, Frankish swordsmen turned outwards, extending the rupture to the front and sides as they came. Halga dashed forward, burying his spear into the shoulder of an attacker as they came within a yard of his position. Edwin and Osgar were already fighting, Horsa's guards all that stood between the Anglian leader and the axe wielding giant. Halga let go the spear in the crush to draw Long Knife in one sweeping movement as he attacked again. The Jute threw himself forward, the force of his shield knocking the nearest Frank back on his heels as he shouldered him aside, and he stabbed out with his seax as he sought to drive them back.

Before he could recover his balance, a Frank raised his own, and Halga saw the look of triumph in the man's pale blue eyes as the blade began to move. But the look of glee lasted less than a heartbeat, as a dark face beneath a glittering helm flashed in from the side to make a mess of his features. Halga grasped the opportunity to push up and break the enemy line as the man staggered back. Dropping a shoulder, he squirmed through the gap made by Arékan's counterattack, coming out into clear space a couple of feet from black beard and his deadly axe. Seeing the Frank was almost up with Horsa's guards, raising his poleaxe high as he prepared to cut a swathe through to the Anglian leader, Halga darted in. With the axe man committed to his attack, it would have been the perfect time to skewer him with a spear. But with his weapon still embedded in a shoulder elsewhere, Halga was forced to crouch, gripping the handle of his seax as he frantically searched for an opening in the armoured giant. The image of the eorle from earlier flashed into his mind, and the debilitating effect a single sword cut had made to the outcome of the duel; but even as he saw that the possibility was open to him, he quickly discounted it. It had taken time, far too much time, for the wound to bring the Frank down, and as he drove the image from his mind, Halga knew what he must do. He went low, down on his haunches as he firmed his grip on the handle of the sword and prepared to strike.

As the poleaxe began to fall, Halga was rising, launching himself upwards as he forced his blade beneath the skirt of mail before him. With the extra power imparted to the blow by the strength of his leg muscles, Long Knife buried itself deep inside the soft tissue of the axe man's groin. The attacker's roar of belligerence became a screech of pain and surprise, and Halga worked the seax with vicious movements to make a bloody mush of his innards. Despite his agony black beard's momentum carried him on, and he crashed into Halga, knocking the Jute onto his back as he came. Spreadeagled and helpless, Halga waited for the avenging blade that would send his soul to Valhall. But as his focus returned, and a blur of figures fought all around him, he recognised the twin forms of Edwin and Osgar straddling him as they pushed the Franks back. His Jutes forced their way to his side, enveloping him in a protective screen as Coella carried the leaping hound banner forward, and as he clambered back to his feet Halga saw that the Frankish attack was faltering. Black beard lay a few feet away, his head attached to his torso by a ribbon of flesh where Anglian sword blades had finished what Halga's seax had begun.

Seeing the failure of their main attack the Franks were beginning to withdraw again, and as the front ranks disengaged Halga looked around him. A quick headcount confirmed that all the members of his comitatus had survived the attack, and he reserved a special nod of thanks to the Hun woman panting with exertion nearby, as he acknowledged that her spirited attack had likely saved his life. The clash of steel on steel ebbed away as the battle lines drew apart, and Halga moved across to Horsa's side as the front ranks reformed, ready to drive off the next onslaught that day.

Both men were too weary now for idle chatter, but as they exchanged a nod of recognition at their part in another small victory, the sound of continued fighting drew their gaze to the north. The sight that met their eyes drove the tiredness away, and Horsa spoke as the rest of the army turned their heads. 'It looks as if the kings have decided that now is the time to force a decision. It makes sense,' he said, casting a rearward look. 'The day is drawing to a close — one of them has to prevail before the light goes, or the bloodletting will have been for nothing.'

Halga added. 'Neither Frankish army are joining in — they are letting the brothers and their oath sworn fight it out.'

Horsa nodded as the rival banners closed in. 'That is understandable too,' he replied. 'If the Franks lose any more warriors, they will lay themselves open to conquest by their neighbours. Both sides, Sea and River Franks, are surrounded by hostile folk. It would be a hollow victory for either king, Merovech or Gundebaud, if they wrestled control of the Franks only for the Alamanns or Frisians to overrun a kingdom stripped bare of the best of its fighting men.' An Angle nearby had overheard, and he caused a ripple of grim laughter among his friends as he made a comment of his own. 'It is a pity they couldn't have thought of that sooner.'

Halga snorted too, especially when the fight that would decide who would reunify the Franks seemed absurdly brief when it came. Clashing together in the dead land between the armies, it soon became clear that the fighting spirit of Merovech's followers outstripped the retainers who had followed his elder brother into exile. But if the fighting was brief, it was no less savage, and as Merovech's named men hacked a path through their Frankish cousins, Halga and Horsa looked on with mounting excitement as the kingly banners met. A sudden surge in the Sea Frank battle line momentarily hid the fight from view, but Gundebaud's war flag when it fell was all the confirmation they needed that the Riverine king had fallen too. With the grassy plain filling with Frankish warriors and chants of *Merovech!* filling the air, Horsa spoke as the first of the River Frank leaders began to make their way across to pay homage to their new king. 'Thank the gods for that,' he said. 'We have a compact with Merovech to provide him with arms for the course of the campaign, but none with his brother.'

Halga said. 'You don't believe Gundebaud would have turned on us?'

Horsa shook his head. 'I doubt that, the Roman reserve

would have been flying across to shore up the line here had Merovech fallen.' He turned back, indicating a hillside thick with mounted troops — Roman equites and German horsemen stationed on higher ground to the rear. A solid mass at the highest point showed where Aetius sat beneath the eagle of Rome, surrounded by his Hunnic bucellarii. But despite the goings-on on the Frankish front, Halga was surprised to see that their attention lay further south. The intensity of the fighting that day had left no time for thoughts of the wider war going on the length of the plain. Halga felt a stab of concern in his guts as he recalled the Hun riders and their unceasing attacks. He switched his gaze — raising his chin to peer along the line, past the Roman *legiones* still fixed in their wall of shields to the mounted Alans beyond. What he saw there caused an involuntary gasp to escape his lips, and the heads of those within earshot turned together, away from the oath giving between the River Franks and their new king and off to the south.

Through the haze of dust that hung on the muggy air, what could only be Attila, the Scourge of God himself, hove into view. The king of the Huns was conspicuous among the mass of guards, standing out clearly in his red felt coat and golden bow as he rode through piles of dead beneath a cloud of banners and dragons.

If the intention was to entice Sangiban's clibanarii from their formation, the ruse was clearly working. Driven beyond reasoning by a day spent in the teeth of the arrow storm, more and more of the armoured horsemen were leaving the relative safety of the line in a bid for everlasting fame as the slayer of the Hun leader. The gaps they were leaving behind were widening by the moment as more and more clibanarii attacked, and Halga and those around him could only look on in horror as the Huns began to fight their way through. Like a river bursting its banks, dark fingers were forcing their way through the gleaming steel of the Alan host, widening, mingling as the trickles became a flood. As the sound of war horns showed where the Roman reserve was beginning to respond to the catastrophe, the first Huns broke through into the clear space beyond.

Further south, the Visigoth reserve could be seen cantering across to help seal the breach, old king Theodoric riding to war beneath his golden Draco. Halga sent an invocation winging its way to the gods that they lend their protection to his brother, who must surely be riding in the king's host.

Before either relief army could arrive, the Alans broke, shattering the allied defence as they hauled at the reins and streamed away to the west. Sensing final victory after a hard day's fight, the Hunnish horde let out a weighty roar, pouring into the breach as the now exposed wings of the Roman and Gothic line began to fold back on themselves in a last-ditch effort to protect their vulnerable flanks. A shocked silence had fallen upon those looking on, and as men's instincts began to switch from fighting to survival, Horsa managed what Halga would have thought impossible by condensing all their thoughts into a single word. 'Shit.'

24

THE TIDES OF WAR

All their hopes now rested upon whether the king of Alans could rediscover his valour, rally his armoured horsemen and lead them back to the fray. Tens of thousands of eyes watched them go, and the groans of the men of the West mixed with the cheers of their enemies as the disordered mass reached the shadows of the woodland and kept on riding. To the rear, the wagoners were beginning to turn their charges to the flanks, scourging the oxen in a desperate attempt to reach the wings before the allied armies pulled back.

At the centre of the line, Aetius had reached the old Alan position now, and his cataphracts, equites, and German horse were making short work of the first Huns to break through. But thousands more were streaming through the line, the Hun and Ostrogoth horsemen feeding into the rupture from all sides, as the centre became a confused mass of mounted bowmen. Halga and his men looked on in horror as the sagittarii shouldered their weapons, running for the safety of the woodland spur as panic spread.

Horsa's voice carried across the plain then, his steady

voice calming the wild-eyed among the Angles as he moved among them, clapping shoulders and pointing out leaders for special praise. If the Frankish peace held he was certain they would be safe, and Halga was about to say a few words to the men of his comitatus when Godwin lay a hand on his arm and spoke. 'The Goths,' he said. 'The king...'

Halga looked, his mind reeling as he watched Theodoric's Draco fall. It was becoming difficult to see through the dust thrown up as thousands of horsemen wheeled and cantered about the plain, but he fixed his eyes upon the spot as he waited to see if it would rise again. Further south, he imagined the men in the Visigoth shield wall looking on in abject horror as the golden dragon was beaten down. As the enemy horde continued to drive forward and the Draco failed to reappear, Halga's fears were confirmed as a mournful groan carried to the army in the north, despite the clangour of the fight in the centre. As Halga looked on, a feeling of dread stole upon him that his brother must have fallen alongside his lord, and a shiver seemed to animate the Visigoth battle line as word spread that their king had been slain. With Theodoric dead, the first Goths could be seen leaving the fight, rounding up riderless horses or sprinting for the hoped-for safety of the woodland edge. Everyone on the field knew that if the Goths broke, it was over. The day would belong to Attila and his invading horde, and the real bloodletting would begin as the horse army of the East rushed forward to slaughter Aetius's fleeing host.

Halga turned back, fixing his gaze upon Horsa like a child to a father in an unashamed quest for guidance and reassurance, as the full horror of what lay ahead threatened to overwhelm him. To his surprise, his kinsman was not looking at the disaster unfolding on the southern wing, and the Jute slowly came to realise that the Angles surrounding him were looking elsewhere too. He followed their stares, lifting his chin to the long crest of the southern ridge as his mind scrambled to comprehend the sight that met his eyes. Horsemen were forming up there, hundreds of them, and he watched in growing wonder as more and more appeared to rise wraithlike from the ground as they ascended the back slope and rode into view. Very soon the entire ridge top had become a mass of horse thegns, a blood-red ribbon as a westering sun reflected from mail and spearpoint. A single word was on every man's lips throughout the Anglian host as a silver point of light rode the length of the formation, a shining star beneath a golden headed Draco of red and green: 'Thorismund.'

Halga spoke as the sound of fighting petered out, and an unearthly hush descended upon the plain. 'Thorismund and his men have been waiting on the back slope until Attila rode forward to join the attack.' He shot them all a look of wonder, as his mind unpicked the weft and weave of the Visigoth plan. 'The recall we heard earlier in the day was as much to fool Attila, as it was to stop the vanguard chasing the Hun scouts back onto the plain. They hope to encircle the king, kill Attila, and finish it here and now.'

Angle, Jute, Roman, and Frank alike looked on as the Visigoth prince and his heorðwerod returned to their places at the centre of the line. Although the distance was far too great for Thorismund's words to carry, the answering roar from the Gothic cavalry was plain enough as the war cry rolled across the Campus Mauriacus like distant thunder. The sound of war horns reached them then, the haunting drone accompanied by a glimmering light as the riders stabbed the air with their spears and lances, and as Thorismund moved downslope beneath a canopy of banners the Goths began to funnel in his wake. Within a few yards the horsemen were forming a *cuneas*, the wedge shaped attack formation that Jute and Angle alike called the swine-head, and the armies on the plain froze and shrank back as they waited for the blow to fall. Thorismund was halfway down the slope before the tide of Gothic horse warriors had cleared the crest, sweeping across the hillside like a breaking wave, and as the air filled with the rumble of hooves and the blare of battle horns, Halga somehow managed to tear his eyes away. In the middle distance the man they took to be Attila was drawing his sword, his golden bow of rank already back in its gorytos as his guards threw a screen to the south. With hope of surviving the day rekindled, Halga looked back, the Jute thrilling again to the sight of a hillside covered with allied horsemen.

Before the Huns could wheel to face the attack, the Goths had dipped from sight, and Halga knew from his time surveying the ground the previous day with Horsa that they had ridden into the dead ground at the base of the hill. As the last of the Gothic horse sank from view, the noise made by their approach was snuffed out like a door slammed shut against a winter storm. Casting a look across the field, the Jute could see that every man not actively engaged with the enemy seemed to be staring at the point they would break cover. Moments later the gaping maw of Thorismund's Draco reappeared, shimmering in the heat haze, and as the prince and his Visigoths swept back into view the plain resounded again to battlecries, the blare of horns, and the pounding hooves of an avenging host.

Attila was riding to meet the charge surrounded by his named men, and with the Gothic battle line cheering their prince as he thundered past, the armies crashed together beneath a storm of arrows and javelins. Witnessing the drama unfolding to their rear the Huns facing Aetius were beginning to disengage, pulling back in small groups before they become stranded or overwhelmed. As thousands of hoof falls changed the air overhead to clouds of billowing dust, Halga threw a look to the west. The shadows were lengthening as midsummer eve drew to a close, the gloom creeping eastwards to gather in the cleft in the higher ground through which they had passed that morning. Away to the south, the crest of the ridge where the Visigoths had begun their charge still flamed like a beacon in the sun's dying rays. But the slopes were in shadow, and Halga knew that whatever they found when the dust cloud cleared away, the fighting was drawing to a close that day.

As darkness came on the Huns would have to withdraw, back to their camp by the river's edge now that their breakthrough had been beaten back. Halga willed them gone, uncaring whether they returned to fight on the morrow or not. The Jute was now the only man without a smile and a cheer for yards around. As alone as any man could be on the Catalaunian Fields that day, Halga steeled himself to recover the body of his brother from among the Gothic dead.

HORSA CAME across as Aetius returned to the fray. 'Thank the gods they have gone,' Oswy murmured, as the Roman and his bucellarii cantered past. 'After a day spent dodging Hunnish arrows, I am less than comfortable having a hundred or so at my back — whether I am told they are friendly or not.'

As the rumble began to fade, the Anglian leader called them across. 'Gather around lads,' he said with a wave of his arm, 'and I will tell you all I know.'

Halga led the men of his comitatus across as the Angles sheathed their weapons, ambling over as the Jutish leader cast a lingering look to the east. It was a habit now, little more than the quirk of a mind that associated the direction with danger and threat. He thought back as he walked, to the juncture they knew for sure that the fighting that day had run its course, as Horsa's men jostled for position. As the rolling thunder made by thousands of hoofbeats had slowly receded, the evening breezes had dissipated the dust cloud, lifting the veil that had fallen over the fighting ever since Thorismund's charge had smashed into the Hun and Ostrogoth wing and turned their victory into a bitter defeat. The sound of fighting still hung over the Catalaunian Fields, but the din was fading almost as quickly as the light. Halga allowed himself to relax for what felt like the first time since the opening Hun attack, as Horsa began his address. 'I will keep it short,' he said, 'so that we can all take a well-earned rest. The latest news is that Attila and his underlings are in full flight, retreating to the laager they made on the bank of the Seine. Prince Thorismund and his Visigoths are hounding them all the way, with Aetius and his cavalrymen preparing to move up to worry the flanks now that they have restocked their quivers with arrows. The rest of the army is to camp here tonight, ready to fight should the Huns move out to try their luck again tomorrow.'

An Angle said. 'What about the Franks? What is going on there?'

'Merovech has been acclaimed king of the Franks, and the leading men of both kingdoms are swearing allegiance to him now,' Horsa replied. 'I don't think we need concern ourselves about the River Franks any more,' he added with a look. 'Any who felt unable to swear an oath to Merovech would have taken off when the Gepids and Alamanns retreated. Even if the lot of them started any trouble now, they would be outnumbered twenty to one by our army. But it does mean that there will be no looting of the Frankish dead.' Horsa saw the dismay in Anglian faces, and he moved to drive the instruction home. 'I am sworn to serve Merovech for the duration of this campaign, as are you through your oath to me. Now that he is king of both Frankish kingdoms, you would be looting the bodies of my lord's fallen warriors.' He fixed them with a stare. 'If anyone takes anything from the Frankish dead and gets caught, I will not only be unable to save you, I will not even try. There are plenty of other dead: Hun; Gepid; Ostrogoth and the like, so do your plundering there.' Horsa waited to let his words sink in before breaking into a smile. 'Finally — well done,' he said. 'That was a fight to keep the scops and poets busy until Woden fights the frost giants at the ending of the world. Merovech knows it, and he has assured me that he will be open-handed in his gift-giving when we return to our ships.'

The Anglian leader came across as the men began to disperse, mostly hurrying south to see what they could loot before the fading light robbed them of the chance. His smile slowly faded as he saw the look on Halga's face. 'What's up?' Horsa said. 'You have fought well and survived to tell the tale.'

Halga cleared his throat. The shadows were deepening — he was running out of time. 'My brother, Oslaf, was fighting in king Theodoric's hearth troop,' he said. 'I need to find his body before he ends up just another naked corpse on the battlefield.'

Horsa blinked in surprise. It was common knowledge that Oslaf had not been seen for several years. 'You are certain?'

Halga nodded. 'Arékan spoke to him before the battle — he would have fallen with the king.'

Horsa's eyes slid across to the Hun, who nodded in confirmation. 'You have my sympathy,' he said. 'But if you are fated to die, I can think of few better deaths than fighting side by side with a king in the greatest of battles. If any man is assured of a seat of honour at Woden's table, it is he.' The Angle turned aside, summoning Halga's friend across. 'Edwin,' he said. 'It seems that Oslaf Hunding was with king Theodoric when he fell. Take a few handpicked men and accompany Halga to look for him — it is getting dark and men will be jumpy, especially when they see a group of strangers with Gepid swords and a Hun in tow.'

Halga nodded his thanks, casting a glance towards the Gothic lines as Edwin rounded up a handful of the toughest looking men from among the Anglian host. The first fires were flickering into life there as the gloom deepened, the men themselves beginning to settle down to see out the short night as others piled weapons and armour looted from the bodies of their Ostrogoth cousins. Halga could see the sense. Not only would the haul enrich every man in the Visigoth army — if the Huns and their allies did return in the morning, at least they would not find a weapon-field to supplement those they had brought to the fight.

By the time he looked back Edwin and his Angles were ready, and the group set off at a fast walk as the first men returned with armfuls of loot. Discipline was more marked as they passed the Roman lines, the men of the comitatenses sat talking in their ranks with just the occasional pedes plundering the dead on behalf of them all. Very soon they had arrived at the dark scar marking the place where the Hun and Ostrogoth charge had broken the Alans and put them to flight. Halga halted at the edge, waiting impatiently as another troop of Roman equites returned to fill their quivers and deliver their wounded into the care of the medicus and his helpers.

The Jute ran his eyes over the tents and wagons as he waited for the riders to clear away. Each of the Roman units had been assigned a medical team to care for men wounded in battle, and some tales of their successes he had heard here in the south were difficult to believe. Spears and darts drawn from faces and torsos, leaving barely a mark to show where the warrior had come so close to death. Slashes and cuts made by swords and daggers, cleaned and stitched like an everyday thing. Stretching to either side of the camp the wounded lay in ordered rows, with men and a smattering of women moving among them administering care, or taking a moment to bring a little comfort to those beyond help. Near the tents, the physician was already coming forward at the horses' approach, wiping his hands on a bloodstained apron as he made ready to assess their wounds.

But it was the sight that greeted his eyes when he turned back that had him catching his breath, and Halga let go an involuntary cry as he crossed the strip of ground trampled and pockmarked by the fighting that day.

Oslaf met him halfway, and the brothers shared an embrace as the Angles and Jutes hung back. Taking a rearward step, the elder Hunding was the first to speak, and Halga laughed as the years rolled away. 'You have grown, little brother,' he said, before plucking at his sleeve to guide him back towards the others. 'But you will not grow much taller if you stand here too long.' The Romans had already dropped off the wounded and replenished their stock of arrows, and now the equites were grim faced beneath the rim of their helms as they made their way back to the fight. The sight of the riders drove the jollity away, and Halga turned to his brother as the Romans cleared the front line and cantered across the plain. 'I was coming across to recover your body,' he said as they walked. 'Were you not with the king?'

Oslaf exchanged nods of greeting with the others as they came across, the warriors hefting their weapons and beginning to make their way back to the Anglian position now that their task was over. 'An arrow struck the king in the shoulder,' he explained, 'throwing him from his horse. Before anyone could react, he had been trampled beneath the hooves of those following on.' The pair paused as Oslaf looked back. Halga allowed his brother to collect his thoughts as the moon rose, and the wolf-tailed star began to flicker into life above the high ground to the west. Oslaf shook his head as he recalled the death of his lord. 'It was all so sudden,' he said, the emotion he felt at reliving the moment etched upon his features. 'One moment we were driving the Huns back, and the next the king had gone. With the remaining guards heavily engaged, we had no option but to continue fighting — even those who had seen the king fall.' The Jute gave a fatalistic shrug. 'There was nothing to be done. No one knew who had loosed the arrow, so we couldn't go after the killer, and following Thorismund's charge the man may well have been dead already.' He gave Halga a look as they walked. 'I doubt that Thorismund even knows that he is king yet.'

The mention of the Visigoth's name drew both men's attention back to the east. The sun was a memory now, the Catalaunian Fields a nightmarish vision as men fought to the death beneath the steely light of the moon and the spectral star. Closer to hand, Roman faces showed red in the light of the campfires as the witching hours came on.

Halga removed his sword scabbard as they looked, taking a backward step to open up a gap between them. 'You are wrong, brother,' he said. Oslaf looked back in surprise, and Halga explained. 'You do have a death to avenge, and the killer is well-known. This is rightfully yours,' he said, gripping the scabbard containing War-spite in both hands, and holding it forward knuckle side up. 'This is *Hild-hete*, our grandfather's sword. I took it from the barrow on the headland above Tiw's Stead, when I placed the urn containing Ottar Hunding's ashes alongside his ancestors. I made a vow then, to regain our father's sword from Garwulf Guthlafing, his killer and the slayer of our kin. Your oath to Theodoric died along with that king. You no longer have ties or obligations to the Goths, you are free to do as you please.' Halga pegged his brother with a stare. 'Arékan told you last night of the burning-in at home and the deaths there, so you know you have a duty of vengeance. But it is not here, it lies closer to home. Lead us back, Oslaf,' he said. 'Together we shall kill Garwulf, and take back that which is rightfully ours.'

25

HENGEST

Arékan nocked an arrow, tracking her target. Halga looked on, studying her movements as she stretched the bowstring. He had it in mind to ask her to teach him how to use the smaller Hun bows after witnessing their effectiveness in the fight — if she stuck around. The Hun released, the arrow flew, and as a yelp of surprise and pain filled the meadow, an answering howl of dismay came from the riders in the column. 'There is more where that came from, you bastard,' she hissed. 'Try wagging your tail now.' Halga and Arékan shared a look, Jute and Hun, man and woman, in perfect agreement as the dog lay panting its life out in the grass. The other dogs scattered as she fitted another arrow to the string and sighted, running back to the safety of Remorum as an outcry came from the army. Arékan called a retort as the men growled in protest. 'Oh, bad woman — how could she do such a thing? Good dog, nice dog — come and get your ears rubbed. Well, we two know another game they like to play when they outnumber you, and they feel a little peckish.'

Halga ran his eyes over the ransacked town as they turned north and cleared the entrance to the amphitheatre, shaking his head in wonder as the events of the past few days replayed themselves in his mind. Barely three days had passed since they had ridden clear of the southern woodland, and laid eyes upon Remorum for the first time. The memories were growing hazy — already a mass of foggy images, the jumbled recollections of a mind hobbled by weariness and lack of sleep.

With Attila's army of the East back on the far side of the River Seine and well on its way to the Rhine, King Merovech of all the Franks had ridden north that morning. Alongside the king rode the best of his warriors, as he strengthened his grip over the lands formerly held by his brother. Before he had gone, Horsa had managed to get a short audience for Halga and Oslaf, the upshot of which was that the king's steward, Dagmer, had been instructed to lead the rest of the army back to Tornacum. Here he would pay off the hired swords, following which he was to accompany the brothers home in their quest to avenge the death of their father. Although the king had forbidden the Franks to fight on the brothers' behalf, Dagmer was to sail north with a shipload of warriors and call on the Jutish king. Here he was to deliver fine gifts plundered from Attila's army, while at the same time letting it be known that the Hunding brothers were friends of the Franks, and of their king in particular. The inference was clear. With the continuing support of the Angles to the south and Oslaf's personal reputation among the Visigoths, the balance of power in the kingdom would shift decisively in their favour.

Halga raised his gaze as they rode, catching sight of his brother as the front of the column made the tree line. Oslaf was riding at the head of his troop, laughing and joking with Horsa at something or other. Halga felt a stab of shame when he realised that a small part of him wished that his brother had stayed dead, or at least believed to be so. Now, with a ship's crew of Gothic friends accompanying him home to reclaim his birthright, Halga had been relegated to the younger sibling again — the spare to the heir. After all the hard work of the past summer forging a reputation as a warrior and leader of men, he felt that he had been usurped, and it had all been for naught. The Jute slumped back into a dark mood as the laughter floated down the column again.

A sharp dig to the ribs jolted his mind from its melancholic daze, and he looked across to see that Arékan had eased her horse to his side. 'Sorry,' she breezed, 'I caught you with my bow.' He watched as the weapon slid down into its gorytos, and she added to the apology with an impish smile: 'that was clumsy of me.' The pair rode in silence for a while, each of them wringing the most from the reality of being out of harm's way for the first time since they had ridden south from Camaracum many weeks before. The day was hot; already the grassy meadow that had acted as a campsite for the competing armies was beginning to recover, with the rasp of crickets loud enough to be heard above the rhythmic clatter of horseshoes on stone setts. Arékan spoke again as they passed from light to shade, and the earthy tang of trees and the woodland floor replaced the sweeter smells of the sward. 'So,' she said. 'I never thought you would be a sulker.'

Halga looked across in surprise, dimly aware that Oswy and Steapel to the rear of them had slowed the pace of their horses and begun to talk loudly about nothing much at all. It was only then that he realised that his mood had affected the lot of them, and he pulled a wan smile. 'You are right,' he conceded. 'Oslaf's unexpected return from Valhall has been bittersweet for me.'

Arékan nodded. 'Is that because you wanted to be ealdorman? Back in Tiw's Stead?'

Halga blew out. 'Overseeing the harvest? Teaching

downy chinned lads and fishermen how to wield a shield and
spear at the moot? Judging which rustic had moved a
boundary stone to cheat his neighbour of a foot or two of
land?' He scoffed. 'After all I have seen here in the south, it
would be a living death. Tiw's Stead means little to me,
whether Oslaf had returned or not. A veil has been drawn
aside, Arékan, and I have glimpsed another world. A place
where a sharp sword and a band of friends can win wealth
and renown, without paying tribute to a distant and
murderous king.'

Arékan said. 'So, why the long face? It seems to me that
you have all you want.'

'There is still a man to kill, and a sword to reclaim.'

The Hun nodded. 'But now you have the means. Less
than a year ago, you were chased from your home with a
handful of friends, barely escaping with your lives. Now you
are a warrior of reputation, a friend of the king of the Franks
with a Long Knife to prove it, returning home at the head of
an army to wreak a bloody vengeance upon those who have
wronged.'

A family group had pushed a handcart containing all they
owned to the side of the road to let the conquering army
swagger past, each of them casting their eyes to the ground as
they waited. Arékan spoke again. 'You are better off than
people like them; even if their home remains, there will be no
crop to harvest. Countless thousands of men, horses, and
oxen have spent the spring and summer scouring the land for
every morsel worth eating. If any crop they had planted has
not been trampled, you can be sure that every kernel would
have gone to feed one army or another by now. Their war
begins when the armies go home — the war against hunger.'
Arékan slipped a band from her forearm and gave a low whistle, tossing the thing across the instant the farmer's eyes came

up. She spoke again as the man snatched it from the air, dipping his head in gratitude as he tucked the band away. 'Even a solitary silver arm ring could be enough to see them through the coming winter.'

It was true that the returning army had left behind more wealth than they had previously dreamed possible on the battlefield that morning. But already the gates of nearby Tornacum had been thrown open, and the population come forward to carry away loot by the wagonload and armful. Halga doubted they had a share-out with those who had suffered in the hinterland in mind. First light had revealed the dead piled in heaps where the heaviest fighting had taken place, with outliers dotting the plain showing where war bands and stragglers had made a last stand. He had walked down to the place where Thorismund's charge had crashed into the Hun formation with Oslaf and his men, the Goths bubbling over with pride as they described the fighting there. A line of Huns and Ostrogoths marked the battlefront like the grim marker of a ghastly high tide, while down in the dip the brook still ran red with blood. They had loaded as many captured horses as they were able before they left, the panniers and saddles festooned with war booty. It was fair to say that there was not a poor man left in the army.

Arékan spoke again, as the column left the cover of the woodland to wend its way through a sunny glade. 'Unlike the chaos beloved of your gods Halga, Tángri Khan teaches us that nothing in life occurs without a reason — if you were a Hun you would know this. If your father had not gone away, you would not have become the man you are now, nor I the woman.' The Hun gave the Jute a meaningful look. 'If I had not felt guided towards the Goth camp that night, I would never have met the brother we all thought dead. Unaware that his father and kin needed avenging and that he was now the rightful ealdorman, Oslaf may well have thrown his life away in a vain attempt at gaining some measure of retribution against the killers of king Theodoric. Then it would have been left to you to recover the lands you say you have no wish to rule, and without the aid of a shipload of Goths. Think on my words,' she said as the horse began to move away. 'I have spent the best part of a year with you now, Halga, and something has changed. The gods are watching over you, I am sure of it, and the battles you have fought this summer are only the beginning.'

Halga watched as she clicked her tongue and the horse cantered away, back to the front of the long line of horsemen, and the brother he now realised she knew better than he did himself. He brightened as he thought on her words, the moodiness driven away as he came to see the truth they contained. Rather than becoming sidelined by the return of Oslaf, he saw it now as a lucky escape, and he relaxed as the men of his comitatus edged forward to his side and the sun beat down. Long before nightfall they were back at Camaracum, and the following week drifted by in a haze of restful rides and leisurely encampments, as the victorious army of the Sea Franks drifted away to their homes in small groups.

Unlike the devastated Roman settlements to the south, the Frankish lands had been spared rack and ruin by the vigorous actions of their king. Supplies were plentiful, the harvest newly gathered, with food and drink sent out from the towns as they passed. Every night the wolf-tailed star had crept a little further east, chasing the army of Attila from western lands, and by the time Tornacum hove into sight the army had shrunk to little more than a war band.

And it was here, at Merovech's city beside the River Scheldt, as Prince Childeric fulfilled his father's pledge to fill their hulls with silver and riches, that a face from the past sought Halga out.

THE FRANKISH GUARD ship sheered away as the mouth of the river came up on the larboard bow. Halga smiled as nostrils flared, and those around him inhaled the salty air with the look of men come home. A cable later and the shallows and mudbanks were behind them, and as the bows came around to the north and the sea beneath their keels turned from silty-brown to grey, the lookouts in the prow called out that the temple was in sight. Ranged alongside Halga could just make out a handful of masts, and he turned to the man at his side as the helmsman altered course. 'Are they Hengest's ships?'

Ægil stretched his neck, squinting into the gathering gloom as his eyes scanned the shore. After a short while, he turned back with a smile. 'Yes, lord,' he said. 'The lads have made good time.'

Halga returned the smile. 'How does it feel?'

Hengest's man blinked in surprise. 'Lord?'

Halga went on as the ship skimmed across a sea as smooth as milk; a two-day journey out from Tornacum, and they had made the island just in time. Away to the east, hovering over the limitless plains and the impenetrable forest men called Iron Wood, the moon and the wolf-tailed star were hardening from the twilight. 'To call me lord,' he said. 'It has been a couple of years since we parted.'

'It feels good, though it makes me feel my age,' the Angle admitted. 'It hardly seems any time since your father dropped you off at Hengest's hall at the beginning of your foster, and now here you are,' he said, 'a drihten, and man of renown. The whole of Tornacum thrilled to the tale of your fight against the Gepid rearguard before the main battle.'

'How many ales did you manage to wring from our friendship, when you told them who you were?'

Ægil's look of innocence only lasted a moment before his face broke into a grin. 'Quite a few — I had been waiting there for your return for the best part of a month,' he said defensively. 'I deserved something.'

Halga chuckled. 'Yes, you did — for that, and for all you have done for me in the past. If I have had any success over the course of the summer, I owe a great deal of it to the training you gave me over the years.'

The conversation had eaten up the greater part of the time needed for the little fleet to reach the anchorage, and Halga ran his eyes along the shoreline as he sought the man he wished to see above all. This close to the festival of Gule, the island that contained the temple of Nehalennia was teeming with folk from the nearby town as the population waited patiently to make their offerings to the goddess. It was a local custom that the first loaf baked from the year's grain was offered up at the site, and the festive mood would add to the reunion between Halga and his foster-father after so long apart.

Forewarned of their arrival by sentinels on the headland the Angles were lining the strand, brickbats flying between ship and shore as the faces of old friends and kinsmen appeared among the crowd. Hengest himself was in view now, and Halga felt his smile broaden as the warlord cupped a hand to swap bawdy insults with his brother in the bow.

The moment that the keel touched the shingly bottom, Horsa was over the side, wading ashore to share a brotherly embrace as Hengest came down to greet them. In no time, Halga was on dry land, hanging back from the pair as joyful reunions took place all around. The delay was enough to enable the men of his comitatus to stand at his back, and

Halga felt a gush of pride as he glanced their way. No longer the group of friends in leather shirts with hand-me-down weapons; now every one of them shone like a newly struck coin in the fading light, their arms and armour the finest that Gepid, Hun and Byzantine craftsmen could produce. But if they now wore the trappings of a successful warrior, the most notable change had come in their demeanour. Gone forever was the countenance that said I don't really belong here — I am just a lad. Now there was a steeliness to their gaze that could not be gifted by a generous patron, a toughness, and self-assurance, that could only be wrung from facing down your doubts and fears in the hard game of war.

Halga turned back just in time, as the brothers drew apart and Hengest threw him a look. 'Who is this? He reminds me of a scrawny lad I knew a while back.'

Horsa smiled too. 'He tells me he is a drihten, and these are his men. They have followed me around all summer. I can't seem to give them the slip.' The smile fell from his face, and he turned back as if an idea had just occurred to him. 'I don't suppose you could find a place for them in your army?'

Hengest marched down the beach, the shingle scrunching beneath his feet as he came. Halga could only smile; even bootless in his shirt and braies, no man could deny his foster-father was a lord of war. 'Halga,' he said as he came to a halt before them. 'Welcome home.' The Angle ran his eyes over the Jutes, the pride he felt in his adopted son shining from his eyes as he recognised their quality. 'You have been busy since last we met. Come, the sun is down and the ale barrels tapped. Gather at the fireside. We have a long night ahead of us, and many tales to tell.'

Horsa and Arékan went first, the Angle and Hun holding Hengest and his men spellbound as they told of hall burnings and Attila's horde. The night wore on, the darkness deepened, and Hengest himself stood to tell of a summer chasing Picts and Scots across peaty moors as ale-flushed faces glowed red in the firelight. And then it was Halga's turn to be called, and as the clash of spear shaft and sword blade on the rims of shields faded into the night, he stood and recounted the story of his year.

If the flight from Thera's tub drew hearty laughs as he knew it would, the sea chase in the fret held them rapt, and as the memories returned he found that he shared their astonishment at all he had achieved. The midwinter rescue of Arékan from a grisly fate, and the witchy night that followed: picking off eastern foragers in Gaul; the fight with the dogs; the night ride and fight with the Gepid rearguard beneath the wolf-tailed star; the battle on the Catalaunian Fields. He showed them the seax that had been gifted by a king, Hengest's Angles exclaiming in wonder as they passed it from hand to hand and saw its worth.

And then his turn was over, and his foster-father, his only father he now realised, was back at his side. They stood awhile in silence as another tale of blood and mayhem drifted across the strand, watching the ships bobbing gently at anchor as the men on guard cast looks of longing towards the gathering. Hengest broke the spell, his words quietly spoken but heavy with intent all the same. 'We have one more tale to add to our summer haul kinsman,' he said. The Angle raised his eyes and Halga followed suit. The clear skies of Gaul had been left behind in the south, and a carpet of grey, flecked silver by the moonlight, drifted northwards on a freshening breeze. 'If this wind holds,' the warlord said. 'We shall sail at first light and begin it.'

26

RED SKY AT NIGHT

Halga looked as the flotilla hurried north. Timing was everything now; in a few days, Garwulf should be back in Tiw's Stead, collecting the tribute that rightfully belonged to his kin. It was the perfect opportunity to catch him isolated and shorn of the protection of his father the king, and he thrilled to the sight of the ships as the wind blew, the sails bellied, and prow beasts porpoised in the swell. Oslaf's Goths were tough lads, almost to a man former bucellarii of the old king Theodoric. The Angles under the brothers Horsa and Hengest were no less fierce — half a dozen snake ships crammed with spearmen beneath the famed dragon banner of their folk. Zigzagging to the rear as it hunted the wind, the Franks. Only a single ship but the finest in the fleet, the serpentine decoration, the sleekness of its lines telling any with a knowledge of seafaring that here was a king's ship. Dagmer caught his eye, and they exchanged a wave. Halga chuckled happily as he saw the joy on the older man's features, and realised just how much it must mean for him to be away from his responsibilities back in Francia for even a short while. Although they would do no fighting, their charge was perhaps the most important of all if the Hundings were to have any future in the Jutish kingdom, following the slaying of the king's son.

With the wind blowing steadily, the majority of the men squatted in groups wherever they could squeeze in. Halga laughed as a cry of dismay went up, the dice clattered on the decking, the marks tallied, and Arékan scooped up her winnings again. A hand on his shoulder caused him to turn, and Halga found that Oswy and Steapel had come to his side. 'A lot has happened since we last sailed these waters, Halga,' Oswy said. 'I wonder what we shall find at home?'

'Things will be much the same,' Halga replied. 'Harvesting, fishing, the same old soaks sat around supping ale as they retell a story for the thousandth time.'

Beorn had joined them, and the gedriht put in with a grin. 'That will be us one day.'

Halga snorted. 'If we go on to do nothing further with our lives, we shall still have tales worthy of recounting.'

Steapel touched his arm, the humour driven from his face as he pointed away to the Northeast. 'There is the channel, lord,' he said. 'I will guide the helmsman, and we should be safely holed up before sunset.'

They all looked as he drifted away. A mile off, the rise and fall of the dunes petered out as the beach became a hook of land. Between that and the small settlement that had grown up on the northern shore, a greenish-grey swatch showed where the passage from Lyme Bay emptied its waters into the wider expanse of the German Sea. It was the same stretch of water they had taken in their mad dash south the previous year, as they had fled for their lives with a scratch crew of ruffians and ne'er-do-wells. But if anything showed just how far his fortunes had risen in the intervening time, a quick glance around the fleet and the men they contained was enough. Halga allowed himself a moment of satisfaction as the helm came over, the braces hauled, and the prow began to turn.

BEORN STUCK his head around the door. Before he could utter a word, Halga could see from the look on his face that it was the news they had been waiting for. 'There is a boat coming down the channel,' he blurted, 'with Coella in the bow.' The gedriht hesitated a long moment, before his mouth creased into a smile. 'He has a dog with him.'

Halga was back in the crofter's hut with its bundles of reeds and rushes racked up outside, and he exchanged a look with the other leaders as he rose to go. 'Well, it is a good cover,' he said. As the returning landowner, and with a ship's crew of Goth veterans to add to the mix, Oslaf had overall command of the attacking force. But Coella was Halga's man, and it was right that he should lead them out. Oslaf, Hengest and Horsa hung back as the boat made the jetty, and a sea of faces turned their way from the warriors camping out on the ships. Coella hopped ashore, looking incongruous back in the garb of a shepherd following a year spent in mail and helm. 'They are here,' he said, as the dog leapt up beside him. 'I saw Garwulf near Tiw's Stead.'

Halga shared a look with his brother; the Hundings eager to wet their blades, and right the wrongs done to their clan. He turned back as the boat bumped alongside the landing stage. 'When was this?'

'They left Tiw's Stead at midday, rowing south — three ships: a snake ship for Garwulf and his men; a smaller scegth to do the running around, and a nice fat trader to carry the *feorm* they harvest. They are summoning the local thegns to the moot as they go, gathering the tribute for the area and moving on at a leisurely pace.'

Oslaf said. 'And why wouldn't they? They have no idea we are here. Still, it is nice of them to farm the rent and supplies for me: it will save me having to do so later.' He turned to Coella. 'And they didn't see you?'

Halga's man shrugged. 'It wouldn't matter if they did, lord. No one takes any notice of a shepherd walking the hills with his dog.'

Hengest laughed. 'True enough! I take it this lad here is from home? It doesn't seem like he is in the mood to let you leave anytime soon.'

They all looked. The dog was at Coella's side, both eyes fixed upon him as he waited patiently for his next task. The one-time shepherd stretched out a hand to tousle his ears, and the dog squirmed with delight. 'He is a good boy,' he admitted with a sigh. 'It will be a wrench for us both when the time comes to leave again.'

Halga was studying the sky, as the toughest warlords in the North became cooing halfwits in the presence of a dog. The promise he had made to his ancestors in the burial mound was drawing close to fulfilment — it was vital that he keep his focus. The day was advanced, the air already cooling, and the southerly that had driven their hulls past the coastlines of Frisia, Saxony and Anglia in less than a week had blown itself out almost the moment they had arrived. Whether it was a sign that the gods were with them, or hurrying them to their death, was yet to be seen. But it did mean that they would be rowing from here on in, slowing their movements to a crawl.

Oslaf had watched his brother's action, drawing the same conclusion, and he turned to the others as Halga dismissed Coella and his disruptive hound with a nod of his head. 'We will have to remain here for another night, and hope that Garwulf takes his time. If we leave now, we will be less than halfway to Wisbey Broad when full darkness comes on.' He threw them all a pensive look. 'We cannot risk showing a light on the bay, not when we are so close to achieving the surprise we need to catch the murderers. If we leave at first light and the wind is with us, we should be in position to spring the trap before they break camp — if not, the men will have to row. They will arrive tired,' he admitted with a shrug, 'but we outnumber them, and have the advantage in quality — it will be enough.'

Halga could sense the Anglian brothers' doubts, and he cleared his throat and made a suggestion. 'Wait until dusk, and make straight for the crossing place opposite,' he said. 'If we lower the masts and stow the sails, we will be difficult to see in the murk. A quick dash across the bay, and we can haul the hulls across the neck of land before full darkness is upon us.'

Oslaf rubbed his chin. 'We are not sailing scegths or færings, Halga — do you think we can get them across?'

Halga nodded. 'Snake ships carry large crews,' he said. 'It is barely more than a sandbank; they will make it across just fine, and it would knock thirty miles from our journey. Not only would we be in position tomorrow morning with the men fresh and rested, but there is far less chance of word of our arrival reaching Garwulf than if we are forced to cross the bay in daylight.'

Oslaf thought for a moment, and then nodded. 'You're right — it is worth taking the chance. Even if we find that we cannot cross the neck of land, we can make camp there. Darkness will soon be upon us, and we can set off from the northern shore of Lyme Bay on the morrow just as easily as the south. As soon as we are ready, we will row the ships upstream and hide in the reed bed 'till sunset and give it a go.'

They all glanced instinctively to the west. 'We have — what? Less than an hour until dusk?' The group nodded their agreement. It was already Harvest Month, the midsummer fight against the eastern hordes a fading memory. Back in the northlands now, the days were shortening quickly — very soon the skies would fill with skeins of geese, Coella's starlings sweeping the air in waves as the wandering birds headed south for winter. 'Right,' Oslaf said, 'let's get to it. The quicker we are in position, the quicker we can make a start.'

Halga moved across to Dagmer as the others made for the ships. The Frank had been forbidden to get involved in any fighting by king Merovech unless they first came under attack themselves, and he could see the disappointment in the older man's face as orders flew, men set to, and the familiar pre battle buzz began to fill the riverside. 'This is where we part,' Halga said. 'I want to thank you for your help.'

Dagmer smiled. 'I am just doing king Merovech's bidding, Halga,' he replied. 'But I would add, that I have not enjoyed myself this much in years. I hope that you take your vengeance on the killers of your kin,' he said, 'and I will assure king Guthlaf that both Hunding brothers are friends of the Franks. Whatever the outcome of the fight tomorrow, I doubt that he would relish facing the combined might of ourselves, the Angles and Goths.'

Halga called across to the crofter as Dagmer turned to go, rummaging in the purse that hung from his belt as the man hurried across. 'Here,' he said, as a Byzantine solidus sailed through the air. 'This is for your inconvenience.'

The man dipped his head, his eyes going wide as he

snatched the gold coin from the air. 'Oh, it was no trouble, lord,' he chirruped.

Halga cut him dead before he could complete his sentence. This close to the fight, he could take no chances on any man's loyalty. 'It will be, when you have to swim out to retrieve your punt from the marsh.'

Halga was walking the jetty, his feet resounding on the boards as the man's stammered reply became lost in the noise of an army preparing for war. His mind went back to the first time he had boarded a ship at this spot as he went, wondering idly if the swordsman he had shouldered over the side that day remained pinned to the riverbed by the weight of his mail. Oswy was holding forth Halga's byrnie when he reached the deck, the drihten wriggling into the mail shirt as men followed suit all around. He cast a look along the line of the fleet as his head reappeared. With the masts lowered, and the sails stowed, the ships looked sleek and deadly, and as the oarsmen poled them away from the bank Halga skipped up onto the steering platform.

The rowers bent their backs, eyes fixed upon the steersman as they did so, and the instant that the man's foot came down to mark time the great blades dipped and stroked. With the first pull, the ship barely moved — but the rowers soon found their rhythm, easy strokes matching the soft thud of the helmsman's foot as it beat a tattoo on the deck. By mid-channel, the snake ship was underway, the dark waters of the river pearling as they burbled past the strakes. Before they had time to pick up speed the trees were drawing back, and as the final outliers gave way to a rampart of sea barley the rowers were already backing the oars, slowing the vessels as lookouts scanned the horizon from the prow.

A few hundred yards to the north the waters of Lyme Bay shimmered like beaten gold in the rays of a setting sun, and

Halga made a shelf with a hand as he squinted into the glare. It took a matter of moments to reassure him that the way ahead was clear, and he swapped a grin and a thumbs up with his brother in the vessel ahead as the plan began to come together.

With the ships in the fleet backed up along the channel, Oslaf indicated that Halga come forward with a wave of his hand. He exchanged a nod and a few words with Arékan as he negotiated the mast. 'You have all the silver now, I take it?' The Hun held up a weighty pouch, her teeth flashing white in the dusk as she replied from beneath a fur rimmed hat. 'Fools and their silver, Halga...' He gave her a look of admiration as he passed. Dressed now in an eclectic mix of northern and Hunnish clothing looted from the battlefield, she would always remain a reminder of the great fight that summer.

Oslaf was waiting for him when he reached the bow. Halga hauled himself up by what remained of the prow post after the removal of the beast heads, as the lookout moved respectfully away. The smiles had gone now as the brothers set their minds to war, and Halga listened as Oslaf shared his thoughts. 'The coast looks clear, brother,' he said. 'There is not a hull in sight.'

Halga nodded. 'Are you suggesting that we make a run for the crossing place now?'

'Why wait?'

Halga hesitated. If Garwulf was forewarned of their presence, he could easily put about and leave Tiw's Stead Broad by taking the northern channel linking it with the bay. If that did happen, he would be long gone by the time they could give chase. He was about to share his fears when Oslaf spoke again. 'I know what you are thinking — that Garwulf could give us the slip. But you said yourself that the shortcut opposite would lop thirty miles from the journey around to Wisbey Broad. Any ship that attempted to take the longer route to warn of our presence would need to show a light to have any chance of negotiating the shoals and islands. Once we are on the northern shore, we will be safely in our ancestral lands — no word will come from there. Even with the Franks leaving us, we still have seven ships, and there will only be enough logs in place to move one ship at a time.'

Halga was convinced, and he said so. 'Yes, you are right. The extra daylight will make the transit of the portage far easier.' They exchanged a smile across the gap. 'Let's get going.'

Freed from his vow of service to Horsa at the culmination of the campaign in the South, Halga and his comitatus had taken ship with his foster-father. Hengest was waiting patiently at the stern as the Jute made his way aft. The sheepdog wagged its tail as he passed, Coella in his herding clothes sticking out like a spare cock in a bawdy house as he whittled a spear shaft into a crook. Halga shook his head, laughter dancing in his eyes as he reached out to give the dog a pat as he went. 'We are crossing straightaway,' he said as he made the steering platform. 'There is naught in sight, and we can use the last of the daylight to help us cross the land bridge.'

Despite supplying the majority of the fighting men, Hengest and Horsa were content to follow, leaving the decisions and timing to the Jutish pair on home ground. Halga knew that it was a reflection of his abilities now as a drihten; he was over-proud. The leading ships were moving again by the time word had been passed back to Horsa and Dagmer further back, and within a short time Oslaf's ship was beam on as it took the first bend. Halga's ship was next in line, and as the bows began to turn, he cast a look to the north. There were still no ships in sight bar their own, and he thanked the gods as the steering oar centred to guide them past the withy marking the entrance to the cut. Soon the fleet had put the shallows and mudbanks behind them — hundreds of oars beating the surface to foam as they raced across the bay.

At the halfway point, Dagmer and his Franks bore away eastwards, the crewmen hard at it as they prepared to step the mast and bend on sail now that they no longer had cause to hide. Halga cast a look aft as they went. The sun lay on the horizon now, the channel from which they had emerged only a short while before already an indistinct smudge against the woodland edge beyond. Oslaf's Goths were sturdy men — built like trolls and twice as ugly. But they were natural horsemen, and no match for Angles at sea. Hengest's crew were no slouches in any company, and a short while later Halga felt the keel give a shudder before the ship slew to a halt, the first to arrive at a shelving beach.

Halga was over the side as soon as the ship came to rest, splashing through the shallows to lead the first party of spearmen ashore. The men fanned out as they ran, darting through sandy dunes and banks of marram grass to secure the landing site as Halga made for the portage itself. The logs were there, cast aside by the last crew to cross the bar, and Halga had the first men shouldering the heavy runners and returning to the ships before the last of them had disembarked.

Oslaf and his Goths were in position when they arrived, twin lines of men ready to haul on a hawser looped around the prow. Further out, shipmates stood knee-deep in the shallows, preparing to lend their weight to the push. They had only moments to wait before the men carrying the rollers jogged down the beach, depositing the heavy logs on the sand with a clatter. As Halga looked on with satisfaction at a job well done, he noticed for the first time that Coella and his faithful hound were hovering nearby. He threw his gedriht a question and a smile. 'Are you waiting for me?'

Coella pulled a thin smile in return and ambled across. 'We two will be off,' he said. He raised his eyes to the sky — Halga followed suit. The horizon was a reddish-yellow, shot through with scarlet as the sun sank from view. 'Red sky at night...' he murmured dreamily, before addressing his drihten again. 'The countryside hereabouts is dotted with small shelters for the use of shepherds, lord. I thought I would make the most of the evening.'

Halga was about to forbid it when Hengest called his name. The plan had always been that they would drop off man and dog at first light, close to the stretch of water they had chosen to spring the trap. Coella was as aware of this as any of the leaders, and Halga was about to say so when he turned back to see that the pair were moving away among the dunes. He made to call after him, but Oslaf's ship slid between them as the Goths heaved and pulled, and by the time Halga had stepped aside the pair had been swallowed by the dusk. The conversation had irked him at a busy time. There was something in his man's behaviour that was troubling, but Halga was forced to push his concerns to one side as the rollers were manhandled, and the Goths heaved the hull again. Halga spat a curse, but Coella's indiscipline was a problem for another time.

27

A TRAIL OF BLOODY TEARS

'There he is!' Halga felt a hand on his shoulder, the relief palpable as he raised his head to look. On the skyline to the north, Coella ambled into view, planting his crook for balance as the dog trotted happily at his side. He shook his head, blowing out as relief turned to exasperation. *Where had he been? Sleeping in? Gone home? Off in a field somewhere, playing fetch with the dog?* The strand had come to life as word spread of the gedriht's longed-for reappearance, and Halga rose from the bench as Hengest snapped out a command. 'Make the signal!'

A quick check to the east as the flag ran up the lanyard, and Halga's heart sang as the dragon banner of Angeln unfurled in reply. Half a mile away on the far side of the bay, Horsa's ships were moving beam on to the strand, their tall prow posts coming about as the oars caressed the surface.

At the centre of the inlet the Goths pulled the first strokes, the snake ship edging forward towards the wider expanse of Wisbey Broad as Oslaf threw them a wave from the stern. Halga cupped a hand to his mouth, calling Woden Luck as they went. He raised his eyes as his brother's ship began to turn, out past Horsa's flotilla on the far side of the waterway and the heather strewn heathland on the island of Moors beyond. The sun was a hand's breadth above the crest; it was midmorning, and with the greater part of the day still to come, the chances of success rose with it.

Halga's mind ran through the plan for the umpteenth time as the warriors came aboard, the oars ran out in readiness, and Oslaf's sternpost became lost from view behind the headland. It was simple enough as all good plans were, but it relied on the enemy to react in the obvious way, and men were unpredictable at the best of times — Coella's antics were proof of that. It had always been intended that his gedriht would pass the night with them here in the camp, before leaving at first light to scale a small hill a mile or so to the north. The rising ground stood on a headland, perfectly placed for their needs at the point where the broad narrowed before doglegging south-east. The vantage point would present Coella with an uninterrupted view the length of the broad as far as the beach at West Strand. This was the only place suitable for the crews of three ships to camp out overnight, and remain within a short ride of the thegn whose tribute they would expect to receive next.

Coella's reappearance told them all that Garwulf's ships had arrived at the meeting place. But if he had wandered off and left them, what then? Although the high ground was little more than a mile distant, it would have taken far longer for a man to circle the inlet that stretched between them. Even then it would have taken some time to think of a good replacement for a shepherd complete with crook and faithful hound, a sight as much a part of the scenery in these parts as the moors and trees. Halga shook his head again as he pushed the irritation down deep. All it needed now was for Oslaf to reappear in the district after years away, for the bloodletting to begin.

. . .

OSLAF PULLED the handle to his chest, the bows swinging
eastwards as the big paddle blade bit. Ahead, the waterway
finally widened into the expanse of Wisbey Broad proper
after the twists and turns of the narrows, and with the sail
stowed the Jute raised his chin to peer past the prow. A flock
of gannets could be seen feeding to larboard, the seabirds
plunging from height to disappear beneath the surface in a
scatter of shimmering plumes. Further north the broad
narrowed again, and beyond that lay Tiw's Stead itself. But if
the surroundings were as familiar from his younger years as
the faces of his friends and kin, the Jute felt only anger as
West Strand and the hulls resting at anchor there hove into
view. His acid faced look had not gone unnoticed by the
others. As the rowers kept their eyes lowered and bent to their
work, his closest friends came across.

Waldmer said. 'It will have been a while since the leaping
hound has been seen in these waters, Oslaf. But I will wager
the dog has not lost its bite.'

The pair raised their eyes to the masthead. Sheltered from
the sea breezes to the westward by the lie of the land, the
wind came in fitful breaths. But it was just enough to tease
the war banner of his folk out to the east, and Oslaf dropped
his gaze as he attempted to make out the figures there and
looked for a reaction. Garwulf's ships were drawing closer
with every sweep of the oars, and he allowed himself the
ghost of a smile as he thought of the men lounging around,
still oblivious to the fact that death was already stalking them.
Waldmer spoke again, the excitement of the moment reflected
in the tone. 'It looks like they are taking the bait,' he said
gleefully. The smaller ship in the trio, the little scegth, was
beginning to edge out into the broad, the oars flashing in the

sunlight as they pulled clear of the beach. The pair watched in amusement as Garwulf's men made for deeper water, pulling for the narrows with lazy strokes. 'Anyone would think they were just going on an errand,' Waldmer said, 'rather than moving up to cut us off.'

Oslaf nodded. 'Let's see what he does when I take her in. We know they have seen the Hunding flag at the mast top, and I doubt they can believe their luck. Whether it is me returning unaware of the fate of my father or Halga looking for a fight, they have us outnumbered and surrounded by fully rested men, while they must assume we have been rowing since sunup.' He laughed. 'Garwulf is already sharpening his weapons, and dedicating our deaths to Woden as we speak.' The Jute put the rudder over, bringing the ship about to head in to shore. Waldmer retrieved his shield, placing it on the deck nearby. He threw Oslaf a look. 'No harm in playing safe,' he said. 'A lucky arrow or spear could take you out, and that would be your ealdormanship over before it began. I will take a stroll for'ard,' he added, 'and let the lads know what we are up to.'

Oslaf scanned the beach as the Goth moved among the crew. The sense of idleness that had hung over Garwulf's men a short while before, had been replaced by an aura of studied calm. Men now moved in groups, deliberately and with intent, while still endeavouring to look unconcerned at the arrival of this longship approaching under the flag of the rightful lords of the shire. As Waldmer returned to the steering platform, they came within hailing distance of those on land. Oslaf ordered the oars backed, and the snake ship came to a halt offshore. Hildric came up and joined them.

When it became obvious that the Hunding newcomer was not about to blunder ashore, Garwulf finally appeared from among the crowd. Oslaf fought hard not to let his hatred of the man show as he called a greeting. 'Garwulf,' he said in a voice laced with surprise. 'What brings you to my father's lands?'

Garwulf struggled to hide his astonishment when he recognised the man before him, but he recovered quickly to paint his face with a smile. 'Oslaf!' he exclaimed. 'Men thought you long dead.'

Oslaf returned the smile. 'In my experience, very few men think at all, so it is little wonder.' Garwulf chuckled at that. But few of his men possessed the guile of their leader, and they stared stony faced from ship and shore. Oslaf ran his eyes over their faces as their leader prattled on with his words of greeting. These were Garwulf's oath sworn, the men who had set the fires and done the killing that morning — the men as responsible for the death of his kith and kin as Garwulf himself. Oslaf allowed the smile to fall from his face. His presence had baited the trap, now came the moment to spring it. 'Why are you on Hunding lands, Garwulf?'

Garwulf shrugged. 'All Jutland belongs to my father, the king — I go where I please.'

Oslaf indicated the trader resting in the shallows. 'My father pays any tribute owed to the king. What is in the ship, and why is it here?'

Garwulf's smile was tightening, but he made one last effort to entice the Hunding ashore. 'A lot has changed while you were away, Oslaf,' he said. 'Beach your ship alongside my own — we have plenty of supplies, and your men can entertain mine with the tales of their trip while I explain.'

Hildric had been keeping an eye on the movements of the scegth while they talked, and the Goth spoke softly as he sensed that the conversation between the leaders was about to come to an end. 'The smaller ship has backed oars, Oslaf,' he said. 'Now that they have cut us off from the northern channel, they are obviously marking time as they wait to see what happens here.'

'There is no need,' Oslaf called as the Goths dipped their oars. 'I am keen to get home. My father can clear up what is happening here.'

The moment the snake ship began to turn away, an arrow streaked from the stern of Garwulf's own. Waldmer raised his shield in a flash, deflecting the dart away from Oslaf as the rowers curled their backs. Another arrow flew, then another; but the Goths were more prepared than the Jutes had anticipated, and none scored a hit. With a full night's rest, and a leisurely row that morning to warm muscles and loosen joints, the ship gathered speed quickly as the oarsmen bent to their task. In no time, they had drawn beyond the range of Garwulf's bowmen, and Oslaf glanced across to the little scegth as the Goths at his side relaxed their guard. The oars on the distant ship were rising and falling as Oslaf bore away, the crewmen onboard clearly straining to cut them off before they escaped. Back at the beach, the big snake ship was beginning to turn as spearmen scrambled aboard.

Oslaf threw his friends a look of satisfaction at what could have been a difficult task fulfilled, as the oarsmen found their rhythm. 'We will let them close, and remain just out of bowshot,' he said. 'That will keep their minds occupied on running us to ground, rather than wondering why we fled.' The Hunding peered ahead as the bows swung around to the south. With bulging bellies, the gannets had cleared away from their path; on a distant headland, a lone figure stood and shouldered a crook. He shot his friends a lupine smile. 'After all,' he said. 'In my experience, very few men think at all.'

. . .

HALGA THUMPED Oswy on the shoulder, sending his drink flying as the anxious wait came to an end. 'Coella is on his feet! The bastards have taken the lure!' He pumped a fist in delight as the figure on the skyline shouldered his staff, every head within hearing distance snapping around to look. 'They are using their oars lads,' he said. 'That should tire them out nicely!'

Despite his erratic behaviour over the past few days, Coella had performed the tasks allotted to him well. Emerging from cover as Garwulf and his crews set up camp on West Strand, the manner of his departure told the fleet that they were chasing Oslaf south. Now, with his distinctive crook resting upon his shoulder, the watching Angles and Jutes knew for sure that they were travelling under oar power alone, and had a good idea how long they had to prepare.

Aboard the ship, a crewman was slipping the lanyard from its belaying pin, dipping the Anglian war flag in the agreed signal to Horsa on the far side of the bay that they were on their way. With no need to set the mast and bend on the sail, the men settled in to wait, their mind's-eye flying to a wide expanse of blue and three ships arrowing south. Halga tallied heads as oars slid into thole pins. 'Where is Arékan?'

Steapel indicated a place near a hedgerow with a flick of his chin. 'She hurried over there, the moment you spotted Coella moving, lord.' Halga looked. The Hun was on her knees, reaching into a pouch at her side to throw handfuls of grey ash into the air as she rocked back and forth. With her face turned away, she was too far to hear. But Halga had little doubt that the ceremony included ritual chanting, as the woman made in invocation to Tángri Khan. He dropped his gaze to the Angles on the ship. More and more were looking in her direction as word spread, and if her actions had unnerved a few, the sight that greeted them when she rose to her feet and started across sent a chill through them all. If the fact that her face was now a pallid mask was not enough, twin nicks cut high on her cheeks were bleeding freely, the channels they made through the ash forging trails of bloody tears. With far more experience of the Huns and their ways, Halga realised that this was her spirit face, the face she would wear to greet her gods and ancestors if she expected to fall in battle.

The silence aboard drew his gaze back to the ship. The Angles looked thunderstruck to a man, as this unearthly vision walked towards them, fixing an eagle feather in her hair. Most men considered the presence of women on a warship bad luck enough: now she had become a wraith. Unlike Horsa's men, Hengest and his comitatus had spent most of their time in Britannia; Huns were rarely seen there, and he was about to lay their fears to rest when his foster-father beat him to it. 'Haven't you lads got things to do?' He hawked noisily, turning his head to send a gobbet of phlegm spinning overboard. 'I am just going to give my sword edge one last lick with the sharpening stone. If any of you want me to hold their hand after that, I will be free until the fight.' Shamed by their leader, the Angles went back to seeing to their weapons, and Halga shifted aside as Arékan climbed aboard.

He was about to make a remark on her appearance when the look on her face warned him off, and she fixed the Cimmerian pools of her eyes upon him as she spoke. 'I want to thank you, Halga,' she said. He opened his mouth to reply, but the Hun held up a hand to still him. Halga sensed the shock of those looking on that a woman could even think doing of such a thing to a drihten, and a drihten on the cusp of battle at that. But she was oath sworn to no man, and by her exploits in the great war that summer, Halga knew that she had earned the right. 'Take this,' the spectre said, pressing a small bundle into his palm. 'I carved it myself, from the shaft of a Hun arrow I picked up on the battlefield. It is scant reward for all you have done for me, but it would please me more than you could know if you would accept it as a gift.'

Halga made to speak again but thought better of it, and he opened his hand to study the object as the woman made her way aft. A tightly wrapped bundle of calfskin and catgut the item was about half the length of his palm, and Halga took himself off to the side of the ship as he picked at the bindings with a fingernail. He glanced towards the stern as he did so. Arékan's attention was elsewhere — staring off to larboard as she prepared her mind for the fight. The parchment opened up as the binding came away to reveal a wooden figure, the facial features and clothing typically Hun. It had to be an idol of Tángri Khan, and the Jute ran the pad of a thumb over the delicate carving as he teased the parchment apart. The inner surface of the skin bore a series of symbols and designs, and although they were unfamiliar, he had little doubt that the tattoos were a protective spell and was grateful.

He looked across to Arékan once more as he tucked the charm away, a thin smile playing upon his lips as he saw that the Angles were still giving her a wide berth. With neither war band nor lord to gravitate towards, the woman was making her way for'ard, her expression deadpan as she plucked arrows from her quiver and sighted along their length as she went.

Halga untied the silk peace bands holding his sword secure in its scabbard, setting his face into a mask as pinewood blades dipped to row the ship into deeper water. The eyes of every man not pulling an oar were on the headland now — willing the stem post of the Goth ship to appear and put an end to their nervy wait. Halga ran his eyes around the men of his comitatus, exchanging looks of grim determination as the ship got under way. The change in their countenance was stark from the last time they had travelled these waters. The hardships and privations of the past year now etched upon features that had outgrown all trace of boyishness in the hardest game of all.

All set now, Halga Hunding hefted his shield, swapping a look and a nod with Hengest as he made his way forward. He would be the first to leap the gap, the first across the wale when the ships came together.

FROM HIS PLACE in the bow, Oslaf Hunding watched the enemy close in. Waldmer and Hildric were still at his side, the big Goths braced against the rise and fall of the vessel as they scanned the heavens for arrows. They were almost within bow shot of the Jutish ships now, and although unlikely, it was not unknown for a sudden gust to pick up a shaft and carry it far beyond its normal range.

They were back at the narrows after the long chase the length of Wisbey Broad, and as the helmsman worked the steering oar and the bows swung to larboard, Oslaf spoke up. 'That is the final turn, lads,' he called. 'We have worn them out, and led them to the place of slaughter. One last dash, and the hunters become the hunted.'

An arrow thunked into the sternpost, causing the steersman to flinch; but the Goths were drawing ahead once more as the rowers arched their backs, and the follow-up splashed harmlessly in their wake. Oslaf looked away from the chasing ships as the narrowing drifted astern. To either beam the land drew back, and upon a rustic backdrop of greens and browns, brighter tones hove into view. With their prey tantalisingly close, Garwulf's ships were rowing hard, hate-filled faces crowding the bows as the prow men — savage fighters — shook their blades.

But the Hunding was not the only one to spot the jaws of the trap snapping shut. The first of the enemy had seen them now — twin groups of snake ships emerging from inlets, flying the red flag of Angeln — and as word spread and arms moved out to point, Oslaf cupped a hand to call a command. 'That's far enough, boys,' he said gleefully. 'Bring her about!'

28

SHOCK AND AWE

A brief look behind confirmed that all was ready, Oswy and Beorn at his shoulders as Godwin tucked in behind. In Coella's absence Steapel was banner man — the leaping hound emblem of the Hundings hanging limp in the still air of the inlet with Arékan alongside. Beyond them the oarsmen were easing the ship closer to the wider waters of the bay with languid strokes, as other Angles filled the centreline ready to hurl their javelins before rushing forward to join the assault. At the stern, Hengest had the steering oar, Halga's foster-father almost hidden behind a screen of shields as he held a steady course.

A sudden tensing to the bearing of the spearmen had his head snapping back, and Halga's stomach turned somersaults as his brother's ship swept into view. The snaca was really moving, long oars beating the waters of the bay to foam as the Goths fled their pursuers. As if to confirm that the enemy were close behind, the point of an arrow flashed in the sunlight as it fell in their wake. Hengest was beating time now, the boards beneath his feet giving a shudder as the rowers bent to their task, and as the first of Garwulf's ships began to emerge from behind the headland the longship gathered speed.

Intent on overtaking their prey, the two ships swept into the bay, and Halga's confidence rose that they would soon bring them to battle with every passing moment. Lifting his eyes, Halga could make out the pointed prow of Horsa's ship about to emerge from the cove, the creamy bow wave at its base betraying its speed. As the first foemen began to point and shout a warning, Angle war horns sang. It was a calculated move for Hengest, Horsa and the others to betray their presence before they came within range, but as the haunting wail filled the bay, Halga saw that it had worked. Shaken and disorientated to find themselves suddenly surrounded by warships, the tempo of the rowers fell apart as the men stared open-mouthed. Oswy voiced all their thoughts as the way bled from Garwulf's ships. 'We have them.'

On either side of the bay, twin snaca were diverging — the rowers whiplashing back and forth as they moved out to slam the trap shut. With the narrows to the north and south denied them by the Angles, Garwulf's ships were doomed, and satisfied that the ploy had worked Halga returned his eyes to the front. The distance was rapidly shrinking as Hengest and Horsa's ships closed in. A short way to the south, Oslaf's Goths had the steering oar hard over, the ship tracing an arc on the mirror-like surface as they doubled back to confront their tormentors. They were within spear shot now, and Halga watched as the shafts curved overhead to land among the enemy in a deadly rain. Seeing the Goths about to engage, Horsa's ship was bearing away, the helm hard over as it prepared to run down the scegth.

He was close now, so close to fulfilling the oath made to the spirits of his kin in their underground lair, and as the bows swept around and Garwulf's snake ship disappeared behind the prow, Halga prepared to leap.

Another volley of spears rained down as the snaca came back into view, and Halga was up on the wale, every muscle as taut as a bowstring as he prepared to vault the gap. One slip here, and he would share the fate of the man he had killed the previous year, pinned to the bottom by the weight of the mail and armour he had always trusted to save him. Hengest was working the big paddle blade as the Angles shipped their oars, skewing the ship on its axis as he sought to come to grips with the enemy. If he could lay the ship alongside while they still had enough forward momentum, the hull would snap the enemy oars like so much kindling, driving the hand grips back into the chests of the rowers and causing bloody mayhem. It was a good plan, and likely to go a long way towards carrying the day if successful.

Trusting to Woden and now Tángri Khan, Halga leapt as the ship came up. But the opposing helmsman was as sharp as a blade, and the Jute's heart came into his mouth as the enemy snake sheered off — looking on in mounting horror as they began to draw apart. An arrow snickered past, so close that he felt the fletching brush his cheek. But by seeking to save the oarsmen from a mangling, the helmsman had inadvertently saved him, and as the ship sheared away the stern swung closer. With the freeboard higher here due to the upward sweep of the strakes, a wall of oak was swinging his way. Halga launched his shield towards the deck to free up a hand and grasp the backstay. A heartbeat later he crashed to the boards, his sword sliding free from its scabbard as he dropped into a warlike crouch. Desperate for support, the Jute threw a look towards the Anglian ship as he did so, cursing his luck as he saw the bows packed with the horrified faces of his oath sworn. He was on his own until Hengest closed again, and he turned to face the enemy as the first attackers came on, screaming their war cries.

Two of Garwulf's men were bearing down upon him, keen to cut down this madman who had the nerve to attack them alone, and Halga was weighing up which to go for when the choice was made for him. An arrow punched into an attacker's brow, the Hunnish fletching betraying its source, and Halga darted forward as the dead man was hurled back by the force of the strike.

If he had hoped to get inside the reach of the spearman before he could react, Halga was to be disappointed. The man sprang back, maintaining the distance between them as he thrust out with his weapon. Without the protection of his shield, Halga was forced to twist aside, but despite doing enough to deflect the point away from his chest, the spear-point struck home. Halga felt a searing pain as the blade tore through the ringlets of his byrnie, punching through the muscle above his collarbone to burst from the mail coat in a shower of glittering steel. Pegged at arm's length by the spear shaft, Halga gasped as his foe shook him back and forth like a hound at the kill. The urge to drop his sword and make a grab for the shank was almost overwhelming, and Halga fought against doing what he knew would only result in his death. Halga staggered as the spearman drove him backwards, pinning him against the sternpost as more enemies rushed forward to finish him off. The man was taunting him now, his face wreathed in a smile as he spoke, and a remark made by an enemy long ago flashed into the drihten's mind as he recognised the voice through his pain.

The Hunding brat? Halga? Not likely, he is already miles away...

The foeman snarled again. 'I have got you now, Hunding — you won't get away this time.' But the words were barely out when a tide of bodies swept him away, and Halga raised his free hand to work the shaft from the post as the men of his comitatus threw a shield fort around him. He gritted his teeth as the point came away, growling a command to Oswy as the man came up. 'Cut this thing off,' he said. 'As close to the shoulder as you can.'

The gedriht had his knife out in a trice, sawing at the spear shaft as Halga gritted his teeth against the pain. Men were pouring over the side now, and Halga watched the fighting spread as Oswy worked. Hengest's Angles were driving Garwulf's men back — already the helmsman had been made to pay dearly for remaining at his post, the Jute's crumpled remains slumped mid-deck at the centre of a slowly spreading pool of blood. Garwulf and his oath sworn had matched his shield fort in the bow, the knot of seasoned warriors already cut-off from the rest of the crew by Oslaf's Goths who were streaming over the larboard side. Despite her earlier fatalism, Halga saw that Arékan had thought better of throwing her life away in a suicidal dash. The Hun perched in the high prow of Hengest's ship — her ashen features drifting from Jute to Jute like an avenging wight as she loosed at the men who had killed her lord in the dawn. With their attention fully taken by the enemy swarming over the deck, the men at Garwulf's side were being quickly whittled down as Arékan's arrows flew in to pick them off one by one.

The fight was almost over, and he had yet to wet his sword; Halga snapped an order as the spear shaft clattered to the deck. 'Come on,' he said. 'We have waited nigh on a year for this moment. This is no time to stand about watching.'

Beorn had recovered Halga's shield from the decking, and he held it out as he led them towards the fight. Halga winced as he moved a hand, his shoulder muscles seizing up as he went to grip the handle. 'You will have to cover me, Beorn,' he said, casting a look of contempt at the sawn-off shaft jutting from his shoulder. 'I can't raise my arm while this thing is still in there.' Beorn swung into place, his shield coming up as they prepared to attack. Halga raised his gaze, taking in the fighting as they settled into a jog. The Goths and Angles had joined up amidships, the Jutes squeezed into shrinking pockets either side of the mast. Further forward, Oslaf Hunding was leading his best fighters in a vicious assault on Garwulf's shrinking band. Off to larboard, Horsa and his crew had already cleared the deck of the scegth, the Angles pointing and whooping like onlookers at the midsummer meet as they lapped up the entertainment nearby.

He would have to move fast if he was to fulfil his vow to the ancestors. But just as he began to despair, his eyes focused upon a face in the ruck. The spearman who had come so close to killing him was less than a dozen paces away, fighting desperately as the Jutish band shrank like ice in the sun. Halga broke his stride, and using his injured arm to pin the scabbard to his side, slid the long sword home before drawing his seax from its sheath. Armed now to fight in the crush, Halga increased the pace, bringing Long Knife around as he prepared to strike. At his side Beorn matched his pace, and with Oswy as his right-hand man and Steapel bringing up his banner to the rear, Halga raced across the deck.

Within a few paces he had reached the lip of the steering platform, and Halga launched himself across the gap to crash into the midst of the fight. Beorn was still at his side, the men of his comitatus following his lead to a man, and as both Angles and their Jutish foemen scattered before him, he lowered his head. The sight of a war band flying through the air had thrown Halga's tormenter back on his heels. But held up by the pressure of those to his rear, the fellow Jute could do nothing, as Halga's steel-clad head crashed forward again and again. Blinded, in a world of shattered teeth and gore, the spearman staggered as Long Knife entered his guts, and Halga pushed forward, twisting the seax in wicked swirls to pulp the man's innards. The next face swam into view as the first man slumped, and Halga was about to raise Long Knife to stab again when the vision burst apart as Oswy's sword blade crashed down to split it to the chin.

With his shoulder a knot of searing pain, Halga was unable to push on, and he took a rearward step to open up a gap as Beorn slid in before him. With his old enemy spilling his guts on the deck at his feet and his oath sworn all around, Halga took the opportunity to raise his gaze. The fight amid-ships was all but over, Angles, and Goths, pouring across the wales from the ships on either beam. The first hands were being raised as Garwulf's crewmen saw the hopelessness of the fight, weapons clattering to the deck as they threw them-selves upon the mercy of their conquerors.

In the bow, Garwulf was in clear view, fighting hard amid the last of his guards as a tide of enemies lapped at his feet. There was little chance that Halga could make his way forward through the crush before the enemy leader's inevitable fall, and he was honest enough with himself to admit that he would be of little use in the fight if he did. There were no striplings to be found among a prince's guard. These were veterans of many fights, warriors of the heorðwerod. Gammy shoulder or not, he would do well to survive the encounter, much less strike the killer blow, and he retreated to the steering platform as he settled in to watch the culmination of all he had worked to achieve. Halga's eyes followed Garwulf's every swing, desperate to see whether the blade was the ancestral sword of his father, the War-bright that belonged in the death mound alongside the man who had wielded it in life. Sunlight reflected dully from gold and garnet as he looked, giving him hope. Halga's hand gripped the figure of Tángri Khan as he sent an invocation to the Hunnish god that he was right.

Before the Jute could strike again Halga recognised the figures of Waldmer and Hildric, the Goths forcing their way through, clearing a path for Oslaf who rushed forward swinging his blade. Garwulf saw War-spite at the last moment, dodging aside as the sword blades sparked in a clash of familial steel. The eyes of every man in the fleet were now fixed upon the duel, and as the last of Garwulf's werod were cut down, the Jutish prince backed against the prow.

If it was a well-know fact that a cornered wolf was at its most dangerous, what happened next had those looking on wide-eyed with wonder. Garwulf scythed what Halga could clearly see was War-bright in a wide arc, and as the attackers ducked and dodged, he grasped the forestay to haul himself up onto the wale. For a drawn-out moment, the king's son swept his enemies with a final look of defiance. As Oslaf rushed across to deal him his death blow, Halga felt his mouth fall open in shock and awe as the prince leapt over-board. If what followed had been Garwulf's intention, he came within a whisker of success. The ship pitched on its beam ends as men rushed to the starboard wale to look, and it was only the presence of Hengest's vessel alongside that stopped it from capsizing. Weighed down by their armour, hundreds of his enemies would have joined the king's son in an undersea army of the dead. But, despite their narrow escape, Halga felt a stab of horror as his gaze fixed upon the spot where the prince had gone in.

Before he could voice his dismay that Garwulf had denied them their prize after a yearlong quest, a dark shape flashed down. Halga just had time to recognise calfskin boots before they were swallowed by the dark waters of the bay, and men craned their necks to look as the surface heaved and boiled. Halga hurried for'ard, keen to stand alongside his brother at the culmination of their struggle, and as he reached the bows and the Goths made way the Hundings stood side by side and stared. A seething patch of spume marked the spot where the two had entered the water, testament to the struggle taking place in the depths, and as the men watched spellbound the surface was broken by a great upwelling marbled by tendrils of red. A hush descended upon Jute, Goth, and Angle alike as they stared at the spreading stain, but Halga felt the weight of his fears lift as a dark shape broke the surface.

Men crowded forward as Arékan swam alongside, and with her murdered lord avenged and the ash and blood washed from her face and hair, the Hun looked a woman reborn. But if her smile told of the joy within, the dagger clasped between her teeth gave her the look of a killer, and the brothers dodged aside as she swung an arm to send something spinning through the air. Even as it sailed past, it was obvious that the straggly ball was the head of their enemy, and as men laughed and joked and kicked it around the deck, Arékan reached out a hand. 'Gelp me up,' she spat through gritted teeth. 'And I'll gish you dish shord.'

GODWIN WAS DEAD. He had to be. Halga ran his eyes over the ship as Beorn began another futile search. Amidships, Arékan was delighting in pointing out to Oslaf those of Garwulf's men who had been present at the burning of his father. Halga watched as the foredoomed were hauled out from the crowd by Goths, admiring their bearing as they said their goodbyes and lined up along the wale. They were Jutes, after all.

The last time anyone had seen his gedriht had been just before they had boarded Garwulf's ship. With their lord stranded and fighting alone, the assault had been more of a frantic scramble than a charge to test the wordplay of poets and scops. His gaze dropped again to the patch of water alongside, as he imagined his friend stretched out on the bottom. Try as he might, he could not completely drive off the feeling of resentment that the man had chosen the very moment of victory to fall. It was just like him, Halga mused guiltily. Not the most outgoing among the gang, the fact that he had given his life for the quest without anyone noticing was perhaps the saddest thing of all.

Oswy returned, shaking his head. Halga nodded. 'There are not that many places to hide on a fifty-foot rowboat. I shall go and see his folk the moment we reach Tiw's Stead. It is not the homecoming I had in mind — but they will watch the ships row up the bay, and hope to see him returned.'

'You will not be accompanying Oslaf home then? There will be a celebration to end celebrations when your mother sees her long-lost son, back from Valhall.'

Halga snorted. Along the ship's side, Arékan and Oslaf were taking turns, sawing blades through bearded throats before shoving the burners overboard and moving on to the next. 'I have the sword *Hildleoma*, my part in this is done. I may have left here callow, but I am drihten now. My first responsibility is to my men.'

29

GUARDIANS OF THE FLOCK

T he crowing of a rooster cut through the stillness, interrupting the drift of their thoughts. Arékan spoke as the throaty call came again. 'Here they come,' she said, raising an arm to point. 'You can't fault their timing.'

Halga looked. Spectral shapes were rising from the misty vale, treading the overgrown pathways that led to the summit. He raised his eyes as the cock crowed again. Out beyond the broad, serpentine swirls filled the hollows and gullies on the slopes of Moors opposite. Higher up, the sun was edging the crest as the celestial horses *Wacan* and *Hræd* — Waken and Hasty — approached. One day, at the end of the world, the wolf, Scorn, will catch the pair, overcoming the goddess Sunna to bolt down the sun. Halga snorted as the apparitions downslope hardened into familiar faces. He had survived one ending of the world that year with the transit of the wolf-tailed star, he would consider himself more than hard done-by for it to happen again so soon.

The peacefulness broken, Arékan nodded down to the scabbard at his side. 'Have you thought of a name yet?'

Halga shook his head. 'No,' he replied. 'Swords have a

life, the same as men. Like men, they reveal the eke-name they will carry for the rest of their days through their deeds and worth.' With a new blade forged by Steapel's father, and a hilt prised from the chill dead hand of a Gepid warlord, Halga's new sword was as fine as any, whether he had bestowed a name upon it yet or not. He cast a look at the death mound of the Hundings a few short yards away, his mind picturing again the trappings of war and celebration contained within. Hildleoma — War-bright — was back where she belonged. Resting alongside the earthly remains of the man who had carried her into battle in the dank and fetid air. Words flit into his mind as he looked, echoing the vow he had uttered what seemed like a lifetime ago:

Vidar, son of Woden, Fenris bane: god of vengeance.

Here, another man's son proclaims that he too is keen to avenge his father.

Already the turfs were beginning to knit. By springtime, there would be no trace left to show where he had entered and fulfilled the pledge. One thing still irked him, and he hesitated before continuing. But his desire for an answer overcame his reluctance to hear the reply, lest it disappoint. With Coella returned to the land, and Godwin rotting beneath the waves, Halga's comitatus had shrunk, despite his successes in the South.

A brief look downhill showed where the newcomers were still a way off as they trudged the paths, and he grasped the chance before they arrived. 'I wanted to ask,' he said, 'why you decided to remain here in Tiw's Stead.'

She glanced across. 'And give your brother my oath?'

Halga nodded. 'That too.'

The Hun hesitated for a moment before replying. She could sense the hurt and disappointment.

Halga's eyes flicked downslope.

She took the prompt for what it was. 'I almost offered to swear,' Arékan said, 'a couple of times. The morning following the witchy visit, and later outside Remorum, when Halga Long-Knife became Halga Long-Face.' The pair shared a chuckle as they recalled the day, and Halga's moodiness as Horsa and Oslaf's laughter had filled the air. Her smile tightened as she came to the reason for her decision. 'You were making me feel my age,' she said, the admission surprising them both in its candour. She pressed on, the words were out and that was that. 'I began to feel like a bitch run ragged by her pups — riding, fighting, sleeping under the stars for weeks on end. You lads revelled in the way of life. But my youth is behind me, and it only made me miserable.' She cast a look back towards the hall. The rising sun had blushed the timbers rufous, gleaming in their newness. 'The moment the ships entered the sound, and the hall hove into view,' she said, 'I knew.' She shrugged, and the ghost of a smile returned as Arékan made another confession. 'Eventually, even wanderers yearn for a place to call home.'

The conversation had whittled away the time it took for his gedrihts to gain the ridge top. Halga threw them both a smile and a question as they came up. 'Said your goodbyes?' Arékan drifted away, unnoticed, as the bond between lord and oath sworn unwittingly shut her out. As soon as Oswy struggled up the rise with the packs they set off, angling northeast to pick up the Tiw's Stead Road. To Halga's surprise he found the footsteps becoming springier, the pace increasing the further they travelled. As the morning mist began to pull back to reveal the mast tops of longships on the strand, he found his spirits lifting too. A short while later they were on the dockside, the sleek snake ships just beginning to wallow as a rising tide lifted their keels.

Horsa saw them double the corner from his place on the

steering platform, cupping a hand to his mouth to call out. 'You are late! We were about to cast off and leave without you.'

The challenge seemed familiar, and Halga raked about in his memory as the rowers exchanged looks and anticipated his response. Then it came, and the expectant smiles widened into grins as he aped the Angle's reply to the river guard outside Tornacum. 'In that case, how can I be late? All it needs is for you to slip the hawser, and I shall be bang on time.' As Horsa's men explained the joke to Hengest's fighters in the ship alongside, and gentle laughter filled the strand, Halga trod the plank. The instant the last man's feet touched the deck the gangway rattled aboard, and as mooring ropes flew and the rowers dipped their oars, Halga ran his eyes over Tiw's Stead a final time. Steapel spoke at his side, mirroring his thoughts. 'Not much to look at, is it, lord? I doubt we shall be rushing back anytime soon.'

Halga made to reply, but his eyes caught sight of a figure watching them from the higher ground to the west, pulling him up short. He squinted to look. It was, he supposed, a scene almost as old as the hills surrounding them. A shepherd and his dog — guardians of the flock. He indicated the high point with a flick of his head. 'Someone come to see us off.' The pair turned back, raising their gaze as the oars dipped, the bows swung to the south, and the longship pulled for deeper water. The mist had risen wraithlike to cover a hillside already speckled by the russet tones of autumn. Beorn came across to join them. The bear-man spoke while they waited for the mistiness to clear. 'The last time we were in a fog like this,' he said, 'we were rowing for our lives.'

Halga nodded. 'It's been quite a year.'

Steapel turned his head, adding an observation of his own as the first sounds of retching carried to them. 'The more things change, the more they stay the same.' They turned to look. Hugging the wale, Oswy spat a mouthful of bile overboard as he steeled himself to face the misery of the seasickness to come.

When the group returned their attention to the ridge, the fog was finally thinning. Gossamer threads drew back into the dips and gills like an ebbing wave, and as the sun broke through to paint the hilltop with its light, they searched the crest but found it empty.

AFTERWORD

The fight known today as the Battle of the Catalaunian Fields or the Battle of Châlons, was famously described in Sir Edward Gibbon's the *History of the Decline and Fall of the Roman Empire* as, 'the last victory which was achieved in the name of the Western Roman Empire'. One of Sir Edward Creasy's contenders in *The Fifteen Decisive Battles of the World,* Attila's invasion of that year was described by a contemporary, Sidonius Apollinaris, a fifth century Gallo-Roman aristocrat in his first-hand account — *Poems and Letters* — as, 'the barbarian world, rent by a mighty upheaval, poured the whole north into Gaul'.

But why did Attila and his allies fall upon the West, and why that year? Of course, we can never be certain — Attila left no record of his motivation for the invasion or any other events in his life — but the answer to that question may lie further east. When Marcian succeeded to the Eastern Roman Empire in 450, he reversed the policy of his predecessor Theodosius II, whereby the Huns were paid tribute to cease the depredations of the later part of the previous decade. With the Balkans largely laid waste by years of warfare, and the only real wealth safe behind the walls of Constantinople, Attila needed to find an alternative source of income with which to distribute gifts to his under-kings and followers. Fortunately for his plans, a legitimate claim to land within the Western Empire arrived at about the same time in a communication from the emperor's sister, Honoria. Valentinian III's sister became embroiled in a love scandal at court, the upshot of which was that she was married off to a dependable senator. Honoria sent a ring to Attila, asking him to champion her cause, a token which Attila chose to view as a timely offer of marriage. The king of the Huns quickly accepted, sending word that as the brother-in-law of the emperor, he would expect half of the Western Empire as dowry. Spurred on by Gaiseric, the king of the Vandals who was in conflict with the Visigoths at that time, it seems possible that Attila thought to replace the Goths in their homeland centred on modern-day Toulouse, while at the same time establishing a client kingdom in the Frankish north ruled by the renegade Gundebaud as he had further east with other Germanics.

Crossing the Rhine in April 451, the Huns and their subjects advanced across central Gaul on a wide front, extorting supplies and provisions from certain cities and either bypassing or ransacking those who refused. The six thousand strong empire-building Roman legions of old were long gone, replaced more than a century before by smaller, essentially defensive, formations known as *Limitanei* and *Ripenses* guarding the frontiers, backed up by the mobile field armies of the *Comitatenses,* and it was not until Attila concentrated his army at present-day Orleans that the Roman general Aetius could assemble a large enough force to confront the invaders. Orleans was the main city of a steppe people of Scythian origin, the Alans, who had been settled there as *foederati* earlier in the century, and there were suspicions, then as now, that their king Sangiban was playing a waiting game, seeing which side looked most likely to prevail before throwing his lot in with the victors. The defence of Orleans was organised by the bishop there, and Aetius and his Gothic allies under king Theodoric arrived before the city could fall, forcing Attila to retreat to the Catalaunian plain. There is still a debate regarding the exact location of the subsequent battle, but I have gone with the area called Les Maurattes, close to the city of Troyes (Tricassium/Tricasses), scene of the famous scourge of God description by Attila — not bishop Lupus, as reported to Halga by Oswy! This agrees with the location given in the *Chronica Gallica Anno 511*, whose entry for the year 451 reads:

'Aetius with king Theodoric of the Goths fought against Attila king of the Huns at Tricasses on the Mauriac plain, where Theodoric was slain, by whom it is uncertain, and Laudaricus the relative of Attila: and the bodies were countless.'

At the end of the Roman Road that was the most direct route for Attila's retreat from Orleans, the topography here matches the description given by the Gothic historian Jordanes. Bounded to the south by the Montgueux ridge, the plain lies approximately halfway between the source of the River Vanne at Fontvanne, and the River Seine. For armies containing tens of thousands of horses and draft animals like Attila's, access to a water source is vital. Each horse requires between five and ten gallons of water per day, and whereas it can survive more than twenty days without feed, that drops to less than a week when deprived of water. Already fatigued from a long campaign under the hot summer sun, and forced to carry heavy riders and their equipment, Attila's army would quickly become ineffective, so moving from water source to water source would have been imperative.

What of the numbers of men involved? The Gothic historian Jordanes puts the dead at 165,000, with a further 15,000 dead on both sides in the Frankish/Gepid clash the previous evening. Hydatius, a contemporary Roman chronicler living in what is now Portugal, gives a total figure of 300,000 dead on the Catalaunian Fields. Although these figures appear implausibly high — most modern-day historians estimate that the rival armies contained approximately 50,000 combatants, with Attila's host including at least the same number of camp followers, slaves, and captives — it does illustrate that to the people living at that time the battle was viewed as colossal in scale and loss.

Written during the following century, Jordanes', *The Origins and Deeds of the Goths* is one of our primary sources for the battle, and although far from perfect, and certainly not unbiased, it appears to be reliable in basic outline. As far as we can reconstruct, the deployment, and battle itself, appears to have been as he described, with the Huns close to victory thwarted by a combination of Theodoric's counterattack and his son Thorismund's charge. The fighting lasted from early afternoon and into the night, as the Huns and their allies retreated to their camp on the Seine.

Jordanes is also our source for the fight between the Franks and Gepids the night before the battle, although whether this was against a prepared position as in our tale, or simply that the leading elements of Aetius's coalition overtook the rearguard on the march, we will never now know.

Further north, at about the same time, it appears that there may well have been a civil war within the kingdom of the Jutes. It is possible that we can catch a glimpse of this conflict when we read the remnant of an Anglo-Saxon tale, known appropriately as the *Finnsburg Fragment*. The action takes place at the court of Finn, king of the Frisians, and appears to involve Jutes fighting on both sides. Many of the elements I transposed to our tale are present in the passage: Hengest; Garwulf; Guthlaf and the sword *Hildleoma.* Rather than describe the rival parties glowering at each other over the course of the winter from the guest halls of the Frisian king until the matter is decided in the spring, I have moved the kernel of the tale back home to Jutland to better fit in with Halga's story.

In dealing with the place names in the Jutish homeland, I have followed a similar path to that taken in my earlier trilogy, King's Bane. Archeology supports Bede's assertion in the early eighth century *Ecclesiastical History of the English People,* that the entire Jutland peninsula was largely depopulated in his day, following the migrations of the fifth and sixth centuries. As a consequence of this, there are very few indications as to the names of settlements, rivers, and bays at this time, so I have anglicised the modern Danish names to better reflect the early form of English likely to have been spoken in the area.

The wolf-tailed star refers to Halley's Comet. The comet first appeared during the night of 18/19 June 451, and was visible until early August. Comets were thought to portend the death of kings in the early Middle-ages, and it was certainly true here. Of the leaders on both sides of the battle at the Catalaunian Fields, the majority were dead, if not by the end of that day, within a very few years.

As we have seen, king Theodoric of the Visigoths died on the battlefield, as did his opposite number, Walamir, king of the Ostrogoths. It is not known for certain that Gundebaud was the brother of Merovech, but he appears to have been the leader of the Ripuarian Franks — the Rhine or River Franks — and is reported to have fallen in the battle. Sangiban, king of the Alans, disappears from history and possibly fell there with an arrow to the throat. Few among the leaders who survived the great battle fared much better. Thorismund, the leader of the charge that rescued the Western alliance, was crowned on the field of battle the following day, but was fated to be assassinated by his younger brother Theodoric II in 453. This Visigoth prince almost certainly fought in the great battle, and was assassinated in turn by yet another son of Theodoric I, his younger brother Eurich.

What of the fates of the two leading men, Flavius Aetius, and Attila?

The king of the Huns died on his wedding night in 453, possibly due to a ruptured blood vessel brought on by cirrhosis of the liver. Bitter infighting among the great man's sons followed, the succession finally won by Ellac, another who almost certainly fought at the Catalaunian Fields. Ellac lasted less than a year before he was killed at the battle of Nedao in Pannonia, in an uprising of Germanic peoples led by Attila's great friend and ally Ardaric, king of the Gepids.

With the Hun threat over, Flavius Aetius was stabbed to death by the Roman emperor Valentinian in 454, who was himself assassinated the following year on the Field of Mars by two of Aetius' former bucellarii, the Huns Optila and Thraustila, to avenge the slaying of their lord.

King Merovech, the semi-legendary king of the Salian Franks — the Sea Franks of our tale — is possibly a son of the Frankish king, Chlodio, who died about 450. Even Gregory of Tours — a Frank himself — writing in the later part of the sixth century, can only write, "some say that Merovech, the father of Childeric, was descended from Chlodio…" If we are on uneven ground with primary sources, it is certain that the later Franks saw the line of succession as Merovech — Childeric — Clovis, as reflected in the naming of the dynasty as the Merovingians. Ultimately, the Franks were the real victors of the fight, beginning the process of reuniting their disparate kingdoms before overcoming those of the Goths, Alamanns, Bretons and others over the course of the following sixty years to form what the Germans still call Frankreich, the English-speaking world France.

Cliff May
East Anglia
October 2021

ALSO BY C. R. MAY

ERIK HARALDSSON

BLOODAXE

THE RAVEN AND THE CROSS

THE DAY OF THE WOLF

KING'S BANE

FIRE AND STEEL

GODS OF WAR

THE SCATHING

CONQUERORS OF ROME

LORDS OF BATTLE

NEMESIS

ALTERNATIVE HISTORIES

SPEAR HAVOC - 1066

BEOWULF - SWORD OF WODEN

SORROW HILL

WRÆCCA

MONSTERS

DAYRAVEN

CHARACTERS

Ægil — Hengest's gedriht.

Ardaric — King of the Gepids.

Arékan — A Hunnish member of first Ottar Hunding's, and then Halga Hunding's comitatus.

Attila — King of the Huns.

Beorn — Halga's gedriht.

Chad — Father of Steapel, Halga's gedriht.

Childeric — Son of Merovech, king of the Sea Franks.

Coella — Halga's gedriht.

Dagmer — A Frank. Steward to king Merovech.

Edwin — Horsa's gedriht.

Flavius Aetius — 'Last of the Romans.' *Magister Militum* — the military commander in the West.

Glappa — A Frankish householder in Tornacum.

Godwin — Halga's gedriht.

Garwulf Guthlafing — Son of the king of Jutes — the leader of the burners.

Gundebaud — King of the River Franks.

Guthlaf — King of the Jutes.

Halga Hunding — Son of Ottar and Hygd — drihten.

Hengest — An Angle — Warlord — Halga Hunding's foster-father, and brother of Horsa.

Hildric — A Goth. A member of king Theodoric's *bucellarii.*

Horsa — An Angle — Warlord, and brother of Hengest.

Hygd — Mother of Halga and Oslaf.

Merovech — King of the Sea Franks.

Oslaf Hunding — The Eldest son of Ottar and Hygd. Halga's brother.

Oswy — Halga's gedriht.

Ottar Hunding — Father of Halga and Oslaf.

Sangiban — King of the Alans.

Steapel — Halga's steersman and gedriht.

Theodoric I — King of the Visigoths.

Thorismund — The Eldest son of Theodoric I.

Waldmer — A Goth. A member of king Theodoric's *bucellarii.*

PLACES/LOCATIONS

Anderida — A Saxon Shore Fort on the coast of Britannia — close to present-day Pevensey, East Sussex, England.

Andreds Wold — the 'forest of Andred' — known today as The Weald in Southeast England.

Aureliani — Orléans — Centre-Val de Loire, France.

Camaracum — Cambrai — Hauts-de-France, France.

Catalaunian Fields — Champagne-Ardenne, France.

Campus Mauriacus — Les Maurattes, Champagne-Ardenne, France.

Duro Catalaunum — Châlons-en-Champagne, France.

Remorum — Metropolis Civitas Remorum — Reims — Grand Est, Marne, France.

The German Sea — The North Sea.

Lyme Bay — Limfjord — northern Jutland, Denmark.

Moors — the island of Morsø, North Jutland Region, Denmark.

The Muddy Sea — Nordfriesisches Wattenmeer, Schleswig-Holstein, Germany.

Old Ford — Hollingstedt, Schleswig-Flensburg, Germany.

The Sley — Schlei, Schleswig-Flensburg, Germany.

Sleyswic — Schleswig, Schleswig-Flensburg, Germany.

Strand — Suderhafen, Nordstrand, Germany.

Tiw's Stead — Thisted, North Jutland Region, Denmark.

Tiw's Stead Broad — Thisted Bredning, Jutland, Denmark.

Tornacum — Tournai, Wallonia, Belgium.

Tricassium — Troyes, Grand Est, France.

Wisbey Broad — Visby Bredning, Jutland, Denmark.

ABOUT THE AUTHOR

I am a writer of historical fiction, working primarily in the early Middle Ages. I have always had a love of history, which led to an early career in conservation work. Using the knowledge and expertise gained, we later moved as a family through a succession of dilapidated houses, which I single-handedly renovated. These ranged from a Victorian townhouse to a Fourteenth Century hall, and I added childcare to my knowledge of medieval oak frame repair, wattle, and daub and lime plastering.

I have crewed the replica of Captain Cook's ship, Endeavour, sleeping in a hammock and sweating in the sails and travelled the world, visiting such historic sites as the Little Big Horn, Leif Erickson's Icelandic birthplace and the bullet scarred walls of Berlin's Reichstag.

Now I write, only a stone's throw from the Anglian ship burial site at Sutton Hoo in East Anglia, England. Scourge of God follows the bestselling Erik Haraldsson trilogy, which recounts the story of Harald Fairhair's favoured son, the tenth century king of Norway and Viking Northumbria better known to history as Erik Bloodaxe.

Printed in Great Britain
by Amazon

21878354R00189